COMING ATTRACTION

COMING ATTRACTION

LAURA CHRISTIAN

Rambling Rhodesy Publishing

For more information, or to book an event, contact:
laura@thelaurachristian.com
http://www.thelaurachristian.com

Book design by Laura Christian
Cover design by Getcovers.com

ISBN - Paperback: 979-8-9871415-0-2
ISBN - Ebook : 979-8-9871415-1-9

First Printing, 2022

To Sandy Lohutko – Thank you for telling me I had a spark. To you, my first book. As promised.

To Pat Bagwill-Brawner – Thank you for fanning the flames. Your faith in me gave me faith in myself.

To Gihan – We have been through so much together. Thank you for being my people – for reading all the first drafts – for being my safe place, and my best friend.

To Gerry – Thank you for sticking with me through the ugly stages of self-publishing and constantly telling me that I could do it and that it was worth it.

To Damon "Sharpe" – Your insane talent pulled me kicking and screaming into the digital age, and because of you, I discovered the great community within social media. It is because of your trailblazing that I dared to take a leap of faith to publish after almost 30 years.

To all of my friends and family for your part in getting me here today. I love you all.

One

Spring 2018 - Filmset, Backstage, Wardrobe: Elizabeth

A box of straight pins clattered to the ground, and Elizabeth screamed, "STOP!"

Everyone froze, clapping their hands over their ears and swinging their eyes to the head costume director. Hundreds of pins scattered, bouncing across the concrete floor of the dressing area. Elizabeth scowled at the intern who had made the mistake and growled.

She studied toes, noting that only one person was barefoot, but she spotted at least a dozen others in sandals. She groaned, throwing her hands in the air.

"Grab the magnets. Everyone else, stay still."

She reached for the magnetic wand in her sewing kit, designed for this purpose. Three of her staff members were also prepared, and they fanned across the room, waving the wands over the floor. When Elizabeth's wand was full, she pointed to a young girl dressed in a cropped flannel shirt with olive-colored pants. "You – get these all into a pin cushion and then go round and see if you can find any more. Take care of *all* of them.," she grumbled, not waiting for the intern to accept the task.

Over the past two weeks on set, Elizabeth had realized that while she hated giving orders, the authoritative tone was necessary. Otherwise, everyone second guessed her decisions and felt free to interject their own thoughts. As the head costume director on the set of a sci-fi drama, she didn't have time for anyone else's opinion. If she wanted it, she would ask.

Elizabeth knew her way around a set, having worked on others previously. This, however, was the first time she'd overseen the entire wardrobe team, and she suddenly understood all the attitude she'd received from former bosses. Today was going to be hard since the principal actors were all coming for their first table read, meaning that she was getting her first chance to measure them.

There were more costumes to design than people realized on the average set. Part of her role was to manage the three lead cast members personally. She had passed out assignments to her staff at the morning meeting, irritated at the obnoxiously strong scent of coffee in the hands of the sleepy faces that had reported.

The first actor was scheduled to arrive in ten minutes, and she stared at her staff collecting pins off the floor. "Will we be ready in five minutes?" she called out.

"Yes," came a chorus of replies.

She turned to her right-hand, Dana, a tiny slip of a woman with a blunt, white pixie cut, a constant tan, and a surprising amount of physical strength for her size. Elizabeth thought of her like an ant that could lift twice its body weight and often felt like an ox beside her: taller, dark-headed and fair-skinned.

Elizabeth pulled at her ponytail, wrapping a chocolate-brown lock around her finger anxiously as she worried. "I don't have time for this this morning. Is my booth set up?" she asked.

Dana nodded, leading Elizabeth to the semi-private area she had cordoned off earlier that morning. There were three folding chairs, a platform, and a three-sided mirror ready. A series of lights had been arranged around the space, and there was a rolling storage drawer unit filled with measuring tapes, pins, chalk, and a plethora of other tools. On top of it was a digital camera and a tiny printer loaded with paper. Elizabeth sighed in relief at the sight. "Thank you so much. I'm nervous enough without feeling unprepared."

Dana rolled her eyes. "This isn't our first project together. I know what your standards are. I'll have the dressing area set up for fittings," she rambled, pointing out other details that she had planned. "I've never seen you this nervous."

Elizabeth sighed, looking around and dragging Dana into the booth. She lowered her voice. "The first actor coming in this morning is my teen idol."

Dana gasped, looking around also then leaning in conspiratorially. "Scott Harper?" she asked excitedly.

Elizabeth wrinkled her nose. "No." She had nearly forgotten about the other male lead who was also a former musician recently popular with the teen crowd. Elizabeth had followed him for a minute as well, but he hadn't captured her heart in quite the same way as her first. "Jared Rains," she corrected and gulped. Merely saying his name out loud threw her stomach into somersaults.

"Who?" Dana's face showed confusion.

"I forget how young you are." Elizabeth sighed. "I guess he was before your time. He had a TV show with four other guys back when I was thirteen. Sketch comedy sort of thing with music and dancing."

Dana's eyebrows were in her hairline as she listened. "You're still hung up on him?" she asked.

"Yes," Elizabeth answered quickly. "And I know it's dumb and immature..."

"It's freaking adorable," Dana interrupted. "I'll run interference for you and make sure no one bothers you while you're measuring his inseam."

Elizabeth's eyes bulged at the statement. "I don't know if I can do that."

Dana laughed. "Go get some water. Be busy for a minute," she encouraged brightly. "Let me find him and bring him here, and you can breeze in and forget he's someone you know and treat him like any other client." She started pushing Elizabeth out of the booth.

"What would be the fun in that?" asked a voice Elizabeth would recognize anywhere.

She turned in horror, seeing Jared Rains standing mere feet away, hands tucked into the pockets of his skinny jeans, stretched tantalizingly over his well-sculpted legs. She hadn't seen him since she was a teenager, and he looked completely different and all the same, standing in front of her now almost twenty years later. His dark auburn hair was cropped short, but his five-foot eleven frame had gotten leaner and certainly more muscular than she'd remembered. His blue eyes twinkled as he regarded her.

Elizabeth stopped breathing, feeling Dana's hands frozen on her hips from behind. It wasn't until her assistant poked her in the side that she remembered to breathe. "Elizabeth Morris," she introduced finally, holding out a hand to him.

"Jared Rains," he offered with a smirk and took the proffered extremity. "I'm here to have my inseam measured," he added, laughing as Elizabeth felt her face turning red.

She groaned. "Well, I guess if the cat's out of the bag I won't have to worry about you finding out," she said, ushering him forward. "Yes, I need to measure your...everything."

Jared's brow arched as he followed her. "My everything, eh?" he teased.

"Well, anything you might need a costume for," she articulated, handing him a clipboard and a pen. "Fill this out for me, and when you're done, we'll get to the nasty business of measurements." She waved him to one of the chairs around the riser. "Even when we source clothes, we'll tailor them to fit. And as you're one of our leads, I'll be responsible for your wardrobe." She presented him a sheepish smile. "It gets a little personal. So – I'm sorry in advance."

He winked, seating himself in a chair. "I can handle it," he promised.

Elizabeth glanced at Dana who was covering her mouth with her hand. The younger woman waggled her eyebrows then darted away. Elizabeth tried not to stare and focused on picking out a measuring tape from her supply kit with her back to him.

The tap of a clipboard on her shoulder ended her avoidance, and she turned to find Jared holding it out to her. "I assume you've been through this before?"

He nodded, kicking off his shoes and bouncing up on the riser barefoot. "The first time was awful," he recalled. "But Janine, the head back then, was old enough to be my mother, so I got over it pretty fast. The other guys and I got used to having our asses assessed by near strangers. I get that it's not a come on."

Elizabeth inhaled slowly for several counts, then looked at his toes forcing the thought of assessing his ass from her brain. "For the record, someone spilled straight pins earlier. I think we got them all up, but I don't generally like bare feet in my area just in case."

Jared nodded his understanding, lifting his arms into a T-pose. "I'm ready. Let the groping begin," he proclaimed.

She couldn't help the squeal that escaped her lips. "Stop it!"

"No," he replied, easily, relaxing as she hopped up behind him. "I don't think I will."

Elizabeth placed the tape against his shoulders, jotting down a number on the clipboard and moving to measure his bicep. She arched a brow when he flexed it, and the tape slipped from her hands. "Were you born difficult or are you trying?"

"Born," he laughed, then relaxed and stood still for the next measurement. "I'm sorry. I might be a little giddy. It's so unusual to be recognized anymore."

"It has been nearly twenty years since your show was on the air," Elizabeth replied gently, slipping the tape around his chest. "Relax your arms."

Jared complied with a sigh. "Damn, I'm old. This movie's a big deal for me. I know it's just a TV movie—"

"It's a streaming service," she interrupted. "That's more than just TV. That's millions of homes. Even I have it."

"Still TV. Not big screen."

Elizabeth could imagine the frown on his face and thought she detected it in his voice. She tried to ignore the fact that she was inches from the boy whose posters had been on her wall while she was growing up and for whom she still harbored feelings. She also attempted to avoid touching him, but it was impossible, and his soapy, sweet cologne was distracting.

"Don't be nervous. You'll be great," she encouraged, slipping the tape lower to find the narrowest part of his torso. She focused, keeping her eyes on the tape. It was inevitable though, his hips were next, and she slipped her hands to the side to avoid touching his behind.

He chuckled. "So, you know my old show?"

Elizabeth stepped off the riser, moving to his side. "Yes," she answered, biting her tongue to keep from telling him she could still quote every line. She stilled her hands before placing the tape against his hip and avoiding his eyes as she dragged it to his ankle. She wanted to apologize for what came next, but she stopped herself. She wouldn't apologize to any other client. Why should he be any different? Boldly, she thrust a hand between his legs, measuring his thigh quickly then lowering her hands to measure his calf. She gulped. She had been disassociating herself from the warmth of his body as she'd touched his arms and chest and torso, but now came the dreaded inseam. She shook out her hands, staring at his exposed ankle.

"It's hanging left today," he revealed.

Her head snapped up, brows scrunching as she studied his face. Why would he say that? Now all she could think about was the thing apparently in his left pant leg.

"Pick your side," he challenged, smirking down at her with a wink.

Elizabeth knew she had just turned purple, feeling the capillaries in her cheeks begin to itch. "You are so wrong," she sassed, taking the measurement on the right leg. She made her notes then set his shoes on the riser. "I'm finished."

He slipped into them then bounced down.

"I don't want it to be weird for you," Elizabeth asserted. "I'll be professional, I promise."

"It won't be weird," he maintained. "We can be friends. It's cool. I know what being a fan is. It would be like if George Lucas walked in."

Elizabeth thought it wasn't quite the same thing unless he was gay. She was disappointed at the suggestion of being friend zoned upon first meeting, but it was probably for the best.

She held out a hand. "Friends," she agreed.

His fingers were warm over hers as he squeezed. "Friends." He released her hand. "I have to be at the table read. Could you point me in the right direction?"

"I'll walk you," she offered. Elizabeth didn't wait for him to accept before she briskly led the way to the reading room. She was a little sad when he didn't quite keep up, always about two steps behind. The set was loud as cameras were being positioned and props were being anchored into place. She sidestepped a maze of cords as they neared their destination. She pulled open the door to the reading room for him and fought not to roll her eyes when he insisted she go ahead. She respected his gallantry, but in a work setting, she didn't think it really mattered who walked first...especially if they were just friends.

Two large folding tables were pressed together with seats around them. On one wall was a table lined with beverages and artfully arranged pastries. A handful of people were seated around the reading table with steaming white foam cups and food near the door, but Elizabeth didn't recognize them. The film's director, Max, a stump of a man crowned with a plethora of curly, black hair was pouring over the script at the head of the table, red pen in hand scrawling notes nervously. He looked up at their approach.

"Elizabeth," Max greeted as she entered. He stood quickly, pulling her into a hug. "I see you've met Jared."

Elizabeth wanted to bounce around in circles at having met Jared already, but, remembering her place as the Head Costumer, not to mention her age, she simply nodded politely.

Max reached to shake Jared's hand excitedly and leaned in to her as if to share a secret. "You may not know this, but Jared has been acting since he was a teenager."

"Oh, she knows," Jared said with a laugh. "We bonded over it while she was taking my inseam."

Elizabeth flushed, watching him hook a thumb in the waistband of his jeans and waggle his eyebrows.

Max glanced between the pair. "You do? Is this going to be a problem?"

"No problem," Elizabeth vowed. "We're friends now. All good." It was never a good idea to get involved with coworkers on a set, and she understood his concern, but it was misplaced. She was the last woman on the planet that Jared would be interested in hooking up with, she knew. The director had nothing to worry about.

Max did not look convinced but focused his attention on Jared, directing him to a chair and talking about the other actors he was expecting. Max had promised to introduce her to their leads that morning, and afterwards she was free to disappear into the wardrobe area to work on the costumes. Elizabeth snagged a bottle of water and paced awkwardly, waiting for the others to arrive. The sooner she could get back to her safety zone, the quicker she could stop making a fool of herself glancing in the direction of a certain celebrity crush.

She was too mature to be so taken aback, she told herself. She had always loved his smile, and in person, it was hard to ignore. Even worse, she had been on the receiving end of one of his wicked, dimple-inducing smirks. She could still smell him and closed her eyes briefly as she breathed deeply. She immediately remembered the way he'd flexed a muscle and made her lose her grip on the tape. Her body was singing with delight thinking about crouching at his feet when she took the last few measurements around his ankles, and that he was especially nice to look up at. She took a long drink of water, trying to clear out her mind.

The reading room door burst open, snapping Elizabeth back into the moment and revealing the female lead actress, Amara Baker. Her honey brown hair was plaited down her back, shining like a shampoo ad campaign. Her lithe body was clad in a summery embroidered sleeveless top with a plunging neckline atop a pair of white jeans with casual wedge sandals, and her stride exuded confidence. Amara wasn't especially tall at five and a half feet, but she commanded the attention of everyone in the room.

Had Elizabeth not studied the call-sheet that morning, she'd have recognized the other woman, but would never have recalled her name. Ms. Baker was a seasoned character actress without any specific movie or show attached to her name. She was the sexy girl next door, the occasional grieving widow, sister, friend of a main character actress who had never had a lead role. Elizabeth was wary. Everyone in the industry could be touchy, but the people who were on a precipice seemed to be the closest to exploding.

Max stopped his conversation with Jared mid-sentence to rise, throw open his arms and veritably skip to greet the newcomer. He appeared beefy and massive wrapped around her slim figure. The embrace lasted moments, and Max was ushering her to the head of the table, introducing her to Jared. They would have no scenes together, Elizabeth knew, but she still felt a twinge of jealousy as they shook hands, each blasting their full celebrity smile at the other.

Elizabeth turned to the door as more people entered, until finally, the last lead actor breezed through the doors, Starbucks cup in hand. He strutted right over to Max, taking the director's hand and pulling him in for a hug either unbothered by or unaware of having interrupted the conversation.

"Scott!" Max greeted in delight, clapping the taller man on the back.

Scott Harper was a face Elizabeth recognized as her favorite member of his mega successful boyband. While he would always be a fond memory for her, she had let go of her schoolgirl crush for him relatively easily when his solo debut turned out to be what she considered an over sexualized plea for attention. Somehow, even though Scott was a celebrity heavyweight, she wasn't nervous about taking *his* measurements. He was just another body that needed clothing. Cute, to be sure, but just a client.

Elizabeth chuckled to herself as she watched Amara take control of the situation again, inserting herself between Max and Scott and cooing for an introduction. She frowned, noting that Jared was now effectively cut off from the conversation. His pose leaning back against the reading table seemed resigned to his fate. Not liking this one bit, Elizabeth strode over to stand next to him, nearly shoulder to shoulder.

"Looks like all my leads are here," Elizabeth pronounced, touching Jared's elbow as she took a turn at interrupting.

Pulled from the messy introductions, Max nodded. "Elizabeth, this is Scott Harper, my good friend and colleague. He's doing us a huge a favor by playing this role. I think he'll make a great on-screen dad," Max prattled.

Scott reached a hand to Elizabeth, shaking it briefly. His ice blue eyes glanced at her before he pulled away, standing tall at just over six feet.

"This is Amara Baker, who you might recognize from *everywhere*," Max continued.

Amara shook Elizabeth's hand. "I hear you're a very important lady here on set," Amara gushed, holding the other woman's hands between both of her own. "I hope we'll be very best friends."

Elizabeth wondered where she'd heard that and returned the gesture lightly before tucking her hands into her elbows. Her professional smile was beginning to freeze, and she breathed through it.

"And *you've* met Jared," Max finished, turning from Elizabeth to the taller man. "Scott, this is Jared Rains, and this is Elizabeth Morris, the genius behind our costuming for the film. When I saw her vision for wardrobe, I knew she was the one. So, treat her right, or she'll put your codpiece in the wrong place."

Elizabeth rolled her eyes. "There are no codpieces," she guaranteed and shook her head. "I look forward to working with each of you," she articulated. "However, lots to do if we're going to start filming next week. So, if you'll excuse me, I'm going to get started on that while you do the table read." She pointed at Amara and Scott. "And I'll see you both after."

The actor and actress both nodded politely.

"Of course," Max acknowledged.

With a little wave, the costume designer started toward the door, cringing when Max called out behind her. "The retreating form of Miss Elizabeth Morris, everyone. Your sex appeal is in her hands!"

She took a calming breath and smiled, doing her best queenly wave as she exited the room. She groaned once the doors closed behind her, releasing the stress of the recent exchange. Why did Max have to bring up codpieces when she was already trying not to think about Jared's pants?

Dana ambushed her as soon as she reached her station. "So?" she quizzed. "You're upright. How was it? Did you get his inseam?"

Elizabeth scowled. "I don't need help like that," she scolded. "And of course I did. How else are you going to tailor his pants?"

Dana gestured zipping her lips shut and pressed them tightly together. It lasted a brief moment. "You're blushing. Tell me everything."

Ignoring the request, Elizabeth set about selecting Jared's costume from the clothing she had procured in advance.

Two

Reading Room: Amara

"Welcome, everyone!" Max announced, and the reading room suddenly quieted down.

Amara watched him closely, surprised that someone flying so seemingly under the radar had hushed the room with just two words. This was her second time in his presence, and she felt obliged to show him respect; after all, he was giving her the lead in his movie.

This sci-fi drama network film had not been her first choice of roles. However, when her agent told her it was a lead, Amara had jumped at the opportunity. This was a step up which would certainly lead to the big screen. Or it would be her last, and maybe she would finally take a short break.

Her introduction to their costume director as the face "you might know from everywhere" still stung. Being a character actor paid the bills, but it wasn't what she'd dreamed of. She wanted her name on the headliner.

Max was detailing what they would be doing and described the process to the greener actors in the room. It was tedious, but this wasn't her first rodeo, and she smiled at everyone. You never knew who was going to turn out to be someone, and it cost her nothing to smile at even the bit players. It also helped to not be upstaged if you were the biggest fish in the room. She considered the other actors and realized that Scott was actually the biggest fish, but she consoled herself with the fact that she had more experience on set than anyone else.

She had done her research on her fellow principals, and she glanced in their direction. Jared, on her left, had a long history of working, but not long-term success, and she felt an immediate kinship with him. He was the oldest and the least successful. She was surprised at how pleasant he appeared, and she wondered if she would have had the same grit he displayed sitting there so serenely smiling at everyone knowing what he'd been through.

On her right, was Scott Harper. He would be playing her on-screen husband. She was familiar with his work but had been too busy with all her hundreds of tiny roles to pay him too much attention. But she didn't live under a rock, so she knew how successful he was. Now, she assessed him discreetly, as everyone opened their scripts. He was beautiful, she thought. His face was like chiseled marble set around his otherworldly silver-blue eyes. His dark hair was wavy around his ears, tempting her fingers to tangle themselves in it. He was the tallest person in the room, she noted happily, thinking how she would fit quite neatly beneath his arm.

Amara was determined to make this role her bitch and finally have her name associated with a film – regardless of its platform. How else would she get better roles if she couldn't hang onto the lead in a small production like this? She glanced to her right as the read began, thinking she could tame this tall man with a flick of her hips and focused her attention on her own script.

The table read lasted for just over two hours, and Max congratulated the cast on getting through it so quickly. For another half hour, he gave out notes to each of them, including Amara who took his commentary with grace. It took another twenty minutes to extricate herself from her fellow actors before she made it through the doors. She hoped Scott would be on her heels, but he was not. She meandered toward wardrobe for her fitting, pleased to find the woman she met earlier near the door.

She rapped her knuckles against the frame of the cubicle walls of the principal's dressing area to alert the other woman to her presence. "Elizabeth, right?" Amara asked. "Like the queen."

The designer chuckled. "I suppose. Right this way, Ms. Baker."

"Oh, please. We're colleagues. Call me Amara," the actress insisted, following Elizabeth to a riser in center of a three-way mirror.

"Amara," Elizabeth complied, handing her a clipboard. "If you'll just fill this out for me so I have some basic information, I can get onto the business of measurements."

Amara groaned. "Everyone's favorite part, I'm sure."

A sympathetic smile answered her. "I know. I know. Don't take it personally. They're just numbers. Everyone has them," the seamstress comforted.

A young woman flitted toward them, and Elizabeth introduced her assistant. "This is Dana. She's my right hand."

Amara nodded politely, finishing up the form. It was blessedly short, asking the sizes she usually wore in a variety of clothing options, including shoes, and her preferences on colors or any known fabric allergies. She finished it up in a quick scrawl and passed it to Dana who stood by with a pencil.

Elizabeth gestured for the actress to step onto the riser, and Amara did so uncomfortably.

"Is this your first time being measured?" the seamstress asked.

"Not exactly," she said. "I've had clothes altered before."

"Ah. Well, this is a bit different. I know it feels intimate, but it's just between us girls," Elizabeth assured, moving up behind her.

Amara felt a light touch from shoulder to shoulder. Elizabeth murmured a number to her assistant, and her hands flew so quickly, she barely noticed when a thin, flexible tape slipped briefly around her bust, her waist, her hips, and so forth until she thought every inch of herself had been measured. "That was quick. Thank you," Amara uttered, stepping down.

Elizabeth flashed a friendly smile. "Well, no need to drag it out. And since you were first, it was nice to have some privacy."

As if on cue, Max appeared with Scott at his side. "You'll know the way next time," he encouraged, clapping the other man on the shoulder. "Take good care of this one, Elizabeth."

"I take good care of everyone," the designer responded, smiling reassuringly as Max departed.

Amara settled into a chair to watch as the seamstress guided the actor to the platform. Amara swallowed her chuckle at his helpless appearance.

Elizabeth flicked her fingers at the riser. "Mr. Harper, if you could stand up here, we'll get your measurements first, and then I'll ask you to fill out a short form for me."

Scott bounded up, facing Amara. "Are you going to watch?" he asked.

His surprised look fanned her mischievous nature, and she leaned forward to prod him. "Consider it method acting, husband mine," she teased.

Scott arched a brow, and she was startled at what an old pro he was, needing none of the instruction she had and virtually flowing with Elizabeth's routine. He even called out numbers as she measured, correct more often than not. He beamed at the three women around him. "I might've done this a few times," he professed.

"Clearly," Elizabeth retorted, passing him a clipboard and pen.

He took a seat, filling it out quickly and passed it back.

Amara eyed him none-too-discreetly. "I'm hungry," she announced. "And I don't want any of this Kraft services stuff." She patted Scott's knee on the seat beside her.

He startled, sliding his knee free of her hand gently. "Oh, well, Max's gonna give me a tour of the set and stuff." He stood slowly, taking a step back.

Blinking, Amara peered from him to the costume director. "Who says I was asking just you? I could've been asking Queenie too," she retorted, splaying her hand out toward the costumer and her assistant. "Maybe I was inviting all of us."

"Oh, uh," Scott stuttered. "Well, the knee and uh..." He fidgeted with his sleeve. "Sorry. I haven't been on a set for a long time."

Amara turned to the costume director. "Hungry?" she asked.

Elizabeth seemed caught off guard by the question. "Me? I'm sorry. I can't today. Too much going on. Another day?" she suggested.

"Sure," Amara answered, tossing her braid over her shoulder. She slipped the phone out of her back pocket and called for a car. "See you day after tomorrow." With a wave, she strutted toward the exit.

If no one wanted to have lunch with her, then it was their loss. She frowned, steps slowing, then turned back around and headed to the wardrobe department. Scott was already gone, but Elizabeth and Dana were still flitting around. They flitted back and forth like birds building a nest, scurrying from one side to the other. Neither seemed to notice her return. "Queenie, could you take a break if I brought lunch back here?" she asked.

Elizabeth whirled around. "Oh. Hi! Um...yes, I could do that."

Amara clapped. "What do you want?"

Elizabeth hummed. "No onions, peppers, or mushrooms. And nothing spicy, please."

"PB and J it is," Amara mocked, then spun on her toes and darted back out to meet her car.

It took Amara a bit over thirty minutes to find suitable fare, collect it, and return. When she did, Elizabeth was hunched over her sewing machine. It was yellowed with age, and some of the dials were worn smooth. The seamstress was flipping switches and turning dials with one hand on the garment. Amara jangled the bag with their lunch, and the other woman jumped.

"I brought salads and sushi," Amara detailed. "Where can we eat?"

Elizabeth held up a hand. "Let me finish one seam, and I'm with you," she answered. The machine whirred, and Amara watched as a dark green-gray silk raced beneath the machine's needle.

"You make that look effortless," Amara breathed over her shoulder.

Elizabeth chuckled. "You missed the last three times I worked over this same seam." She pulled the garment free and cut the threads, holding it up to her chest for Amara to see. "I'm working on yours first." She smiled.

The actress reached out to pick up the raw edge and smiled. "You just started it today?" She shook her head. "I do not understand how you crafty people work so fast."

Elizabeth shrugged. "Practice. The first garment I made took me a day just to cut the pattern pieces and another three to assemble it. And it was wrong." She laid the garment out as Dana rounded the corner, holding up two skeins of elastic.

"Will one of these work?" Dana called, looking between the two samples as she came to a stop. "I can start dying them if they will. Oh, hi, Ms. Baker."

Amara smiled and waved, watching as Elizabeth took the samples. "Don't you have Jared tomorrow morning?"

Elizabeth nodded. "His clothes are sourced, not hand made. Dana's already done the alterations during the table read, and he's just test fitting them tomorrow between blocking scenes. I decided to start on the most difficult outfit first." She examined the elastic from the younger woman and selected one. "I don't need it dyed. I'll make a pocket."

Amara shook the bag again. "Dana, join us. I got plenty."

Dana led them away, more interested in lunch than either of the other women. There was a picnic bench slightly outside the exit under a pop-up tent, and Dana took the bag from the actress, spreading out the contents with a hum of approval. "This is a feast," she complimented.

Amara slipped into the bench opposite the other two women and picked her meal from the bundle. "So how long have you been designing costumes?" Amara questioned the wardrobe mistress.

"Since I saw *Pretty in Pink* and Molly Ringwald made that awful prom dress," Elizabeth explained wryly. "I figured if everyone thought she was a genius for that monstrosity, I could definitely do it. Then I just had to learn to sew."

Amara chortled as the other two studied the remaining containers, and she gestured to them. "Not everyone is big on sushi, so those are all cooked, for the record."

Elizabeth pulled one box toward her, eyeing it cautiously. "I've never tried sushi."

Amara was shocked. "Never? In LA?"

Dana snickered softly. "Elizabeth is very sheltered," she tattled. "It was a big adventure the first time she had tacos on the set."

Amara wanted to laugh but thought that might not incur favor, so she kept it to herself. This woman was either hiding something or did not understand her own worth. Amara wanted very much to know which. Her hesitation gave her companion an opportunity to speak.

"So, what got you into acting? It seems like a very hard gig." Elizabeth changed the topic.

"What? Memorizing lines and regurgitating them in front of an audience?" She blew raspberries. "That's easy."

Arching a brow, Elizabeth popped a slice of sushi in her mouth and chewed thoughtfully.

Amara saw her chance and leaned in toward Dana. "First time you worked with Queenie?" she asked.

Dana's forehead wrinkled as she shook her head. "Why do you call her Queenie?"

"Queen Elizabeth," Amara enlightened.

Dana's eyes widened over her grin. "I like it."

"You may not call me, Queenie," Elizabeth said to Dana then turned an eye on the actress. "And you're avoiding a question."

"Ooh! You're as sharp as a needle," Amara retorted. "I've always had a flair for the dramatic. Acting is all there is for me."

The ladies passed the time convivially, but Amara noticed that Elizabeth veritably shoveled down her food, excusing herself to get back to the work within minutes.

Amara watched her go, alone now with Dana and half her meal. "Is she always like this?"

Dana nodded, stirring the ends of her salad around the plastic container. "We've worked together for three years now?" She lifted her eyes skyward, counting, then nodded.

The actress took another bite and waited for more details.

"She doesn't really get out much – all work and no play, you know?" Dana finally volunteered.

Amara nodded, thinking she could work with that. She wanted to win over this cast and crew. That's what leading ladies did, she reasoned as she began cleaning up the table.

"Thanks for lunch," Dana acknowledged. "If I'm gone too long, I'm afraid she might stitch herself into your costume."

Amara glanced curiously at the assistant.

Dana chuckled. "I, um...keep a lot of bandages on hand. When she rushes, she turns into a human pin cushion."

Laughing, the actress waved, and she watched Dana dart back inside.

Before the door fully closed, it swung open again, revealing Max and her leading man. Amara was glad she stayed.

Max seemed surprised to see her. "Fitting go badly?" he asked as they approached.

Amara shook her head, smiling brightly. "Not remotely. Elizabeth is great. In fact, I brought lunch back for her and Dana."

"That was thoughtful," Max complimented. "I've noticed she forgets to eat or to let her staff eat." He frowned. "Hey, I was about to show Scott where the trailers will be. I expect them to get here this weekend if you guys want to bring a few things to leave here. Clothes or music or phone chargers or whatever."

Amara nodded.

"You want to come with us?" Scott suggested.

She studied her costar's face, watching his half-lidded eyes glancing from his hands to her face, then to the asphalt lot and back.

"I'd love that," she replied, staring at Scott. She fell into step beside them, listening as Max rambled. As they walked, she began to worry that she was going to have to carry the other actor through the entire film. He was entirely too pretty to be good, she judged.

When Max stopped at the location where their private trailers would be installed, he stuffed both hands in his back pockets. "Amara, you have been totally under-utilized, and I think you're going to shine in this. And, Scott, man. You're gonna make every woman in the audience want to be married to you. I'm gonna be so jealous."

At this Scott laughed. "You couldn't handle more than one woman," he teased.

Max bounced lightly from one foot to the other trying to deny it but couldn't. "Well, I guess I won't see either of you tomorrow. Jared will be in, and we're fitting most of the extras tonight and tomorrow."

"Is there some space for us to run lines in the background?" Amara asked.

Max shrugged. "Nowhere quiet except in wardrobe, and that's a hot mess today. They're still finishing the set." He scanned the area around them. "I mean, you're welcome to come back and find your own spot."

Amara turned to Scott. "You game? I really feel like we need to get started and work on our chemistry."

Scott scratched his head. "Sure. We can do that."

Amara named a time and instructed him to meet her at the picnic bench near the back door to the set and strode away. On the ride home, she contemplated their lengthy table read. Part of her wished that Scott and Jared's roles were reversed. Jared was equally hungry for the success she assumed from his resume. She bet he was prepared and knew all his lines within a few days of getting the part. He was fit and definitely limber looking, but there was no chemistry there. Something about Scott's presence felt like a dad who would pack up his family and move across the galaxy to pursue his work.

The following morning, Amara arrived on set before Scott, sporting a simple green spaghetti strap tank and denim shorts. She paced in her new straw wedges, admiring them as she did so. A long, silky scarf was wrapped around her head holding back her hair, and its excess tickled over her shoulders in the breeze. She scanned the lot, looking for Scott and glancing at her watch. He was five minutes late. She scowled. This was not a good start for their working relationship.

Amara seated herself at the picnic table, leaning back and crossing her legs. She sucked in a deep breath, one foot tapping restlessly. When she spotted him strolling toward her, she waved her script and pointed at her watch.

He sped up, jogging toward her. "Sorry. I got lost," he explained when he reached her. "Again. I've figured it out for tomorrow."

Amara arched a brow at him as his cheeks pinked, and he sat down on the bench next to her, leaning on one knee and looking at her. "So, true confessions," he revealed, scratching the back of his neck. "I'm used to having people sort of take me where I'm supposed to be and someone else sort of manages me. And I'm a little lost without that person. Last night, a lawyer showed up on my doorstep threatening to kick me out because I hadn't paid my mortgage. Someone used to do that for me, and it slipped through the cracks. Thank God they accepted a check, or we'd be having a very different conversation right now."

Amara had the grace to laugh. "Feeling a little lost, eh?"

He nodded. "But I'm serious about this movie," he promised. "I needed a change from the music, and I don't want to let Max down."

Amara couldn't help her sigh of relief. She set a hand on his knee. At least he was trying. "I've got your back. Stick with me, and we'll get through this together." The resulting smile she received melted her insides. "Ready to run these lines?"

He nodded, pulling the script out of his back pocket and flipping to a specific scene. "I was hoping we could start here." He showed her the page number. "I'm kinda struggling with how to play this one. I'm getting the impression that there's some tension unwritten in here."

Amara was familiar with the scene, and she agreed, taken aback at his assessment.

"You look surprised," he noted.

"You just told me you nearly lost your place because you forgot to pay your mortgage," she demurred.

"Fair," he answered. "Look, this isn't my first acting gig. I did a show when I was a kid. I know how to be an actor. Nothing on this scale before."

Amara flipped the script to the indicated page. "Let's run through it," she suggested. "I think there's some movement in here we'll need to play with, too."

Scott took a position and started the scene.

Amara played along, and within a few lines, they were the characters. She was no longer Amara. He was no longer Scott. She was his wife, and they were talking about the potential pitfalls of moving their family to Mars to follow his research. When Scott finally called, "Scene," Amara found herself a little breathless.

Scott beamed at her.

When the clapping started, Amara watched his cheeks pink and felt hers begin to do the same, not having realized a small crowd of crew had gathered around them.

"Not bad for a first try," Jared complimented, separating himself from the crowd that was beginning to dissipate.

Amara curtsied at him. "Good to see you," she greeted.

"I wish we had some scenes together," Jared said sadly, looking between Amara and Scott. "The way this thing is written is crazy."

"I know. I think you're like my great, great, great grandfather," Scott teased.

Jared winged, looking at his shoes. "I know I'm the old fart on set, but that's a little harsh, man. I've only got four years on ya."

Scott clapped him on the shoulder. "It's okay to be older. It just means you're not dead yet," he consoled.

Jared laughed, shrugging his hand off politely. "Stop," he insisted. "You guys are really getting a jump on this. It's sounding great."

Amara agreed. "Thank you. Want any help running your lines?"

Jared chuckled. "No, thanks. Most of my scenes are me talking to machines and staring furtively at a computer screen – and then there's the rats." He shivered visibly at the remark.

"I do not envy that," she sympathized. "Some of your scenes get pretty brutal mentally."

Jared tilted his head. "I'm hoping none of it rubs off on me."

"It's a great role though. So open to interpretation," Amara assessed. "There's a lot of depth in your character beyond the cruelty if you're open to it." Amara's eye was drawn to her leading man who was glancing at his watch.

Scott shot a look between the two of them before he spoke. "This is fascinating, but don't keep Elizabeth waiting, man. I saw the looks she was giving you before the table read."

Jared waved him off. "Old fan. They're thin on the ground nowadays, but they resurface every once in a while."

Amara quirked a brow. "Really?"

"Don't make it weird," Jared begged. "I do a fine job of that all on my own." He lifted a hand and waved. "I'm off like a prom dress," he announced, then disappeared into the building.

With Scott's approval, Amara picked another, quieter scene, and the pair began their makeshift practice again. When Scott had shown up late to their appointment, Amara had started to write him off, beautiful or otherwise. But as they continued working through the scenes, and she listened to his thoughtful take on how to play certain aspects of the role, he began to gain her respect. It had been a little begrudging at first, but this man knew his way around a script at least. She hoped that when it really came time to perform, he would deliver. If this movie failed, she doubted she'd get another chance. If she had to act *his* way through it to get there, she would. Amara pushed all her judgements aside, reaching for her character's voice. Scott didn't know how lucky he was, she thought. They were both going to be a success if she had her way. And she would. She almost always did.

Three

Backstage, Wardrobe: Elizabeth

Elizabeth arrived early to set to continue working on the costumes for two of her principals. She was making good progress. Amara's tunic was nearly complete, and she was putting the finishing touches on the waistband of the matching capri pants when she heard singing.

Out of the corner of her eye, she saw Jared approaching, seemingly in his own world. He wasn't walking, exactly. There was a hint of dance in his steps, and he proceeded as though no one was watching. His hands lifted as he snapped silently to a beat only he could hear, and his hips jutted forward.

"Good morning," she called out.

His head snapped up, and he straightened, stuffing his hands into his pockets. "Is it morning still?" he asked.

Elizabeth nodded avidly. "It's like ten o'clock."

At this, Jared chuckled awkwardly. "No... it's going on one," he corrected.

She balked, picking her cell out of her back pocket and grimacing. She surveyed her staff, shuffling slowly at their stations, sending away another batch of extras who'd finished trying on their costumes. "Lunch!" she called out to a collective moan of relief. "Sorry!"

Several of them waved back at her, and she turned back to Jared. "Well, I guess you're ready for the fitting," she noted, making a beeline toward a waiting rack.

"Not if you're breaking for lunch," he rebuffed. "I don't mess with union lunches."

She waved him off, picking up three hangers and holding them out to him. "Nonsense. I'm your person. Not them."

He arched a brow. "When are you going to eat?" he asked. "I can't have my very own fan passing out on me while my pants are down."

Elizabeth's face flushed briefly, and she shook her head at him. "You don't stop, do you?"

He shook his head, accepting the items. "You stop, you die." He frowned at the words. "Or gather moss, or some such proverb."

She chuckled. "Be careful with that before someone overhears you and reports you for harassment or something."

The frown on Jared's face and resulting, "Oh," made her pause.

"Look, it's okay with me," she assured. "We're friends, I know. I just...want to protect you."

He nodded. "Thanks. I'll try to be quieter about it. Where can I try these on?"

She indicated a pair of screens that gave him plenty of privacy and turned her back to further insulate him. She listened to the sound of his zipper being undone and squeezed her eyes shut. "You're in a good mood today." The sound of fabric sliding to the floor heated her cheeks, and she was grateful as he picked up the thread of conversation.

"Yeah, heard one of my favorite artists in the car this morning," he explained. She heard another zipper and sighed in relief.

"So, what is Mr. Rains driving at the moment?"

"A 2002 BMW 325i," he enunciated proudly.

Elizabeth's heart skipped at the pride in his voice. "Very nice," she admired.

She heard footsteps and turned to see him emerging as he pulled the white lab coat over his outfit, adjusting the collar. "It's 2018," he pointed out.

She shrugged. "So? It's not a Yugo."

He sprung onto the riser, holding out his hands to her. "What do you think?"

She scrutinized his form , trying not to sigh at the way the tailored outfit hugged him in all the right places. "How does it feel?"

He shifted around, tugging at the coat again and nodded. "Surprisingly comfortable. It looks tight. Is it tight?"

Elizabeth shook her head. "Fitted," she corrected. "Not tight." Instead of telling him to do a circle for her, she walked around him, reaching to tug his pant legs. "I can see your ankles. I'm not sure if I like that," she mumbled.

Jared looked down his legs then to her. "What's wrong with my ankles?" he questioned.

She laughed. "Nothing. You have perfect ankles. I'm trying to decide if it's right for your character."

"Isn't that a Max question?"

"Probably. When Dana gets back, I'll send her for him." She eased away, assessing him from the shoulders down. "Can I see it without the coat? I want to make sure it's not going to bulge or anything if you take the coat off during a scene."

He complied, letting it fall behind himself and, in one smooth gesture, slung it over his shoulder dangling by his index finger. He jutted out a hip and rested his other hand on it then struck his best model pose and met her eyes.

"Do I have any unsightly bulges?" he murmured. His face contorted, lips wriggling until finally one corner of his mouth curved upward.

She rolled her eyes, pulling the jacket from his grip and laying it over her arm. "I'm glad you're amused. I want to give the audience every reason to look at you."

"What's with the *Rush* shirt?" he asked, pulling at the band shirt he was wearing till it puckered around his torso.

"Every nerdy scientific dude I've ever known has been into either *Rush* or *Marillion*. Count your blessings that *Rush* is easier to source, or you'd have some freaky nutcracker looking kid on your chest right now." She shivered at the memory of the album cover she had picked out for an ex in her youth.

"Spoken like a real-life experience," he noted.

She nodded, feeling his eyes following her as she walked. "Yes, we all make mistakes in our past." She sighed, focusing instead on his outfit. The fit was right in the seat of his pants. Even the T-shirt followed the form of his torso. "Where are the shoes?" she asked, then turned back to the clothing rack. A heavy plastic bag contained a pair of worn, white tennis shoes and socks. She passed it to him, and he moved down to accept it and sit in one of the chairs.

"I had the shoes sanitized, but I still recommend socks," she encouraged, watching as he treated the socks like vipers. "The socks are brand new."

He frowned. "I simply hate socks. I avoid them at all costs." He gestured to his bare toes perched on one knee. "Which is why you can see my awful ankles," he cajoled.

"Your ankles aren't awful," she ceded. "Hairy, but not awful."

He laughed at this, and Elizabeth went in search of Max. She dragged the director back to the fitting area, explaining her concern as they walked.

"He still needs hair and makeup. I'm thinking maybe a messy wig or something," Elizabeth was saying as they joined Jared.

Max eyed the actor, and Jared bounced up on the riser again. "I like the ankles. It's sort of... absent minded," Max decided.

Elizabeth frowned. "Did you roll the socks down?" she asked, reaching to see that he had done just that. The mid-rise tennis shoes bulged at the top. "I'll get you some no-shows," she promised.

Max asked to stay to see the next outfit, and when Jared disappeared behind the screen, he pulled Elizabeth away from the booth. "Everything okay?" he whispered.

Her brows furrowed. "Great. Why do you ask?"

He sighed. "When he announced the inseam thing at the table read, I worried that he was maybe a little forward."

Rolling her eyes Elizabeth waved him off. "I meant it when I said we were good. I'm like his little sister or something," she affirmed.

"Guys don't talk about their inseam with their sister."

"It's fine. I promise I'm not feeling harassed. If anything changes, you'll be the first to know."

"I'd better be," Max insisted. "I don't want our names in the mud over this."

She sighed. "It's kinda funny," she admitted. "I don't mind."

Dana approached the pair, sticking her head in close. "What are we whispering about?"

"Things okay with him?" Max questioned, pointing toward the screen.

"Very good. She's laughing." Dana squeezed the director's forearm. "I'm watching," she promised.

Max seemed satisfied at this, all three turning to face the actor who was patiently waiting on the riser. His brown plaid suit, sweater vest, and T-shirt looked both awful and perfect at once.

"Oh, yes. That is our professor," Max declared, clapping his hands as Jared took a bow. "And we absolutely need to see his ankles with this," he added.

Jared lifted his pant leg and waggled a foot at the group. "Who has time for socks when there are discoveries to be made?"

Max nodded. "I like it. Let there be ankles," he announced. "Send him to hair and makeup. Get pictures. I'll pick the final look. One character nearly done!" he broadcast happily as he walked away, hands in the air.

Elizabeth and Jared exchanged a look, and while he fist-pumped the air, Elizabeth hugged her elbows to her sides and twisted her hips in a happy dance. "Okay, let's get you to hair and makeup. How do you feel about some glasses?"

"I resemble that remark," he joked, jumping down and following.

By the end of the day, Jared's costumes were sorted, and Elizabeth and Dana were making copious notes and zipping his outfits into garment bags with a photo of each in a baggie stapled to the lot. Jared insisted that he and Elizabeth go with Max and Dana for drinks, and by the time they had found their way to a nearby watering hole, Amara, Scott, and half a dozen other crew members had joined them as they crowded the bar waiting for their first round.

"To small victories," Jared toasted his costars.

"To people who get the vision," Max added, clinking his bottle to Jared's. He eyed Elizabeth and the principal actors. "I'm excited to see what tomorrow brings."

"Me too," Amara agreed, sipping her drink. "She had half of my costume done yesterday, by lunch."

Embarrassed, Elizabeth hid behind her opaque martini and sipped it. The corner of her nose twitched. It was strong and tasted like coffee.

"Time is money," Max declared. "I hired the best."

The group split up, the crew finding themselves a table and the actors drifting toward another with the director. Dana and Elizabeth didn't seem to fit at either table and tucked themselves into a small table between the two. They discussed what they were drinking, surprised when Amara grabbed each of them by an arm, Max scrambling behind her.

"No. I will not allow this," Amara asserted. "The whole point of drinks it to get to know each other, and you two have a head start."

Max pulled chairs up to the actor's table, and the others scooted closer together. When Amara returned to her seat between Scott and Jared, she barely fit, but she giggled as she shouldered her way between them.

"I want to know everyone's worst thing they've ever done for money," Amara asked the entire group.

The table oohed at the provocative question as Elizabeth and Dana settled into their chairs.

"I'll go first," Amara decreed. "After high school, I did singing telegrams for a minute. And I was once sent to a board meeting dressed as a Teletubby."

The entire table shrieked, demanding to know which color and what she was singing. Amara held up her hands, refusing to give any additional details other than being grateful that her face was covered, and no one knew it was her. She demanded someone else have a turn.

Max went next followed by Dana, and Elizabeth squirmed, anxious to hear what Jared had been up to in the last twenty years. When he spoke, she was on the edge of her seat. "I was once paid to dress as Barney at an outdoor flea market to entertain kids while it was 110 degrees," he confessed.

Elizabeth clapped a hand over her mouth as the rest of the table broke out singing the infamous "I Love You" song the purple dinosaur had made popular. She shook her head, almost not hearing when Scott confessed to trash collection at the end of a particularly nasty roller coaster at an amusement park. All eyes turned to her, and she froze. She was still thinking about Jared in a Barney costume sweating to death.

Dana nudged her, and she jumped. "Cleaning toilets at a shop where the guys would wait till I got there to take their daily...movements so I'd have to clean it in a cloud of stench."

The resulting groans prevented additional questions.

"You're looking at that drink like it's one of those toilets," Jared pointed out.

"There's coffee liqueur in it," she complained, frowning.

"And this is a problem, why?" Amara questioned.

"She hates coffee," Dana answered.

Everyone at the table regarded her appalled, and Elizabeth used that as her excuse to stand. "You're welcome to this if you want. I'll see if I can find something else I can drink," she excused, darting for the bar. She ordered a simple amaretto sour and assessed the tables of people from the set. Max had disappeared from the actors and insinuated himself into the table of crew, clinking bottles and laughing at something. She noted begrudgingly that he had stolen her chair. Dana was perched at the edge of the table still leaving Max's previous seat available.

She braced herself as she returned, taking the last available seat...next to Jared. She thought for a moment she had evaporated into flames when he winked before turning back to Scott across the table. She sipped her drink, listening quietly.

After an hour, the crew left, citing early call times, then Scott peeled off, and Amara next leaving Elizabeth with Jared, Max, and Dana.

"So, what even is that?" Jared pointed to the untouched milky looking concoction. The martini glass had been sitting in the center of the table, its contents separating into murky layers while Elizabeth nursed her new drink.

"It was supposed to be a chocolate martini, but that's full of Kahlua," she explained, wrinkling her nose. "A proper chocolate martini shouldn't taste like anything besides chocolate."

"You're not picky at all," Jared scoffed.

"Of course she is," Max agreed. "That's why she got the job. That's why we had a whole conversation about your ankles."

"My *hairy* ankles," he amended.

"Okay, yes, I'm a big dirty fan," Elizabeth admitted. "But I'm always going to tell you if you have spinach in your teeth. It's not kind to hide stuff like that from people. And your ankles are just as nice as the rest of you." She watched Jared's face as the last words left her lips, sighing relief inwardly when he smiled.

Dana giggled, hugging the older woman, laying her head on her shoulder. "And this is why we love you," she articulated.

"You're a good egg, Lizzybeth," Jared praised before swigging the end of his drink.

Elizabeth turned an eye on him. She didn't have nicknames, and when people had tried to shorten her name, it was usually Beth, and she hated that. The kind affection in his voice pinked her cheeks, and she toyed with the straw in her drink.

Max groaned. "Okay – I need to get this out in the open because it's been bugging me all day. I don't need any harassment suits, guys. Please. So – if you two want to fraternize, can you please keep it on the DL? Like seriously, on the DL."

Startled out of her happy glow, Elizabeth turned her eyes on the director. "Dude, I do not understand the obsession with this," she protested. "We are not fraternizing. Do you not have any friends?" she asked, suddenly realizing that she did not. "People tease each other, and it's cool. If I'm cool, and he's cool, why can't we all be cool?"

Dana pulled the glass out of Elizabeth's hand. "I think you hit your limit."

Elizabeth wrinkled her nose. "Yes. I'm at my limit of one." She rose from the table, gathering her purse and pulling out her keys. She turned an irritated eye on their director. "I will conduct my affairs in private. Have no doubts." She waved sweetly first to Dana and then to Jared. "I will see you both later."

Not waiting for Max to respond, she turned on her heels and stalked toward her car. With each step she grew a tiny bit angrier. She knew that Jared wasn't interested in her. He'd said so from the start. He was a nervous actor possibly getting his last opportunity to make good on his acting career, and he had rushed through the door she'd opened when he found out she was a fan. And she was a grown ass woman, she reasoned. If Jared Rains wanted to play-flirt with her, she would take it. It's not like anyone else was trying. And in a few months, this whole gig would be over, and she'd be alone again. She may as well make hay while the sun was shining. She hadn't felt this excited about her work ever.

She locked the doors of her apartment behind her once she was inside, feeling like at each turn of the tumbler, another part of the world was being shut away. She felt free in her own space, despite her dining table being used for a makeshift sewing room, designs and fabric scraps scattered somewhat haphazardly across its surface. Her actual sewing room, which was technically a second bedroom, was too full of materials and tools to work freely.

She dropped her purse in its hidey hole behind the couch and plopped down at the table, pulling out her sketch book. She began salvaging fabric swatches to build the base for the next thing she wanted to make. She wondered if she could convince Dana to model it for her but scratched the idea. She didn't feel it was fair to ask someone who worked for her to give more time – unpaid no less.

Suddenly tired, Elizabeth retired to her bedroom, pulling on a pair of loose, comfortable sleep pants and a nightshirt. She spied the pictures still taped around the edges of her dresser mirror. A few, small magazine pictures of Jared still clung to its surface. The habit was a holdover from her teen years. Her father had not cared if she had pictures from magazines all over her bedroom. He was more concerned about pinholes or tape residue on the walls, which had led her to find creative ways to hang her teen idols all over the room. The one that had infuriated him the most was when she started taping things to her enormous dresser mirror. She had left approximately an eight by three-inch patch open where she could see her bangs and curl them with a hot iron. That was all she needed.

At thirty-three, she still had a few pictures taped to the glass, though far fewer than in the past. They framed her life in the images that gave her joy, and she started to feel a little guilty about the ones of Jared now that she'd measured his inseam.

Part of her considered carefully removing them and tucking them in the box with the others she had collected. He was not even eighteen in the photos, she realized as she slipped between the sheets. But the good news was, he would never see her bedroom mirror. And in a matter of weeks, she would be finished with this set and off to the next, and he'd be gone. She may as well enjoy the fantasy while she could. Releasing the guilty from her pleasure, she drifted to sleep.

Four

Backstage, Wardrobe: Amara

Construction on the set was nearly complete, and without the constant buzz of saws and hammering, Amara was amazed at how loud the staff in costuming actually was. There were lots of instructions being barked as actors with smaller parts were fitted by the other staff. She wound her way through the organized chaos until she found Elizabeth and Dana hovering over a rack of clothing in the principals' dressing area. She approached quietly, not wanting to interrupt.

Dana was the first to see her, smiling broadly and waving.

Elizabeth followed suit, passing her clipboard to her assistant. "Can you go make sure all the other fittings are going well? Feel free to crack the whip in my name."

Dana waggled her eyebrows. "I can't wait." She skipped off quickly, leaving the actress alone with the costumer.

"Are you ready to become your character?" Elizabeth asked, rubbing her hands together gleefully.

"I am," Amara agreed. Excitement surged as she placed her handbag on one of the waiting chairs. "Bring it on." She waited impatiently as she was handed three hangers and a pair of hard-soled slippers.

Spying the dressing screens, Amara hurried behind them. She placed the hangers over the screen edge, eyeing the green-gray silk tunic. She

"

had seen the workings of it the day before but hadn't expected it to feel so lush in such muted tones. The garment was accented with emerald leatherette around the neckline, hem, and shoulders, giving it a surprisingly geometric shape. She shimmied into the tunic, pleased when the seemingly too tight garment fell into place, snug in all the right ways.

She struggled to look over her behind herself unsuccessfully. A large portion of her back was exposed in a diamond shape, and she felt her bra strap cut straight across it. "Am I supposed to wear this without a bra?" she called through the screen.

"Yes, and no. I'm still sourcing the right long line for you. Leave whatever you're wearing on for now," Elizabeth replied.

Amara pulled on the matching emerald slacks. They tapered down her legs, and Amara straightened the chevrons at the front and back of her mid-calf. "Wow," she cooed, running her hands up to her waistline where they snapped around her hip.

"Fitting okay?" Elizabeth asked.

"Yes. This is very different from having my clothes altered," Amara expounded. She wiggled her toes into the slippers and stepped out from behind the screen.

Elizabeth clapped. "Up," she instructed. "Up on the riser."

Startled from her stupor, Amara stepped up, turning to face herself in the mirror. The pants were somehow snug and modest all at once. She loved the way the tunic brushed her hips in an asymmetrical hemline, soft over the buttery pants. "I feel almost too sexy to be a mom," she muttered.

Elizabeth laughed. "You're the wife of a big exec type. You've got some means. The others are going to be dressed...differently." She tugged on the pant legs and lifted the bottom of the tunic. "Can you move in it?"

Amara stretched, squatting low and nodded.

"My fear is that it won't breathe," Elizabeth fretted.

"Prettiest pair of pants I've ever worn," she flattered. "I like it."

"Why don't you test it out? Scott should be here soon, and you can go find Max together. See what he says."

Amara sneered. "He's probably lost." She fished her cell from her purse and punched in the number from the call list. She waited while it rang.

"I'm here!" Scott's voice called out across the building as the back door banged shut. "Had to get gas." He jogged to a stop in front of the ladies, catching his breath. "Did you know that there's an arrow on the dashboard to show you which side the gas tank is on?"

Elizabeth chuckled, turning her back on them.

Amara nodded gently. "And how did you figure that out?"

"Kid on the other side of the pump told me after griping at me for taking up the wrong side. It wasn't pretty."

Elizabeth thrust a set of hangers at him and pointed toward the dressing screen. "Well, you're here now. Let's get you outfitted and see how you work together."

Rushing to comply, Scott slipped out of view.

Amara patted the seat next to her, looking at the seamstress. "Don't you ever sit?"

Elizabeth laughed. "All the bleeding time," she said, but took the seat anyway.

Leaning comfortably back, she tried to distract herself from thinking about the man stripping off his clothes within hearing distance. She couldn't see him, of course, but her brain was painting an intimate picture while she remained quiet. "How late did you stay for drinks last night?"

"Until Max made it weird, and I had to leave," she groused.

"What's that about?" Amara asked, wondering at the on-set drama.

"Sincerely, it's a molehill that he's turned into a mountain. I don't want to be censored in my own studio."

Amara arched a brow. "Censored how?"

Elizabeth shook her head, standing again. "I'm an adult, and I'm allowed to decide for myself what people can say to me." She paused, and a proverbial black cloud passed over her face. She met the actress' eyes, pointing for emphasis. "And the worst part is, Dana took his side!"

Dana appeared at that moment, smiling weakly at the other two ladies. "We're cool," she pledged.

Elizabeth's shoulders softened. It was a blessing when Scott stepped out to display his costume, immediately climbing onto the riser. "Do we get socks?" he asked.

Elizabeth gestured to Dana, who disappeared. "You can have all the socks you want," she answered.

Scott tugged at the sleeves of his jacket, shrugging as it all fell into place. "This is nice," he praised.

Amara assessed him in his navy blue and gray attire. It amazed her that his suit was so reminiscent of one without being one. She was beginning to see the vision as he stood before her.

"It works for you," Amara noted appreciatively. It was a fight not to lick her lips, and instead she bit the tip of her index finger to cover the curling of the corners of her mouth.

Dana returned with socks, and Scott sat on the chair beside Amara to put them on. He perused the actress appreciatively. "I married up," he ribbed.

Amara blinked at him, feeling the corners of her mouth hinting at a smile. "Yes, you did," she countered, standing and doing a full turn for him. "Let's go find Max and see this set they're building for us."

Scott agreed, holding an elbow out for her. "I figure we should get used to walking as a couple," he explained.

"Practice makes perfect."

They started away, and Amara hid her amusement as he seemed unsure of what direction to take. She guided him toward the set, keeping one eye open for Max as they circumvented the cords, and cameras, and tracks that were now in place.

"Did you bring your script?" he asked hopefully, dodging a passing catering cart.

Amara tapped her head. "Up here," she countered.

"Impressive. The whole thing?"

She tilted her hand back and forth. "Most of it."

Ahead of her, Max was studying a gray wall of the set with the art director next to him. The other man was holding up paint chips, and Max was squeezing his chin.

At their approach, the director turned, applauding. "So much better than paint! You guys look great," he enthused. "Come here. Sit here, but don't touch the walls 'cause they're still wet." He ushered them to a prop couch, seating them side by side. The director pulled back assessing them with the art director and returning to the paint chips.

Amara turned to her on-screen husband, schooling her face and meeting his eyes as she recited one of her character's lines. She expected him to be dumbfounded, but Scott's gaze darted away from her. When he turned back, he was in character, matching her intensity note for note, reciting the next line perfectly.

"Okay, okay, you showoffs," Max insisted. "Save it for the shoot. Go back and get changed…I know you have at least one other outfit each."

Amara stood, curtsying. She waited for Scott to follow, silent as they headed back to wardrobe.

He was pretty, she thought, dissecting him as they moved. He ticked her box for height; he was slim, and the costume he currently sported showed him to advantage. She wondered how taut he was beneath the fabric, but his piercing blue eyes were like walls of water cutting her off from anything more than a physical assessment.

Experience had taught her that once the filming began and they slipped deeper into their roles, some flirting would be inevitable. As a character actress, her job was to make a quick and strong impression on people – grab viewers in one scene and make them care about her murder, affair, mistreatment, etcetera. And more than once, she had costars enamored with her.

Some of them she kept secrets about, but as she felt the familiar need rising in her brain, she thought that on a long-term set like this, slaking her thirst with the tall drink of water next to her might back-fire. If she wanted to unearth his specific mysteries, she'd have to play the long game so that when he got bored and they parted ways, at least filming would be done. No – if she had an itch to scratch, she knew where she could find a solution with far less on-going drama.

"So, after we finish with wardrobe, you wanna go to the reading room and run more scenes?" Scott proposed, holding the door between the set and the back areas open for her.

She nodded. "Of course. You can't over practice a scene, right?"

His resulting smile was charming. The rest of the fitting was a blur. The second outfit was far less successful, and Elizabeth vowed she would have it right before filming started. Scott's outfit was perfect, tucking into his shoulders and highlighting his behind perfectly.

She ran lines with Scott as promised, finding that she believed the words passing through his lips. It was more like playing than working, she thought as they developed their performance.

"I think I'm finished for one day," she proclaimed.

He smiled, nodding agreement. "I think we're going to nail it. We're gonna knock this out of the park."

She laughed. "*If* Max likes what we've done."

"It's like muscle memory," he insisted. "I feel like we're really in the groove together."

She smiled. "We're doing great. Let's hope our fictitious kids can keep up."

"Oh, that Catherine? I think she's going to act circles around us," he retorted, gathering his script as she collected her purse. "She was on the ball at the table read."

"She also has the fewest lines. If Sean doesn't nail the last scene, we've done all this for nothing." She sighed.

"Have a little faith. Not everyone in the universe is out to get us," Scott consoled. He paused as she reached for her phone.

"I notice you're always calling for a rideshare," he pointed out. "Is your car in the shop?"

Amara shook her head. "No. I gave up driving about ten years ago," she explained. "LA's getting busier every day, and why risk it to go through the hassle of maintenance, insurance, and all that when I can use the drive time to go over the script?"

"I never thought of it that way," Scott said. "That's pretty smart."

She did a little twirl and curtsied. "Thanks."

"Well, I'd be happy to save you the trouble and give you a ride," he offered.

Amara tilted her head at him, trying to figure out his intentions. "I'm probably out of your way."

He shook his head. "I don't mind. I've got nothing better to do."

Amara didn't answer, analyzing the way his cheeks dimpled around the corners of his mouth. His silver-blue eyes crinkled as he awaited her answer.

"We can even grab lunch...or is it dinner now?" he asked looking at his watch.

Amara cast an eye at her phone. "Lupper?" she asked. She *was* getting hungry, and the thought of not having to cook or order in would be a nice change of pace. She sighed languidly, flipping her hair over her shoulder and fluttering her lashes dramatically with a deviant grin. "Okay, but you'll have to wow me," she directed.

He smirked. "That, I know how to do." He pulled his cell from his pocket as he led her to the car, sending out a quick text. "You active on social media?" he asked.

Amara nodded, posing as he held the phone up in the air, his long arm angling the phone easily. She smiled saucily as he snapped a photo. "I'll post it after we eat, but I wanted to send it to Geno before we get there. We get good food; he gets all the fan business when I post the picture on social media after we leave."

She chuckled. "Clever. You must have a lot of favors in your pockets still."

He nodded. They had reached his Mercedes S-class now, and he held the door for her.

Amara slipped inside the luxury beast, still smelling dyes and leather. "So...you get lost on set; should I be concerned that you'll get lost on the way to the restaurant?"

Scott laughed. "I deserved that. But no – going out on the town...I've got," he reassured her, pressing the start button next to the steering wheel. The engine purred as he snapped his seatbelt into place.

Music filled the car, and Amara eased back in her seat, allowing the sound to wash over her. His fingers drummed the beat against the steering wheel. Other than acting, this was the most at ease she had seen him since their first meeting.

"After the movie, do you think you'll go back to recording?" she asked casually.

"Probably. It's in my blood," he reasoned. "No matter what I'm doing, I'm always composing in my head."

She nodded, thinking she was very often acting and wondered if the interest she was showing him now was feigned or not. She appraised his profile, loving the way the fading sun was deepening the shadows around his cheekbones and emphasizing the curve of his full lips.

"What's been your favorite role to date?" he asked, "And this movie doesn't count."

She thought back, humming as she evaluated the many roles she'd had. "Probably the time I got to play the daughter of a woman who was dying. Lot of meat in that role even though it was one episode." She wanted to ask him the same question, but his career had been the same note for almost a decade. Music with the same band, followed by an unsuccessful solo album. It felt more like prying.

"Role you wish you hadn't turned down?" he asked before she could think of a question.

She hummed again. "I've turned down very few roles, and the ones I did were mainly because I wasn't ready to disrobe," she answered. "You'd be surprised how many offers I get for porn."

.The sound that escaped his lips was pure joy, as his face relaxed. "Same! Like I could ever say yes to that."

"Don't get me wrong. I like porn as much as the next person, but I don't need to star in it. I'd rather have this kind of leading role than that."

"Talk about your short appearances," he joked.

"Speaking from experience?" she countered, eyeing him playfully. "I don't know about you, but I don't do *short* appearances." Her eyes narrowed, inhibitions evaporating in the privacy of the car as he navigated around the city. "Kinkiest place you've ever gotten your freak on?" she challenged.

He glanced from the road to her and back. "Seriously?"

"Seriously," she insisted, crossing her arms defiantly.

His lips pinched in thought as he eased to a stop light. "Behind a club between a pair of dumpsters," he answered.

She nodded. "Brick wall. Nice."

"Your turn."

"What gave you the impression this was quid pro quo?" she asked innocently.

He eased the car into the restaurant driveway. "Sex usually is," he retorted.

The car rolled to a stop, and she sprung her door open before the valet could reach her. "And the best sex always leaves you wanting more," she countered, slipping coyly out of the car.

Scott fumbled his keys to the valet and scrambled to hold open the front door for her. She winked at him as she sauntered past.

True to his word, the owner was waiting for them, having cleared a special table in a back corner and plying them with food and drink immediately. When they were finally alone, Scott leaned forward, dangling a fork over his plate. "So, I know you're an actress, and you're bold and smart...tell me something about you I don't know," he encouraged with a smile.

Amara felt like all the spotlights had turned on her, and she'd forgotten to take off her facial cream while standing naked in front of her high school classmates. She blinked at him.

"Is there something specific you'd like to know?" she asked slowly. What was his game? They had been having fun in the car, and now he was getting personal.

"I'm not asking what kind of birth control you use. I'm talking about like, best vacation spots...how many siblings... nieces and nephews. Least favorite food. Things a friend might know."

"I think I'd rather talk about birth control," she drawled, focusing on the plates in front of them. "Your friend must like you. He's showing off." She pointed at the food.

Scott's smile faded slowly, and he speared a bite. "He does. He's making me fat." He frowned.

Humming in delight at her first taste, Amara relaxed. "But what a way to go." She released a sigh. "I want to be friends with Geno."

Scott eyed her carefully. "So have I sufficiently wowed you?" he asked.

She nodded, taking a second bite and chewing slowly. The flavors were bold and exploded on her tongue.

They ate in silence for a bit. "So how do you know Max?" she asked, hoping to get him talking.

"He directed a few of our videos," he answered. "He was always so good with us. Really clear direction and easy to work with."

She saw something akin to sadness cross his face and wondered what she'd said to spark this. "Do you not see the band anymore?" she asked gently.

"They're pretty busy. We all are, I guess."

"How long were you on tour?" she questioned.

He shrugged. "I don't actually know. I lost track. You have someone that tells you where to be. Someone that dresses you. Someone that feeds you. When you come back from that, trying to be a real person sometimes is...challenging," he admitted. "I think it was a few years all told. Because, I remember holidays on the road. Families don't really understand being gone on the holidays, which is odd, since we never had a poorly attended show that time of year..."

Scott's face shifted, and he seemed very far away. She could only guess what he'd been through, and it sounded lonely. "That must have been difficult to be in such tight quarters with the same people for that long. I usually get a few days with people, and then everyone goes their separate ways."

"No," he refuted. "It's good. I miss them. We're all doing other stuff now. After a while, you get used to people, and then it's weirder when they're gone than when you're with them."

The faraway look had returned, and Amara frowned, trying to think up some other topic to distract him. "Favorite season?" she asked.

"Summer. Perpetual summer," he answered quickly. "Yours?"

She thought for a moment. "I like the crisp air in the fall and cuddling by a fire in the winter."

He smiled softly at her as he listened, and Amara found herself somewhat unnerved. "So, tell me something about yourself that only a husband would know," he prompted, twirling a fork around his plate.

Amara arched a brow. "Why?"

"I'm thinking about the intimacy people like our characters have. And if I have to play your husband, I thought it might help. You know – little inside jokes and stuff."

She blinked rapidly at him. All that came to mind were her fetishes, but she certainly wasn't ready to share that with him. "Mmmm...I've never had a husband. I'm not sure how that works."

He cast a withering glance at her. "But you've played a wife on TV before. Surely you can guess. What's something that I would know about you if I was your husband?"

Amara balked at the suggestion. She realized his questions were coming from the perspective of the actor playing her husband, but she still hesitated. She mentally went through the list of things her past partners had never figured out about her. "I especially enjoy being tended to – whether I'm sick or not."

Scott nodded. "Princess... got it."

"I'm not a princess," she snapped.

He held up his hands defensively. "I mean it in a positive way. You want to be treated like royalty. And you should," he retorted.

Her eyes narrowed as she speared a vegetable with a fork. "Usually, people don't mean that in a good way when talking about adult women."

Scott scooped up a large bite, answering absently, "I do. I'm all for spoiling the right woman." He shoveled the bite into his mouth, cheeks bulging as he chewed.

Amara let the subject drop, then her face assumed a wicked expression as she swallowed. "So, tighty-whities or boxers?" She laughed as he started to choke on his bite.

He wiped tears from his eyes as he caught his breath.

"Something only a wife would know," she clarified.

"My character wears boxer briefs. No lines," he answered hoarsely.

Amara wagged her fork at him. "That's good."

"Siblings?" he asked.

She shook her head. "Just me. You?"

"One brother. One sister. That I know of," he clarified.

She cast a sidelong glance at him. "That's an unusual answer."

"I'm adopted."

Amara's gaze snapped up in shock. "I'm so sorry. I didn't know." She wanted to sink into the ground for what turned out to feel like an incredibly insensitive question.

"I'm not. My adoptive parents were amazing. I was young – I didn't really know any different. I, you know, don't look a lot like them."

Amara ate a few more bites and set down her fork. It wouldn't do to gain weight now that the costumes were prepared. "This was delicious," she proclaimed.

Scott's brows furrowed. "You're not done already, are you? You hardly ate."

"Such is the life of an actress." She sighed. "After I get fitted, I'm afraid to eat lest anything should change. Maybe I could take it home?"

He nodded. "You don't mind if I finish, do you?"

She shook her head. "Take your time. Scenery is pretty enough," she countered sipping her water. She watched his cheeks pink, and his eyes darted back down to his plate. She peppered him with questions about where he was from, how long he'd been in the industry, and how he'd gotten his start. It felt a little like pulling teeth, but once prompted, he volunteered the information freely. She noticed that if she wasn't asking a question, the conversation lulled, and she didn't like lulling conversation. After all, the purpose of going to eat was to get to know each other.

When he finally took her home, she was never so grateful to see her house. She thanked him for dinner and waved as she skipped up the walkway to her front door. She paused at the entrance and pointedly watched as his car rolled slowly away then picked up speed. She thought about him as she let herself into the house.

He was an enigma. On fire when he was acting, but as a person, she didn't understand how he had achieved heartthrob status and maintained it for so long. Sure, he was pretty to look at, but she doubted a man who couldn't carry a conversation would be very good at holding any other court with her. She was far from tired, and the earlier exchange about starring in porn films had her body begging for attention.

She stripped out of her studio clothes, peering into her closet. Shiny fabrics twinkled at her in the warm bedroom lights, begging to be donned. She realized it was barely nine, and she was pretty certain she had friends lounging at the club, Dragonfly. She slipped into a pair of soft black leather hot pants and a matching crop top then tugged on a pair of vampy black stiletto thigh boots and went back out.

Her heels clicked confidently across the concrete walkway as she strode into the club and directly to the smoking patio in back. As she ordered a rum and coke from the patio bar, long arms snaked around her waist from behind. She could think of simply one person on premises would be so bold, and she shivered at the touch.

"Hey, babe," purred a familiar male voice.

Her body puckered at the warmth of his breath on her earlobe, as she leaned back into the embrace. She didn't have to guess who it was. She recognized the voice and the tattoos brazenly puling her back toward the sinewy body behind her. Taking a swallow of her drink, she murmured, "Frankie, you naughty boy." Cautiously, she asked, "And where is that wife of yours?"

She and Frankie had been playing this game for years now. The attraction between them was undeniable. Despite their serious re-lationships with other people, whenever they were near each other, sparks flew.

He pulled away and turned her to face him. He stretched his arms out to drape on either side of her head, elbows resting on her shoulders. "She's left me. I'm a free man, babe," he informed her.

She arched a disbelieving eyebrow. "Is that so?" She had heard this before. The last time he'd said something similar, the wife had been on vacation with her girlfriends.

"You want proof?" he asked. Before she could respond, he leaned down, arms drawing back till his hands were on the back of her head, twining in her hair as he kissed her until she was breathless.

This was new. They had ridden so very close to the line for years, but this was definitely crossing it.

Startled, Amara drew back and stared up at the lanky man. Licking her lips slowly, she tasted the beer he must have been drinking earlier. Part of her was angry he hadn't asked about her entanglements and kissed her senseless. However, she had shown up alone in hot pants and gone straight to the patio where she knew he would find her.

"So, stick by me tonight, babe," he bade, drawing her in to his lean body.

Amara exhaled slowly at the way they fit together like puzzle pieces, and an erstwhile part of her howled greedily. She remained motionless in his embrace for fear of losing control, her eyes meeting his, mentally chewing on the proposition.

The rest of the evening was a blur. Frankie lavished attention on her, and she went along, shell-shocked. During all the time she'd known him, Frankie had either been engaged or married to the woman who had finally left him. Amara had even fancied herself half in love with Frankie during one tumultuous year. Now, after all this time, here he was wrapping her up in his arms. He was fulfilling her long-dormant fantasies as he periodically nibbled at the sensitive spot just behind her ear or tugged her hand to his lips to kiss the inside of her wrist.

As the club closed, Frankie twined his long limbs around Amara again and told her to come back to his place. "Come on, babe. Car's this way," he urged when she hesitated.

She eyed him in the moonlight of the patio, challenging him. "I'm done with relationships, you know," she advised. "Can you do this casually?"

He stared back, kissing her sensually. "Whatever you want, babe. I'm yours."

Taking a deep breath, she nodded and closed her eyes. She could feel her heartbeat in her throat as Frankie pulled her to him and kissed her deeply. Her knees nearly buckled as his hands gripped her behind. Moaning softly, she broke away. "Let's go," she gasped.

Five

Backstage, Wardrobe: Elizabeth

Dana was sprinting away as Elizabeth tried not to cry. She should have been used to the tools of her trade by now, but she had lost focus while threading the machine and felt the sharp sting of the needle as it jabbed her finger. She scolded herself, eyes feverishly going over the garment near her machine. At least she kept the blood to herself. This latest poke had been deep, and she was sadly sucking on her finger when Jared joined her.

"Are you trying to turn me on?" he asked coyly.

Chuckling despite the pain, she offered him a wry smile. "Who says this is for you?" she asked, nearly forgetting the coppery taste of blood on her tongue.

He gasped. "Lizzybeth, is there someone else on set for you?" He spun around, eyes darting over the room. "Who is it? Is it Greg, the camera guy with the saggy pants?"

She shook her head with an amused smirk.

"It's the saggy pants, isn't it? My hairy ankles turned you off." He sighed, grabbing at his heart. "Curse my excess body hair," he bellowed, dramatically dropping to his knees. "Please don't make me wear baggy pants to win your affection...or shave my legs."

"No, dear, it's just you for me," she croaked. "Hair and all." She popped the wounded finger back in her mouth, hoping the bleeding would stop soon.

He beamed, standing and dusting off his knees, nodding at her hand. "What'd you do to the finger?"

"Stabbed myself on the sewing machine needle trying to put in the replacement too fast. I've done it before, but this one was deep."

"I'd offer to kiss it and make it better, but you've slobbered all over it." He made a yuck face.

Elizabeth flushed, pulling her finger free to investigate. "Dana's bringing me a bandage." She scowled at the tender spot as blood began to pool again.

Before she could put it back in her mouth, Jared flourished a tissue at her. "Here. This should stop it."

She accepted it gratefully, smashing it to her fingertip.

His eyes were on her as she squeezed the injured appendage. "Is it bad? I can find the medic," he offered.

Elizabeth shook her head. "I'll be fine."

"If you're sure," he added, then leaned closer to study the garment near the machine. "Whose costume?" he asked.

"Catherine's. The nine-year-old that plays the daughter. She claims it's pinching her under the arm, and it's easier to fix myself than hear about it again."

"Where'd you learn to do all this?" he asked, curiosity lighting up his features and making him look ten years younger.

Elizabeth averted her eyes and shrugged. "Self-taught, mainly," she replied. She felt his heat behind her, and she breathed a sigh of relief as Dana rounded the corner with a med kit in her hands. She accepted it with many thanks.

"Where's my costume?" Jared asked.

Dana took over, passing him his outfit and sitting beside Elizabeth as she doctored her own finger. "Do you want gloves?" the assistant asked.

"No. I can't work in gloves," Elizabeth complained.

"Finger condoms," Jared called out through the screen.

Dana's eyes were wide. She blinked rapidly, her mouth hanging open in both horror and delight.

Elizabeth turned to the screen, watching as Jared's head poked out.

"To cover the bloody finger," he explained, brows furrowed. "Get your mind out of the gutter," he scolded, grinning cheekily before his face disappeared again. "What else would you use them for?"

Dana looked at Elizabeth, jaw still on the proverbial floor.

Elizabeth shook her head, chuckling. "Have you had a lot of bloody fingers?"

Making an ugly face, Dana shook her head violently, and she slapped her boss's knee, motioning for her to be silent. "No," she mouthed.

"Um...I'm not going to touch that," Jared answered, stepping into view. His folded clothes were in his hand, and Dana jumped up, holding open a monogrammed bag.

"Whoa, is that a custom bag?" he exclaimed, dropping his clothes inside.

"Yes," Dana noted. "Elizabeth made them up once the contracts were confirmed. We don't have lockers, and this will keep everything together for you."

"I'm flattered." He gazed at the costumer as her assistant offered to store it for him.

"You coming to set today?" Jared asked. "I don't see you sewing for a while with that finger."

She nodded. "Yeah, I want to see the costumes in the right lighting. See if there's any adjusting required." Her eyes roamed up and down him, his white lab coat highlighting his figure as he tucked one hand in his pocket. She shook her head. "But yours is pretty perfect. Guess you don't need hair and makeup today?"

He shook his head. "I'm praying for my hair to grow out some. I'm afraid someone will bring up a wig again."

She covered her face, splitting two fingers apart to peek at him. "You have beautiful hair," she complimented. "I don't know what possessed you to cut it all off."

He rubbed his fingers together as they walked toward the set. "Lot of maintenance costs. Money that a broke artist like me doesn't have." He eyeballed the parking lot over his shoulder. "May I refer you back to my sixteen-year-old car?"

She smirked. "Well, I hope you make bank on this and grow it back out."

He rolled his eyes as they found Max on set, and he walked ahead of her. "Rains, reporting for duty," he announced with a salute.

Max saluted him back then waved behind him to where Elizabeth was standing.

"You're doing the blocking today, right?" At Max's nod, she folded herself into one of the canvas chairs settled near the main camera. "I want to see what it's going to look like on film in case I need to change anything."

Max sent Jared to the set, asking him to move around and walk. Elizabeth stood beside the director at the backside of the camera watching the tiny screen. She was fascinated by the seeming magic she saw through the lens, and the way the wafting light changed the tone. However, when Jared began dancing, she burst out squealing and clapping as he jumped around the set.

"Enough! Don't go popping any splits and pull something," Max scolded.

"Dude, I got my start as a dancer in show business," Jared retorted. "I know what I'm doing."

"Famous last words," Max warned.

Jared held up his hands in concession. He winked at Elizabeth from across the set when Max ducked behind the camera again and instructed him to walk behind the fake lab equipment.

"Look good?" she asked Max.

He nodded. "Yeah. He's good to go. I'm more concerned about the others. That fabric reflects light differently." He gestured toward Jared.

"And seriously. You nailed his costume. He couldn't wear anything else. I'd change the set before his clothes."

She bowed happily. "Thanks," she answered. It felt good to be recognized. The last job she'd had did nothing but criticize. It was a welcome change. "I'm going back then. Got to get Catherine outfitted."

"Good," Max inclined. "I've met her mom." He caught her arm as she turned. "Actually, I have something to throw at you."

Elizabeth frowned. "What kind of thing?"

He scratched the back of his neck as he answered. "So, you know early on we talked about a cameo role," he began.

"Right. The belligerent passenger," she recalled. "But you hadn't had any luck on the right person."

He nodded. "But I do now. And he's coming in this afternoon for measurements. Because you're so fast..." he cajoled. "Can you take the fitting tonight and have something for him by Monday? I really want you on this and not one of your assistants."

She sighed. "I don't have anything in the tank for that."

"But you could do it, right? Something simple...basic"

Her jaw dropped before she quoted her favorite movie. "You keep using that word. I do not think it means what you think it means!"

There was clapping behind her on the set. "Good quote!" Jared called out.

She gave him a thumbs up for recognizing the line and returned to scowling at Max. "I'll figure it out." She sighed. "What time today?"

"Well, he has another appointment, and when that's done, then he's supposed to swing by. I'll bring him back when he gets here."

She sighed. "It's a good thing this is my first big gig, or I'd consider leaving you stranded. This is the last one," she insisted.

Max held up his hands defensively. "Yes. The last. I swear."

Elizabeth put him behind her, heading back to wardrobe. Her head was swirling with thoughts of what materials she had in stock or could get easily.

She was suddenly tired, and when she arrived, she found Catherine, her mother, and Dana chatting. Dana's voice was high pitched and unusually fast, Elizabeth thought. She sighed, slipping on her very kindest smile.

"Catherine!" she greeted. "It's so good to see you again. I heard about the trouble you're having in your costume."

The young girl rolled her eyes. "You can't expect me to have something poking me all the whole movie."

Elizabeth nodded. "Of course not. That would be absurd. I've been working on it this afternoon. I found the problem, and it should be all good now. Let me trim a couple threads, and your mom can help you try it on again, if that is okay with you."

"I can do it myself," Catherine insisted. "I don't need help."

"Yes, right." Elizabeth started to give her a thumbs up and saw her bandaged finger looking a little less dainty than she was willing to show her young client. She gestured to Dana. "Would you snip those threads for me and hand it over?" she asked.

Dana complied quickly, passing off the tiny costume and motioning toward the changing screen.

Elizabeth reached for the med kit and fished out another bandage with her back to the others. She opened it and swapped it out quickly, pulling it tighter in hopes of stopping the oozing wound. She examined the rolling drawer where a stack of small rubber rings. She squinted then fought the urge to groan as she rolled a finger condom over the fresh bandage.

Catherine emerged and stepped up on the riser for Elizabeth to assess. "It's less pokey," she conceded. "Thank you."

The costumer nodded and crouched down to examine the hemline. "Hmm, I don't think this tunic is hitting you in the right place," she noted. "Let me make some notes, and we'll have it sorted for you by the time you start on Monday."

"Yes, thank you. I thought it was crooked, but maybe that was on purpose," the young girl agreed, standing up straight as Elizabeth dropped to her knees to pin the hem.

She had nearly finished when a commotion interrupted. Elizabeth carefully pinned the fabric on the young girl and was about to investigate the waistline of her capris when the thunderous footfalls stopped behind her.

It was Max. "Elizabeth, our cameo has arrived."

Elizabeth started to call back that she was busy, but she wanted to give him the courtesy of saying it to his face and turned to do so. Her eyes lit first on the curly-headed director before shifting to notice he wasn't alone. She recognized his counterpart, and she nearly swallowed the pins tucked in the corner of her mouth.

Max's face was covered in pride, chin pointed slightly skyward, and he even had one hand poised on his hip. "Chris, this is our costume director, Elizabeth."

Keenly aware of her position on the floor, she held her breath as Christopher Stone bent over and reached a hand down to her.

"Greetings and salutations," the actor acknowledged.

Elizabeth stretched up to shake his hand, and it took every professional instinct not to spit the pins from her lips to ensure she didn't swallow them. "Pleasure to meet you," she replied.

Before the exchange could go any further, Catherine's mother, Barbara, leaped forward to introduce herself and her daughter.

The actor kindly shook her hand and drew back, listening and nodding as Barbara talked about her daughter and herself.

"I think you're finished," Elizabeth said softly to Catherine.

Rising slowly, the seamstress brushed off her knees, turning to Dana. She pinched the spare pins from the corner of her mouth between her fingers. "Can you take Catherine back to her usual dressing room and bring her costume back?" she requested quietly.

Catherine was looking bored, and the moment Dana reached for her hand, she accepted it, leading Dana away. "Mother!" she called over her shoulder.

Barbara stopped, mid-sentence and waved before trailing after her daughter.

"Looks like a party all the time," Christopher teased, glancing between Max and Elizabeth.

Max grimaced slightly. "Always something happening back here," he added.

"So, you're our very special cameo," Elizabeth mused, tucking her hands in her elbows to hide her wound.

"So, I hear," he said, leaning in conspiratorially as his voice lowered. "Your director looked like he was going to piss himself when I walked through the door." He chuckled, adding, "Your man on set in the lab coat handled it well." He rubbed his hands together. "I'm here to participate in the age-old practice of invasive measuring. Is there a...sign-up sheet or something?" He was waggling his eyebrows.

Elizabeth chuckled. "Right this way."

He stepped onto the platform.

"You're in good hands, Mr. Stone," Max vowed. "I'll let you get to it so we don't waste your time. We're really glad to have you."

Christopher waved silently, effectively dismissing Max.

"I'll take it from here," Elizabeth pledged as she extracted a measuring tape and a notebook from the storage bin. She raked her eyes from Max to the exit discreetly.

Max crossed his fingers and pressed his hands together in a praying motion as he backed away and finally disappeared.

"This is a big operation you have going here," he noted conversationally as she searched for a pen. "You handled that kid's mom well, and your assistant is well-trained."

"We're a team around here," she eschewed, stepping up behind him and beginning with his shoulder measurements.

He appeared loose and comfortable as she moved around him. She felt it as she touched his limbs, muscles pliable to the touch.

His head turned slightly to follow her path, and he spoke up again. "So, what kind of look are we in for? No codpieces I hope."

She giggled. "No. Futuristic, but no body suits or matching uniforms. People still have a fashion sense and choice. Any favorite colors?"

"No. No. I wear what I'm told. I do try to avoid yellow. It makes me look like a walking puddle of piss," he mumbled.

Elizabeth snickered. She liked him. He was charming. "Not a fan of yellow myself," she stated. "Think upscale tunic style suits. The little actress I was working with will be in the scene with you."

He nodded, chuckling when she slipped the measuring tape around his chest. Elizabeth grinned. Calling it a chuckle was generous. It was really a giggle. "Ticklish?" she asked.

He cleared his throat. "No, that was a very manly response to a tunic," he defended coolly. He smoothed his hand over his sides where she'd touched, composing himself.

"I'll try to be more careful." She lowered the tape carefully to measure his torso then down his hips. "Good?" she asked as she stepped down.

The actor was biting his lip to hide another titter. "From you? I don't mind."

Elizabeth smiled back at him, making quick work of the last measurements. She had seen him clothed, but she had a good picture of his exact shape. She was looking forward to designing his costume, and she started to picture him in shades of silver with blue trim. Her cheeks felt warm as she studied at him. "Hopefully, you won't hold my forward hands against me."

"Only in your favor," he supported.

She couldn't help the resulting grin that lit her face. She tapped his foot lightly. "You're finished."

"What? So soon? That's it? You didn't even *accidentally* touch anything interesting," he complained.

At this, Elizabeth cackled. "The last thing I need is your shoe size."

"And here I was hoping you might want my number...or be willing to give me yours. You know, in case I have anything else that needs to be measured."

Her breath caught in her throat as his gray-green eyes stared down at her confidently.

"I think that could be arranged." Smoothly, smoother than she'd ever felt in her life, she retrieved a business card from the top drawer of the cabinet and passed it to him. "For all your measuring needs," she teased.

He grinned, taking it from her and slipping it into his pocket. "Excellent," he cheered, jumping to the floor. "So, is it even possible to make something from scratch by Monday?"

She nodded. "I can't promise it'll be pretty inside, but it'll look good on camera," she promised, eyeing his neck and picturing a penny round collar.

He bit his lip again. "Well then, you have your work...*cut*...out for you," he chuckled. "Oh, that was bad. I heard it when it came out. Sorry," he apologized.

"Well, I appreciate that you tried," she excused.

"What time on Monday should I be back?" he asked, sliding on his shoes.

"Would noon be okay?" she asked.

He adjusted his collar. "One would be better for a fitting. So, we'll have time to finish lunch," he clarified.

The heat that flooded her cheeks was instantaneous. She fought not to fan herself, hoping he didn't notice, but there was no hiding it now. One small comfort was that no one else was around to see it. She allowed her eyes to roam his face. He was leaning in expectantly.

"One it is then," she agreed.

"Excellent! I look forward to it." He rubbed his hands together in satisfaction. "I'll see myself out." And with that, he was gone.

When Dana returned, Elizabeth was still staring after him in shock. Had that truly happened? All this time she had spent drooling over Jared, and this well-known actor had simply waltzed in, taken one look at her, and asked her to lunch.

Dana pinched her boss sharply on the upper arm. "That was Christopher Stone," Dana observed. "Even *I* know who he is."

Elizabeth nodded. She blinked a few times, looking at Dana until she could focus on the other woman's face. "I think he just asked me out."

The tiny woman's eyes turned to saucers, jaw dropping open. "Tell me you said yes," she pleaded, squeezing her hands together.

Elizabeth nodded dumbly, drawing back as Dana bounced and clapped.

"What are you going to wear?" the younger woman pressed, dropping into the chair beside her boss.

"I haven't even thought about it. It's a lunch before his fitting," Elizabeth reasoned.

"Well, okay, a little black dress is out of the question, but something black...and low cut. And tight..."

"Dana...." Elizabeth frowned. "That's not very me."

The assistant jiggled her brows. "But it should be if you want his full and undivided."

Holding up her arms, the head designer regarded her own shoes. "I did fine this way. I'm not going to stress about it."

Dana slid closer. "How did it go measuring his inseam? Was it worse than Jared's?"

The question gave Elizabeth pause as she considered her answer. In Christopher's case, she didn't know where his third appendage was after it was all said and done, unlike Jared. She fanned herself. "Well, no. It was all neat and professional. I think I was in a little bit of shock. He just...showed up."

"Ah. No time to foster nerves," Dana concluded. She pursed her lips and tilted her head as she asked her next question. "How long were you twisting over knowing you were going to meet Jared?"

"Three weeks?" Her own answer surprised her. She remembered getting the details from Max after everything was finalized and staring in shock. It had taken her a full day to believe it. She hadn't told anyone for fear of being too distracted to do the actual work when the time came.

It surprised her too that taking this mega star's measurements had been like anyone else. Of course, that was before he'd asked her to lunch. Maybe that was how she had gotten through it. Switching back to her professional brain, Elizabeth refocused her attention. "I'm going to need more fabric. I have another costume to make."

Six

Frankie's Residence: Amara

Amara stretched lazily Thursday morning, her body aching in all the right places. Frankie's bed was surprisingly comfortable, but her internal clock was nagging loudly that she had places to be that weren't his bed. Namely, she was due at the studio in about ninety minutes, and she wanted coffee before she addressed her adoring public.

She extricated herself from her lover's arms to shower. Her clothes from the night before were strewn somewhere between the front door and his bedroom, and she used one of his duffle bags to corral them. She refused to do a walk of shame to the studio in thigh boots and hot pants, and there would be no time for a pit stop at her house. Resorting to his wardrobe, Amara pulled a black T-shirt from his closet. It was thin and patterned, nearly see through in places, but it hugged her curves cheekily, and she thought it would do. She squeezed a pair of his ripped jeans over her hips and rolled the cuffs around her ankles. She found a pair of his slip-on house sandals to cover her feet which were shy of comically large to complete the look. When she was ready to go, she woke Frankie and pressed him into his clothes.

"Studio. Now," she instructed as she buttoned his pants.

He was cranky, she thought, for someone who had been so well sated less than six hours ago. But he acquiesced, kissing her neck naughtily as they made their way to his red Corvette. The trip to the studio was a blur, and she concentrated on sipping her coffee as he drove.

"Hey – those are my clothes," he pointed out shy of the parking lot.

"Yes," she answered.

"When am I getting those back?"

She shrugged. "We'll see."

He pulled through the studio gates, allowing her to direct him. She instructed him to stop at the back door where the increasingly familiar picnic bench sat empty in the shade. When she opened the car door, she was assaulted by the loud beeping of large vehicles backing up.

Amara stepped out of the car, looking around. The cast RVs were being delivered, she realized, watching as a trailer was backed into place. She felt a pinch on her ass and jumped, twirling to face the driver.

"Naughty," she scolded, wagging a finger at him.

Frankie had the audacity to look at her innocently before licking his lips. "Can I pick you up tonight? Get my clothes back?"

She leveled a gaze at him. "No strings," she reminded. "I'll call you." She closed the door. The engine revved behind her, and she heard it squeal away. Amara slung the duffle over her shoulder, sipping her coffee as she started toward the door.

Chills raced up her spine, when she felt a pair of eyes on her and turned to see Scott standing next to his car, watching her with a slight frown on his face. She wondered how long he'd been there. Something about her felt suddenly dirty despite a thorough shower that morning, and she rushed inside. She nearly barreled through someone exiting and caught her balance just before she hit the ground. She grumbled an apology, setting the person to rights and darting inside the building. She stopped again, spinning around and opening the door to peek outside.

Movie icon, Christopher Stone, retreated, and she considered chasing him down to apologize further. His pace slowed, and he stopped in front of Scott. At this distance, Amara couldn't tell what they were saying, but it was animated, and then Christopher pulled a cell from his pocket and handed it to Scott, who held it out and snapped a photo of them together. Not caring to watch any more, she let the door slam and reported to wardrobe.

Jared was passing Elizabeth a white lab coat as Amara arrived. He winked at the costume designer before grabbing a monogrammed bag from Dana and disappearing behind the dressing screen. Elizabeth's neck was splotchy red, and her usually tidy hair was mussed.

"What's up, Queenie?" she greeted. "You look like you're having a rough day."

"It's been pretty full," she agreed.

"Did you get to talk to Christopher Stone?" she asked, setting her bag on the floor and settling into one of the chairs. "I literally ran into him a second ago."

Elizabeth nodded, turning her back to Amara. "Yes, I saw him. And so did Catherine, Barbara, and Max...and he mentioned seeing Jared on set who was the only one who didn't piss himself when they saw him. Bravo," she called behind herself to him.

Jared cheered, and both women jumped when they heard a loud noise, and the dressing screens suddenly crashed to the floor. Jared was shirtless, hands outstretched about a foot away from the screen in an apparent effort to catch it. Amara wasn't sure if it was the string of expletives that passed his lips or the sight of his muscular body that caused her to feel heated.

"Wow!" Amara giggled. "You kiss *anyone* with that mouth?"

"Sorry," he muttered, reaching to right the fallen items.

"It's okay. You just...got a little excited," Elizabeth forgave. "It happens." She lined the partition up with its mate, her hands at a notable distance from his.

Amara exchanged shocked glances with Dana and watched in fascination as the pair fumbled around each other, watching Elizabeth handing his shirt to him daintily. Jared stretched upward, sliding the garment over his head and tugging it down.

Amara tore her gaze away from his well-sculpted torso and groaned dramatically throwing one arm over her eyes. "My eyes! You're supposed to finish putting on your clothes before coming out here," the actress corrected.

"I'm a boy. It's not a big deal," he retorted, patting his stomach.

"Uh, it is when you are obscenely ripped," Amara disagreed. She had seen enough of his eight-pack to make her stomach do an objective flip-flop. Thinking about Frankie again, she sighed dreamily.

She heard Jared chuckle. "You look like you had a good night." His brow was arched knowingly.

Amara agreed with a simple nod, standing. She wondered how he could tell, but the thought passed quickly as Dana was already handing her a costume, and Amara retreated behind the dressing screen to shimmy out of Frankie's jeans and T-shirt. She listened as Jared bid farewell to the seamstress then called a goodbye to her as well.

She perked up at the sound of Scott's voice in the distance as he and Jared exchanged greetings. Footsteps approached then stopped nearby.

"The weirdest thing happened," Scott began. "I'm on the way in, and Christopher Stone stopped and asked for a selfie for his teenage daughter. She's apparently some huge fan."

Amara chuckled under her breath listening to Elizabeth reply, "Most girls of her age are or were." Amara began tugging off her pants behind the screen.

"I don't know about that," he refuted. She could hear the embarrassment in his voice and bit her lip when he changed the subject. "I'm ready to get started."

"Well, Amara's changing now," Elizabeth interjected. "But as soon as she's finished..." Elizabeth trailed off.

Amara was grateful to see the promised undergarments in her kit. "I'll be quick," she called out. She smoothed her hands over the costume once it was in place, feeling her character come to life inside her, and she could suddenly hear the voice she wanted to use. Moments later, she rejoined them, and Scott scurried past her to the changing area.

Amara caught Elizabeth's gaze, brows knit, and pointed between herself and the actor in confusion. He hadn't even said hello, just run past her. She wasn't sure why she was getting the cold shoulder. How was he making drama already? They'd barely known each other a few days, and she thought they had been getting along well. She had even stopped herself from hitting on him. He had better not carry this onto the set. She stepped onto the platform in front of the mirrors.

The seamstress lifted her shoulders toward her ears, holding up her hands to gesture her lack of understanding. She shook her head in commiseration.

"How's it look?" Amara finally asked, turning slowly for the costumer's appraisal.

"Looks right. Everything underneath comfortable?" Elizabeth asked.

Amara felt the seamstress plucking at the fabric around the exposed back and beamed back at her. "Perfection." She faced forward. "I'm headed to the set."

"Me too. I need to see the fabrics under the lights. I'll make sure Scott's squared away and join you there."

"Don't wait on me," Scott called. "I'm good."

After a few reassurances, Amara linked arms with the costumer and led her away. "He was weird in the parking lot, too," Amara rambled, thinking of the look of disapproval she had felt rolling off him all the way from his Mercedes.

"Why do you think that is?" Elizabeth questioned.

It had to have been the sight of Frankie dropping her off. He was jealous, she thought. Her lips curled upward knowingly, and she added a little extra swing in her step. "I don't think he liked my ride."

"What was special about your ride?"

Amara giggled, proudly. "Well, I might've hooked up with someone last night who dropped me off this morning right as Scott was getting out of his car." She sashayed a few steps ahead with her hands on her hips and allowed her face to split into a grin. She was quite pleased with herself and didn't hesitate to show it to the other woman.

"Saucy!"

"A girl's got to get her freak on," the actress cooed. "It's good to have people available. So, what was Christopher Stone doing on set?" she questioned, looping her arm back through the other woman's.

"Oh. He's doing a cameo in the movie."

"That's fantastic." Amara beamed. She tilted her head to one side, glancing meaningfully at her newest friend. "What do you do outside of wardrobe and costume design?"

"Not much," Elizabeth replied.

"And what about the special someone in your life?"

"Married to the job. Which is ironic because I could design my own gown."

Amara chuckled with her. "What else do you design?"

"I've been thinking about this business clothing line but with like superheroes and comic book characters. But I don't know where I'd sell them or if anyone would buy them."

The actress thought this sounded like an amazing idea. "Well, the internet, of course. It's 2018...everyone has a website, and everything sells there. And with all the superhero movies this year...you'd better strike while the iron is hot. I'll even model if you want. I could scrounge up a few acquaintances, so you have variety if you need."

The look of shock on Elizabeth's face was satisfying. "Yes, that would...well, I'd appreciate that a lot."

As they neared the set, Max called for them to hurry, and the ladies trotted quickly toward him. Amara swanned around the set, reclining on the sofas and posing dramatically. The costumer and director behind the camera nodded and pointed as she moved again.

She was startled when Scott joined her on set, sitting beside her and scooping her into his arms with a grin. His fingers grazed her bare back, and Amara shivered. Involuntarily, her eyes slipped shut, grinning, and she inhaled his woodsy scent. When her eyes fluttered open, she was greeted with his face large in her vision, smiling down at her. His eyes crinkled at the corners, and she wanted to reach out and caress his cheek. She refrained, schooling her features. Remembering herself, she sat up straight, effectively ending their embrace.

Her words were meant to be friendly, but they came out as something closer to a purr. "Well, hello." Amara felt pinned by his gaze as he stared at her face.

"How's it going out here?"

Inwardly, she sighed, mesmerized by his silver-blue eyes. "Good," she answered. "I think they're liking what they see." She turned back at the cameras where a small crowd was gathering, pointing and debating as they stared at the monitor.

"Let's run some lines," he suggested.

Liking the idea, Amara nodded quickly, picking a scene in her mind. She launched off the couch, taking Scott's hand and leading him to the corridor, facing the cameras. The script called for him to guide her down the hall toward the couches then ease her onto one. Now that she was immersed in the set, sinking into the role felt like second nature, and she no longer saw Scott, but his character. She took a deep breath and began reciting her lines. Following her lead, Scott placed his hand on the small of her back to guide her forward. His fingertips slid upwards 'til they met naked flesh, and he made tiny swirls over it. Amara's skin prickled viscerally, and she was grateful her undergarments were so heavily lined. She stopped abruptly, nearly tripping and shaking her head.

Breaking character, Scott released her. "Am I doing something wrong?" he asked.

"No, no," Amara retorted. "It's me. I'm...a little exposed." She tried unsuccessfully to look at the open back of her costume.

"Oh, yeah." He leered in a way that let her know he'd noticed her bare back. "I kind of thought that might show their relationship. If I had the chance to touch my wife's bare skin in public, I'd do it every time. But if that's, you know, inappropriate or something..."

"I think it's beautiful," she countered. "I'll get myself under control."

"You can lose control with me," he pledged, smiling wickedly. "I've got your back."

"Literally," she teased, a little too loudly, drawing the attention of the others.

Scott placed his entire palm in the open diamond, then ran his fingernails over it lightly. "Well now we know how he got his wife to move to Mars," he teased.

Even on the heels of her night with Frankie, the touches had her body ready and willing all over again. "Be careful," she warned. "When someone hands you the keys to a Ferrari, you'd better know how to drive it." She blinked, fearing that if she stayed, she'd start to reconsider getting to know him better. Instead, she stalked toward where Max was now alone behind the monitor. His focused his attention on her approach.

"How's it looking?"

"Great. You guys have great chemistry. I'm hoping it doesn't dwindle between now and Monday."

She patted his shoulder in reassurance. "We've got this," she declared. "You won't have to worry about us." What she didn't say was that she would be doing all the worrying for him. Scott's embrace was a tantalizing trap she would have to guard herself from falling into, if it wasn't too late already.

Seven

Backstage, Wardrobe: Elizabeth

Saturday morning found Elizabeth at the studio, and she marveled at the quiet. Without a dozen staff running around, things were pretty calm. There were the occasional sounds of the set crew dropping tools or hammering, but otherwise she was alone with the machines. Sketching out her design for Christopher had taken most of the night. That morning, she had pulled all the fabrics and cut them. Now, she was putting the finishing touches on the waistband of the trousers for their cameo actor and finding herself quite distracted as she imagined him putting them on.

Christopher Stone had been one of the first movie actors she'd liked. As a teen, she found herself sneaking all his movies into her playlist when her parents were out of town and buying up old rental copies at the grocery store rental counter. She was never sure if it was him or the roles he chose, or some combination of both. But she knew how she felt after watching one of his movies. She was feeling it now as she snipped the threads off the garment under the needle.

She wondered about the lunch they were going to have on Monday. What had generated that much interest from him toward her to insist on lunch? They'd scarcely met. She started calculating their age difference. It was more than ten years, and she wasn't entirely sure how she felt about that. Plus, according to Scott, he had a daughter old enough to have the hots for the leading man.

The sound of a slamming door interrupted her train of thought, and she pulled her hands free of the machine before she could undergo another poking. The last one had nearly required an ironic stitch of its own, but the medic on set had a drop of glue that felt like fire that had closed the wound. Today, it had calmed down to simply pulsing with each heartbeat to remind her to be more cautious.

She craned her neck around the corner, surprised to see Jared jogging toward her.

"I thought that was your car," he called out as he approached, grinning wide.

"What are you doing here?" she asked, matching his smile. Despite being friend-zoned, the thrill of looking at him had not yet completely disappeared. And, if she was honest with herself, it probably never would. Even if he hadn't been her teenage celebrity crush, he was still one of the most attractive men she had ever seen. Something about the combination of his blue eyes, button nose, and swagger kept her enthralled.

"Wanted to swing some stuff by my new trailer while I had time. Then I saw your car and thought I'd say hi."

She warmed at the thought. "That's sweet. I was working on our cameo's costume."

"Ah, the elite Mr. Stone," he mused, taking a seat.

Elizabeth nodded. "No matter how long I'm in the business, it's still overwhelming when you come across certain people."

"Like me?" he teased, puffing out his chest comically.

She chuckled. "Yes, like you." She winced as she tapped her index finger on her knee. "He's kind of a big deal, you know? And very friendly," she recalled. The whole encounter had been amazingly fast, and she still wasn't sure she believed it had happened.

He laughed. "Oh, so now I have to share you with him?" he hassled.

She quirked a brow at him and returned to pinning a section of material. She studiously avoided his gaze.

"Oh shit," he uttered slowly. "You're into him. Isn't he old enough to be your father?"

"No," she snapped. "And what do you mean share me? *We're* friends."

"I just meant your attention," he clarified easily. "You're like my last remaining fan. Stone has tons of them."

"You don't know that." She turned back to him. "Speaking from a fan's perspective, it's hard to support you when there's nothing to buy and nowhere to find you." Elizabeth felt her pulse racing and paused. "Sorry if that came out harsh," she apologized, glancing his direction. "After this movie is released, you'll see there are more of me out there." She turned fully toward him and away from the machine.

His posture was relaxed spread across two of the three chairs, an arm poised on the back of one. "You know I put out an album," he pointed out.

She nodded. "Yes, I am aware. Self-titled. It's in regular rotation in my car, along with the three songs you released on MySpace, and I have the CDs from that weird thug phase you went through," she added. "And the board game."

"Did you have the dolls?" he challenged.

She shook her head. "I've seen them for sale once, and they were $500 each. So, no."

He was beaming at her, and clearly fighting to keep a straight face. "So, you're only a *little* bit of a fan?"

She pinched her fingers together in demonstration. "And on that note, I need to preserve what's left of my dignity and get back to work so that when I go to lunch Monday, I'm not embarrassed."

"Why would you be embarrassed at lunch on Monday?" he asked.

Elizabeth turned her full back to him now as she answered. "Our cameo star has a fitting after our lunch, so I'd better have something for him to wear."

"Is this a date?" he needled happily.

"Maybe," Elizabeth drawled.

"And you're worried about impressing him?"

"Well, I've already impressed you. He's all I have left," she teased boldly. If the possibility that anything could ever transpire between them were a joke, she couldn't be disappointed.

"You mean I'm first?" he balked. He moved into her line of sight, watching as she rethreaded the machine's needle.

Elizabeth laughed, thinking he sounded either vulnerable or proud, and she refused to answer.

He straightened up smugly. "For that, *I'll* take you to lunch *today*. And if you stick around, I'll take you to a bar that I'm certain serves better chocolate martinis. I'll make sure of it."

She rolled her eyes. "You don't have to do that."

"Sure, I do. How else am I guaranteed to look better in my costume than he does in his?" He raised his hands to emphasize his point as though he had no choice in the matter. "My treat," he added with a bow.

"I can be bought with drinks. Good ones," she emphasized sternly. Elizabeth bit her lip, trying to be serious and hide the giggle fighting to escape.

"Yes, Mistress," he swore, saluting.

The word sent a shiver through her spine, and she shook her head vehemently. "Okay, no. You cannot call me that."

"Why not? You're the wardrobe mistress," he reasoned.

She sighed, trying desperately not to think of all the images that him calling her Mistress dredged up. "People could get the wrong idea."

His eyes flicked around. "What people? We're alone. You can relax today. Nobody's looking."

She sighed. "Thank God for that."

"Amen," he agreed. "I mean, seriously...if I'm saying anything that bothers you, I feel like you'd have the balls to say so to my face. Or are you too polite?"

Elizabeth held her breath for a moment. "I'm definitely not that polite. And for the record, you have not offended me in any way, shape or form," she expounded.

A smirk quirked his mouth to the side, and he took one step toward the door before asking, "You're saying you wouldn't be my mistress?"

She sighed, looking at him squarely. "Call me mistress, treat me like one. Them's the rules," she sassed.

"Lizzy," he said, laughing. "I didn't know you had it in you. But I like it." He pointed at her as he sauntered away.

Elizabeth enjoyed the sound of his mirth as it faded into the distance, silenced finally by the studio door slamming shut. She was still chuckling as she ran another seam. Maybe she wouldn't ever live out her teenage fantasies about kissing the boy that had recently wandered away from her, but she was beginning to think that being his friend might be almost more fun... especially with Christopher Stone waiting in the wings.

The machine whirred, and she watched a perfect row of stitches pass before her eyes. She pulled the garment happily from the machine, cut the loose ends and sighed. Today was going too perfectly. Something had to be wrong. The trousers were complete. The tunic still needed sleeves and buttonholes, and maybe some detailing to the cuffs and collar to set it apart from Scott's costume. But otherwise, she was right on target to get the garment completed before the one p.m. fitting on Monday.

She replayed the encounter with Christopher, suddenly worried that it was simply a business proposition he had in mind. That would be a perfectly reasonable explanation. The more she thought about it, the more she was convinced that's what had happened. Lunch was a pretty casual affair, and lots of people liked to have business meetings at lunch.

She didn't have long to worry before Jared whisked her away, treating her to the best pizza she'd had since she'd made it to LA a decade ago. She chewed slowly, watching the way he ate, cheese strings connecting him to each bite before he would pull them away and gather them like noodles in his mouth, licking his thumb and forefinger with each bite. It wasn't really much different from the way anyone else ate a slice, but Elizabeth was enamored.

"You're staring," he pointed out before swiping a napkin over the pepperoni grease on his cheeks.

"Sorry," she apologized, turning back to her own slice. She felt like a teenager again, living the life she had never lived but imagined would have been exhilarating. He barraged her with the usual questions about where she was from and how much family she had and how had she wound up in LA. She recognized this as standard practice and rolled with it.

"What about you? What part of LA do you claim?" she questioned, picking a string of cheese from her pizza and piling on the slice before taking a bite.

He chuckled. "At this point, all of it. None of it. It's all sort of made up anyway. In fact, I'm thinking of moving soon. My lease is up in the fall, and I have some decisions to make about my career."

She frowned. "Please tell me you're not quitting," she whined, heartbroken at the mere thought of it. She set her slice down, waiting on his answer.

"No, nothing that dramatic. We'll see where this acting thing goes. I'm not ready to give up music or dance, but you know, not sure I can physically dance professionally forever."

"Fred Astaire did it."

"Not breakdancing on a cardboard square," he countered.

Elizabeth leaned on one elbow, tucking her hand at the nape of her neck. She couldn't help the grin that infiltrated her next words. "It must be terrible being so talented and have all these choices."

"Yeah, I know. I see you playing the tiniest violin for me from here." He laughed. "It's that, talent isn't what it used to be. It's about social networking and being open to hard work. I know a lot of talented people that have given up and seen a lot of semi-talented people with incredible drive be mega successes. It's a numbers game," he rationalized, almost sadly, she thought.

She nodded. "It's just you to support then?"

He sucked on his straw for a moment, meeting her eyes. "Lizzy, are you asking if I'm single?"

Flushing to the tips of her roots, she shook her head. "No. No. I was thinking about the pressure you're under. It's different if you have other people or pets to support."

He shook his head. "How are you still single?" he mused, swirling his straw around his cup. "You are so genuine."

Elizabeth fought not to choke on her pizza and decided it was time to abandon the slice. "Work. Lots and lots of work. Besides – I sort of like not answering to anyone. No one's counting on me for dinner. Case in point, here I am on a Saturday, and I'm not rushing home for anyone. It's kinda nice."

He nodded. "I was thinking of adopting a dog, but now that I'm on set... I'm not sure it would be fair to the dog. Maybe when we're done filming."

"You don't have to wait long. It's like what, eight weeks? Ten tops?"

"Yeah. I can wait for anything for eight weeks. Well, most things." He waggled his eyebrows. "So, what is Lizzybeth going to wear to lunch Monday?"

"I don't know," she hesitated. "I still have to work."

He shook his head, clicking his tongue in response. "A designer who doesn't know what to wear? Shameful," he mocked, biting into a corner of crust.

"That's why we become designers," she expounded. "Ever in the pursuit of what to wear and never satisfied."

He swallowed, waving her off with one hand. "I say be comfortable," he encouraged.

"You're trying to make me tank," she protested. "Besides, I'm sure it's a request for custom work. People in this town always have some event."

He frowned. "Why do you say that?"

She remembered very specifically the moment he first saw her. She cringed as she retold the story. "Well, the first time he saw me, I was crawling around on the floor at Catherine's feet. I can't fathom I gave him any good reason to want to meet for anything other than that. I was so not prepared for his arrival. He wasn't supposed to show up until late afternoon."

Jared grimaced. "Well, if it's any consolation, maybe his mind's as dirty as mine, and he thinks it's a turn-on to see a woman on all fours."

Something resembling a groan escaped her lips, and she covered her face in replacement shame for the words he'd uttered. She tried for another moment to not hear what he'd said, but it was too late. She leaned on her hands to look back at him. "The sad part is I know that was intended to be comforting," she responded wryly.

"That's what I'm here for, baby," he taunted holding his arms out wide. "To stroke your ego."

She laughed. "Hey, that's my job as your vintage fan."

Jared opened his mouth to speak, then shook his head and busied himself gathering their table trash.

Elizabeth wasn't accustomed to being waited on, and she reached for her portion before he could get it all.

Jared slapped her fingers. "I got it, Mistress," he stated, one eye trained on her face.

She stared as he turned and walked toward the garbage. Sighing, she slid out of the chair, pulling her purse strap over one shoulder and sauntered past him. "Have it your way," she conceded, leading the way out of the shop and back to his car.

The sound of his glee followed her, and Elizabeth sighed dreamily. For all the hours as a teen she had spent thinking about him, it was a relief that he was every bit as charming and kind as she had hoped. "What I can't figure out," she said, strapping on her seat belt, "is why in the world *you're* still single."

Jared peeked at her before pulling back out into traffic. "I didn't say I was single," he corrected.

"Oh." Elizabeth went rigid in the seat, sealing her mouth shut and looking out the window. How did she back pedal from that? "But you said earlier..."

"There's someone," he confirmed. "Just nothing regular or what you'd call a relationship. I like to keep my options open."

She nodded, thinking that made sense. She changed the subject, and the ride back to the studio felt three times longer than the ride to the pizzeria. She loved the friendship that had been developing between them, but part of her was clinging still to the idea that perhaps one day he'd see her as more than a fan – more than a friend. But he wasn't even going to look, she realized. And she felt her heart crumbling slowly at the thought of being so close and still not having an opportunity.

Eight

Principals' Trailers, Backlot: Amara

The first day of filming started for Amara at 8:30 a.m., but by 6:00 that morning, she was already on set, watching a cup of coffee brewing in the single-cup maker in her very own trailer. She'd never had an RV of her own before.

She was taking a break from pacing, calling this portion of her process meditation as she watched the stream of dark, translucent liquid cascade from the machine directly into her cup. It swirled under the premeasured creamer turning it a pale shade of caramel. The rich scent permeated the air around her, and she breathed deeply. It was going to be a good day.

They were taking on the story-telling scenes today where she and Scott would be explaining to their on-screen children the history of the process by which unconscious individuals were teleported from one place to another.

She had read through the scene schedule, grateful for the spacing from easy to difficult and back to give the actors an opportunity to reset themselves for each scene. She and Scott had run through all their scenes more than once, skimming the ones they felt good about and working on others. But both knew working out the scenes with Max on set was going to be the game changer. He could throw them for a loop at any moment.

Amara felt herself beginning to spin out of control, and she focused on the stream of coffee again. This magic liquid would fix everything, she assured herself.

When she finally emerged from her trailer closer to 7:00, she started with hair and makeup. There was a surprising amount of activity on set as extras were filing in and out for quick touch ups and some interesting hairdos, Amara thought. She eased into the chair, prepared for the beginning of the transformation. By 8:15, she was standing behind a changing screen completing the metamorphosis from actress to character. With Elizabeth's approval, she marched toward the set, finding Max relaxed in the director's chair.

He waved her forward. "You look perfect!"

She nodded graciously, looking around the set. "Seen my mister?" she questioned.

"You just missed him. He stopped by to clarify some points with me before prepping for his monologue."

It had not occurred to her that the first scene they would be filming rested so squarely on her partner's shoulders. A bead of sweat formed on the back of her neck, and she had a sudden moment of panic.

"That's perfect," Max encouraged. "Channel this. You need to project that sense of nearly falling apart as you listen. Don't forget – you're more skeptical about teleporting for the first time than your kids are. You're not just nervous for yourself; you're nervous for your whole family."

Amara put a hand to her forehead to forestall any worry lines that tried to crop up, and she walked away, pacing slowly and practicing her breathing techniques. The sound of the set door slamming shut made her jump, and she twirled to see Scott confidently striding toward her with one of their film children on either side.

He touched her shoulder. "Child actor. I got this. I promise." He gave her a wink before placing a hand on the bare skin of her back to direct her to the starting point for the scene.

Amara tensed briefly, but then leaned into the sensation as the character, feeling the transformation come together. For a moment, he was her husband, and she felt herself come home in his face. She was vaguely aware of the extras milling around her. She shook herself out, preparing. She examined the actual child actors, memorizing the way they moved, watching as they began shaking their shoulders out. She saw Catherine's mother beside her, doing jumping jacks with her. She squeezed Scott's hand gently in solidarity.

At 8:45, Max stood abruptly and called everyone's attention. Amara could barely hear him as she breathed intentionally, counting her inhales and exhales as Max waxed on about his faith in this project and everyone involved. Finally, he called places, the clapboard snapped, and it began.

On the set, with their two children fidgeting between them, Scott delivered his entire monologue with perfect elocution and timbre. She felt his eyes on her. A blush heated her cheeks as she averted her gaze toward their kids, reaching to push a stray hair behind Catherine's ear. The little girl pretended not to notice, going about her part as though this was a normal occurrence between the two.

When Max called "Cut!" Amara took a few beats to break character.

Max applauded madly along with the rest of the camera crew. Scott stood, taking a bow.

"Can you not touch me again? I think that's weird," Catherine noted to Amara. "My mom doesn't do that."

Amara sighed. "She should. But I won't do it again."

Max bounded toward them. "That was perfect, Harper! Can you do it again?" he begged.

Scott nodded. "Yes, if I can get a water first.".

Max snapped at one of the grips and pointed. He turned to the cameras, darting toward them and speaking in rushed tones.

Amara felt Scott's eyes on her. She was still feeling the buzz from her character, and she swallowed seeing the anxiety pinching his brows together. Part of her wanted to reach up and smooth the area in soothingly, but she stilled her hands. He was her husband only on-screen. Comforting him wasn't her job.

"Was that okay?" he murmured.

She gave a thumbs up and nodded, watching as his body relaxed, his eyes snapped shut as he exhaled. He wanted her approval, she realized.

Scott beamed at his fellow actors. "You guys are great," he applauded. "You're giving me tons of stuff to bounce off of. Thank you!"

For a moment, she thought he was making fun, but as he fidgeted and sucked down the bottle of water handed to him, she realized his words were sincere. She watched his lips curling around the bottle, and her eyes followed the water's course down his throat, and she caught herself biting her lip.

The day proceeded this way until they finally called for lunch. It was surprisingly exhausting to simply watch Scott complete his monologue multiple times to allow for different camera angles. She could barely hold her laughter in as Catherine stretched beside her then ran for the bathroom with an announcement that Amara didn't pretend to understand. Scott and their "son" Sean headed toward the buffet area, play fighting as they reached first for the same bottle of water then for the same paper plate.

Amara considered briefly mingling with the rest of the cast, but her head was scrambled with emotions, and she needed time to break character to disentangle the feelings making her want to cry every time she tried to speak. She disappeared into her trailer with a cold sandwich and an apple that she promptly deposited on the counter before dropping down onto the couch to stretch out. She closed her eyes, thinking of a black void where she deposited all the feelings coursing through her veins. Scott was her husband and the father of her two children. She imagined their wedding vows and following him passionately across the galaxy. Amara shed those feelings, calling up the night she'd spent recently with Frankie and thinking she needed a repeat, possibly even that night if she could decide on the lucky recipient.

She reached for her cell, scrolling through the contacts. Her lips snarled downward at several, beginning to question her own judgment before deleting a few of names and setting it on its charging stand. She needed to move. She was ready to talk to people as Amara and not the anxious and extremely devoted character she was portraying.

She had two bites of her sandwich before turning up her nose at it. She grabbed the apple, tossing it from one hand to the other as she went in search of wardrobe. She wanted to steal some of Elizabeth's calm and was surprised when she found Dana alone in the now familiar principals' dressing area.

"Where's Queenie?" she questioned.

The assistant's jaw dropped. "You haven't heard? I thought the whole set was abuzz. She's out with Christopher Stone."

Amara's face went slack, and she kneeled into one of the chairs, gripping its back. "Tell me everything."

Dana beamed, sitting beside her. "He's doing the cameo this afternoon. And when he came for the fitting last week, he asked her out. And they're at lunch now before his final fitting and filming this afternoon."

"Wait, she stopped working for more than five minutes?" Amara balked, incredulous.

Dana giggled. "She made this huge deal about how she'd worked over the weekend and not being gone too long."

Rolling her eyes, Amara waved off the statement. "Oh, please, like we all wouldn't have jumped up and down on one leg like hyperactive flamingoes while wearing a tutu if he'd asked."

Dana shrugged. "I don't get it. I mean, he's charming, but..." she trailed off. Her lips curled into an ugly wrinkle. Her next words appeared to taste sour. "He's so old!"

"Shut your mouth," Amara scolded. "He's not old – you're just a baby."

"I shouldn't be gossiping about it. I've never seen her leave the set with someone," Dana confided.

Amara let out a happy gasp. "Well, good for her."

"If you stick around, they should be back any minute."

Amara nodded and took a bite of her apple.

Dana busied herself moving racks and sorting hangers before

speaking again. "So, I heard applause more than once this morning," she divulged proudly. "And I heard Catherine's mom talk about how you and Scott were flaming on the set."

"Flaming?" Amara repeated after swallowing a bite. He'd mostly been giving a monologue all morning, and she'd sat and reacted to it. Her brows furrowed. "How so?"

"I'm telling you what I heard. But she was so jealous," Dana added with a giggle. "She said you had this smolder going, and she'd never seen someone act so much without saying a word."

Amara grinned, relaxing in the chair and displaying her apple like a prop. "Years of practice," Amara pronounced shrewdly, satisfied with the report. She was ready to change gears though and did so with her next statement. "What other projects have you and Queenie worked on together?" She took a giant bite, listening to the assistant prattle on. "Do either of you do work outside of set? Like gowns for events and stuff?"

"I don't, but Elizabeth does." Dana pulled a business card from the rolling drawer and passed it to her. "You have something coming up?"

"Not really. But you never know, and it's never a bad thing to have a few people on speed dial for when these things happen."

As if summoned by too much conversation, the Head Costumer strolled in, one hand tucked under the arm of none-other than Christopher Stone. She was laughing, and Amara barely recognized her. Her hair was down instead of its usual ponytail, fluttering below her shoulders. That morning, she'd seen Elizabeth in a T-shirt but now the woman sported a black low-cut, silk wrap-style top and some fitted jeans that flared slightly at the ankles over a pair of dress sandals.

The actor Elizabeth was holding onto was smiling beatifically, extending a hand to Amara as they approached. "You must be Amara Baker," he greeted. "You are an amazing actress. You've had so many roles, and I believed you in all of them," he commended. "I know how tough it can be to spread yourself so thin."

"That's so kind," Amara gushed, taking his hand and shaking it lightly. "It's an honor to get to work with you on this film. I've learned so much from your extensive career."

"Thank you," he accepted before he smiled, pointing at the seamstress. "I taught her to say fuck." His grin stretched wickedly from one ear to the other.

Amara gasped, looking at Elizabeth who was releasing his arm and heading over to the garment rack to pull a costume free. "You don't say that," she accused.

Elizabeth redirected her gaze, red-faced and seeming speechless.

Shifting in her chair, Amara turned the apple in her hand and grinned. "I'm sticking around to see how this costume came out."

"Let the disrobing begin!" The actor laughed, taking his costume from Dana and heading to the screen.

Amara twisted off the apple stem and threw it at Elizabeth to get her attention. Amara pointed at the seamstress then at herself before pinching her hand open and closed indicating that they would be talking later. Then she grinned and picked at the bottom of her neckline, giving the seamstress a thumbs up.

The dark-headed woman's neck turned splotchy red, and she tugged the shoulders of her top back to hide more of her cleavage. It didn't work very well, and Amara clamped a hand over her own mouth to stop her laugh from escaping. She was less successful at holding back her snort.

When the actor reappeared, he was outfitted in a silvery tunic style suit similar to Scott's, but finer with a great deal more detail, and she gasped. "Bravo!"

Christopher did a slow turn, hands up as he assessed his shoes, pants, and the front of his shirt. "I look like a rich asshole!" he announced happily, before stepping on the riser. "Perfect."

Elizabeth was covering her face loosely with one hand, but Amara could see and hear the amusement there. She decided in that moment, that she and Elizabeth were going to be best friends. As actress and clothing designer, they had nothing to lose and everything to gain. She began plotting a party at her house to get to know her better.

When Christopher was suitably dressed, and Elizabeth had stopped fussing over imaginary lint, Amara offered to escort the actor to hair and makeup. "So, I feel the need to threaten you about our costumer's honor or something."

He chuckled as they walked. "My intentions are honorable...less than noble maybe, but honorable," he admitted.

"Oh good," she replied. "Threats are so dull." Amara took a seat beside him as the makeup artists gave her touch ups and made quick work of the veteran actor beside her.

"So, tell me about Scott Harper," Christopher requested softly, eyes closed as makeup was applied.

Amara drew back. This was a pretty public venue to ask the question, and she wondered at his purpose. "What do you want to know?"

"Nothing specific. Something to tell my daughter. She's a huge fan. I sent her a picture Friday, and she nearly jumped through the phone at me all weekend. I had to bribe her not to come to the set with me today. But then I told her I had a date, and she backed off." He released his trademark chuckle, and Amara fought every instinct not to jerk her whole self to stare at him.

"Classic," she agreed. "You should bring her. Let's ask Scott when we go out there. And we can talk to Max and see when might be good for that. Although, she missed his monologue this morning. It was frighteningly impressive."

"Ooh, that is a tragedy."

They were quiet then until they were ready, and Amara led him to set.

As they neared the crew, Christopher broke the quiet. "Set the scene for me. Max told me that I'm supposed to fight being gassed and be a nervous passenger. I got the impression there's no actual lines."

She nodded. "The script is unclear other than you're supposed to make a ruckus and be far too important to be traveling commercially."

"I see..."

They arrived on the set to find Scott entertaining the kids by juggling three apples he must have pulled from the buffet. Even the pint-sized actress was clapping, declaring his work to be very good.

"Mr. Harper," the actor beside her called out. "I wonder if I might extract from you a favor, not that I have any right to do so…"

"Ask," Scott proffered, catching the apples, and handing one to each of his small costars.

Catherine scoffed, shaking her head and setting it down.

"If you recall I mentioned the other day my daughter is a big fan," Christopher began. "She was climbing up my a–" His eyes stuck on the child actors nearby. "My posterior to come with me today to watch you work. Your costar here seemed to think you wouldn't mind an audience."

Scott's cheeks flushed. "Oh, well," he stammered bashfully. "Um, maybe. I don't want to disrupt the whole set on my account."

"Maybe we could arrange something after we're done for the day," Amara suggested, watching their exchange with interest, surprised by the way her costar had put the cast of this movie before his own need for attention.

"Preferably somewhere off set?" Scott added, standing a little straighter.

"That would really make me dad of the year," Christopher noted. "Are you sure you don't mind? She's seventeen, so it could be a little awkward."

Scott nodded, waving him off. "Fans, I've got," he assured.

"Bring her to my trailer," Amara volunteered. It had been her idea, after all, and it wouldn't do to have a big fan of his inside his private space. "It's quiet, and there won't be a big scene on set."

"Perfect," Christopher mumbled, patting his outfit and coming up empty handed. "Left the phone in wardrobe. I guess I'll text her later."

Max joined them, walking everyone through the next scene including his plans for the big cameo. Max called the cameras operators over as well, hoping to get it all in one take.

The main characters took their places, and Amara slipped into her role as a mother and wife.

When the scene started, Amara saw out of the corner of her eye as cameras pushed past her, focusing on the actor behind her. She heard the fuss as Christopher struggled on his couch. "No thank you," he refused.

"I'm sorry, sir, but every passenger is required to use the gas before passing through the portal," the extra playing the stewardess/nurse insisted kindly.

"Get away from me with that bottled fart water," he groused.

Amara's screen son began to laugh, and Max cut the scene.

Christopher looked over his shoulder, smiling wickedly, and Amara felt like she was on the set of one of his early movies the way his face was shining

Max scolded Sean, asking Christopher to try again. They started over, and this time, they got to the attendant explaining to the passenger why it was critical and mandatory to take the gas. His next refusal was funnier than the last, and Scott snorted first. Each take got worse until Max threw the husband-and-wife team off the set so he could get his take.

They retired to Amara's trailer, collapsing onto her couch laughing. "What a genius," Scott admired. "He's going to make this scene, and people are going to watch just for him."

Amara nodded. "That's not the main reason," she insisted. "You're so engaging. It's day one, and I'm blown away. I'm ashamed to say I'm not familiar with your earlier acting work," Amara confessed.

"Aww, thanks, and it's good you don't know my child actor days. I'd like to forget them myself," he said.

"And the way you are with those kids," she commented, sighing and remembering it. Her brain replayed the scene for her, and she felt her ovaries dance in response. She watched his lips move as he spoke again, leaning ever so slightly closer.

He chuckled. "I remember what it's like to be a kid on set, and it helps me not be bored. Everybody wins."

She thought she was winning as she ogled him semi-discreetly. She liked that he wasn't opposed to making a fan happy and his sole objection had been not to subject everyone else to the squealing that was likely to ensue. "Also, it's very kind of you to meet with Christopher's daughter."

"Well, it's not like you gave me a lot of choice. You'd volunteered me before you guys got there."

Amara flushed. "Oh...well..." she stuttered.

"It's okay. Usually fans are nice, and it makes such a big difference to them. It doesn't cost me anything really. Besides, fans are the reason I got as far as I did. And if we can't be good to our fans, we shouldn't be celebrities."

"That's a really beautiful way to see it." She turned on the couch to face him, leaning on one arm and staring. "What does a retired pop star do for fun these days?"

"Retired," he repeated scornfully. "That's kind. I'd go with failed."

"You're not failed. You've got a lead role in a big deal movie. What's a failure about that?" She frowned. It had taken her a lot more work to get her first lead role. However, when she counted the years since he'd performed with his band and added in years as a child actor, she realized he'd been at it even longer than she had.

He shrugged. "It's not music. My heart's..." Scott paused. "Music is my passion. This is fun, but it's not the same."

Amara's knee jerk reaction was to be affronted by this. Her whole life she had toiled and sacrificed to get to this point. He was dissatisfied because he wasn't getting to do his preferred art form? But as she recoiled from her expression, she softened. She saw that he felt the same way about his art too – it was simply different from hers. And maybe that made him less competition and more kindred spirit.

"Acting is an amazing profession," he continued, "and I like it, too. I...I didn't think I'd ever have to reinvent myself after the success I was so blessed to have had. I didn't mean to offend you."

She sighed, not sure how to respond and grateful when there as a knock at the door. She leaped up to answer it.

"Yay! Someone's home!" It was Jared, and he beamed. "Can I come in?"

Amara stepped aside making space for him.

Jared paused on the second step, one hand frozen on the door handle. "Oh, am I interrupting something?" he asked, looking between the two quickly.

"Come on in," Scott insisted. "We got kicked off set because we couldn't stop laughing. Our guest cameo is a riot."

Jared crested the steps and slipped in past the actress. "That's what we wanted, right?"

Scott nodded. "I thought you didn't have scenes 'til later tonight," he prompted.

"I don't. But I've been setting up my trailer," Jared answered.

"With what?" Amara questioned, pulling a bottled water from her fridge. She offered one to each of the others, and Scott accepted happily. Jared refused, easing into her dinette.

"You're actually bringing stuff here?" Scott questioned.

"Sure," Amara affirmed. "I brought this magic elixir maker." She performed her best Vanna White impression on her single cup coffee maker. "I also brought some clothes just in case. Thinking I might stock the bar, too."

"I sense a party," Jared cooed.

Amara nodded, pointing to the tip of her nose and then to him. She loved the way he smiled back like he'd found the door to a secret VIP entrance.

"What'd you bring to yours?" Scott questioned the actor.

"Recording equipment," Jared detailed as though it was the most natural thing in the world. "Thought I'd set up a makeshift studio so that when the muse strikes, I can get it on tape. All my takes are at night, so I got lots of time to burn."

"And here I thought you'd be all over Elizabeth," Scott razzed.

Amara's attention was torn between the two boys, surprised at the personal interaction.

Jared chuckled and shook his head. "Why?"

"I saw you two," Scott joshed good naturedly. His face beamed like sunshine as he stared knowingly at the other actor. "There's something there, man," he insisted. "First time I met her, she was right at your side, like she was defending you."

Jared rolled his eyes blowing him off. "That's what fans do. Loyal to a fault. She doesn't know me at all."

Amara knew about Jared's career based on her thorough internet search, but she wouldn't have recognized him otherwise. Amara oohed, doing the math. "If she's really a fan, she goes all the way back. Like, twenty years..."

Jared's answer was soft. "Seems that way."

Amara noticed the way he reached for the back of his neck and how his usually cheerful attitude started to evaporate. Scott was grinning like a child on the couch watching the reaction across from him. Amara decided to put an end to Jared's misery. "Well color me jealous for the dedication. I only get the crazies and the inmates."

Scott's eyes turned to the actress, face awash in surprise. "Inmates?" Scott repeated. "For real? I never had an inmate."

"That you know about," Jared joked.

Amara sighed in relief as the oldest of them returned to his usual bright personality.

Scott chuckled, leaning forward toward the other actor. "Hey, tell me about this studio. What are you set up to do?"

The two devolved into the finer details of musical recording and what gear Jared had procured that fit in his space. She sat back watching them and drank her water. They were both pretty, she thought, but vastly different. Scott was so tall, he made Jared look short, and Jared was so thin he made Scott look fat. But something in their spirits seemed to click like twins when they talked about music. In short order, the boys disappeared to Jared's trailer, and she wondered if they'd noticed they'd left her behind. She'd bet her Gucci handbag that they hadn't. Normally, that would make her pout, but the way Scott lit up as he talked about music warmed her heart. She was glad he found a friend in Jared. She realized too, that Jared probably filled the empty spot Scott's former band had occupied for half a decade.

After a moment, she wandered back to set to see if Christopher had finished his scene. When she approached, the camera guys were doubled over laughing, and Max was wiping tears from his eyes. She pivoted instead to the wardrobe department in hopes of a friendly face and details about the lunch with their cameo star.

Nine

Backstage, Wardrobe: Elizabeth

"Finished for the day?" Elizabeth questioned as she saw Amara drawing near. She nodded to her assistant to get the actress' street clothes but stopped when Amara shook her head.

"No. Your new boy toy is so funny I can't be in there, or I'll ruin the take. Max kicked us off set, and now *they're* all in there laughing."

Elizabeth cleared her throat. "He's not my boy toy. We had one lunch."

Amara chuckled. "He told his daughter he had a *date* today," she goaded. "Sounds like more than lunch to me."

"It was nice," Elizabeth admitted. "He ate a salad. I'm not sure I've ever seen a man eat a salad." She remembered the site of him spearing lettuce so expertly and wondered if he ate a lot of salads. It was both refreshing and altogether unnatural.

Dana chuckled, and Elizabeth squelched it with a glance.

"I saw you when you came back," Amara prodded. "Someone plugged you into 220. There's got to be more to tell than salad."

Elizabeth got the distinct impression that Amara was not going to give up until she spilled all the beans. "I don't know. We talked the whole time. And he's pretty funny...clever."

"Well, you looked great," Amara approved. "And how did you feel about it?"

She eyeballed her "date" clothes and thought she had done well. He had complimented her on sight, and she hadn't felt the least bit awkward on his arm. But she had also felt warm under his gaze, a bit like how a mouse might feel when confronted with a cat. She'd had very few dates in her life, and none felt as important as this one. He was a brilliant conversationalist. If he knew he had rescued her repeatedly, he hadn't let on.

"It was lunch. There's not much to feel a lot about," she replied.

Amara's gaze pinned her, and Elizabeth fought the urge to cover herself as the actress probed, "Would you go out with him again?"

"Sure." Elizabeth was grateful when the other woman's gaze turned away. "Nothing to lose, right?"

The actress turned her scrutiny toward Dana, clearly searching for secrets.

Her assistant squirmed awkwardly, then stuffed her hands in her back pockets. "Hey, I'm going to check on the B team," Dana announced and didn't wait for Elizabeth's approval to disappear.

Once they were alone, Amara leaned in and lowered her voice. "You can tell me to back off...but...do you not have a lot of experience with guys or something? Because it's like you swallow your tongue every time one of them looks at you."

"No one's looking," Elizabeth countered.

Amara's expression broadcast her disbelief. "You mean except for Christopher *and* Jared?"

Elizabeth tripped over the rolling bin, nearly knocking it down before she steadied herself and posed next to it as though she had done nothing of the sort. "Okay, Christopher maybe," she confessed. "But definitely not Jared. He's come right out and said so, and he's got some mystery partner waiting at home for him. He told me so himself over the weekend."

Amara gaped at her, blinking repeatedly. "Why were you with him over the weekend?"

"Nothing really. I was here working, and he was here playing around in his trailer. We're nothing more than friends. I don't know why no one believes us."

Amara threw her hands up. "I believe whatever you tell me," she protested. "Even if you did just call yourselves an 'us.'"

Elizabeth found it hard to scowl at Amara's grin, but she did her best. If she wanted to get out of this intense line of questioning, she was going to have to turn the tables. "And what about you, Ms. Fling-with-an-old-friend?"

"Flings are the best," Amara answered glibly, but Elizabeth saw the way she averted her eyes suddenly. "I don't do relationships. I had one once or twice, but it wasn't my bag."

Elizabeth saw a too-perfect smile and interpreted it avoidance. She had struck a nerve, she knew, and she decided that poking it would be like taking a stick to a hornet's nest. She advised softly, "I think we have time for what we want to have time for if we're honest."

"Maybe," Amara conceded. Her eyes squinted toward the designer. "You're not on the rebound, are you? Because celebrity relationships are tough on any level without that baggage."

Elizabeth shook her head. "No. My last relationship was before I moved to LA."

Amara's hand flew to her chest. "Tell me you did not admit to not having any kind of...relations for however long you've been here...because you've been with Dana for three years she said..." She started fanning herself in distress, looking expectantly at Elizabeth and leaning forward.

Feeling her cheeks warm, Elizabeth turned back to the actress. "I said nothing of the sort," she denied. She cleared her throat, rummaging through one of the drawers in the rolling cabinet. "So, where's Scott if you're both kicked off set?"

"In Jared's trailer. He set up some kind of recording studio, and the boys went off to play with their toys." Amara frowned.

"Ah. He mentioned bringing stuff in Saturday but not that." She wondered if he kept it secret so she wouldn't ask him to sing. Her heart did a happy flip-flop in her chest, but her brain shut it down. Jared had someone waiting for him at night. She had no reason to let him know any more about how intense her crush was or had been. Besides, she'd spent the afternoon thinking about how comfortable Christopher had been with her.

Jared spent all his time making innuendos, but Christopher talked about life and the world, and while they'd had a surprisingly meaningful conversation about the "f" word, he hadn't said a single thing that she would have to worry about anyone else overhearing. He'd taken her to a nice restaurant with a sophisticated menu and had tipped their waiter generously. He'd even signed a few autographs while they were out, and he was incredibly gracious to his fans. His maturity was a definite turn-on, and she'd found herself staring at his mouth more than once.

Elizabeth flushed when she realized Amara was talking to her, and she'd tuned out as she'd wandered down memory lane.

"Fourth of July is coming up," the actress was saying, "and I was thinking I'd throw a pool party for the entire cast. Would you come if I did?"

"Oh...sure." Elizabeth pressed the corners of her mouth up in a nearly convincing expression. She didn't fancy the idea of being in swimwear around co-workers, but industry parties were almost required if one was invited. Networking was integral to success in this town.

Amara's face split open in a grin. "Oh! You can invite your 'lunch date.'" She threw the last two words in air quotes. "It'll give you an excuse to see him again after today. Although, if he's smart, he'll find other excuses if you show him you're interested. Or I'll ask him for you."

Elizabeth held up one hand. "Slow your roll. I can ask him myself," she retorted.

"Who are you asking what?" interrupted the actor in question.

She saw Christopher approaching with a grin, rubbing his hands together. "Oh, Amara was thinking of throwing an Independence Day party at her house," Elizabeth explained.

"A pool party for everyone in the film," Amara added, standing. "Including you."

"Will you be attending?" he asked the costumer pointedly.

Elizabeth nodded. "I think I've been drafted, yes."

He turned to Amara. "I'll get the details from Elizabeth, and we'll see you there." Christopher disappeared behind the screen.

Amara fanned herself.

"Well, if you're back here, I expect Max'll be wanting me on set," the actress noted. She left, waving at the costumer then skipped away.

The seamstress was beginning to think she needed some light music going in the fitting area to cover the noise of people unzipping their pants. She listened as Christopher finished getting ready and waited on one of the chairs. She pulled out her phone and opened a mindless game to distract herself from the sounds of fabric sliding on skin.

Out of the corner of her eye, she saw his head peeking out from the screen before he sauntered into the open.

"We're alone," she assured gently.

He grinned as he faced her. "Well, that's enough rich asshole for one day. I'll go back to regular asshole." He smoothed his hands down from his shirt to his pants, making sure everything was to spec.

"I don't think you're an asshole," Elizabeth disputed, shaking her head.

"That, my dear, is because I'm an actor." He gave a bow with the statement then righted himself. "You know, I don't play dress up with most women on a first date," he teased.

"I thought I was pretty clever getting you out of your clothes without so much as a handshake. Twice," she countered, feeling a wave of heat roll off her face. She fought the urge to hide behind her hand and winked at him. Jared was rubbing off on her.

He chuckled. "So, you were." He smiled quietly, eyes searching her face. "I had fun at lunch," he confessed breaking the silence. "I hope you did, too."

She nodded. "I did, thank you. I'd do it again," she volunteered.

"Well, that saves me from the fear of rejection when I ask again." He grinned at her then began fumbling in his pockets, sighing relief when he produced a phone. "I've got to call my daughter," he explained, glancing up at her. "Scott's offered to meet her in Amara's trailer."

"That was nice of him," she said, going behind the screen to collect his costume.

"I hope this hasn't been dinging the whole time I've been away," he apologized, indicating the phone in his hands.

"I heard a few vibrating noises," she admitted as she approached the rolling rack. She glanced at him, seeing all his focus diverted to his phone as he scrolled, thumb flicking the screen repeatedly. She shamelessly eavesdropped on his call as she began hanging his clothes, melting at the tone of his voice when he called his daughter "sweetie."

"How long do you think they'll be filming?" he asked.

It took her a moment to realize he'd hung up the call and was now speaking to her. "Oh, I don't know. It's hard to tell. How long before she gets here?"

"She's not far. I think part of her was expecting that I could make this happen."

"Well, of course, dad. Didn't you hang the moon?" she teased. "You're her hero."

He harrumphed as he sat beside her to tug on his shoes. "It's a rare occasion these days. She used to be my little princess, and now I feel more like a warden. Did you have this thing with your dad at this age?"

"No. He was begging me to get out of the house," she confessed. "Insisting that I'd never meet anyone online. It was me and my sewing machine trying to be original."

"No wonder you can't say fuck," he harassed.

"Perhaps not, but I can certainly appreciate it."

Christopher's eyebrows shot up. "You appreciate fucking, huh?"

Elizabeth's face flamed, but she grinned and shrugged demurely, arching a single eyebrow in reply. "That would be telling," she whispered.

Suddenly, the empty chair between them felt half its size, and were it not for the doors bursting open from set and a swath of cast pouring in, Elizabeth wondered what might have transpired.

Cast members were marching past them toward the rest of the waiting wardrobe staff as Scott and Amara filtered into her space. She popped out of the free chair while Amara grabbed her change of clothes and headed to the screens to change.

"We're wrapped for today," Scott confirmed. "Well, at least we are. They're setting up for Jared now." He took a seat beside Christopher, and as he tugged off his shoes, Dana arrived, taking them from him soundlessly.

"You are a saint," Elizabeth whispered to her assistant.

Dana bestowed a pleased grin and brought forward the actor's street clothes, plucking away Amara's costume as it appeared over the edge of the screen. "I'll go get these pressed and ready for tomorrow."

"I don't pay you enough," Elizabeth apologized. "Thank you."

Dana approached, lowering her voice to a near-whisper and sassed, "You can thank me with details about lunch, which I have been waiting for all day."

Amara chose that moment to appear between the two ladies. "Me too," she hissed conspiratorially.

Elizabeth felt sweaty. "I swear there's nothing to tell." She found Christopher's eyes on her, a grin parting his lips as he rested on one knee.

"You wouldn't be telling tales, would you?" he dared.

She shook her head her lunch date. "I feel like I should've made you a cape to introduce your daughter to Scott."

His face balled in confusion briefly, but as understanding dawned, he launched himself from the chair, landing solidly on both feet, fists firmly on his hips, and puffing out his chest. "I am super dad," he declared.

Amara clapped her hands. "Did you reach her yet?"

"Yes. She's not far. She's practically at the Starbucks across from the gate already. I didn't think you'd wrap so soon. This is pretty great."

Amara sniggered, glancing over her shoulder as Scott passed by her to change clothes. "The whole crew was worn out from laughing so hard. And Scott keeps getting everything right on the first take. It's so annoying."

Scott poked his head out from the screen and gave them all a beatific smile, a dimple forming on one cheek. He disappeared behind the screen again.

Amara held out an elbow to the cameo star. "Scott, I'm taking your fan's father to my trailer. Join us when you're ready."

"Okay," Scott called, "but I'm going to swing through makeup first to get this gunk off my face."

"Take your time," Amara encouraged, and Elizabeth watched as Christopher was escorted away.

Elizabeth diverted her eyes until they landed on Dana. "Where's Jared? He should be here getting ready."

She shrugged. "I thought I saw him poking around earlier. I'll go check his trailer," she offered.

"Wait. When?" the designer questioned.

"Oh, maybe ten minutes ago? It hasn't been long."

Ten minutes ago? Elizabeth thought back ten minutes and nearly swallowed her tongue. "Was he like, *here*?" she interrogated further.

Dana nodded. "Yeah, he was around here somewhere." She gestured around the area, brows furrowing when she didn't spot him. "I'll check his trailer in case I was hallucinating. Don't worry. I'll find him in plenty of time before they're ready for him on set." She breezed away equally quickly.

Before Elizabeth could worry about it too long, she realized she was suddenly alone with Scott for the first time. He was behind the screen, and she saw his arms flailing over the top as he pulled on his clothes. The silence felt awkward after the chaos that had recently ended. She certainly didn't want to talk about her worries, and she racked her brain for a safe topic.

"How's the costume been working out?" she finally asked.

"Perfect," he acknowledged. "It really helps put me in character."

"That's the best compliment," Elizabeth enthused. She leaned back against the sewing machine table. "You guys are going to have me spoiled for any other cast after all this flattery."

"Well deserved," he praised. He joined her moments later, suit folded neatly over his arm and extended it to her.

She took it from him and set to hanging it for Dana to have cleaned.

"Your adoring public is waiting," Elizabeth spurred gently when she noticed him fidgeting with his shoelaces. "And somehow, I feel like you're dreading it."

He groaned. "Don't get me wrong. I'm incredibly grateful for fan support. It ...reminds me how it's all over. It's kind of embarrassing...and depressing."

"Only if you let it be," she encouraged. "Every actor on that set would trade you places."

"Because they haven't been there," he countered. "You can't go anywhere or do anything without drawing a crowd. I'm enjoying being on set and everyone treating me like a normal person."

"You are a normal person," she encouraged.

His face softened. "You'll have to get used drawing a crowd in public if you're going out with Stone," he cautioned. "And not all of them are going to be nice. Some fans tend to think of us as their property and act accordingly."

"There were some fans at lunch," she admitted. "But they were very respectful. It wasn't a huge deal."

"Chris is a veteran. He knows how to handle the cool ones." He tied a shoe. "Have you ever been to a movie premiere?"

Elizabeth shook her head.

"I get offers all the time that I turn down. Tell you what...the next premiere offer I get, I'll get three tickets for us and Amara, and you can see what I mean. You should know what you're getting into."

Her head tilted involuntarily. It was a generous proposition for someone she barely knew. She liked him on principle alone, and she began to regret her initial assessment of his solo work. The man before her did not need to beg for attention, nor did he seem to want it.

"Thank you. It sounds like fun," she accepted. She wanted to repay the favor but had nothing to offer. She realized the one event she could reciprocate with wasn't even her party. "You hear about Amara's pool party?"

His face brightened. "I might've heard something about it."

"You going?"

He looked away noncommittally. "Well, I'll need an official invitation first."

She furrowed her brows in confusion. "Well, she said it's for everyone, even Christopher," she revealed. "I'm pretty sure as her on-screen hubby you're at the top of the guest list."

He smirked. "I hope so."

Elizabeth squinted at him. "Well, you might get uninvited if you stall much longer. The quicker you get there, the better Amara looks."

Her words landed, and his face split into a boyish look of delight. "You're right," he yelped. With a quick thank you, Scott darted away toward the principals' trailers.

Ten

Principals' Trailers, Back Lot: Amara

Amara walked Christopher to the gates, watching as he jogged across the street to the aforementioned coffee shop and returned with his daughter. She was about his height and seemed far older than the seventeen he'd claimed as she bounced along behind him. As she drew closer though, Amara recognized the telltale signs of actual youth: glowing skin without a stitch of makeup, shiny curly hair, and exuberance. The excitement on her face alone made her look like a child, and the way she clung to her father's elbow was adorable. She was quiet as they walked back to her trailer, listening to the girl bubble about getting to meet Scott and thanking her father repeatedly for setting it up.

Christopher gave her a sidelong glance and a sigh as he held the trailer door open for the ladies. "Sorry," he mouthed silently.

The actress waved him off, seating his daughter on the couch and asking about what pictures she might like to take with her hero. For a moment, she thought the young woman was going to melt into the floor at the suggestion of a photo op.

"There's a mirror in the bathroom through that door if you want to freshen up," Amara suggested.

The young lady darted away.

"You'd think she's never met a celebrity before," Christopher joked as he slipped into the dinette comfortably.

Amara chuckled. "I remember that feeling. But I have yet to run into my idol, so I can merely guess what she's going through. In fact, I'm not even sure I'd *want* to meet him," she added, pursing her lips thoughtfully. She seated herself on the couch and regarded the door. Surely Scott wasn't lost again. "He was right behind us," she reasoned aloud. "Said he had one more stop to make. It shouldn't be long." Amara wondered who she was trying to convince about Scott's tardiness.

Christopher's daughter emerged from the restroom and paced slowly from one end of the trailer to the other. Amara distracted her with a bottle of water and a line of questions about her upcoming senior year, asking what she was doing with her summer. Amara thought an eternity had passed before there was a brief knock at the trailer door, and it opened to reveal Scott.

He veritably bypassed the stairs and launched himself into the space. He looked young and innocent, Amara thought, and every bit the teen idol he had been a few years prior. She could see he'd asked hair and makeup to do him some favors, every hair in place. She grinned, thinking that this fan was about to be blown away.

"Hey," he greeted, eyes automatically lighting on the young girl frozen between her father and the couch. "I'm Scott." He extended a hand to her.

The teenaged girl gasped for breath, giggling. Her face was glued to his, beaming. "Hi," she squeaked reaching for his hand, then froze again.

Christopher spoke up. "Scott, this is my daughter, the ever-eloquent Elaina." He clapped his hands together once to punctuate her name.

This seemed to break her from her stupor. "Hi. Elaina," she pronounced.

Scott opened his arms, enveloping her in a hug. "It's so good to meet you," he continued as he released her. "Your dad's told me what a fan you are, and I wanted to say how much I appreciate your support."

She flashed all her teeth happily, one toe making circles on the ground as she stuffed her hands into her pockets. "It's my pleasure," she murmured.

"So, tell me, what's your favorite song?" he inquired.

Amara watched in awe as Scott charmed his little fan, sitting on the couch beside her. Amara settled across the dinette from Christopher, gesturing for his phone silently. He unlocked it, and she began filming the encounter. She winked across the table when Christopher motioned his understanding, leaning forward to watch.

After a few minutes of conversation, Scott offered to snap some selfies with Elaina's phone, and she squeezed in with a shiver and a giggle.

Amara turned the camera slowly, capturing the whole thing. She was shocked when the young girl turned to her. "My dad says I have you to thank for setting this up. I will never be able to repay you."

The actress grinned, glancing at Scott as she stopped recording. Scott patted Amara's shoulder, squeezing it gently. "Oh, he's such a softie. He wouldn't pass up an opportunity to meet one of his biggest supporters." She clasped the hand on her shoulder, sneaking a glance up at him. He was a good celebrity, she thought. If she ever got a following like his, she wanted to remember this exchange and replicate it.

"How long have you two been together?" Elaina questioned.

"What?" Scott balked.

Amara snapped her attention to the fan, feeling like someone had dumped a bucket of ice water over her head. She pulled her away from Scott's grip, folding her hands in her lap as her acting skills kicked in.

When she spoke, she knew her face projected the essence of serenity, lightly tinged with confusion. "I'm sorry?"

Elaina waved them both off. "I won't tell anyone." She gestured toward her father and rolled her eyes. "I'm very discreet," she promised. "You've clearly kept it incredibly quiet. I'd have never known if I hadn't seen you together."

"Baby, you can't ask questions like that," Christopher scolded gently. "We've talked about this. It's not about you being discreet – they may not be ready to tell. You put people in an awkward position."

She sighed. "Sorry, Dad." She turned sad eyes to the actors. "Sorry, Scott and Amara."

"It was an innocent question," Amara pardoned, smiling brightly, as if she weren't blushing twenty shades of burgundy inside.

Christopher stood, taking his phone from Amara. "Come on, Ellie. Let's leave these nice people to their business. We'll go get some boba. Thank you both so much for your generous hospitality. I hope I can fit her head through the door on the way out."

Elaina nodded, then in a surprise fit of excitement, she squeezed Scott around the waist, pressing her head to his chest and squealing.

Scott chuckled, patting her back lightly with one hand and looking at Christopher.

Her father pulled her away, sighing. "Sorry, man," he apologized to Scott. "Thank you both. See you on the fourth," he added, lifting one hand and leading his daughter from the trailer.

"Bye," Amara and Scott both called.

Elaina waved at them both with another thank you, and when the door closed, the silence was deafening. What had just happened? Amara played the last few minutes over in her mind, trying to figure out what had prompted the girl's response. They had barely said two words to each other, and in fact, she was still a bit frustrated it had taken him so long to join them.

Amara turned to Scott with a stunned expression. "So...that was weird."

He sighed. "Sorry – I uh...I have this thing I do with fans, and they really like it. Puts them at ease."

She shook her head. "Not what I'm talking about," Amara clarified. She studied his face, squinting her eyes. Had Elaina's assumption truly not bothered him? "I'm talking about that girl thinking we were together. What in the world gave her that impression?"

Scott blinked at her. "I don't know." He tilted his head to the side in thought. A terrifying pounding raced in her heart as he gazed at her, and she suddenly wanted nothing more than to kiss the confusion off his face until she had him begging on his knees in front of her.

Swallowing hard, she stuffed that idea to the darkest recesses of her brain and chewed her bottom lip.

She stared at him a long moment, waiting for him to reveal anything else. When he didn't, she frowned.

"It's early days, and I like you, so I want to put all the cards on the table, Scott." She paused, making sure she had his attention before continuing. "I don't do relationships, and I don't do people from work. Ever."

Scott's face was turning red as she watched her words land on him.

"I've worked on enough sets to know that things can get…emotional," she continued. "Especially for actors like us who are playing a married couple. It's easy to assume those emotions we're projecting on each other are real. But it's purely a job, Scott. Once filming is done, you'll see that."

She wondered which of them she was trying to convince. Either way, it had to be said. She would not allow this to happen. A romance or the inevitable breakup was a distraction a leading lady couldn't afford.

He blinked at her, rapidly. "Just like that? You feel no attraction whatsoever?"

"Exactly like that," she stated firmly. "I like you, Scott. But those romantic feelings? That's left-over character emotions. Come on? What do we really even have in common?"

Scott didn't answer her, but she felt his gaze locked into hers. He breathed out his next words in measured tones. "Is that really how you feel?"

Was it? She nodded. "Of course. Take it as a compliment to your acting skills." She knew she was right. He might be a lot of beautiful man stuffed into one package, but there was no gain to their relationship. He didn't need the press. She wasn't willing to foster a relationship simply for press, no matter how much she wanted to pin him down to hard surface and claim him. No. They were merely afflicted by their character's romance.

Scott tucked his into his elbows across his chest. "What about all that stuff about knowing how to drive a Ferrari?" he questioned.

Amara held her breath briefly as she drank in his commanding pose. She blinked, suddenly recalling how he had toyed with her bare back the first time she'd been in full costume, and she'd cautioned him not to rev her engine. She shivered in memory of his fingernails running so lightly over her skin.

"That was actor flirting," she clarified. "It helped get us in character."

He stared at her face intently, and she felt his eyes boring into her. He seemed to be searching for something, but if he found it, he gave no indication. His face turned hard, and Amara watched his jaw twitch for a moment. When he spoke again, his voice was purposeful, almost parental.

"It's cruel to play with someone like that," he reproached. "You're a great actor, Amara, but you shouldn't use your acting skills to manipulate people off the set."

She scowled at him. "Is that so? You didn't use your acting skills on that innocent young girl?"

Scott matched her expression. "I did it to make her feel comfortable. It wasn't for any kind of personal gain."

Amara shrugged. "Po-tay-to, po-tah-to," she enunciated. "It worked for the roles we're playing. Your character needed to be chasing for keys to a Ferrari." She was unsure how to tell him she was right any more clearly. He was still so...naive, she thought, despite his apparent innate talent and years in the entertainment industry.

His eyes narrowed as she spoke, and Amara got the distinct impression something very fragile had broken. He stood, without meeting her gaze. "I'll see you tomorrow," he pronounced and stalked toward the door.

Amara's face wrinkled, watching in shock as he passed her. "Yeah," she agreed, but before she could say more, he was gone, the door slamming in his wake.

She frowned, crossing her arms over herself. She didn't know what he was upset about. It had to be said, she reasoned. If Scott was developing feelings, it was best to stop it now. It was the considerate thing to do. If she was honest, Amara had given the speech to herself as much as to him. Watching him with those fake kids all day had her stomach in knots and her biological clock beating her upside the head with its ticking. He made her want babies, and rose petals, and long walks on the beach at sunset holding hands.

She grumbled to herself. Going home alone tonight was not in her best interest. She flopped onto her stomach on the couch to scroll through her phone. Surely, she knew someone suitable for the evening. She needed someone to remind her that the emotions coursing through her were strictly hormonal, and nothing sated that thirst like something quick and rough.

After donning the little black halter dress she had tucked in her trailer, she then slipped into some matching pumps and called for a taxi. Tonight was about power. She stalked the patrons around a dark Bellaire bar, finding a lone stool under a single pin light. She was setting a tableau, a lonely actress who wanted to have some peace, drowning her sorrows in a martini glass. She wanted to look like a rescue.

Her ploy worked like a charm, and within the hour, she had drawn her prey into her spider's web. But the encounter was unsatisfying, leaving Amara scowling in the hired car all the way home. She ticked off each moment, recalling how smoothly she had drawn in her treat. He was a delicious investment banker who'd bought his first luxury car. He was trying to awe her with his prowess, ordering her a second drink and requesting top shelf liquor. He acted as though he hadn't known who she was. But he couldn't help referencing that he secretly knew her face.

She'd worn him out quickly, then shimmied back into her dress and left. He hadn't even been worth sticking around to see what happened after he caught his breath. She hadn't even removed her bra. The last time she felt this disappointed, had been during her last serious relationship. And she had thought she'd loved that poor bastard.

Concern niggled at her for the rest of the night, trying to figure out what had been wrong. The boy banker had a perfect body – muscled and young. There was nothing wrong with his performance specifically. But she was bored.

She showered off the event quickly, pulling on her pajamas and climbing into bed. Her eyes closed, and unbidden, she thought of Scott juggling for the children on set, and her insides twisted.

"It's just a job, Amara," she spoke into the darkness. "He's just a job, and you're both just actors."

Even so, that night she dreamed of silver eyes and a sinful mouth that, alarmingly, whispering three small words into her ear that startled Amara from her sleep.

She didn't have those emotions. Those were fake things that she pretended to know on screen. She knew how to long, or mourn, or desire. But love? That wasn't a real thing, and she paced the house for hours before finally dressing and calling a ride to the studio.

Eleven

Backstage, Wardrobe: Elizabeth

Elizabeth was ready when Dana returned with Jared, and she ushered him behind the dressing screen. Tonight, one of his awkward scenes involving an award ceremony was on the filming schedule. Jared squirmed when he emerged for inspection in his brown, tweed suit and vest combo. It was at least a size too big for his lean frame, despite some of her careful tailoring, but the effect was perfect. It was as though he had borrowed his father's suit: too big and out of date. He tugged at the bottom of his sweater vest.

Elizabeth clapped at the figure he presented. "Excellent!" she complimented. "Perfect mixture of poor geek and legendary genius."

She pointed him in the direction of the raised platform and reached for the lint roller. She indicated he should stretch out his arms.

He did so with a deep exhalation, eyes darting to the ceiling while she ran the roll of tape over the costume.

"So, I heard you got your studio set up in your trailer," she commented, trying to put him at ease. She could feel the tension in his shoulders as she worked.

"Where'd you hear that?" His question was quick, and she felt him jerk around to see her.

She pursed her lips, cheerfully regarding the floor. "Amara hung out with me after the two of you abandoned her in her trailer to go check it out."

"Oh, right. I guess we did do that," he realized. "We may owe her an apology."

Elizabeth ran the lint roller over his legs before setting it aside. "It couldn't hurt." She offered him a genuine smile, glad to see him relax slightly. She lifted each pantleg to investigate the loafers he sported, shaking her head at the auburn hair on his ankles. "You're ready," she proclaimed.

"Come watch us film," he pleaded. "I could use the support."

"Let me clean up in here, and I'll come watch a few takes."

Jared stepped off the riser, patting her on the shoulder. "That's my girl." He jogged off in the direction of the set, and Elizabeth shivered. He must be incredibly nervous to want his "fan" there for moral support, she reasoned.

She found his street clothes in a pile on the floor, and as she folded his warm T-shirt and jeans and folded them into his duffle, she sighed. Why were all the good ones taken? Fate seemed cruel to allow her this access to him now when he wasn't available or interested, for that matter. Of course, this same fate had brought her someone else, equally charming, that was interested. She waited until Dana had returned before slipping onto set like a mouse in search of cheese.

A bunch of extras in some sort of semi-formal ware were milling about, and as she watched the monitor, her heart thrilled. Her team had done an excellent job. The camera panned, zooming in on Jared as he was greeted by the head of his fictitious lab and introduced to some sketchy looking supporters, who, according to their wardrobe, could buy and sell him over without missing the change.

He was no longer Jared – he was the nerdy scientist who had stumbled upon a discovery that would change the world. She believed his character, and when Max called cut, she exhaled, suddenly perturbed that there wasn't more to be watched. Max called for an additional take, barking orders to two of the cameras to change position and giving some guidance to the lab investors on how to turn themselves.

She squeezed Max's arm when he returned, beaming at him. "This is genius," she whispered.

He nodded knowingly at her. "I know. Wait till the world gets a load of him. Did you see how his eyes painted the whole screen? Like you could practically see the mathematical wheels turning in his brain. The camera loves him."

She nodded.

Max's face wrinkled. "You're not objective on this."

"Maybe you're jealous that I've known about him so many years longer than you. And if you'd had the good sense to find me sooner..."

"Well, we're here now. I'm hoping that there will be a spin off series born out of this."

Her brows raised at the information, and she pressed in closer. "How would that work?"

He shrugged. "Couple ways it could go. But I could easily see a series of the discovery itself and all the dark testing that went down and such. Like a real prequel to the movie."

"Well, get him while he's available."

Max nodded, then turned his attention to the set.

Jared's face quirked up in a smile. For her. She gave him two thumbs up and was rewarded by him blowing her kisses and pressing his hands together with a minuscule bow.

She saw Max grunt out of the corner of her eye. Several of the crew chuckled, and Jared thanked them as well.

She watched the next take, then slipped out equally as quietly to go compliment her team. When she was finished, she returned to the principal's dressing area where Dana was curled around her phone.

"How come you're back?" Dana asked. "I saw you watching on set."

"He needed a little boost," she reasoned. "He's fine now."

Dana rolled her eyes up to her supervisor. "For as dedicated a fan as you are, you are a *bad* fan. Get over yourself. If he needed your support at the beginning of the scene, he needs it now too. You make a difference, Elizabeth. Besides, he's your main responsibility now, so go hang out with him. I'm cool back here."

The head costumer smirked. "He is pretty amazing. Wanna come with me?"

She shook her head. "No thanks. I'd rather make noise back here than watch you swoon silently."

Elizabeth pivoted. "Have it your way," she kidded then sneaked back onto the set.

She loved watching him work. It had been years since she'd seen him on television, and this new, mature version in a dramatic setting had her captured. For all his playfulness, when he was performing, nothing existed but the scene. Max rolled his eyes at her several times but said nothing.

When the director wrapped for the evening, it was nearly midnight. She jumped up, clapping and joining him as he danced toward the changing area.

"You were really great."

He nodded. "It felt so good. I hate doing those awkward scenes, but when they go well, I'm pretty proud of them." His mouth froze in an "o" as she handed him the duffle bag of his street clothes. "Thanks for hanging out on set. It helped to know I had someone who'd root for me no matter how I did."

She smiled shyly at him. "Thanks for the invite."

Jared was busy opening his duffle bag, and he jangled it in his hand. "I'm taking this with me when filming is over," he declared before disappearing behind the screen.

"I fully expected you would. That's why I did it."

"You're a peach," he called out.

Elizabeth tried to focus on any other noise than the sound of his clothing coming off and the zipper of his pants coming back up. She had heard these noises thousands of times, but none of it seemed to affect her the way this did.

"Wanna go for drinks again?" Jared asked.

She sighed. "Are you paying again?"

"Yes. For not making me wear those tunics." He laughed. "Your boyfriend looked ridiculous."

"Not my boyfriend," Elizabeth denied.

Jared appeared from behind the changing area. "I got to hear how he taught you to say fuck."

Elizabeth gasped, turning away from him. Something about the word coming from his lips made her insides turn into flowing lava. It would not do to let him know.

"At least he didn't teach me to do it," she countered cheekily.

He beamed at her. "Good one! You're learning, Padawan. But how did you get started talking about that anyway?" he asked, the curiosity clear across his furrowed brows.

"I was telling him about the first time I saw one of his first films. Most of my favorite quotes included it."

"But you don't say it now. In fact, you won't even say it in a conversation about it." He sat on the chairs to put on his shoes. "You about ready?"

Elizabeth was busy inspecting the clothes he'd left behind the screen. Again, they were warm with his body heat. She rushed through putting them back on the hanger and frowned.

"Did you spill something on this?" She turned her eyes fully on him, finding Jared looking suddenly away.

"Hurry up. I'll drive."

"But you out-drink me," she cited. "Why don't I drive?"

"And risk having to hear myself on your stereo?" He shook his head. "No thanks. Are you ready yet?"

She arched an accusatory brow in his direction. "If someone hadn't spilled something on their costume, I might be."

"Well, I don't know who that would've been," he stated. "But I bet they've learned their lesson and will never do it again."

She arched a brow slyly at him. "As long as that's the truth...I'll allow it." She wondered if he would recognize one of Christopher's more obscure lines from a canceled television show.

"You didn't," Jared groaned. "You can't be quoting him. You're *my* fan."

"I think *you're* the fan for recognizing that. But a good chocolate martini covers a multitude of sins," she resolved, grabbing her purse.

Elizabeth led the way to the parking lot, exchanging banter with him as they strolled. "So how is it," Jared mused once they were ensconced in a booth with a drink in front of each of them, "that you are still so uptight in Hollywood at this level?"

"Years of training," she expounded, taking the first sip of her martini and humming in delight. "You did a good job with the bartender. It's perfect."

"The Mistress asks, and she receives," he teased, easing back in the booth. "I have a little experience talking to bartenders; waiters who make the right requests get bigger tips."

She smiled. "Smart. I am lucky to be the beneficiary of your hard work."

He frowned at the statement.

Elizabeth mimicked his expression. "Did I say something wrong?"

He shook his head. "No. Having some morose old man flashbacks," he retorted.

"You're not old. And trust, you look a lot younger on screen than I happen to know you are."

"Thank God and good genes." He sighed. "And you know you're old when people start telling you that you're not and then finding ways to justify how old you don't look or act despite the facts."

Elizabeth chuckled, thinking he was right as he took the first drink of his beer.

"So, when are you and honey bunny going out again?" he questioned.

"Oh, stop it," she retorted. "It's not like that."

"See?" he added. "Uptight."

"I don't see you giving out any details about your love life," she pointed out. "Why are you so interested?"

"Living vicariously through others." He took a long swig of his beer. "Besides, what else is there to talk about?"

She shrugged. "Well, until you're prepared to talk about your bunnies, tell me what movie you're going to see next."

He finished his beer and flagged a waitress for another. "Marvel," he answered. "They've got this huge schedule of films. Did you see *Infinity Wars*?"

She shook her head, and he cringed.

"No! We can't be friends anymore," he said with a sigh.

For a moment, Elizabeth panicked, but she spoke quickly, surprised at her own boldness. "Now see, a proper friend would offer to educate me, not disown me."

Jared leaned forward with a grin. "How committed are you to this friendship?" His eyes sparkled as he awaited her answer. He wanted her approval, and she couldn't deny him.

"Straitjacket level," she confessed.

Jared leaned in closer. "Are you multiple-movies invested?"

Fascinated by the passion in his plea, Elizabeth leaned toward him. "How many is multiple?"

"Enough to get caught up before the next one comes out in the theater this summer."

Elizabeth drew back. "Isn't that like more than five?"

He nodded. "Close to twenty, if you go back to *Captain America*."

She sighed. The thought of sitting with him for twenty movies was intoxicating, but her grown up brain protested that she had responsibilities. "It'll be hard to find that much time."

"I'll loan them to you," he challenged.

The grin on his face was impossible to resist. "Maybe I can use Amara's trailer and watch while you're filming," she mused aloud.

"I'm hurt. You can use mine," he insisted. "I'll bring the first one tomorrow. We can start while they change cameras for my set."

She sipped her martini for a beat. "Okay. I'll give it a shot." She leaned back in the booth and proceeded to pepper him with questions about his history, sneaking more details about his stint as a purple dinosaur she'd learned about recently. She noticed how he warmed to the gentle interrogation, and she wondered if he was practicing for press. Giggling inwardly, she tested the theory, sliding into questions about the movie they were filming.

"What's your least favorite part of this movie?" she asked.

"The scene with the rats," he answered immediately. "I am seriously dreading that."

She grimaced in sympathy. "I will be in hiding that day. Giant boots," she detailed.

"They assure me the rats are well trained..." he trailed off as his fresh beer arrived, and he accepted it gratefully. He took a long pull and leaned back against the booth, looking around the bar. "The music in here kinda sucks," he noted.

"You have the power to change it," she encouraged hiding behind her drink.

"If only," he said with a sigh. "It's not about talent."

Elizabeth frowned. "I wish it was. Although, if it was, we wouldn't be having this conversation because you'd be off doing concerts and posing for teen magazines."

"Your lips to God's ears. I'm hoping to record during my down times," he confessed.

"Tease. You can't tell me these things and not share with me."

He eased back in the seat, , swigging his beer with a self-satisfied smirk. "Keep stroking my ego, and my head won't fit through the door."

Elizabeth couldn't help but waggle her eyebrows back at him until they were both laughing too hard to remember where they'd started. Almost an hour later when they departed, Elizabeth floated all the way to her car after ensuring that Jared was passed out safely in his trailer before she left for home. At least he wouldn't miss his call time. She began plotting to deliver a case of water and some appropriate food to his trailer the next morning.

She sighed, wondering about the "someone" in his life. He never talked about this person, and she suddenly thought maybe this person was another man. That would explain his tight-lipped approach and why he felt so comfortable making so many innuendos to her. This was a disappointing turn of events, she thought, and then her brain recalled an image of him leaning on the table and laughing, and none of it mattered.

Elizabeth realized as she navigated the city streets that she'd had lunch with Christopher Stone, and she hadn't thought about him once since Jared had arrived on set. It had been a great lunch. The restaurant had been off the beaten path, and the service had been amazing. They'd been seated in a quiet booth and gone through all the usual pleasantries. Conversation had come easily. He had seemed genuinely amused when he charmed into telling on herself with the story about the first time she'd seen the full version of one of his early movies littered with more f-bombs than she had ever heard at that point in her life.

Something about the way he watched her face as they talked, she felt stripped of any pretense or defenses. It was something entirely different from having drinks with Jared. Maybe it was the emotional maturity level. It felt like such an adult event. Her phone dinged from its haphazard location in the bottom of her purse, and she stuffed a hand inside to fish it out. At a stoplight, she received a text from the man in question. A grin curved her lips, and rather than risk reading it at the wheel, she punched keys on her car's navigational screen until a call connected, ringing over the speakers.

"She calls," Christopher greeted after half a ring.

Elizabeth smiled devilishly at the roads ahead of her. "She does. I'm driving, so I couldn't read your text. I was hoping maybe you could tell me what it said. I'm better at phone calls than text anyway. I'm a little old school that way."

"Hey, that was going to be my line," he protested with a grin.

"Well, then, maybe we should hang up if you're all out of lines," she teased.

"Oh, no. I'm perfectly capable of pulling something out of my ass for such an occasion."

Elizabeth frowned but laughed as she replied. "I'm not sure I want any part of something that came out of your ass."

"Then I'm screwed because it all comes out of my ass," he crowed. "Elizabeth, you make my inner thirteen-year-old so happy."

For a moment, she realized she'd been channeling her inner teen all evening – with Jared. Probably gay Jared, she reminded herself. "I do what I can."

"I'm really surprised you're still up. And driving you said?"

"Mhmm. Filming ended about midnight, and Jared and I went out for drinks. Headed home now. He's sleeping it off in his trailer."

"Ah." There was a pause. "So, maybe I should ask before I make a fool out of myself...is there something going on there?" he asked.

"No – not at all," she replied easily. "We're nothing more than friends. He doesn't really get to film with the others, so there's no one else to entertain him. Think of him like the older brother I don't have," she clarified.

"You're sure?"

"Certain," she insisted. "He's got a mystery partner he's not talking about."

"In that case...I was thinking that after a successful lunch, it's time that we take the next step and have dinner."

"Ooh – dinner. That's a bigger commitment."

He snickered. "I think we're ready for it. I was texting to see when you were free again. I know the movie's barely getting started..."

She cringed. "I'm not sure. I think we've got a day off scheduled around the fourth of July..."

"That's too far away. Maybe I could sneak you out for drinks later this week? Or a midnight picnic? Something?"

She blinked at the proposition. "Well, that sounds charming."

"Less of a commitment than dinner, and there will be wine," he teased.

Elizabeth didn't really like wine, but she liked the concept of it, so she made an approving noise before she continued speaking. "So, I know why I'm still awake, but why are you still up?" The dashboard clock told her it was well past the average person's bedtime.

"I've been listening to my daughter gush about meeting Scott and tell me I'm her hero all night. She passed out, and I am finally alone with a bottle of scotch."

"That sounds lonely."

He sighed, and she heard ice clinking in a glass. "Not tonight."

Elizabeth was grinning as she pulled into the parking lot at her apartment complex and navigated to her reserved spot. "I'm glad you texted while I was driving, and I was forced to call."

"Yes, otherwise it might've devolved straight into sexting."

She laughed. "I wouldn't know how to do that."

"Oh, I'd be happy to teach you," he teased. His voice lowered as he spoke again. "So...what are you wearing?"

Grateful to be sitting in park now, giggles bubbled up from her throat that she'd been holding back while driving. "Wouldn't you like to know?"

"I have quite an imagination," he warned. "If you don't tell, I'll be forced to let it run wild." He snickered softly.

She joined him under her hand. "Something tells me that will be far more interesting than any costume I could dream up."

"Isn't that your job?"

"Well, yes, but I've never designed anything appropriate for this conversation."

"Maybe you should. I'd love to see those sketches over our picnic," he taunted.

"I hope you like stick figures."

"Ooh! Skipped straight to the wood. Good choice," he retorted. "Or if describing it is too hard, you could send pictures."

She howled now. "I'm hanging up. I'll reply to your text tomorrow after I've checked the schedule."

His glee crackled over the phone, and she hoped no one was near enough to the car to hear him through the speakers. "I look forward to it. Have good dreams," he encouraged.

Twelve

Backstage, Wardrobe: Amara

The previous night's forays were still occupying Amara's mind when she barreled into wardrobe the following morning, and Elizabeth called her out.

"What's crawled up your behind sideways?" the seamstress mumbled.

Amara struggled to answer. She remembered climbing into her ride home, and the frustrated feeling returned in force. She growled at nothing in particular as she dropped into one of the waiting chairs. Even though they were alone in the small area, she lowered her voice. "I had a perfectly lovely evening last night, and it wasn't even remotely satisfying. Got the engine all revved up and stalled."

The seamstress' brow shot up as she reached for Amara's garment bag. Elizabeth gave it the once over including a discreet sniff test before she passed it back.

"I'm sorry?" she asked. "I'm sure I don't understand what you said."

Amara took her outfit behind the screen wriggling out of her street clothes and into her costume. She spoke very little as she got on the riser and allowed the costumer to adjust the fit and roll away any lint. Amara focused on her breathing in an attempt to prepare for the scene. But the previous night's ventures were forefront of her mind, and it was blocking her flow.

"I just wanted sex," she confessed. "A nice, steamy little exchange. And *he* was satisfied. This has never happened before. I always get what I want. And I'm not even sure it was his fault!"

"Sounds terrible," Elizabeth mocked, moving to the back of her tunic.

Over her shoulder, she peered at the top of the other woman's dark head as she felt the trim on the cutout on her back being smoothed down. She lowered her voice. "You have had sex, right?"

"Of course," Elizabeth huffed not meeting her eyes.

Amara wasn't sure she believed her. "I think we need to have a girl's night so I can grill you like a cheese sandwich."

Elizabeth gave her a suspicious look. "You make it sound so appetizing."

"Oh, come on. I have this big, empty house, and I know the best delivery services," she coerced.

She studied Elizabeth's face for an indication of her answer and tried not to frown as she avoided eye contact. Finally, Elizabeth met her gaze, and Amara saw the excuse forming before she heard it.

"I don't have a lot of free time. When you go home, I've got to be here until Jared's finished filming. And now I've committed to watching a crap ton of movies with him..."

Narrowing her eyes, Amara turned to the seamstress. She was far from one to judge, but something about the statement piqued her curiosity more than the disappointment. "So, be straight with me. Are you sure there's really nothing going on between you two? Because I thought you'd be all over this Christopher thing."

Elizabeth's head whipped around, and Amara watched her cheeks flare red. "Not here," she whispered, her eyes darting all over the room in a frenzy.

Sensing the opportunity, Amara seized it with an ecstatic smile. "Girl's night it is." She jumped off the riser. "We can sort out the details after shooting," she promised, not giving Elizabeth a chance to protest. She waved and headed off to hair and makeup.

Scott was already seated in one of the chairs, quiet as the people there coiffed his hair. His eyes were closed, and his body was relaxed, except for the tight set of his jaw. She suspected he was still stinging from their conversation in her trailer the afternoon before.

"Morning, Mara!" the makeup artist greeted, waving her to the empty seat.

She watched Scott for a reaction, but there was none. A knot of discomfort wedged itself in her throat, forcing her to swallow hard. She chatted amiably with the makeup artist, wanting to give no indication of her disappointment with her rendezvous the previous night. It was one thing to tell Elizabeth – future bestie – but an entirely other thing to confess in front of her costar who she'd just rebuffed. And worse, she suddenly seemed to crave his respect. What was happening to her? Since when did she want anyone else's approval?

Unable to take the silence between them, she waited for her makeup artist to finish, then blurted. "Good morning, Scott."

"Morning," he hummed, calmly, eyes still closed as the artists worked. "Have you seen Sean or Catherine yet?" he asked, referring to their on-screen children.

"No – just Elizabeth." She gestured to her costume.

There was a long silence while his hair was sprayed into place, and his eyes slipped shut again. "I think this is the last scene in the airport...travel center. Whatever this place is called."

Amara studied him through her mirror. His expression was neutral, posture eased comfortably in his chair as the crew worked around him. Not ready to admit defeat, she countered, "I think you're right. I guess today is big scream day."

Scott was finished first, and Amara's heart dropped into her stomach as he left without even a goodbye. It wasn't too many more minutes before she was finished, and Amara stalked toward set.

Max was waiting for her when she arrived, but her eyes were scanning for her costar, who she did not see. She realized he hadn't been in costume and must have stopped at wardrobe next, and her frown deepened.

Max was talking, explaining what was to happen and how he wanted her to play the scene, and she nodded absently. When Scott did finally arrive, Max pulled them both together, discussing points of how they would need to act toward each other and walked through blocking before turning his attention on their "son."

Amara studied her co-star. "Good night's sleep?"

He nodded. "You?" he reciprocated.

"Sure," she answered. "Ready for this?"

"Born ready," he answered. At that, he turned and began talking to the camera guys, and she listened to the technical details, steam nearly pouring out her ears. Why wouldn't he talk to her? Because she'd prioritized her professional career over a quickie? She huffed, thinking two could play at this game, and she wandered over to talk to the sound crew.

When Max called everyone to places, she swaggered toward her coworkers and stepped to her mark. Nothing else mattered now but the lines and the scenes, and she sank down inside her character. In her place was solely her character, a wife and mother of two realizing the horror of what had happened to her son. She thought of every disappointment she'd ever faced – every role she had tried out for and lost – every bad thing in her life that she could reach and mixed in a little of the frustration from the night before and the anger with Scott.

When the director called "action," Amara was ready, and she acted her ass off.

If Amara had not buried herself so deeply below her character, she would be distracted by thoughts of her past relationships. She would be thinking about that first on-set fling she'd had so many years ago now. She hadn't realized it was merely a fling until his number had been disconnected. They'd spent a glorious weekend together with no holds barred after filming her guest role on his show. When she'd called to set up dinner, the number was out of service.

Then there was Thomas, and Michael, and too many others to name really. Early in her career, she'd had a boyfriend. They were both young, and in hindsight, stupid. When her career began to pick up, he had grown increasingly frustrated with the long hours she would be away. Heaven forbid she ever got a major role. She had recently allowed herself to believe that she was worthy of being someone's priority.

Unlike her character who had given herself up to move to Mars for her husband's work, Amara was not ready to give up her dreams for anyone. As a reward for her character's sacrifice, her son goes insane. Amara was quite happy to live vicariously through her character and skip the soul crushing rewards life liked to throw.

She let her emotions pour out, listening as Sean began the infamous scream. Tears coursed down her face as she fell to her knees, and she turned her rage to Scott. Her fictions husband should never have told their son that story about teleporting while conscious. He had given their son the idea that had stolen his sanity. She voiced these thoughts, whimpering her accusations, getting stronger with each repetition.

When Max called cut, Sean flopped back on the couch, and she felt Scott's arms wrapping around her.

"Shh," he soothed, pulling her to his chest. She felt his hand smoothing over her back. "Come back to us, Amara," he encouraged.

Amara tried to surface again, breathing in the soapy scent coming off her costar. She inhaled deeply, sitting up and wiping the backs of her hands against her cheeks to clear the tears. A laugh spilled from her lips amidst the onslaught of misery as she pressed it all back down. "Sorry," she sobbed.

"Oh, thank God," Scott sighed, pulling back.

Amara opened her eyes, seeing Scott's forehead pressed to hers. "Sorry. I went a little deep for that one," she breathed.

"Yeah, you did," he agreed. He released her gently. "Maybe not so deep on the next take."

"Amara, are you okay?" Max worried. She wasn't sure when the director had joined them, but he was suddenly kneeling in front of her, face full of concern.

With a deep breath, Amara stilled her crying. She nodded at the director, slowly rising and took a bow. "The dramatic stylings of Amara Baker, at your service," she volunteered shakily.

She swore the director sighed relief as he and Scott began clapping until the rest of the crew joined. She curtsied with a cheeky grin.

The director squeezed her hand, and without a word, the hair and makeup team set upon her with water and flying makeup brushes and sponges. Others swarmed Scott, though he towered over them.

The crew was buzzing as they reset the scene and double checked the lights. Amara heard the little girl near her groan, throwing her arms up in the air. The small actress rolled over on her couch and turned to her on-screen brother. "You did a really great job if other people didn't steal your spotlight," she groused rather loudly.

Feeling a bit ungracious, Amara leaned away from the team repairing her face and blew raspberries at the little girl.

They ran through the scene a dozen more times, but Amara managed to collect herself, giving the right amount of motherly terror in the next takes.

She watched Scott, seeing the heartbreak on his face each time they pretended to watch their son lose his mind. She kept thinking about the way he had instantly pulled her close. It was as though he knew what had happened.

His hands had felt large on her arms and back. Her skin puckered remembering his touch. Why had she felt so...safe? It must have been his superb acting skills pretending to be her husband, she reasoned.

When they moved onto another scene, she was grateful, stretching and looking forward to lunch break. She downed a bottle of water and collected a plateful of fruit from the buffet. She plunked into a seat at an empty table and popped a grape into her mouth.

After the morning's work, the tumultuous parts of her history that she had been squashing down for decades began trickling through her brain. The scene had broken a piece of her carefully constructed wall. She watched as Scott tended to Sean, offering him suggestions to soothe his throat, gesturing to his own throat as he pointed out different things.

Max interrupted her reverie, taking a seat at the corner of the table unceremoniously. "Hey, that was a little intense in there today. You okay?"

She waved him off. "Of course. I was channeling some old wounds trying to imagine if I'd seen my son destroying himself that way."

The director nodded. "It was actually a beautiful take. I'm hoping to use some of it in the final cut. But it felt kind of personal."

"Good," she approved. "At least it was all for something."

"And did I sense something between you and Scott?" he pressed.

"Sense what?" she asked, playing dumb. She actually batted her eyelashes at him. "You know I'm strictly professional," she assured.

Max smiled and nodded. "Of course. Let me know if something changes."

"Naturally," Amara answered.

The director excused himself, and Amara was surprised when Scott took his place. After his earlier treatment, she was relieved to see he was speaking to her again.

"How are you feeling?" he questioned.

"Proud," she countered, enjoying the confusion that crossed his features.

"I was not expecting that," he admitted. "You were pretty far under on that first take," he noted, opening a bag of chips.

His vocabulary choice surprised her. "Under?" she repeated.

He nodded, reaching in the tiny bag with two fingers and extracting a chip which he placed into his mouth and chewed.

Amara's gaze was focused on his fingers and lips, and she caught herself zoning out for a second. "That's a very specific term," she pointed out.

"I'm aware," he answered, reaching for another chip. "But that's what you did."

She rarely heard the term used outside the bedroom, but as she considered, he wasn't wrong. "I can see how it would look that way from your perspective." She paused as he chewed again, and she had a sudden craving for chips herself. "You knew exactly what to do," she observed. "You have a lot of experience?"

"I've been there before," he answered smoothly.

Every muscle in her body tensed, and Amara forgot to breathe. When she remembered, she started to choke, some saliva trying to escape down the wrong pipe.

"You are having a rough day," Scott sympathized. He didn't take his eyes from her 'til she had settled.

She changed the subject, discussing the scenes they had planned after lunch. She neatly avoided any further questioning by retreating to her trailer for a short rest. Somehow, she'd patch up that wall in her mind, and a nap seemed to be the ticket. Unfortunately, after her nap she was still feeling vulnerable to Scott. She wasn't sure how he'd sneaked through that weak point and remained inside her mental barricades, occupying her mind, and Amara was none too pleased. She was smart. She would find a way to shut him out.

Thirteen

Backstage, Wardrobe: Elizabeth

Elizabeth was waving a magnetic wand over the floor on one end of the changing area, and Dana was crawling around on the other side doing the same. Elizabeth had been preparing to do a quick service on her poor old sewing machine, but she was tired from staying out too late the night before, and her hand had slipped while turning the screwdriver. She had heard the tiny screw from the machine housing bounce against the floor, but so far, neither woman had turned up the offending item.

"Why are they always so ridiculously tiny?" Dana complained. "Also, when we find this, I am going to buy some of those foam puzzle piece mats so that things don't bounce all over, and we can find them easier."

"Don't go through the trouble," Elizabeth countered. "As long as no one rips their costumes, we won't have that much more sewing to do anyway. I should've waited to service it at home."

"Ladies," greeted an appreciative male voice. "To what do I owe the pleasure?"

Elizabeth groaned, recognizing the voice. "Either help us find a screw or go away, Jared," she griped.

"You..." his voice stuttered, and she didn't bother to turn around to look at him. "You're looking for a screw?" His laughter filled the room, and she heard Dana's foot connect with some part of him. "And you want my help?"

"Too far," Dana groused. She crawled around for another moment before proclaiming, "Found it!"

At this, Elizabeth did turn and see her assistant on her knees, holding up the minuscule part carefully between her fingertips. She handed it to Elizabeth then pushed herself to her feet.

"Little bugger," the seamstress swore before trying to rise. She groaned as her knees creaked.

Instantly, Jared's hand appeared to pull her up, and she accepted, hanging onto the little part that had caused all the trouble in the first place.

"Thank you," she replied, smiling at him. "You look surprisingly well rested. And early."

"Thanks for making sure I was safe last night and for the delivery this morning. I got a little carried away," he confessed.

Elizabeth felt Dana's eyes on her, before the assistant stood bodily between the two, prying the fastener from her hand.

"Let me do this. I'm good with an oil can and a brush," Dana insisted, turning to the machine and seating herself.

Elizabeth frowned, but let her do it, worried suddenly that Jared had worn out his welcome with her. She turned her attention back to the actor at hand. "What's up?"

"Well, I went home and showered and came back." He held up three DVD cases, beaming at her. "The next movie comes out right after Independence Day. And if you're going to see them all in time, we'd better start now. I've got it all hooked up in my trailer."

Elizabeth frowned.

"Start what?" Dana asked, turning in her chair to look. "Are those Marvel movies?"

Jared nodded, his grin seeming to nearly stretch past his ears as he waved the cases at Dana. "Lizzybeth's never seen them before, and she promised last night to watch them all with me before *Ant Man and the Wasp* comes out."

"*Ant Man and the Wasp?*" Elizabeth repeated incredulously. "What did I get myself into?"

"Oh – they're worth the time," Dana promised. "I can't believe you haven't seen them yet."

"I'm more of a *Harry Potter* or *Lord of the Rings* fan...Superheroes haven't been my thing." Elizabeth turned her attention back to Jared. "Looks like I'm odd man out on this one. But I really am supposed to stay here even though they're filming in case something goes wrong."

"I've got it," Dana insisted. "It's almost lunch anyway."

"Oh right. Food," Elizabeth remembered.

"We'll be in my trailer," Jared informed Dana. "So...not far in case you need her." He held her elbow and tugged lightly.

"Leave the door open," Dana harassed.

Elizabeth balked.

"Unlocked – not open," Jared countered. "Too much noise and too much light." He stared at Elizabeth squarely in the face. "You coming? I'm due on set in like five hours."

She stared between Jared and her assistant. Dana waved her on with a wink. "Well," Elizabeth said with a sighed. "All right. Here I go." She virtually had to jog to keep up with him, and he rambled as they walked.

"I really think you're going to be hooked right away. I'm hoping to get through the first *Captain America* and the first *Iron Man* before my call time. Then you can finish up *Hulk* while I'm working."

"You mean there's parts of the parts?" she fretted.

Clearly amused by her question, Jared slowed his pace as they neared his trailer. "It's fun. And then we can talk about it." He vaulted up the steps, opening the door and holding it for her to squeeze past him.

The entire trailer smelled like popcorn, and she noticed that the TV was already cued up to the movie menu. The dinette had been converted into a pallet, and pillows and blankets rested on both it and the couch.

"You were pretty certain I'd follow you today," she noted as he closed the door.

"You promised. And when fans promise, they usually mean it."

She turned to see him grinning and rolled her eyes affectionately. "Where's all this recording equipment? I thought you had it set up."

"It's in the back bedroom," he expounded as he opened the microwave and pulled out a bag of popcorn, dumping it evenly between two bowls on the counter. "Soda? I've got Coke and Pepsi...take your pick."

"Pepsi," she snapped. Realizing her tone had been harsh, she backpedaled, biting her lower lip and softening her expression. "That was a little aggressive. Sorry. I'm just strongly anti-Coke."

He laughed. "I prefer Pepsi, but Coke doesn't offend me." He passed her a bowl and turned to the fridge. "Couch is mine. Fan gets the dinette."

Elizabeth couldn't help but grin as she took her treat to the pallet he'd made for her and curled up happily. This almost felt like relaxing, and Elizabeth had begun to think she'd forgotten how to do so.

Jared passed her an individual bottle of Pepsi as he passed, dropping onto the couch and reaching for the remote. "Got your phone handy in case you're needed?"

She waved it at him. "Ringer volume all the way up."

He nodded. "I'm setting an alarm for fifteen minutes before call time." With that, he started the movie. "Get ready to realize precisely how awesome I am for hooking you up with this."

Elizabeth rolled her eyes again as she made herself comfortable. She found it difficult as the studio logos appeared on screen not to stare at her companion. He caught her staring at him. "Eyes forward," he scolded.

"Yes, sir." She saluted with a laugh, turning her eyes on the screen and watching. To her surprise, the movie was actually riveting, and she watched in fascination as the plot unfolded. There was something incredibly satisfying to hear him laugh with her or clap when she had an appropriate reaction. He paused it occasionally, asking if she'd caught certain things until she chided him to let her watch, and they could discuss it at the end. About halfway through, he disappeared to bring back real food from the studio.

When the first movie ended, Elizabeth giggled as Jared gushed about the film. "You were right. I liked it. And there's a part two?"

He nodded. "Yes, but you're not ready for it yet. You should see *Iron Man* next."

She laughed at his enthusiasm but surrendered. "I'm going to use the facilities in the studio and check on Dana. I'll be back."

Jared nodded already pulling the first disc out of the player and placing it reverently back in its case. "Hurry up. Want more popcorn?"

She shook her head. "I'm full after the first round and lunch. But I'll bring back something sweet if I can find it."

He gave her a thumbs up. "Hurry up or we won't finish this before my call time. And you still have to dress me."

She fought the urge to shrink back into the trailer as she opened the door, squinting at the extremely bright outside. "There he is – the diva."

Jared threw one hand on his hip and pointed at her with the movie case. "You know it!"

She burst out laughing, nearly stumbling down the stairs. She actually jogged back toward the studio, the Pepsi screaming at her to be released. She used the facilities before sliding into the wardrobe area. She could smell the cleaners and oil in her old sewing machine and smiled, seeing Dana stretched across all three chairs with a magazine open over her head. A small Bluetooth speaker was quietly playing some unfamiliar music.

"Everything okay in here?" Elizabeth asked.

Dana sat up with a wicked grin. "Okay, be honest. Are you watching movies or making out? 'Cause you can't do both at the same time unless you're doing it wrong."

Elizabeth rolled her eyes. "Just the movies."

At this, Dana groaned. "Things are dead here. Even the extras are sorted. We're all bored."

"I'm sorry."

Dana waved her off. "You always let me go do stuff, so it's my turn. There's a card game around the corner if I want to get crazy."

"Okay – well thanks. Text me when you hear filming break," she requested.

"Will do. Go. You're barely gonna finish the next one before they get back, and I don't think Amara wants to be here without you."

Elizabeth cooed. "It's sweet. She's reaching out. You know actors have a hard time making real connections."

"Except for your boy crush," Dana prodded, giggling.

"Stop it," Elizabeth hushed. "You know I'm going out with Christopher again," she pointed out.

"All these years, I didn't think you had it in you to juggle two men, but here you are. Doing it."

"I'm ignoring you," she stated, turning on her heel to leave. She swung by food services and picked up a few candies, taking them back to Jared's trailer.

"Did you get lost?" he accused when Elizabeth opened his door and stepped inside.

She tossed a candy bar and some Twizzlers at him, impressed when he caught both easily. "I'm sorry. I had to talk to my assistant."

He waved her off. "Well close the door. I'm starting, and this one's funnier than the last, so buckle up."

Elizabeth dropped into the dinette and curled up with her pillow, peeling open a candy bar and nibbling the corner of it. As promised, Elizabeth was immediately immersed. About halfway through, the door latch drew her attention, and after glancing at Jared to find him equally surprised, she craned her neck behind her. Dressed in her street clothes, Amara slipped in silently, pulling the latch closed as softly as she could before pouncing next to Elizabeth and curling up.

"Do I need to rewind?" Jared breathed.

Elizabeth shook her head. "Can we finish it?" she asked quietly.

"Yeah. It'll be tight, but yeah."

She glanced at the actress next to her who was quiet and beaming.

Elizabeth sighed and tried to focus on the remainder of the movie, but she kept glancing at her phone for the time. She felt guilty for Dana having sorted out both principal actors. Why hadn't she texted? She would have to make it up to Dana.

The moment the movie finished, Jared stopped the player and jumped up. "Everybody out. We're up!"

Elizabeth felt Amara stir next to her and squealed when the actress tickled her side. She stumbled out of the booth, surprised when Jared caught her. Her heart skipped a beat as his arms wrapped around her. She felt the tip of each finger against her arms as he straightened her up. She should have thanked him, but in that same moment, his inner drill sergeant surfaced.

"Out!" he barked, clapping at them both.

The seamstress scurried out the door and jogged toward the studio, Amara and Jared on her heels. She wasn't even a little surprised when Jared sailed past her, disappearing into the building.

"He could at least have held the door," Amara grumbled.

Elizabeth would have concurred, but she was running out of breath, and she had to be at her post before Max discovered she was missing or Dana simply quit. She reached her base in record speed. Jared was curled up on the riser and fake snoring. Dana stood over him, arms crossed and tapping one toe.

"Sorry," Elizabeth called, catching herself on one of the waiting chairs. "I'm here. I'm here."

Behind her, Amara skidded to a stop and grabbed her shoulders. "Let me; let me," she begged quietly.

Without explaining what she wanted permission for or obtaining the subsequent approval, the actress dashed forward pouncing on Jared, fingers digging into his sides. Jared was instantly alive, squawking and fighting back. They rolled off the riser with a thud, Jared breaking their fall. Amara fought back furiously, straddling him, fingers a blur as she reached for his stomach.

Jared was laughing, grabbing her wrists easily and holding her off before rolling them 'til they were on their sides. He tried to coral her hands into one of his so he could tickle her back, but Amara was quick and extricated one hand to reach his neck.

As the seamstress watched, she felt a little green monster rearing its ugly head inside her. Part of her wanted to be trapped beneath his taught body. Elizabeth turned away, looking to Dana as though there was nothing of interest happening within a foot of their feet. "Scott get on alright?"

Dana nodded. "Nice guy. I like him."

The head designer nodded then stepped toward the riser. "Okay, enough. You two are going to destroy my area," she scolded. She reached down, boldly hooking a finger in Jared's back belt loop. She tugged, snickering at the way he had Amara easily snared in his thick arms. The actress squirmed, trying to tickle his armpits to relax his grip, but not quite reaching. Jared's face was red with delight as he held on.

The tug on his jeans was what it took to get him to loosen his grip.

Amara jumped to her feet, brushing herself off and straightening her hair.

"Sorry, I fell asleep waiting for wardrobe. I was here on time, and there was no one to help me," Jared goaded.

"What am I? Chopped liver?" Dana objected.

Jared brushed himself off as well. "No. You are the world's best assistant to whom I am indebted and will be looking for ways to pay you back."

"I'm partial to pizza. And Imagine Dragons," she added quickly.

"I got you for pizza, lady," he vowed. "Any toppings you want. Because we only got through two movies. We're behind schedule."

Dana sniggered. "I've got this," she assured.

Elizabeth watched the whole thing with a bemused detachment, thrusting his costume for the evening into his hands. "Get dressed before daddy finds out we've been skipping school."

Jared snatched the outfit and ducked behind the screen. There was a swish of fabric against skin and then fabric over fabric. "I gotta say no matter how many times I do this, it's weird to be stripping down with a room full of women within ten feet of me."

"And here I thought you'd like the ratio of men to women," Amara called, settling down on the chairs.

"Well..." His head popped over the partition, eyebrows wagging.

Amara punched Elizabeth's arm lightly with a grin. She fanned herself.

In no time, Jared was headed out to set, leaving the ladies in his wake. Elizabeth sighed.

"He's fun," Amara cooed. "I see why you like him."

"She likes Christopher. He's just a pretty distraction," Dana spoke up.

"What you gotta do tonight, lady?"

"Undress the distraction when he gets back," Dana teased.

"You're not starting on that too, are you?" Elizabeth frowned. "I need an ally."

"Jared's your ally," Amara cooed with a conspiratorial glance at Dana.

Elizabeth sucked in a deep breath and turned to her machine trying to ignore them both and change the subject. "Nice work on the machine," she complimented. "You are so much better at this than I am."

Dana smiled.

"What are the odds I could steal her for the rest of the night?" Amara asked, wrapping both hands around Elizabeth's arm.

Dana threw up two thumbs at the actress. "Pretty good. Night shift is easy. It's just Jared. Besides, I went home early last night."

Elizabeth groaned, remembering. "Yeah. They finished about midnight. And then we went for drinks."

"Save your secrets 'til we've gotten to my house, dear," Amara cautioned. "You drive, right?"

Nodding, Elizabeth examined her assistant. "Are you sure? You've been alone all afternoon."

"Of course," Dana insisted. "I say what I mean. And also, when you're not here, I act as your proxy, and it's fun to boss people around in your name."

Amara needed no further encouragement to pull Elizabeth away.

"Let me get my keys," Elizabeth begged, extracting herself and collecting her things. She hugged Dana's shoulders. "Thanks," she replied. "We all owe you."

"I know. This business is built on favors," she responded. "And I'm making it rain."

Fourteen

Amara's House: Amara

By the time the ladies arrived at Amara's house, at least three deliveries were due to arrive any moment. Amara bounded out of the car with gusto. It had been a long while since she'd invited anyone inside. She wasn't even crazy about letting people pick her up or drop her off from her own front door. But the prospect of having an actual friend – one who didn't seem concerned about her success – was exhilarating. She wanted Elizabeth to feel welcome. For a moment, she wanted her to move in, but she recognized the neediness in the sentiment and backed down. She was perfectly fine and happy by herself. She liked it that way.

She welcomed the seamstress inside, as she tossed her keys into the bowl on the table.

"Wine or vodka?" she offered.

"Vodka," Elizabeth selected, frozen in the front hallway. Amara watched her looking around uncomfortably. "Do I need to like...take off my shoes or something?"

"If you'll be more comfortable, yes. But I don't have any weird house rules," she excused. "Make yourself at home." Amara headed to the kitchen, pulling vodka out of the freezer and then inspecting the fridge.

"I've got Coke, OJ, ummm..." She paused. "I think I have some other tonic water or club soda or something."

"OJ is fine," Elizabeth said as she picked her way to the couch and set her handbag on the coffee table.

Amara presented her with a drink minutes later, settling onto the couch opposite her. "I'm glad you came by tonight," she began. "There's things you simply can't say at the studio."

Elizabeth scoffed. "Doesn't feel like it's stopped anyone."

Amara laughed. "You've gotta have a thick skin. People only pester you if they like you," Amara coached. Her years as a character actress had taught her that Elizabeth's behavior stemmed from a place of trauma. "Who made you think people don't like you?"

"No one," Elizabeth answered, sipping her drink. She choked, face turning bright red as she tried to swallow.

Eyes narrowed, Amara shrugged. "I like them strong."

Elizabeth sputtered setting the drink on an end table. "I'll be careful then."

"No, no! That's the idea. Drink up! How else am I going to get you to loosen those lips?"

The seamstress balked. "You're tight-lipped too. I know nothing about you besides your encounter with an old friend who delivered you to the studio."

Amara thought back on her night with Frankie and purred in delight, leaning against the back of the couch as she faced the other woman. "Ah, Frankie," she sighed. "Have you ever had one of those people in your life where you think it could be mind-blowing and life changing, but you're both always involved with other people?" When Elizabeth shook her head, Amara continued. "Frankie is my person. It was years of build up for that one night."

"You're satisfied with one night?" Elizabeth questioned.

Amara nodded, smiling at the memory of all the things they'd done to each other.

"Where is he now?" Elizabeth's shoes slipped off, and she tucked her legs up under herself as she listened.

Amara shrugged. "I don't do relationships. And Frankie's a little clingy. Which is great for a night here and there. But who wants all the drama?"

Elizabeth sighed. "It's interesting that you think of it as strictly drama. I always thought the right relationship would make even the most mundane things worth doing."

Amara stared as she considered the statement. "Well, Frankie is always drama. We'd be constantly fighting to be the center of attention. In any relationship, one person has to stand down. And it's not going to be either of us. We're like...fire and gasoline." She trailed off. "But I already know all about me." She waggled her brows. "Tell me about you and Jared," she prompted.

Elizabeth took up her drink and had a healthy swallow. "I've been his fan since I was thirteen," she explained. "That's the full scoop. At heart, I'm just a silly little fangirl."

Amara sighed. "You're precious," she cooed. "He must love that." She considered Jared for a moment. He was the right age. He was fit, and from the way he had held her during their tickle fight, she got the distinct impression he knew how to move his body in all the right places. Her lips curved up wickedly as she contemplated a naked tumble with him. Her tongue flicked out over her lips dreamily. But then, her eyes landed on Elizabeth, and she saw the crestfallen look on her new friend's face. It was all she needed to push the notion aside. "So why are you not all over that?"

Elizabeth frowned. "What do you mean?"

"You've clearly got a thing for him," Amara contended. She studied the woman across from her. This is what her father had wanted for her – a modest existence, hidden behind a camera and never in front. Amara wondered what her life would have been like if she hadn't pursued acting. If she'd followed her father's wishes and gone into teaching or nursing or some other essential but essentially wrong-for-her career, would she be more like the designer across from her now? Confused and lacking confidence?

"He's not interested," Elizabeth said, shrugging. "I'll only ever be a fan to him. Maybe his friend... but you know, it's a little one sided. And besides...I'm starting to think he's gay." She sighed.

Amara thought otherwise. "What makes you think that?"

"I don't know. He's a little cagey about his personal life," she answered, reaching for her drink and swallowing another large gulp.

"Well, so am I generally," Amara pointed out. "That doesn't make me gay. This is Hollywood. You don't talk about your unmentionables."

"Okay, okay. Fair," Elizabeth conceded. "I don't know. Something about the way he said it last time we talked about it... made me wonder."

Amara arched a brow. "Explain."

A sigh escaped her lips, and Elizabeth's eyes fell to her feet. "He was giving me crap for being single, so I turned the tables on him. So, I say something about not knowing why *he's* still single. And he gave me this look..."

Amara wished there was a way to see what the other woman was recalling, because the expression on her face was pained.

When she spoke again, her words were fast and clipped. "He got really quiet and said something about how he'd never said he was single. And whatever it was, it sounded like something serious...long-term and definitely secret."

Amara was all too familiar with the concept of not being involved in a relationship but having someone to warm her bed whenever the need struck, and she jumped to his defense. "Or something casual. He might have a little black book like I do, you know."

Elizabeth blinked, pausing for a moment. "I don't know. If something's casual, wouldn't you say you're single? Or say you've got a casual thing?" she challenged. "The more I thought about it, the more real the possibility that it's another dude felt."

It was difficult to refute the woman's reasoning, but Amara was 99.9% sure she was wrong, nonetheless. But it sounded like she wanted to be right, so the actress let her. "Don't get all in your head about it," Amara placated.

The seamstress calmed slightly, but Amara could practically smell the smoke as the other woman's wheels turned. "Well, if he's not gay, and if he's seeing someone...why is he always making innuendos and calling me Mistress and crap?"

Amara cackled at the statement. "He calls you what?"

Elizabeth's face flamed again. "Mistress."

She pictured the other woman wrapped in a shiny, black provocative costume cracking a whip and fought the urge to cackle. The image fell apart quickly, and she bunched up to her knees, looking expectantly at her. "Why? You're about the nicest, most accommodating person..."

"Exactly!" Elizabeth exclaimed. "I think he does it to embarrass me."

"And why would it?"

"What if someone overheard and really thought that?"

Amara stared at her. It certainly wouldn't be the worst thing to be called, Amara knew. In fact, she tended to like it. She dared the other woman to say anything negative about it, forcing Elizabeth to be next to speak.

"But we're not...I'm not...like that."

"Like what?" she challenged. "Sexually confident?"

"Ha, ha," Elizabeth replied. "Quit trying to make me feel bad about my sex life."

"I'm sorry," Amara apologized. "I feel bad for you. Come on, I can see it on your face you'd give your left ear to do the horizontal tango with that man."

"Amara!" Elizabeth shrieked.

The actress grinned unapologetically. "I stand by my statement. I mean, what would be so bad with other people thinking that you're doing the naked mamba with Bo-Flex McAbs?"

Elizabeth scowled, curling into herself and setting her drink aside. "Who I'm sharing my bed with is no one's business."

"You worry too much about the wrong stuff. All I know is that anytime I've been around you both, there's a bond there, and it feels right." She finished her drink, setting the empty cup on the coffee table. "And what about Christopher? When did you hear from him last?"

"Last night. After drinks. We talked on my drive home." At this, Elizabeth reached for her glass and swirled the ice around. "Should we get to planning this pool party you want to have?"

"No. I didn't abscond with you all the way to my place and ply you with drinks to get put off so easily. What did you talk about?" Amara pressed.

Elizabeth giggled, covering her face briefly before confessing. "Well, it was mostly innocent, but then he brought up sexting. I mean, do people really do that?"

"Um, yes!" Amara swore. "Girl, have you been living under a rock your whole life?"

Frowning, the other woman answered, "Sometimes it feels that way. I was raised in a very sheltered house."

"Me too," Amara replied. "But I've been making up for lost time for years." She laughed, lifting her arms over her head and couch dancing for a moment.

Elizabeth shook her head as the doorbell rang, and Amara scurried to answer it. The next minutes were a flurry of activity as her deliveries arrived one on top of the other, and Elizabeth was at her side, carrying food to the kitchen while Amara signed for the orders. Elizabeth awed at the variety, remarking at the overwhelming spread.

They perched on bar stools at the kitchen counter, picking out bites from the trays, and Amara grinned as she watched Elizabeth evaluate each dish before picking at it. "So, since you won't tell me about Jared and all your squishy feelings about him, tell me about your past boy-friends."

Elizabeth's face scrunched up. "That's not much of a conversation."

"Tell me anyway. Pretend I don't know much about you." Amara busied herself eating, giving Elizabeth space to spill her secrets. She listened closely to the tale and offered Elizabeth another drink, which she refused.

"I thought you went out drinking with Jared all the time. You don't even actually like liquor, do you?" Amara was beginning to wonder about what this woman did for fun. No sex, and now no alcohol? This friendship was going to be a stretch, but maybe she needed a little reservation in her life.

"Sure I do."

"Uh-huh. Like, 'of course you've had sex,'" Amara derided throwing up air quotes. She rose to refill her own drink.

"I have," Elizabeth protested. "It...I'm not entirely sure why everyone gets so excited about it."

"You're doing it wrong," Amara contended. She reached for the seamstress' hand. "You deserve to have somebody rock your world. You need a Frankie. Or a Michael, or a Bret...or anyone." She giggled at the red face staring back at her.

"Maybe," Elizabeth agreed.

"Well, I think you get your mitts on either Jared or Christopher, and you'll change your mind about sex." Amara sighed.

"I'm not worried about it. Been living a long time without it."

"Surviving," Amara corrected. "Not living."

"Well, it's not like I could walk out the door and find someone."

"Yes, you could." Amara studied the other woman again. Did she not have a mirror? Had she not met herself? She realized her companion needed some encouragement and laid it on thick. "I could take you out tonight, and you'd have half a dozen guys begging you out of those sensible panties in an hour."

Elizabeth shivered in disgust at the word. Her mouth puckered like she'd sucked on a lemon. "I don't say that word."

Amara repeated it, thinking she suddenly understood why Jared liked to torture her. She was super reactive, and in a place like Hollywood, it was difficult to believe anyone was being genuine about being this innocent. But the costume designer didn't seem to have an ounce of self-preservation in her system to ward off the vultures. Amara felt the urge to protect her. "When were you last not single?" she asked.

Elizabeth's eyes turned skyward. "I guess about seven years?"

"Did you break a mirror or something?" Amara contemplated not having sex for that long and shuddered.

"A heart maybe." She released a sigh. "But we were together three years, and when I realized I still couldn't say I loved him...I ended it."

Amara balked. "No one else in that time?"

"I don't get out much. I moved here, started working... no one's ever interested, so I stick to the work. At least that's rewarding. I have a big wedding dress booked for after the movie. One of the cast members from one of the shows I worked on asked me for this fall."

"Wedding gowns? You do a lot of those?"

"No. I've sourced a few for different shows and altered them—"

"Like Molly Ringwald," Amara filled in, remembering the detail she'd shared on set recently.

Elizabeth nodded. "Yes, except not ugly. And definitely not pink." She giggled. "Oh, I think the alcohol is hitting me," she professed. "I'm over my limit."

"Eat more. Soaks it up," Amara encouraged. She thought back on what she'd heard so far. "Three years is a long relationship. Why'd you let it go on so long?"

"It was my first relationship," Elizabeth explained. "I had nothing to compare it to. I was so excited to have someone to call my boyfriend...I never stopped to think if it was right. I can make anything work, you know?" Elizabeth took a bite of food and chewed slowly. "After three years, I realized I liked his family better than I liked him. I was afraid that we'd be that couple no one invites to things because he had anger issues. Snarly all the time, and everything was someone else's fault."

"I know the type. I had one of those, but it didn't last more than a few dates." Amara snatched a piece of sushi from one of the containers. "Well, the good news is, you're moving on to greener pastures. And I don't think Jared's gay."

"I hope not," Elizabeth inclined. "But I want him to be happy, whatever that means for him."

"You really mean that?" Amara pressed, but she knew the answer already. She could see it on the other woman's posture. "And what about you?"

"I'm fine. I've got Christopher on the horizon anyway, and he's proposed a picnic."

"Ooh!" Amara purred. "Romantical. I like his style. But I refer to surviving, not living. Is it enough to be fine with someone? Is that fair to either of you?"

Elizabeth frowned. "You can't go heavy on the vodka and then ask me real questions."

"It's the one chance I have to possibly get some answers." She grinned wickedly at her companion. She was going to get the information she craved whether Elizabeth liked it or not.

"I guess I do wait to pounce on Jared for answers while he's drinking."

Amara burst out laughing. "Lizzy! I didn't count you as diabolical."

Seeming to take this as a compliment, Elizabeth's posture widened as she leaned back in her chair, shaking her head. "And that boy can drink!"

Before Amara could express her concern at the news, her phone alerted the neighborhood to an incoming text. It was a booty call from Frankie begging for the return of his clothes, preferably peeled from her body. Amara squeezed in close to Elizabeth, snapping a photo and sending it to him to convey she was busy. Frankie's reply was quick, promising to accommodate whoever and whatever kink she wanted, and Amara groaned in aggravation. She schooled her features and smiled prettily at her friend, encouraging her to continue as she tucked her phone beneath her thigh to ignore it.

"So, what about Scott?" Elizabeth questioned.

Amara's brows wrinkled. "What about him? He's my costar. You know how it is about shitting where you eat."

"We work with Jared, and you're all up in my grill about him."

Amara growled and pouted. "Fine, fine," she acquiesced, remembering begrudgingly the few early on-set disasters she'd survived in her past.

"You gotta admit, Scott's very pretty. And he's such a nice guy. Little helpless sometimes, but very nice," Elizabeth needled.

Shaking her head, Amara answered quickly. "Not happening. I already gave him the talk."

"You did not," Elizabeth accused, eyes bugging. She placed one hand over her mouth and mumbled through it in disbelief. "You told him this?"

Amara nodded. Why wouldn't she? Honesty saved so much time.

"And how did he react?" Elizabeth was literally on the edge of her seat waiting for the answer.

Amara's face pinched. "Not well. When you act in roles like we are now...sometimes emotions get mixed up. You don't even realize you're projecting it until after you've had a little space. Then he got all snappy with me for saving us both a lot of trouble."

Elizabeth's face fell. "No! He was telling me that he was going to get us all movie premiere tickets. For you and me and him."

This new information froze Amara's hand mid-way to her open mouth.

"You'll catch flies like that," Elizabeth teased.

Amara set down her hand, depositing the morsel onto the plate.

Elizabeth's mouth formed an "O," and she grinned widely. "Oh, so the big, bad Amara has a little crush on Scott," she sassed.

"I do not," Amara denied.

"That was way too fast," Elizabeth said with a giggle. "Tell me all about it. It's his eyes, isn't it?" she prodded. "He has really nice eyes. What would you call that blue? Ocean?"

"Silver," Amara answered, then realized her mistake by not only a hasty reply, but also a specific one.

"I knew it!" Elizabeth clapped in delight.

Amara waved her off. "I stare at his eyes on set all the time. Of course I know what color they are."

Elizabeth shook her head. "If you were purely looking on set, you'd have said blue. But you said silver because you thought about them after the fact," she reasoned.

Amara sighed, plucking the drink from the other woman's hand.

"Liquor is supposed to loosen your lips, not sharpen your wits," she scolded.

The seamstress giggled, taking her drink back and swallowing down the rest of it. "What's so bad about thinking he's pretty anyway? He is."

"Because he's my coworker. And maybe it would be all magical roses and satin sheets for a night, but in the morning – when reality kicks in, it's always ugly. And then I have to go to work and pretend he's my husband. And no."

"Yes, but who says you're going to have an opportunity after the movie's over? What if after it's over, you regret not at least sampling some of that?"

Amara rolled her eyes. "He's not the only fish in the sea. He's basically the closest one."

"Well, you won't convince me." Elizabeth stared curiously at the remains of their appetizers. She reached for something fried and nibbled it carefully. "Are these pickles?"

It was well after eleven when Elizabeth's cell rang, interrupting a conversation they were having about hair products. Amara snatched it with surprisingly good aim after her third concentrated cocktail. Her mouth formed an "o" in delight as she saw Jared's name scroll over the screen. This was a perfect opportunity to torture him, and she skipped across the room to prevent her friend from seizing the phone back. She clicked the green answer button, pressing it to her ear. "Hello?" she answered brightly.

"Lizzybeth?" Jared asked, sounding confused.

"No, of course not," Amara scoffed, dancing away from Elizabeth's grabbing hands as she continued the conversation. "But I know who this is."

"Is this Amara?" he asked.

"Bingo."

"Where's Elizabeth?"

"She's not in any danger, so you can stop worrying. I've absconded with her to my house. We're having a splendid time."

"Why do I have the feeling she'll need to be searched for contraband when I get her back?"

"Oh, stop being so overprotective. She's a grown woman. She can have all the contraband she wants," Amara groused to the disembodied voice on the phone. "We're having a little girl time."

"Can I talk to her, please?"

"Hmm," Amara considered the option, twirling past the seamstress. "Well, if I was to let that happen, I really feel like there needs to be some sort of payment first."

"Excuse me?" he barked.

Amara grinned broadly at her companion as the other woman crossed her arms over herself and glared.

"It'll be easy," Amara encouraged. "We've been having a little discussion, and you are the onliest one who can settle the matter."

She heard Jared sigh on the other end. "Okay. I'll bite. What do you want to know?"

Amara reached out, squeezing Elizabeth's hand. "So, tell me, hot stuff. Are you playing for the home team?"

"What?" Jared's reply sounded more than confused. It sounded angry.

Amara released Elizabeth and turned her back to her, heading toward the patio. "Well, you know how girls talk. And I was wondering if you'll be bringing a Joe or a Joanna to the pool party on the Fourth of July?"

"You're holding me hostage because you want to know if I'm gay?"

"Well," Amara thought about throwing Elizabeth under the bus, but looking at her face now, she couldn't do it. "You never bring anyone around, and we didn't want to assume you were straight. But it would explain why you haven't pounced on Lizzy yet."

"Or I could be a stand up kinda guy who doesn't pounce on people."

Amara was starting to rethink her proposition and relented. "You're right. I'm sorry. Let me give you Lizzy." Feeling properly chastised, she passed the cell to her friend, turning away to give them some privacy as she heard Elizabeth greet Jared. She began putting the leftovers away, making plenty of noise in her wake.

She nearly had it all covered and stowed before Elizabeth returned to the kitchen, sitting on a barstool and leaning her elbows on the counter. She rested her face on her hands, staring dreamily back, and in that moment, Amara was certain that Christopher could be the best man ever and execute their picnic date perfectly, and it was never going to work out. Because Elizabeth was completely smitten with Jared.

"Everything okay?" Amara asked.

Elizabeth nodded. "He was surprised when he came back to wardrobe, and I wasn't there. He wanted to watch *The Hulk* tonight. They finished early because everyone was creeped out by the rats."

Amara shivered, grateful there were no rats in her half of the film. "Ah."

A yawn distorted Elizabeth's face. "Exactly how much OJ was in that vodka?" she asked. "I still have to drive."

"I don't think you're in any shape to drive." Amara gestured toward the other side of the house. "I've got a guest room ready. I'll get you some clothes to sleep in."

Elizabeth started to protest, but Amara wouldn't hear of it. She dragged her to spare room, hugging her tightly. "I can't have you getting hurt. I only just found you," she reasoned. She shared some pajamas with her guest before skipping to her own bedroom.

She realized her last words had been a bit dramatic, but she meant it. She didn't remember the last time she'd felt like a girl or even a person. But she had since meeting Elizabeth. And she wasn't ready to risk losing it.

Amara tossed and turned as she played over the events of the day. She skimmed over her acting scene, choosing to remember nothing more than Scott's arms around her as he called her back to herself. In the dark, in the privacy of her bed, buried bodily under her Egyptian cotton sheets, Amara could admit to herself she had feelings for Scott. Or maybe it really was a projection of their acting skills. But she refused to act on them to find out. After the speech she had given him, she'd look like a flake if she ever changed her opinion. Turning it over in her mind, she fell into a tumultuous sleep.

Fifteen

Amara's House: Elizabeth

When Elizabeth woke, it took her a few minutes to remember where she was and why everything hurt. It came rushing back with one flip of her stomach as she opened her eyes, then immediately squeezed them shut again. She was at Amara's, and somehow, she'd had far more than her limit of one drink. Her head felt like a broken glass wrapped in gauze. She touched her forehead to make sure that there was no actual gauze or broken shards protruding. She sighed, scolding herself for her lack of judgement and reaching for her cell that somehow had gotten plugged in overnight. There were three messages from Dana, one by voice and two by text.

The voicemail she ignored, squinting at the words on her screen. "Assuming you got carried away with Amara and overslept." The second text was shorter. "Covering 4 u. Let me know u r safe."

Elizabeth tapped out a message then pried herself from the bed and began changing clothes. She didn't like the idea of showing up to set unwashed and late, but here she was: nailing it. She began to fret as she pulled the sheets up over the bed that she would have to wake her actress. She couldn't very well use up the woman's hospitality and then leave her without a ride to the studio. She pulled the door open and rushed toward the kitchen.

"Oh, good. You're awake," Amara said gently.

Elizabeth jumped, screaming in surprise. She hadn't expected to encounter anyone in the house yet. She held a hand up to her chest to calm her breathing, looking away and then to the actress who was standing calmly at the counter, stirring what smelled like coffee in a stainless-steel travel cup.

She was bright-eyed and bushy-tailed, and Elizabeth wasn't sure how she'd done it. The actress was chuckling now, holding up a bottle of pills and a large glass of OJ. "Take this for your head," she instructed.

The sight of the juice began to summon what she'd consumed the night before, and she covered her mouth with the back of her hand, groaning and closing her eyes. "Can I..." She held back the belch that was trying to force its way up. "Maybe some water, please?"

"Coming right up." Amara pulled a bottle free of the case in her pantry and passed it over.

Calming herself, Elizabeth accepted it gratefully, swallowing back four pills in a single gulp of water.

Amara's eyes were wide as Elizabeth came up for air. "Impressive."

Elizabeth frowned. "Why? Because I can swallow a gob of pills at once? We swallow a lot larger amounts of food in a single bite," she rationalized.

The actress shook her head. "You're too smart for being this hungover, and yet somehow you missed my swallowing joke. Jared would be so disappointed."

Elizabeth froze, putting the pieces together and groaned. "That is nasty."

"You're *definitely* doing it wrong," Amara maintained, eyes on the microwave. "Are you ready? Because we should get moving."

Nodding, Elizabeth led the way to her car, buckling in quickly and starting the engine while Amara locked up the house.

"Sleep well?" the actress asked as she settled into the passenger seat.

How was Amara so calm? Elizabeth channeled her inner Indi-race car driver as she wove through traffic, grumbling when she was forced to slow down. "Yes, thank you. Best guest room I've ever stayed in," she complimented.

"Turn right at the next corner. I know some side streets," Amara directed.

With help from her passenger, Elizabeth made decent time and rushed inside to get started. She thanked Amara for the hospitality again but denied the offer to go scrounge for breakfast. Scott was already sorted when she rounded the corner to her station.

"Good morning," he greeted energetically.

She couldn't help but respond in kind. "Morning," she answered. "Looks like Dana got you all figured out."

"Child's play at this point," he scoffed. "But it's nice to see your smiling face," he added.

Elizabeth tucked her purse under the sewing machine. "Mind if I have a look-see at the costume?"

Scott obliged, stepping onto the riser for assessment.

She adjusted the ankles of his trousers, making the cuffs lay neatly over his feet and picking a thread tattle off the back of his tunic. He appeared perfectly ready. "Looks like you've already done hair and makeup."

He nodded.

"I feel so guilty," Elizabeth gushed, standing back and waving him to the floor. "First, I missed you coming off set yesterday, and then I was late today. You must think I don't care about this project at all. But I really do."

Scott ran his hands over the intricate cuffs of his sleeve. "Hardly. I can see your passion in your work." He took a seat in one of the chairs, and Elizabeth worried that may have been where he picked up the loose thread. "Speaking of...do you design clothes outside of the studio?"

Elizabeth nodded, reaching for one of her business cards. "Sure," she answered, passing it to him. "I can work pretty fast, but I always appreciate as much advance notice as you can give me."

He tucked the card into the duffle bag he'd stowed beneath the chairs. "My bandmates will freak when I scoop them on a designer."

"You still in touch with everyone?" she asked.

"Oh, sometimes. We all got really busy," he replied. "You a fan?"

"I saw some shows," she answered casually. "And I wasn't living under a rock. You were on TV a lot and radio too." She swore she saw him sigh with relief. "This must be a big change for you, being in one place for so long."

He nodded. "Very much so. It's been years since I came to the same place every day for more than a week."

"Is it only a week?" Elizabeth mused. "Feels like longer and like we got started at the same time."

"Agreed," Scott answered. "But we're really kinda nailing it out there. As long as Stone's not on set." His smile stretched wider. "He's really funny. I didn't realize he could adlib like that. You seeing him again?"

"I think so," she answered, surprised at her willingness to confess to him. "But we're pretty busy around here, and I can't keep abandoning you."

Scott paused before speaking. "It's really good for your assistant though. You're really giving her some trust, and there's no better way to breed loyalty in your assistants than to trust them to do what you hired them to do."

The statement rang true, and Elizabeth heard the wisdom in his words. "I think you're right."

Amara joined them at that moment, carrying a plastic plate full of pastries, fruit, and foil burritos. "I brought breakfast," she announced. "I heard your stomach grumbling the whole way here, so don't deny it."

Elizabeth wondered if the actress had seen her costar yet and got her answer when she froze on her tip toes briefly.

Amara's shoulders straightened, and her pace slowed as she approached. Her voice was like velvet as she spoke. "Morning, Scott."

"Morning." Scott carried on about his business.

If she was as completely unaffected as she claimed, Elizabeth thought Amara wouldn't have missed a beat. However, the hitch in the other woman's step had spoken an alternate volume.

"Thanks," Elizabeth accepted, trading the actress her plate for a garment bag. She was expecting Scott to leave, but he did not.

Instead, the actor straightened, looking directly at Elizabeth, hands together and pointing in her direction. "So, I got tickets to a movie premiere like we discussed. Next Thursday. You game?" he asked.

Elizabeth felt a little apprehensive about preparing for such an event, but she didn't want to hurt Scott's feelings, and he was probably right that experiencing it with him and Amara would be easier than going to her first one with a date. "Let me check the filming schedule."

"Amara?" Scott asked.

"Yes?" the other woman called from behind the screen.

"Movie premiere. Thursday. I already know I'm free, and if I am, you are. You in?"

There was no answer. "Amara?" Elizabeth called.

"Sure. What's the movie?" the actress answered smoothly.

"I don't remember. Does it matter? The idea is to take Elizabeth to a premiere so she knows what it'll be like to date a celebrity," he enlightened.

Amara popped out from behind the screen and onto the riser. "Oh, well of course I'm in for that. Need to make sure our little bird can fly before we kick her out of the nest."

Elizabeth studied them when Scott agreed. "You both know that I'm a grown woman, right?"

Scott laughed and reached out a hand to fondly touch her shoulder. "Yes, but you're *our* grown woman."

The seamstress rolled her eyes, checking Amara's costume briefly. "I approve you for set duty," she pronounced to them both.

Amara stepped down and called Elizabeth's attention. "Here are the keys to my trailer if you need to nap or something while we're filming."

Elizabeth felt a little like melting at the kind offer. The headache was clearing up, and the foil burritos were starting to smell good. She wasn't used to being tended, and the tenderness on the actress' face seemed genuine.

"Thanks," she acknowledged, accepting the keys. "Break a leg today." She blinked. "Well not really."

"We know what you mean," Amara assured, patting her hand. Then the actors were gone, and Elizabeth unwrapped her burrito as she searched for Dana.

She found her chatting with other staff members and joined the conversation as she ate. Seeming to sense her desire to talk alone, Dana excused them both, and they headed back to the principal's changing area.

"I owe you an apology," Elizabeth started when they were alone.

"No need," Dana dismissed.

"But there is. Your job is to follow up after me – keep me on schedule."

"And sometimes that means that you're not here, and I hand out the costumes. We're down to maintenance and cleaning. You're wasted here anyway on set. We've already completed everything they're wearing. I'm sincerely enjoying this. For the first time since we met, you're actually taking time for you."

Elizabeth felt her eyebrows knitting together, and she tucked her free hand into her elbows. "I want you to know how much I appreciate it."

Dana stared at her, and Elizabeth looked away. "I don't know if you remember, but two years ago, I was going through that ugly divorce. You insisted I take care of my business. You covered for me more times than I could count. It's my turn to repay the favor. I feel like you've finally found your people. You've got men falling all over themselves for you," she cajoled, sniffing the air. "Is it your perfume?"

Chuckling, Elizabeth shook her head. "You've got me."

"Well, whatever it is, I'm excited for you. Someday you'll be so rich you won't even want to work, let alone need to. And when that day comes, I hope you'll have someone to wake up with."

They were silent briefly before Elizabeth spoke. "I'm the older one. Like a lot older. How did you get to be so mature?"

Dana poked her companion in the arm gently. "Because someone helped me figure out how to balance my personal life without giving up my career. And it gave me some perspective."

Dana's expression gave Elizabeth pause. She remembered how protective she had felt of her now-assistant when Dana was going through her divorce. She didn't think her current situation warranted the same apprehension, but she cherished the action. "Well, aren't you the lucky one?"

"Let me do this for you. I know Jared's gonna want to watch more movies. He told me so last night, and he's ordered pizza for me today for dinner. So go – live a little."

Elizabeth sighed. "I guess I do need to fill the creative well," she conceded.

Dana snickered. "Someone wants to fill your well," she taunted then groaned, clapping a hand over her mouth. "Oh no. He's rubbing off on me."

They laughed until they cried and then hugged each other.

When Jared arrived at ten a.m. to collect Elizabeth for their movie binge, Dana shoved Elizabeth out the door, threatening to quit if she stayed.

She walked beside him as they headed toward his trailer, but it was awkwardly silent. Elizabeth had the distinct impression that she'd done something wrong and wracked her brain for something to say. "So, Amara held me overnight," she blurted.

He nodded as they walked, not looking at her though. "I thought she might. She's kind of a force of nature."

"But good hearted," Elizabeth pointed out.

"True." He paused for a few steps, then asked, "Was she very drunk last night?"

"Tipsy maybe. But not drunk."

He frowned, this time looking at her. "I felt a little attacked you know."

Elizabeth matched his expression, and she was sure now why he was giving her the cold shoulder. She had been mortified when Amara grabbed her phone the night before, but it had all happened so quickly, she wasn't sure how she could have prevented it.

"I'm so sorry," she spouted. "She grabbed my phone, and I thought I was going to melt into the floor when I heard what she said."

He was quiet as they reached his trailer, and he preceded her in, holding the door. "Why were you talking about my sexual preferences to begin with?"

The TV was already on, and while there was no popcorn, a case of Pepsi adorned the counter. She almost cried. "I don't know. She was asking if you were single, and the idea kind of popped up." Elizabeth cringed. That wasn't entirely true, but she didn't bother to elaborate.

He switched off the lights and settled onto the couch, staring at her. "I'm very private about this kind of stuff."

She felt suddenly shy and ashamed of herself for allowing Amara to pry. A worse thought came to mind. "Is it because you don't trust me?" she asked quietly.

He shook his head. "There's a lot of reasons. Mainly because a lot of that stuff's painful and I don't like to spend time wallowing in the past. I've chosen to move forward."

She felt sheepish for not having asked him directly and instead telling a third party. "Whatever you choose to tell me or not, I really do respect your privacy." She wanted him to understand where she'd gotten the idea. "The other day when you said you weren't single and then got so weirdly quiet...it did leave an impression that you didn't want to talk about it because you were still in the closet. And I wasn't planning to ask you about it because I didn't want to make you uncomfortable."

"Bang up job," he jibed.

"I'm sorry," she apologized, blinking back the sudden tears that threatened her.

He sighed then, meeting her eyes. "Not gay. Obsessed with girls. And there's someone I'm seeing, but it's not serious, and I'm not ready to label it yet. Satisfied?"

"Yes," she whispered. She wanted to promise him she wouldn't pry again, or swear she'd meant no offense, and a hundred other things. But anything else she wanted to say sounded simpering and unimportant, so she simply nodded emphatically.

"Well, this movie's a little dark," he muttered. "So, I guess we've set the mood now. You ready?"

Elizabeth nodded. Part of her was surprised he wanted to keep watching, but maybe he had more mercy in him than she deserved, and at least he wouldn't kick her out over the faux pas.

He pressed play on the menu, and they were silent for the remainder of the film. It took her a bit to get immersed, worried that something between them was irrevocably broken, but slowly she was drawn into the plot until she completely forgot that Jared had seemed cross with her at its start.

In the middle of the third movie, Elizabeth's phone started blowing up. First it was Christopher, making plans for their picnic date, and then the texts from Dana began. She frowned, asking Jared to pause the film. "Hey, I gotta go. Duty calls," she apologized.

He nodded, and Elizabeth winced when he turned on the indoor lights. She stretched gently before standing, meeting his eyes. "I'm sorry about last night," Elizabeth apologized softly. "It's none of my business, and I should never have said anything to Amara about you," she added.

"It's over. We're good," he promised, then, much to her surprise, held his arms open.

Elizabeth blinked for a moment then accepted the offered hug, grateful at the seeming forgiveness. She squeezed him tightly by way of apology, and he squeezed back.

He released her a moment later. "I'm sorry I have a chip on my shoulder about this. I'm working on it," he pronounced.

She shook her head. "You're allowed to feel how ever you feel about things, and me assuming I have the right to ask about them is the crime here."

Jared waved her off. "Go before we start saying who's the worst. I'll bring you the keys when I come to wardrobe so you can watch more alone if you want. Or grab the disc."

Elizabeth nodded, waving as she slipped out of the trailer and headed to the studio. It was a relief to know that they'd smoothed that over and things were back to normal. And she hoped nobody saw the last few skips that landed her in front of the studio door before straightening up and stalking inside to sort out whatever mess had started in her absence.

Three days later, she found herself accumulating more debt to Dana as she slipped away from the studio and seated herself in Christopher's Audi. She giggled as he sped away. "Someone's in a hurry."

"Eh, I know how films are. You think you've escaped, and then they drag you back in kicking and screaming. The surefire way to get by with it is not to let them see the whites of your eyes."

She nodded her agreement. "Well, Dana's a dream at taking over, and I'm always available by cell if it comes down to it," she expounded.

"The golden handcuffs of the golden age," he mused.

She stared out the window as the city blurred by between traffic lights. "Where are we going?"

"Well, it's going to look a little suspect, but I promise it's not," he chuckled. "Ideally picnics happen in parks, right?"

She nodded.

"But LA is a bit short on those if you don't want to accidentally sit on a hypodermic needle," he ruminated. "But what LA is NOT short of is high rise buildings. And I happen to have access to one with a rooftop garden."

She watched his face as he gave a quick, proud smile from the road to her. "Clever," she complimented.

"And the view at sunset's pretty good. If I hurry, we should be there right on time."

She was amazed, watching him, and her stomach felt a little wobbly at the thought of the man next to her and the consideration he'd seemingly given this. However, his words rang true, and she raised her brows to meet her hairline as he whipped into the parking garage of a hotel. He parked in a reserved space near an elevator and popped out and around to hold her door.

The attention left Elizabeth tongue-tied, but she sucked in a deep breath to calm herself. She was allowed to enjoy this. He was so charming, and it was virtually impossible not to grin like a girl when he turned his wry smile and sparkling eyes her direction.

Christopher grabbed her hand as though he had been doing so for years and led her to the elevator. "Now I know what you're thinking. Where's the picnic basket?" he stated as the doors parted, and he pulled her in with him. He punched the button for the top floor.

She giggled, thinking that was not the first question on her mind.

He held up a finger to announce his next thought. "Where we're going, we don't need picnic baskets."

Elizabeth's giggle turned full laugh now, and he seemed to buzz at the sound of her enthusiasm. "You are entirely too clever for my good," she sassed.

"That's the plan," he agreed easily, pulling her out when the doors opened again. She was surprised they were not in a rooftop garden as promised, and she wondered where they were exactly. A pair of ugly, worn double doors was ahead of them, doing little to mask the din beyond them. Christopher pushed through unceremoniously. "Edward!" he called in a sing-song voice.

Elizabeth was suddenly surrounded by the sounds of a kitchen vibrating with life. At least a dozen people manned cutting stations, stoves, ovens, and a variety of other equipment, and she could hear the constant flow of water in the distance and the squeaking of dishes being washed punctuated by chopping knifes and sizzling grills.

A man, shorter than Christopher, emerged from the seeming chaos, thrusting a hand in their direction. He had a towel flung over one shoulder of his chef's jacket. "Chris! You made it up the secret elevator."

"Just like a spy," he exclaimed and squeezed Elizabeth his side. "This is Elizabeth. I managed to steal her away for a few hours to visit your fine establishment."

The newcomer, presumably Edward, shook Elizabeth's hand. "He exaggerates. It's nothing but our rooftop garden. We source a lot of our own herbs and some seasonal vegetables." He gestured for them to follow him as he wove through the staff toiling over boiling pots of water and pulling trays out of ovens. The clattering was loud enough that she barely heard anything he said as he directed them to a door off the enormous kitchen. It led to a room lined with shelving and spare kitchen gadgets. There was a stairwell leading up, and Christopher stepped aside to let her go first.

Edward spoke again as they reached the top and lifted open a pair of doors on what appeared to be a sloped ceiling. "Here we are," he stated.

The sky opened up before her, and Elizabeth was immediately aware of all the warm string lights tracing a path around and hanging over raised garden beds covering the entire rooftop. She smiled at the charming area, smelling the herbs and growing vines and feeling the wind swirl around her.

Christopher emerged behind her, hands in the air and face bright as he announced, "Behold! A picnic." He snickered at himself, turning in a circle.

Elizabeth's eyes landed on a giant blanket spread out near the edge. On one corner were several plates and a bottle of something chilling on ice. Nearby was a charcuterie spread and a few other dishes she didn't recognize at a distance.

"Thank you, Edward," Christopher said, effectively dismissing him from the evening.

Elizabeth made her way to the blanket, glad she'd settled on some comfortable jeans and a blousy pullover. The wind made her feel like a princess as the fabric fluttered around her arms. "Well, this is magical," she admired. "I'm not sure I'm worthy of all the trouble."

He laughed. "I'll be the judge of that. And I declare you: WORTHY."

She felt her face flush, and she giggled as he gently tugged her hand to lead her to the edge of the rooftop. She was grateful there was a significant railing around them. "How do you know Edward?"

"When you live in LA for this long, you know people. Probably fifteen years ago, I met him at some other restaurant, and he's been taking care of me ever since. He showed me his garden the last time I was around, and I thought it might make pretty unique picnic grounds.

Sometimes it's hard to do stuff like this in public for me. One of the hazards of the job. So, it's cool to find little secret workarounds."

She was suddenly thankful to not have to deal with any fans this time. The privacy felt suddenly special. "I have a confession," she admitted.

"Uh oh. Let's hear it."

"I'm embarrassed to say that I don't get out much and might not be up to date on what you've been doing lately. Kinda been stuck in career mode for longer than I realized."

The smile he gave her was forgiving. "Me too, so I sympathize with the work you're doing now. It's a little refreshing to be with someone who doesn't know everything about me. But so you're aware of my time constraints, I'm working on two series now. One live-action, and one animated." He made his way to the blanket and eased down, perusing the offerings Edward had set out. "Let's see what we've got here. Ah. All the essentials it looks like. Some sort of crusty bread...check."

He recounted what was set out before they began to nosh. He seemed comfortable, and his disposition curled her lips into a smile as she listened to him talk. She fought him for the rest of the brie when the last piece remained, splitting the last bite with him and grinning mischievously as she licked the remains from her fingertips.

"Tease," he groaned, licking his fingertips in reply. "See? Not the same effect."

She giggled. "I dunno. You could give a girl ideas."

He waggled his brows as Elizabeth eased to her back to watch the sun as it began to set. The sky wrapped them both in an amber hue, and the wind toyed with a handful of his hair, and it waved at her in the breeze.

It felt like slow motion as he reached for a grape, lowering it to her lips. She was mesmerized by his fingers, and her lips pulled the fruit from their tips. His eyes met hers as she chewed, and he eclipsed the sunset as he leaned down and gently pressed his mouth to hers.

She caressed his cheek, lifting her head to meet his. She felt him stretch out beside her. They snuggled together, kissing and touching lightly until after the sun had completed its descent. His kisses were tender and reverent. She wasn't sure which of them was snuggling closer, but when they parted, there was little air between them. Elizabeth felt like she was floating, despite the hard ground beneath her.

"I like your lips," he murmured.

She grinned at him, running her fingers through his hair. "Yours are pretty nice, too," she purred.

He didn't bother moving away. "I could stay here all night, but no telling what Edward would find if I did." He trailed the tip of his index finger down her cheek to her chin. "And if I keep you out too long, Max might come after me."

Elizabeth sighed. She was quiet in the moment, staring openly at his face. So close up, there was no hiding, and she allowed herself to study each hair in his eyebrows, the curve of his eyes and nose. She even raked her eyes over his earlobe. "Are you trying to get rid of me?" she asked.

"No. Trying to make sure there's a next time. We barely got to the wine."

"We had better things to do," she pointed out.

"Agreed," he mumbled before kissing her languidly one more time. "Okay, let me take you back like a responsible adult."

She bit her lip as she grinned, and they righted themselves. "I almost feel a little guilty not cleaning up," she said.

"That's the beauty of this park. Setup and cleanup are included," he said with a laugh, leading her down the stairs and back through the kitchen. His friend was nowhere to be found, but he told someone that they were going before they slipped back down the "spy" elevator to his waiting car.

The ride was silent, but he reached for her hand as he drove, and Elizabeth beamed at the city passing slowly by the windows. When the car rolled to a stop at the entrance to her workshop, Elizabeth sighed, turning her eyes on him. "I had a wonderful time," she confessed.

"Me too. Maybe we can do it again next week? Say 8:00?"

She named the day, and they agreed. With one last kiss, she exited the car, dashing inside to find Dana.

To her surprise, Dana was not alone. Jared was lounging in a nearby chair, and their chat stopped as she approached.

Dana squinted at her. "What's wrong with your face?" she asked.

Elizabeth touched her cheeks and nose worriedly. "What? It feels fine."

"You're smiling," Dana noted.

"And your mouth is all swollen," Jared added.

Elizabeth rolled her eyes to their obvious amusement. "Oh, shut up. Tell me you didn't finish early."

Jared shook his head. "Neh. Had some technical issues with the lighting, and there's no one else on set for this part. I'm just hanging out."

"Which I would've known had I been here," she said, sighing as she mentally berated herself for abandoning her duties. If she wasn't careful, she could slide down the food chain in a tenth of the time it had taken her to climb.

Jared waved her off. "Stop apologizing for not wasting your life sitting around hoping there's a wardrobe malfunction," he challenged.

"That's my job," Dana added.

Elizabeth held up her hands. "Well, then I won't feel at all guilty when we go again next week."

"Or when we finish *Thor* tonight after filming," Jared added.

"And I'm supposed to sleep when?" she asked.

"When you're dead," Jared replied easily. "Stop moping because people want to spend time with you. You're not the martyr here; you're the queen."

"Mistress to you," she teased, then slapped her hand over her mouth. "I did not say that."

"Oh, but you did," Dana cooed.

One of the crew popped around the corner at that moment calling Jared back to set. "Don't watch *Thor* without me now that I know you've been out cheating on me," he ordered.

Elizabeth saluted. "Yes, sir."

He shook a finger at her as he retreated, and Elizabeth turned to Dana.

"Why do you call him sir if you're the Mistress?" the assistant asked audaciously.

Shaking her head, Elizabeth decided not to attempt answering the question. "Go on home," she instructed. "You've been covering for me all day. I've got the rest of this. Easily."

"Normally I'd argue to put on a good show, but you're right." Her assistant turned and collected her backpack. She twirled to face Elizabeth before leaving. "Was he everything you hoped he'd be?" she asked.

"And more," Elizabeth recalled touching her lower lip without realizing she'd done it 'til it was too late. "Rooftop picnic," she told the assistant.

Dana whistled. "Nice touch." She gathered her things quickly. "Don't go making out twice in one night," she called several steps toward the exit.

Elizabeth winged, watching her go. She contemplated the constant razzing from Amara, Dana, and even Max though in a far less friendly way. She loved the thought that there could be anything more than a sibling style relationship between herself and her teen idol. But that was not to be. And he was an amazing friend. She worried that if he was getting the same treatment, he might decide the hassle wasn't worth it and ghost her the moment filming was over. At the moment, she had the world by the tail. Making out with Christopher under the stars and watching movies with her new best friend in his trailer. She wondered how long it could last.

Sixteen

On Set: Amara

Grumbling, Amara shook out her hands as Max cut the scene for what felt like the billionth time. In fairness, it was probably no more than the seventh take. But they still hadn't gotten a good one, and that was unlike Scott. Especially since they didn't have the problem of the young actors today. She wasn't sure what had him jumpy, but he kept forgetting his lines and missing cues.

She frowned at him as the cameras reset. "What's blocking you today?" she asked as they waited.

He sighed, stretching his shoulders and rolling out his neck. "I don't know. I'm sorry. My brain is on that premiere tonight," he confessed. "I'm worried about the limo being on time and if I brought right socks and shoes..."

"Did you plan that all yourself? Don't you have a PA for that?"

He arched a brow. "Do you?"

"No, but I've been managing myself for years. You've just started. You need a PA."

Scott sighed. "You may be right. But that won't help me now."

Tenderly, as her character, Amara touched his forearm. "I'm sure you did everything right. It'll be fine. It's nothing more than a movie premiere," she assured. "And it's not even ours." If Amara was feeling confessional, she would have told him that she was excited about it as well. She'd rummaged through her closet for an appropriate outfit, coming up with a puffy white satin top that plunged into the waistband of a flowing, floor length, black skirt. It was simple, but she'd felt elegant in the mirror when she'd modeled it for herself.

When she'd arrived, she'd hired Dana to have it steamed and ready for her after set with the quick slip of a C-note. She remembered someone slipping her a Benjamin once while she was on one of her fateful singing telegram jobs. It was what had inspired her dive headfirst into a career as an actress. She'd always loved acting, but if someone tipped her that much for her performance, she must have something to offer the world.

She and Scott positioned themselves on their marks, Scott reviewing a nearby script and tossing it back to one of the crew. When the director called "action," they began, but this time, Amara flubbed a line. She scowled at herself when Max called "cut." She shook her head, thinking that perhaps Scott's seed of self-doubt had taken root in her mind.

"If I flub again, I'm going to keep going. Is that okay?" Amara questioned.

"Roll with it. We'll see where it goes."

Today, they were filming a scene where Scott's character would try to convince hers that teleporting was safe, and that the move to Mars was going to be the easiest and best thing for their family, and for her. She was dressed in a slinky V-necked T-shirt tailored with elastic at the sides paired with a simple pair of heather gray yoga pants. At least she was comfortable. If she could deliver her lines, she could move on to the more exciting portion of the day. She gave a thumbs-up to the director, took a deep breath, and stared at her costar.

Scott winked at her, and Amara felt herself go deep into character, seeing her husband beside her, not an actor. This time, they made it through the entire scene, Max clapping when he finally called for a cut. "I think we actually got everything we needed in that take," he called.

Amara shook herself back to reality, and the pair headed for the buffet.

"Finally," she groused as they relaxed in the nearly empty room. They could hear the crew moving the set around for the next scene. After so many takes, it was nice to have a break.

"Sorry I needed so many takes," Scott apologized.

"Shit happens and then you flush," she excused. "But maybe it took all those do overs to get to the right head space." She crunched on a baby carrot stick, watching as he opened a bag of chips. "Thanks for the tickets tonight, by the way. I don't get invited to these often, and certainly not something as big as a *Jurassic Park* movie."

"It's gonna be...a lot tonight," he warned her. "My fans are still rabid, and I'm pretty sure the really dedicated ones will be there. I still can't grab a coffee without getting mobbed."

"Still a luxury problem," she reminded.

He nodded. "I know. It's a lot for the people around me. I've gotten used to it. Social media is a double-edged sword."

Amara agreed. She had a huge following who loved to see the pictures she was posting from set in costume every now and again to garner interest for the film. She had not experienced the full-on mania she was sure Scott had, but she had felt the pinch of social media in other ways. Every picture she posted made her vulnerable to critics who could say some pretty awful things in anonymity. "Well, at least you won't be alone tonight," she comforted.

He chortled. "I've been imagining the headlines since I accepted the tickets. You realize we're going to be the poster throuple for a while."

Amara had not thought of this, and she crowed. "Lizzy isn't going to like that."

Scott grimaced, leaning on the table's edge. "I'm not planning to tell her and hope she doesn't see it."

"You might get lucky. I promise not to rat us out." She reached for a celery stick this time from her plate and crunched on it as he ate his chips. "You are coming to the pool party, right?"

He cringed. "Will you be hurt if I don't?"

"Yes," Amara snapped. "It's our only day off for the rest of the shoot. I've gone through a lot of trouble arranging this."

He groaned. "But it's our only day off for the rest of the shoot," he repeated. "I thought you might want to see other people."

"But I like these people. Let me do this. It'll be fun. All we do here is work, and I've got a karaoke machine, and a bartender, and everything lined up already."

Further conversation was halted as the doors burst open, and Dana skidded to a stop at their table.

"Amara! We need you in wardrobe now." The woman's tone was like a stage whisper filled with urgency.

"But –" Amara began.

"Now." Dana grabbed hold of her hand and pulled.

Seeing the look on the assistant's face, Amara stood without another word, trailing after her. Before they reached wardrobe, Amara knew what the problem was. She could hear Frankie's voice loud and clear.

"I know she's here," he demanded. "And I've seen you on her Instagram, so I know you *know* where she is."

She found Elizabeth standing tall, opposite him, unflinching with her arms crossed over herself. "She's on set," Elizabeth explained. "If you'll have a seat..."

"I will not," Frankie argued, pressing his face in closer. "Take me to the set."

Amara was shocked at the juxtaposition seeing six foot tall, rail-thin Frankie, covered in tattoos, wearing a grungy ripped sleeveless T-shirt and leather pants inches from Elizabeth's face. In contrast, the designer looked short and wholesome like something out of a greeting card commercial. Although, Amara was impressed that Elizabeth had seemingly held her ground and appeared completely unfazed.

"Franklin Carol Whispers, that is quite enough," Amara hushed in her most domineering tone. She slowed her pace until she was a few feet away, one hand poised on her hip.

He whirled away from Elizabeth. "Mara," he cooed, slinking toward her.

Amara held up a hand that arrested him mid-step. "That's close enough," she ordered.

"Baby, where have you been?" he asked. "It's been weeks."

The actress cringed inwardly when she realized Scott had followed her and was standing behind her stock still. "I'm working," she stated. "And you know this."

He sighed, inching toward her again. "Baby, I don't like casual. Not with you. I thought you'd died or something."

Amara rolled her eyes at the drama. Part of her wanted to go to him. He was certainly the best bed mate she'd had to date. But she knew him better than she cared to admit. She'd watched how he'd treated his wife – hopelessly devoted one minute and a hand half up her own skirt in the next. Frankie did what pleased Frankie in the moment.

"You stole my best T-shirt, baby," he purred, closing the gap between them and resting his hands directly on her hips. "I'm so cold—"

Amara smacked her lips, pushing him away. "I'm busy. Can we talk about this later?"

Frankie tipped her gaze to his face with a single finger under her chin. "Why? Afraid you can't resist me?"

"I think I'm doing a fine job of it at the moment," she rebuffed. There were times when she loved Frankie's possessiveness of her. Now was not one of those moments.

"Do I need to find security?" Scott suggested from behind her.

"No. No. Frankie was about to leave," she assured him.

The musician growled, weaving his fingers into the hair at the nape of her neck and tugging gently. "You'll call?"

The tug made Amara's senses flutter, and she felt a lust-fueled chill shiver over her body. "Yes," she whispered. She pulled free of his grip and cleared her throat. "But you have to leave now."

Frankie's face melted into a satisfied grin, and she watched him cast a side-long sneer at the man behind her. "Later, babes," Frankie promised before pivoting on one toe and swaggering toward the exit.

"Who was that?" Scott asked.

She sighed. "An old friend." She heard a tiny gasp, and her eyes landed on Elizabeth who suddenly turned her back on everyone and fussed with the top drawer of her rolling cabinet.

"Are you okay?" Scott fretted as he moved beside her. "How did he even get in here?" His hand was resting on her elbow, and she wondered if he was himself or still in character or some of both.

"I'm fine," she insisted. "He's harmless."

"He didn't look harmless," Dana groused. "I didn't really want to leave Elizabeth alone with him, but I figured you might get him to leave faster."

"Good call," Amara agreed.

There was a commotion behind them in the direction of the set, and they all turned to see Max stalking toward them. "Every time I turn around my main characters are gone," he complained. "We're ready for you if you feel like working today."

Amara flinched at the tone. It was unlike Max to sound so condescending, and she assumed it was because of how long it had taken to get a single scene filmed that morning.

"Coming," Amara called, taking Scott's hand and stalking past the director to the set. She heard Max trying to keep up but didn't slow her pace.

The rest of filming seemed to go more smoothly, and they were finished in plenty of time to get ready for their evening. Amara headed to hair and makeup for an evening reset. When they discovered where she was going, they giggled, seeming to enjoy the task of giving her a more glamorous look.

"Go get Lizzy, too. I'm betting she'll need the help," Amara suggested. She giggled as one of the assistants ran. She hooted in delight when she spied Elizabeth in the mirror, the assistant tugging on her sleeve to pull her to a chair. The seamstress was clearly unnerved and uncomfortable, and Amara reached for her arm to comfort her. "Oh, darling. It'll be fun. Let's see what you look like all dolled up Hollywood style. Sit. My treat," she offered, watching as the seamstress sighed and relented, collapsing into the waiting stylist's chair. "And when you're finished, bring your stuff to my trailer. You can change there."

She didn't give the other woman an opportunity to protest. The moment her own makeup was complete, she tipped the artists for both women and scurried to change in her trailer. She found her outfit hanging over her bathroom door with a note from Dana. It took a mere moment to dress. She giggled in the mirror as she adjusted the top to scandalous levels, leaving a glimpse of side boob open for all to wonder how she kept her breasts suspended and covered all at once. She was dangling a rhinestone necklace down to her navel when there was a knock at the door.

She scurried to admit Elizabeth. The other woman's usually long hair was wound up elegantly, and she'd never seen her with so much eye makeup.

"Are those lashes extensions?" she asked as the seamstress climbed inside, garment bag over her arm.

"Yes. I look like a clown, don't I?" Elizabeth fretted.

Amara froze. "No. You look like a movie star. Now go get dressed." She ushered the woman into the back room then resumed assessing her necklace choice in the mirrored cabinet door.

When Elizabeth rejoined her, Amara was pressing her earrings into place and slipping on her shoes. She should not have been surprised that the designer's garment was perfect.

"Tell me you designed your own gown," Amara gushed. All the answer she needed was provided when the other woman turned a shade of scarlet. Amara clapped delightedly. "Oh, you sly fox. I love it."

Elizabeth picked at her dress. "It's not too much?"

Amara shook her head, asking the woman to turn so she could admire the seemingly simple design. She was wrapped in a violet sheath dress that stopped below her knees with a band of sequins then ended in roughly three inches of satin pleats that showed off the curve of her calves. The top layer was a sheer white netted material with splatterings of gray that vaguely resembled flowers. It accentuated the bodice of the dress, flowed up over her shoulders and fluttered behind her just down to her backside. "It's right. I'm so proud of you for seizing this moment. Everyone will want to know where you got it. Where are you going to carry your business cards?"

Elizabeth beamed, then slipped two fingers delicately into a seam at her hip and extracted a card from a secret pocket.

"I love it! You should make everything with pockets."

"It has occurred to me," Elizabeth agreed. She began fussing with a pair of drippy rhinestone earrings that complimented her updo, and the actress warmed at the camaraderie she felt watching the action.

There was honking from outside, and Amara scowled. "Rude!" she exclaimed. "Scott should have come to collect us."

"Does he know we're in here?" Elizabeth countered.

Amara frowned. "He should. We agreed to meet here. Oh, and we're late. Let's go." Amara locked up, tucking the keys into her clutch and ushering Elizabeth toward the waiting limo.

"What's the racket?" Jared called.

Amara spied him hanging from the door frame on his trailer, looking around before stepping out onto the top stair.

Before she could answer, Scott called from where he stood next to the limo. "We're going to a movie premiere."

"Who's..." Jared began but stopped, his eyes landing on Amara and her companion.

"Aren't we gorgeous?" Amara called, twirling for him then hugging an arm around Elizabeth.

"How were we watching movies all morning, and you never mentioned this?" he accused, eyes clearly on the costumer.

"I gave you my full and undivided attention, Jared dear. I wasn't thinking about this," Elizabeth comforted.

Jared stepped down to the pavement, looking at all three of them. "I feel supremely left out."

Scott stammered. "Sorry, dude. I just knew you'd be filming tonight, and I knew Amara and I would be free."

"And someone's got to train this one how to handle crowds before Christopher sweeps her off her feet," Amara added wickedly. She clasped the designer's hand, lifting it and twirling her around for inspection. Amara choked on the laugh she felt rising in her throat as she watched the other actor popping a boner, eyes glued to the turning seamstress.

"We're going to be late," Scott cautioned. He made an apologetic motion to Jared. "We can hit one up after filming," he promised. "I'm getting offers all the time."

The driver, standing next to Scott, pulled the door open, and Amara waved to their fellow actor.

"Oh sure. Abandon me to do all the work," Jared taunted.

"We're leaving our film in your capable hands," Scott answered as Amara and Elizabeth slipped into the waiting vehicle.

With a nod to Jared, Scott joined them. She had barely had a chance to admire his well-cut suit. He was wearing a silvery sports coat over a black button-down shirt. He wasn't wearing a tie, leaving the top few buttons undone to show off a silver chain if you were close enough to see it.

"You ladies are both gorgeous," Scott complimented once they were on their way. "If I had known, I'd have taken you sooner."

Amara cast a wry look his way. "You hate these things. I can see it all over you."

"At least it's a good movie. And press is nothing new. I'm an old pro. You'll see when we do the press junket for this."

"When does that begin?" Elizabeth questioned. "I can throw something together if you like."

"Yes, please," Amara beamed. "Maybe some of that stuff you were talking about for your line."

"You have a line coming out?" Scott balked.

"No. Nothing official. Just something I've been dreaming about."

"I've offered to model for her when she's ready," Amara asserted. "For the mere price of clothing," she added merrily.

"Reasonable rates indeed," Elizabeth kidded.

The ride passed quickly, the three of them discussing the original *Jurassic Park* movie in preparation for the film they were about to see. As they approached, Scott explained to Elizabeth what was about to happen.

"I don't need to have my picture taken, do I?" the seamstress asked.

Amara rolled her eyes. "Of course you do! Besides, it'll be nice to have a good photo of us all," she encouraged. "Plus, it will be good publicity for your dress."

When the limo doors opened, Scott motioned for Amara to go first. "You sure?" she prompted.

He nodded avidly, motioning her to go. "Absolutely," he confirmed.

The actress reached for the valet's hand, unfolding herself to the snapping of cameras. She heard her name called by a handful of people as she stepped forward, putting on her press smile and waiting for her companions to join her.

She felt it as Scott appeared from the vehicle and the camera flashes tripled. The crowd gathered around the red carpet surged, calling his name. She realized with a start that he hadn't wanted to steal the spotlight from her. By letting her get out first, she received all the attention even if it was for a brief moment. She turned and reached out to him.

Scott rewarded her with a toothy grin, taking her proffered appendage and pulling Elizabeth behind him.

Amara squeezed his hand. "Pull her closer," she whispered.

Scott complied, and carefully, Amara scooped Elizabeth away from him, linking arms and guiding her toward the entrance. Someone called her name and she glanced up to see a friendly reporter she shown favor to in the past. She pulled Elizabeth with her, releasing her once a microphone had been positioned close enough to speak.

"Amara, it's so great to see you on the red carpet," the reporter gushed. She was a middle-aged woman with long red hair that curled around her shoulders. Amara thought she could've chosen something flashier to wear to the event. However, she recognized the fact that the understated black pantsuit kept focus on the actors and actresses when the reporters weren't competing for attention, and she appreciated the respect.

Amara smiled sweetly, bunching up her shoulders. "You, too. It's been a minute."

"Are you a big fan of the *Jurassic Park* franchise?" the reporter inquired.

"Oh yes, of course. We were just talking about the original on the ride over here."

"What have you been up to these days? Any scoop?"

Amara beamed. "Well, actually, since it's you...I am in the middle of a project for a network right now," she confessed. "We should be wrapping soon, and it's a really great cast. I just came from set, in fact."

"Can you tell us about it?"

Amara bit her lip as though she was about to spill a giant secret. "Well, it's a movie," she admitted, "And I'm playing the female lead." She covered her mouth with her fingertips as though she couldn't say any more.

Scott joined her then, pulling Elizabeth between them.

"And there's my on-screen hubby now," she told the reporter.

He greeted Amara's reporter kindly with a handshake.

"Aren't you all stunning? And who's this?" the reporter asked, looking pointedly at Elizabeth, now standing between Amara and Scott.

"This is our Head Costume Designer Elizabeth Morris," Amara answered. "Give her your card, darling," she instructed.

Shyly, Elizabeth pulled a card from her dress and passed it over.

"Is that a pocket?" the reporter gushed. "Is this your design?" she asked. When Elizabeth nodded, the reporter squealed. "Do you take requests?"

"Yes, she does," Scott answered. He reached out to shake the woman's hand again. "It was so nice to meet you, but I think we might need to keep moving."

"Of course. Of course. Thank you, Amara, Scott, and Elizabeth."

Scott ushered them toward the main photo backdrop covered in the movie logo. They stopped for photos, Amara getting some singles, some duos, and some trios of the group before she relented to finding their seats.

"That was...a lot," Elizabeth whispered, as she settled on Amara's left in their seats.

"I'm glad you got to experience that with us the first time," Scott agreed. "If you came with..." he inspected the people around them to make sure no one was listening before naming him. "...Chris...it would have been ten times worse. People ask the most invasive questions."

"They don't mean to pry," Amara excused. "They just think you're great, and they want to know everything about you. You'll get the hang of it," she encouraged.

"Can I get you ladies some snacks or anything?" Scott inquired.

The ladies shook their heads.

Amara's phone ding from her clutch, and she pulled it free. Notifications were already beginning to pop in about her name appearing in the press. She scrolled through, flashing the screen at Elizabeth first and then to Scott. "We're adorable!" she gushed.

Scott nodded. "True. But now Jared's going to be super pissed. I'm sure he'd have loved the publicity."

Amara frowned. "I know. But he's filming. And he'll get the press for that instead." She turned her phone off and tucked it back in her bag. "This will give me something to take my mind off this afternoon." She didn't want to think about Frankie, or the way he'd pulled her hair. Amara balked when Scott asked about her visitor on set that afternoon, as if reading her mind.

"I've known Frankie for years," she divulged casually. "He plays in a band at a club I've been going to forever. We're buddies."

"Looked like more than good buddies. I was a little afraid for you, in fact," Scott divulged.

"Oh, don't be. He's all bark and no bite." Unless he was asked to, Amara thought before shaking the thought away. He was scrambling her brain. She turned her attention instead to Scott, but before she could speak, the house lights dimmed, and moments later, the movie began.

Amara barely paid attention. At the mention of Frankie, her brain ran a mile with the suggestion. She wasn't sure why she didn't go back to him now that they had their first chance to be a couple. It's what they'd both been wrangling with for years. Should they, or shouldn't they? And once they had, Amara's curiosity had been satisfied. She'd do him again, she thought. But she felt like now it would be rewarding him for showing up on her set unannounced.

She wrestled with the idea until the house lights came back up, and she joined the audience in clapping.

Scott ushered them out with deceptive quickness and back into their waiting limo.

"How in the world did you get them at the head of the line?" Amara asked as they were closed inside.

"I gave very specific instructions, and I also know the best limo drivers in LA," he explained.

"Thank you so much for inviting us," Elizabeth enthused. "I've never felt so glamorous."

Scott nodded happily. "Once you get past the reporters, it is pretty cool to get to see these before the rest of the world."

Amara rested in her seat. She realized her error in letting Frankie take over her thoughts during the film. Now, her body was revved up and needy, and neither of her companions were appropriate outlets. She slipped her phone from her clutch, turning it back on. She had scores of notifications on different outlets. What she had not expected was a message from Frankie. "You. Me. Talk. Fuck?"

She snickered at the brazen request. She bit her lip, eyes on Scott. She definitely wanted to unwrap him and see what sweet morsels lay inside, but she refused to compromise her work ethic for a tawdry affair. Even if he had been tending her every other need, spoken or otherwise, since they'd left the studio.

"Talk," she texted Frankie. "About an hour."

His reply was surprisingly fast. "I know where you are. Come to my place."

Amara tucked the phone in her clutch again, feeling Elizabeth's eyes on her. She arched a brow, daring her friend to say something then shook her head.

When they reached the studio, Scott jumped out, helping Elizabeth out of the car. "I asked my driver to give you a ride home. Just give him your address," he offered.

"That's very generous of you," Amara answered.

Scott smiled at her, no hint of pretense in the gesture that she could sus out. "It was my pleasure. Thanks for going with me tonight," he added.

"Anytime," she pronounced, surprised at the quickness of her own reply.

He closed the door, and she gave her driver Frankie's address. In no time, she was pulling up to his place.

He answered the door in nothing but his leather pants which were riding low. He had barely closed the door before she was on him, clothes disappearing as they stumbled toward a soft, flat surface.

Two hours later, she was in a taxi on her way home, having sneaked out of Frankie's place while he slept. She was absolutely furious. The encounter had left her more needy than before. Oh, sure, Frankie had passed out satisfied, but this time, she just...wasn't.

When she got home, she packed up the clothes she had borrowed from him to courier over the next day. She didn't want the reminder in the house, or the excuse to keep him looking for more from her. She included a brief note saying she had moved on. With a frown, she took a shower to attend to the ache she still felt, gasping out Scott's name as her release crashed over her in waves. This would *not* do. She had to get the man out of her system somehow, and the usual methods just were not working. Maybe once filming was done... She refused to finish the thought, shaking her head to clear it before she slipped between her cool cotton sheets and drifted off to sleep, exhausted.

Seventeen

Opening Night of Ant Man and the Wasp: Elizabeth

Elizabeth squealed as Jared rounded the corner and whipped his car into the theater parking lot. "I won't be able to see the movie if I'm dead," she complained.

"We have worked too hard to get to this movie for us to miss even one minute of it," he justified. "I've been driving for years and haven't died once." He turned off the car and bounced out.

Elizabeth followed his lead, barely keeping up as they crossed the parking lot.

He held the door for her, and she hurried through. "It's not fancy like your movie with Scott, but I got digital tickets," he bragged, flashing his phone at the waiting employee. "I got us reserved seating, too. Bet Scott didn't have that."

Elizabeth laughed. "You're right. He did not."

Jared flashed a smile as he held the next door for her then led them to their reserved seats in the middle of the row behind the handicapped section. Elizabeth cringed as they tip-toed over the other patrons who had arrived earlier to get to their seats.

"Everyone hates us," she whispered. "We got the best seats in the house."

"Of course we did. I ordered these tickets months ago with my rewards card access," he scoffed.

She studied him with quiet pride. He was so different from Christopher. He was sitting in a crowded theater, and no one seemed to notice. She hated for Jared's sake that she seemed to be the lone person who recognized his face. She'd preserved so many magazines, T-shirts, pins, and even cereal boxes over the years just to have his picture. She was also fairly sure no one else in in the building had their very own board game. Even Christopher didn't have that.

Something in his statement struck her. "Wait. I didn't know you months ago. Who were you planning to take?"

He shrugged. "I had some ideas. I just knew I wouldn't go alone. So, I bought two tickets."

She considered his words briefly. Part of her wanted to spiral thinking he had planned to take his girlfriend or some other friend, but the fact that he had eschewed all the other known quantities to take her was flabbergasting. She tamped the emotions down. They were only ever going to be friends. She started to sigh and stopped, turning instead to thank him for his generosity.

"Thanks for investing the time to get me up to speed," she told him gratefully. "I'm actually excited to see this."

He sighed, rubbing his knuckles over his shirt. "It was hard work watching all these movies that I love so I'm all refreshed for this, too."

She snickered.

He turned to her as the lights went down. "This is very important," he said sternly as he lowered his voice. "No talking during the movie. We'll talk in the car."

Elizabeth nodded avidly as they turned their attention to the screen. The previews seemed to take forever, but she grinned as Jared gave her a thumbs up at the end of each preview that he liked. She had no time to contemplate any further as the movie started. After over twenty films, getting to experience his first viewing at the same time as hers was a little bit of magic, Elizabeth thought. There was a particularly funny battle scene, and Elizabeth was squealing. Before she realized she was doing it, she was slapping his hand as she squealed. She sneaked a peek at his face, watching tears of laughter rolling down his cheeks, and he squeezed her fingers in response.

Elizabeth gulped, grinning at him. She pulled her hand away a moment later, curling up into her chair. By the end, she was emotionally wrung out. She felt like she'd run a marathon as she was seated beside Jared in the car.

She sighed when he pulled away. "That was amazing."

"It was. I'd ask if you enjoyed it, but I heard you," he teased.

"Same," she agreed, pinning her eye on him and yawning.

"Did I keep you out past your bedtime?" he jeered.

Elizabeth nodded, leaning against the window. "I was never a night owl," she confessed. She turned her head to see him. In profile he was relaxed, and she admired the way the moonlight highlighted the button tip of his nose. She had always adored that about him, though she was loathe to admit it. In the dark, she hoped he didn't notice. Although after all this time of working together, she assumed he'd gotten used to it.

Why was she thinking about Jared, she wondered, and not the man she'd been canoodling? Her eyes slipped shut, thinking of how Chris' scruffy beard roughed up her cheek. It was a feeling that had taken some getting used to, but there was something visceral about it. Something unique to him.

When her eyes opened, they landed on Jared's baby-smooth face.

"Thinking about Christopher?" he asked.

"How could you possibly know that?" she questioned.

He chuckled. "The look on your face."

She sighed, turning to look out the window again.

"Why don't I just drive you home? I'm actually a little afraid that you'll fall asleep at the wheel."

"No," she yawned, "I'll be okay."

"Don't make me pull over and force your address out of you," he demanded. Jared passed her his phone. "Here. Put it in the map for me. I'll even come pick you up in the morning."

"It's very gallant of you, but you realize it's after two, I have to be there at like seven a.m.," she reasoned.

"I'll risk it. I can sleep in the trailer now that there's no more movies to screen."

Elizabeth stared at him for a moment but figured she was not going to win this argument. She opened the map app and input her address, settling it into the holder on his dash. "That okay?"

"Perfect," he replied, listening as the app rerouted him. He fiddled with the radio, settling on a rhythmic dance music mix.

Elizabeth tapped her knee to the beat, and before she knew it, she felt Jared poking her arm.

"Wake up, sleepyhead," he murmured.

She stirred with a yawn, looking his direction as she heard the engine stop. "Sorry. I didn't mean to fall asleep on you. So rude."

"It's okay. You've just proven me right," he crooned, flashing her a knowing smile. "Come on. I'll walk you in."

Still waking up, she did not protest, leading him to her door, yawning so wide her jaw popped. She fumbled with the key in the door 'til he took it from her hands, inserted it smoothly, and opened the lock before passing the keys back to her.

"You have a dead bolt I assume?" he asked. At her nod, he added, "I'm going to stand here until I hear it turn. And I'll text when I'm on my way in the morning."

She nodded with a sleepy smile. "Thanks for the movie and the ride home." Elizabeth gave a wave and added, "Text me when you get home too."

Jared nodded, and she closed the door, turning the deadlock swiftly to make a loud clunking noise.

Elizabeth wound her way to her bedroom, peeling off a layer every few steps 'til she collapsed into bed and waited to pass out again. She thought the movie had been worth a midnight showing. Being among true, long-time fans of the series had made it more exciting. Her mind went back to him squeezing her hand during the funny bit. It had been so intimate – warm and reassuring and purely natural. They were just two people connecting over something great. She could never have predicted that at any point in her life she would be a close friend of Jared Rains. She never thought she'd be anything to him but a fan. Her eyes drifted to her mirror to his old picture, and she grinned, slipping off to sleep.

Elizabeth woke to a banging on her apartment door, and she frowned. The sun was beginning to glare through her window. Before she could understand what was happening, her phone started ringing. She reached for it groggily. "Hello?"

"I'm here," Jared called, knocking at the door again.

She scowled, looking at the bedside clock, and a full-blown panic set in. She cursed softly. "Sorry. I'm coming," she answered, hanging up the phone. She jumped out of bed, darting to the front door and tripped over her jeans in the hallway. She cursed again, remembering that she was virtually naked in nothing but her underwear and wondered if she was having a stress dream. This time when she cussed, it was quite loud and long as she struggled to stuff her arms into a bathrobe and pick up the remaining clothing stripped off the night before. She fumbled the deadlock open and dashed back to her bedroom, calling out, "It's open!"

She hoped he didn't see her as she slammed her bedroom door shut, but it was anyone's guess. She dropped the pile of collected items on the bed, shimmying back into her jeans. "There's water and stuff in the kitchen. Help yourself," she yelled through the door.

"I'm good," he called back. "Actually, can I use your facilities?"

She frowned. "Yes, give me a second." One of the drawbacks of her place was that the single bathroom was attached to her bedroom. So, any time she had guests, it meant inviting them into her super private space.

Elizabeth finished pulling on her clothes, grabbed a hairbrush and an elastic band then threw open her bedroom door, one hand raking the brush through her tresses as she did so. "In here," she called, slipping into the hallway to allow him passage.

Jared made haste, and she cringed at how thin the walls were as she heard him peeing. By the time he'd finished and she heard the faucet running, she'd pulled her hair back and was rinsing her mouth with a cup of water at the kitchen sink.

"What the fresh hell is this?!" he yelled.

She couldn't imagine what he was yelling about. For a moment. And then the horror set in as she ran to find him standing in front of her dresser, looking at pictures of himself taped amongst her family and friends.

"Uh – you weren't supposed to see that," she groaned. "In fact, can you pretend you didn't?"

He blinked at her, frozen for a moment, and then he was all in motion again. "Let's go," he instructed, breezing past her and to the car.

Elizabeth was stuffing her feet into canvas loafers as she raced behind him, locking up and meeting him at the car.

"You have my picture taped to your mirror," he stated as he began driving.

She wasn't sure what to say, so she said nothing.

"I get that you were a fan...but we've known each other for going on two months now, Lizzybeth. Fuck, I gave you a nickname!"

She tucked her forehead into her knees and simply groaned. "I know," she mumbled. She groaned again, this time half crying as she did so. "First of all, if you're really a fan of something, you never stop being a fan of it. Second of all, I kind of forget they're there. I put those up when they were new and just never took them down. And most importantly," she emphasized, "you were never supposed to see those. I could not have predicted you would ever be in my bedroom."

"Really?" he prodded. "What if I had fallen madly in love with you at first sight and dragged you back to your room to have my wicked way with you?"

Elizabeth cocked her head, one eyebrow perched in her hairline. "Uh-huh," she said flatly. "Because that seems a very likely possibility."

"And what about when Christopher is having his wicked ways? It doesn't bother him?"

She frowned. "We're not having wicked ways yet."

The car slowed. "Well, you'd better take those down before you do."

The ride was frighteningly quiet. All the progress they'd made as friends felt to Elizabeth like it was evaporating. She grappled for something to say and tried opening a dialogue about the movie from the night before everything had fallen apart. He didn't seem to take the bait. She sighed, gathering all the courage and strength she'd felt as the Head Costumer on the set and sat up straight in her seat, twisting to face him. "I'm the same Lizzybeth that you were at that movie with. The same one who made a fool of herself the first time we met. The same one you've spent so many hours with watching all the movies. Why is this different now?"

Jared glanced from her to the road.

Elizabeth did not avert her gaze, challenging him to reply. She wanted to goad him into a response, but it felt like a dangerous approach, and she opted for the safer option of letting him think.

He squinted at her again, this time with a scowl. "You can understand why I might be a little freaked out."

She considered his point of view for a moment. "It's not like it was a shrine with candles and poems and weird creepy tributes. They were pictures that YOU posed for, and you knew were published in magazines."

"They're over twenty years old. And they're in surprisingly good condition," he noted.

"So, I take good care of my things. That's what I do."

He was quiet again.

She sighed, turning forward in her seat. "Well, I'm sorry I freaked you out. I will take them down tonight and you can rest easy knowing that no one has your picture up on their wall anymore." As soon as the words left her lips, they felt bigger and far harsher than she had intended. Well, that was the end of that. It was inevitable that he was going to not be part of her life soon anyway. She may as well rip the bandage off now while she could still look at him. And she wouldn't take the pictures down, she told herself. He'd never be in her bedroom again, that was for certain.

When they arrived at the studio, they met Dana exiting her car. She couldn't miss the shocked expression on her assistant's face, even though she knew the other woman was trying to hide it.

Jared made a beeline for his trailer without a word, and Elizabeth walked toward the shop with Dana. Before any questions could be asked, Elizabeth volunteered, "After the midnight showing of *Ant Man*, I was too tired to drive home, so he gave me a lift and then picked me up this morning."

Dana whistled. "That's a good friend." She paused, and Elizabeth felt the younger woman's eyes on her. "It actually sounds like more than a good friend."

"Well, don't worry about that. I'm not sure we're friends anymore. Which I guess is fine. Because we'd probably never see each other again once this movie wraps."

Fortunately for Elizabeth, Dana said no more, and they set about their day with no more talk about Jared. She had never been so grateful to see Scott and Amara as she was that morning, prepping them for set.

Elizabeth began looking around her station, starting to plan the eventual tear down. She frowned, realizing that everything was just perfect and still necessary in her cube, and then she began wandering the set with the call list and called a staff meeting to set schedules for the remaining days.

She dismissed everyone for lunch, dialing up Christopher to see if he was free. He raced to pick her up, making haste to depart the set. "This is an unexpected pleasure," he greeted once they were off the lot.

She smiled at him, feeling the tension in her face as she did so. Truthfully, she simply didn't want to be on the set and potentially run into Jared. The wounds were still fresh, and she certainly didn't want to tell the man beside her what had happened, despite the growing intimacy between them.

"So how was the movie last night?" he asked. "I can't believe you went to a midnight showing!"

"It was so good," she enthused, gushing over the plot and the humor and the characters, relaying her favorite lines as best she could remember them.

They found their way to a café, and he donned his protective jacket, hat, and glasses to disguise himself as they valeted his car. She did not recognize the restaurant. They were seated quickly in a booth in the back, obscured from most of the potentially prying eyes. She wondered if he ever got tired of hiding in public. But she recognized suddenly that he was doing this for her benefit. She had called and asked him out, she realized. "Thanks for coming at the drop of the hat. I didn't even think to ask if you were busy."

He quirked a brow, sipping his water. "Well, I'm flexible. I've got a voice-over scheduled for this afternoon. Your schedule is actually timing out pretty well with mine," he complimented. "Dating someone not in the industry can be difficult sometimes."

"I can see that. And speaking of timetables, good news/bad news. After the *Jurassic Park* premiere, I lined up more work for when our movie is finished."

"Ah, yes," he noted with a grin. "My girlfriend the famous third to Scott and Amara."

Elizabeth blanched. "Third what?"

"Partner."

She began sinking into the booth. "Like...for sex?" she whispered.

He laughed at her assessment, leaning into her, shoulders wriggling. "Their toy. Yes. Haven't you seen the speculation?" he asked, pulling out his phone. He was scrolling and glancing at her.

"What speculation?"

"I'll take that as a no." He snickered. He tapped the screen and passed it to her.

Elizabeth's appetite died as she viewed a picture of the three of them. She remembered being dragged into the pose with Scott between the two women and then the damning photo of the three of them after the movie as they escaped the crowds. Scott had one arm around Amara's waist, and he was dragging Elizabeth by the hand. She saw the word "throuple" mentioned and passed the phone back without reading more. If she hadn't been the subject of the picture and known better, the reporter's argument sounded viable. "You know that's all lies, right?" she asked, tucking her trembling hands beneath her.

"Of course. It's kinda funny though." He grinned. "How do you feel about a threesome?"

"I don't think it's very funny," she countered.

Christopher rolled his eyes. "It's what the press does," he assured her. "It will blow over. But hey – you're already getting work from it, , so mission accomplished. You can laugh all the way to the bank."

She frowned. "But you have to know I didn't go with any of that in mind. It was all...organic," she defended. "I'm not...manipulative like that."

He scooted closer to her in the booth and pulled her hand free, lacing his fingers with hers. "I know that. Which is part of why I'm here with you now." He kissed her fingertips slowly, looking at her face as he did.

She smiled, feeling herself begin to calm under his ministrations. "Okay. Thank you."

"You know you can set up a notice on your phone so that any time you're mentioned in the press, it'll ping you," he suggested.

She nodded. "I knew it was possible, but I've never thought to set one up for myself."

He hummed, kissing her cheek then scooting back to his place as the food arrived. "I'll help you set it up after lunch." He placed his napkin in his lap. "And you should know there's already rumors about us, too. Very faint, but word is starting to spread."

Her head tilted in disbelief as she reached for her silverware as well. "We've hardly gone anywhere together," she balked.

He shrugged. "It's part and parcel for me. Can you handle that?"

She thought about it for a moment as she picked up her wrap. "I think so. It is true after all. But I'm not used to being seen, and I definitely don't know how to pose," she said.

"Me neither. I always look so awkward. Like a deer in the headlights."

She chuckled, taking a bite and chewing. She had seen the photos he referenced and didn't disagree. "Well, God blessed you with an amazing face to make up for it," she replied.

One corner of his mouth quirked up in response. "Thank you." They passed the rest of lunch discussing their arrangements for the pool party they were planning to attend the following weekend.

Eighteen

Amara's House: Amara

The afternoon sun was brutal outside the shade of the tents Amara had set up around the pool for her party. She was roaming through the crowd dressed in a red string bikini with a sheer sarong tied at her hip. Beads lined its edge, and she liked the way they rustled as she sashayed from guest to guest. Her pool was full of crew members splashing around, and she eyed the buffet. Guests were lined up with plates, happily chattering, and she knew she had done well.

She spied Christopher as he carried a frosty pink beverage toward a chaise lounge where Elizabeth was sprawled. His linen shirt fluttered attractively in the gentle breeze. Amara made her way toward them, watching as he planted a kiss on the costumer's mouth before handing her the drink and sitting on the lounge chair beside hers.

"That's enough, you two," Amara interrupted, taking a seat at the foot of Elizabeth's chair. "You're making all us single people jealous."

Christopher beamed. "Guilty as charged." He leaned back.

"You guys get any food?" she asked noting their lack of plates. "And why aren't you in a bathing suit?" she prodded, eyeing her friend's shorts and tank top.

"You can't expect us to eat and get in the pool at the same time," Elizabeth retorted. "Pick one."

Amara frowned. "Nope. My party. I can do what I want," she sassed.

Christopher tugged at the waistband of his shorts. "These are technically trunks, so I'm dressed and ready to go."

Amara turned her eyes on Elizabeth. "And what's your excuse?"

"We just got here," the seamstress supplied. "I thought I'd soak up a little sun first. And I'm deciding if I want to be seen in a bathing suit," she confessed.

The actress arched a brow. "You did bring one, right?" she asked. When Elizabeth nodded, Amara slapped the other woman's thigh. "Go. Go now and put it on. I'll keep your seat warm. You know where everything is." She scooted closer, effectively pushing the costume designer from the chair. When it was vacated, she eased back, glancing at her new companion.

"Pretty successful party," Christopher complimented.

She nodded. "Thank you, thank you. Although, I haven't seen my costars yet," she grumbled.

"Well, your little actress is here somewhere, and Elizabeth has been warding off her mother for me since we arrived."

Amara's eyes roamed over the guests, spying her on-screen daughter in the buffet line arguing with a server about something. "She's so precocious. Way too serious for her age."

"I dunno. I could work with her. I always prefer serious child actors instead of ones doing it just because it's funny or someone told them they were cute once."

"A wry but valid assessment," she concurred. "So, looks like you and Lizzy are getting along well."

"Yeah, we are," he answered.

His clipped reply gave her the impression that she was about to tread on too personal a conversation, and she backed down. She barely knew the actor, and she thought that digging into the details of his personal life may not be a smart approach. The last thing she wanted to do was offend him. If this person was important to her new friend, he was important to her.

She felt rescued as a shadow fell over her. She turned to see Jared beside her.

"I should've guessed I'd find our host lounging by the pool," he teased.

"I'm so glad you made it. I was afraid you might not," she greeted, leaping up to hug him.

Jared hesitated. "Wow, you went full Leia on the suit," he noted before hugging her gingerly, not making bodily contact and patting her shoulders.

She giggled at his chaste gesture. "I am the host. If I don't set the tone, who will?"

"Well, now I feel overdressed," he joked.

Amara peeked at her companion. "Jared, you know Christopher, right?"

Jared nodded at her and then to the actor. "We've met. Good to see you," he acknowledged.

"Likewise," Christopher stated, gazing out over the pool.

She watched the tight exchange of greetings between the two and took Jared's arm. "Did you bring the music?" she asked. She turned to Christopher, excusing herself and guided Jared inside the house.

He pulled a thumb drive from his pocket. "My special mix." He snickered. "Perfect for a pool party."

She beamed at him until they reached the kitchen. "I wondered what you'd been doing in your trailer now that the movie marathon is over."

The beginnings of a scowl formed on his face before it relaxed. "I've never had a problem staying busy." He scanned the kitchen. "Where do I plug this in?" he asked.

She snatched the drive from his hand. "I'll get it to the DJ in a minute. I just...wanted to put some distance between you and Chris."

"Why?" he asked, a decidedly neutral expression settling on his face as he rested one hand on his side.

Amara recognized the schooling of his features and saw right through him. "Uh, if you don't think I noticed the tension, you're dumber than I thought." She crossed her arms over herself and stared him down.

Jared rolled his eyes, taking the drive back. "I'll get it to the DJ. I'm starving, and he's right next to the food," he excused, turning to exit the kitchen.

As he did, there was a great slapping of skin as he collided with Elizabeth who was heading toward the patio doors at the same time. Amara gasped, rushing to the pair as Elizabeth landed ungracefully on the floor. She remembered him seeing her dressed for the movie premiere and wondered if he would react similarly to the sight of her in a bathing suit.

"Are you okay?" Amara asked, helping the other woman up.

Elizabeth nodded. "Fine. Sorry. Didn't see you there," she apologized in Jared's direction.

"I should've been looking where I was going," he absolved, also industriously studying the thumb drive in his hand.

Elizabeth righted her one-shouldered suit. "Um, my drink's melting," she excused herself and then rushed toward the patio.

"Well, that wasn't awkward at all," Amara muttered, eyeing Jared. "What did you do?"

"*I* didn't do anything." He ran one hand through his growing hair, flashed the thumb drive at her, and headed toward the DJ.

Amara crossed her arms over herself. Through the patio door, she watched Jared's hair flame red in the sunlight as he wove through the guests. The pool was alive with a beach ball being batted lightly between guests inside and out. Everyone was having a good time, but she lingered in the kitchen wondering what she was going to do about Jared and Elizabeth. They couldn't stay broken like this.

Fortunately, straying behind allowed her to see the front door open slowly. Scott poked his head through the opening tentatively before walking all the way inside. His eyes landed on her, and he seemed to relax. "Hey," he called from across the house.

Amara skipped toward him, strangely pleased to see her outfit appreciated by her new guest whose loose board shorts did little to hide his interest. She hugged him tightly. "I was beginning to think you weren't coming."

"It had crossed my mind," he admitted, squeezing her back.

Amara pulled away. It wouldn't do to give too much too soon, she thought. "Well, I'm glad you did. Can you imagine the scandal of having a cast party without one of the principals?" she asked. She eyed the bag slung over his shoulder, pointing him down the hall. "Go get changed," she instructed. "Bathroom's at the end of the hall or you can use any other room. Just lock the door first. I've got a killer barbecue buffet, bartender, DJ out back. In fact, it looks like Jared's out there still harassing him. I'd better go save one of them." She turned, not waiting for a response. The beads on her sarong jingled against her thighs.

After sorting out the music, she returned to Christopher and Elizabeth.

"Lizzy, can I borrow you?" Amara requested with a hand extended.

"Hey, you keep taking her away, you'll negate my reason to be here," Christopher protested. "And the tiny actress's mom will come after me again."

"I just need a few minutes," she said, pulling on the other woman's fingers as she led her into the house.

"What's up?" Elizabeth asked as she followed along. "I love your sarong. I should've thought of that."

"I've got a spare if you want to borrow it," she offered. "And thank you."

"I might take you up on that. I'm feeling very naked," she complained wrapping her arms around herself. "How can I help?"

Amara hooked a finger to follow and led her back to her bedroom. She was pleased that the door was open, and she pulled Elizabeth inside, locking it behind her. "What the hell happened between you and Jared?"

"What are you talking about?" Elizabeth asked, meeting her eyes.

"He was all shirty with Christopher, and then when you literally ran into each other, you both just bolted. You two are practically joined at the hip usually. You didn't even say hello."

She blinked. "I don't know what you're talking about."

Amara took a long, patient sigh. "Okay, out with it. You went to the movie premiere and then it's been crickets."

"We're just coworkers," Elizabeth alleged. "I'm busy with Christopher. At least that's going somewhere."

Amara squinted her eyes, moving to her dresser and opening a top drawer. "I don't believe you. He's usually in wardrobe giving you grief or something, and I haven't seen him on set at all." She saw the other woman beginning to pace. "I know you want to tell me. I see it all over your face. You're sweatin' like a whore in church." She pulled a spare sarong out and passed it over.

Elizabeth scrunched up her face as she accepted the item. "That's gross," she groused as she unfolded the sheer fabric and busied herself tying it on.

"I'm waiting," Amara prompted.

Adjusting the knot on her hip, Elizabeth did not look up when she spoke. "So... he saw the pictures on my dresser mirror and freaked out."

"What was he doing in your bedroom?" Amara gaped. She was briefly hopeful that something romantic had transpired between the two, but Elizabeth dashed it quickly with a scowl.

"Nothing gross like you're thinking." Elizabeth leaned against the closet door, folding her arms around herself.

Amara smirked. "I didn't say it would be gross. And you don't think it would be either," she scolded. "So, how did he get to your bedroom, and what happened that's so bad?"

"It was after two when we got out of the movie, and so he drove me home."

"Because he's a saint like that," Amara punctuated.

"And then in the morning, he came to pick me up to take me back to my car at the studio, and he had to pee, so he had to come through my bedroom to use the bathroom."

"That's very specific. Go on," Amara agreed, motioning for Elizabeth to hurry the story along. Then the light donned on her, and she nodded. "Oh...What pictures did you have?" She suddenly wondered if the woman had been sneaking photographs stalker style and pinning them up in effigy.

At this, the seamstress turned bright red and covered her face with her hands. "Pictures of him from teen magazines from back in the day," she answered.

"Lizzy!" Amara exclaimed. "Why do you have teen pictures of him in your room?"

"I told you I was a fan. I put them up when I was a teenager. I just never took them down. And I never in a million years thought he would ever see my bedroom mirror," she whined.

"Oh, no." Amara couldn't help the laughter that bubbled out of her throat. The questions that followed flew out in a steady stream. "How many pictures are there? I want to see them! How old was he?"

"I don't know. Seventeen?" Elizabeth guessed. "Maybe younger."

Amara fell onto her bed laughing, clutching her stomach. "I can't wait to give him shit!"

"Please don't," Elizabeth begged. "He hasn't talked to me since."

Her mirth turned to a sad cry. "Why?"

She shrugged. "I wish I knew. I don't know if he's embarrassed or mad. It's so stupid. It's been no secret that I'm a fan. In fact, our whole relationship is built on it. And now...now he's freaked out like they weren't there the whole time I've known him."

"Yes," Amara reasoned, "But now he knows. Although, he's such an ego maniac, I'm surprised it bothers him. But, that's still awful. I'm so sorry." She started giggling again at the thought of "teen dream" pictures of her costar.

Elizabeth shifted uncomfortably. "Is that all you wanted?"

Amara rested on one elbow as she nodded, her glee subsiding. "Is that all that happened?"

"Yes," she answered quickly. "I'm going back to my date."

Elizabeth unlocked the door and hurried through. Amara followed, looking down the hallway and seeing Scott appear from one of the rooms. He had a bag in one hand, and he seemed lost, she thought. Amara decided to rescue him in all his shirtless glory.

"I'll walk you out," she called, running ahead of him and sliding the patio door open. He followed behind her then easily closed the door. She gestured toward the buffet, bar, and karaoke machine. "And I fully expect you to serenade us at least once."

He chuckled. "As long as it doesn't have to be one of my own songs."

"Absolutely," Amara agreed. "I insist it has to be someone else's. I always find it very telling what someone chooses to sing for karaoke." Amara led him to the station, pulling out a black binder and passing it to him. "If you start now, maybe you can be the first."

He flipped through it. "I'm not sure I'm drunk enough for that yet."

"Oh, please. With your background, you probably sing anthems in your sleep."

He snorted to Amara's delight.

Watching as the sun highlighted his skin, smooth and taut over his muscles, she wanted to reach out and squeeze his biceps, but she refrained. "In that case, let me direct you to the bar."

Scott set the book back where she'd extracted it and followed suit. "Looks like everyone's here," he noted, gesturing toward the pool where their on-screen kids were having a splash fight.

"Oh, I hope someone's filming this. Catherine actually looks like a little girl for once."

He shook his head as they reached the bar. "You really don't like her very much, do you?"

"I want to," Amara admitted. "But she's so...unnatural. I don't know what to do with her."

"You don't like kids?"

She shrugged. "I like some kids. Just like people. I've always put my career first. I've never given much thought to having a family." She shielded her eyes from the sun to assess him as he placed a drink order. "You?"

"Yeah, some day. You know, when you're adopted, family is kind of a big deal."

Amara waited for her proverbial jets to cool after his statement conjured the perfect family unit involving him, a white picket fence, and two and a half children. Having children did not fit her career plan, especially poised near the top of her mountain. She cleared her throat to push the thoughts away and ordered a drink of her own, toying with the straw lasciviously as she stared back at him. She wondered what she was doing as she met his gaze with the tip of the straw between her lips. She felt her cheeks cave inward as she sucked on it.

She watched Scott's eyes focus in on her mouth, and she grinned. She started toward an empty pair of lounge chairs, pleased when he trailed behind her. "So, how's it coming hiring a PA?" she asked, sitting on an empty chair and looking up.

He blinked, shaking his head and took a drink. "I'm not making a lot of progress. I made the mistake of posting an inquiry on my social media. Got some entertaining replies." He took the seat next to her.

Amara laughed. "Oh, my word. You are helpless," she scorned. "Go through your agent. Let them rustle someone up for you."

Scott's jaw dropped open. "I should've thought of that."

Amara refrained from agreeing with him, sipping her drink. She was about to say more when a huge splash from the pool interrupted, and Amara gasped, barely holding onto her drink. She regarded at her co-star, water dripping from his face and running down over his pectorals.

"Get in the pool!" Sean yelled.

"You did not..." Amara accused, then screamed along with half a dozen other people that were splashed in the wake of Scott cannon balling into the pool! The young actors screamed happily as he began chasing them with splashes while threatening to catch them and splash them more.

She spied Jared sneaking out of the house and closing the patio doors behind himself. Grateful for the distraction, she scurried to his side. "Are you seriously wearing Spiderman trunks?"

Jared's face pinched, and he looked down at himself. "Are you seriously asking the question?"

"Okay, maybe I'm wondering where you found them in a grown-up size! I love it!"

A smile broke over his face. "Somewhere online at two in the morning, I'm sure," he answered.

"I love them," she complimented. She linked arms with him. "So, I talked to Lizzy," she began, pulling him to the chair she had just vacated. She heard him groan, but she was unprepared to stop. "Tell me about the pictures," she prompted.

She saw his jaw twitch. "I'd really rather not."

Unperturbed by his response, Amara reached for her drink again, to hide behind it and pretend she hadn't seen his back teeth clenching. "I gathered they were old. But here's what I don't get. Why are you freaking out? Was it, like, a shrine or something?"

"Why do you care anyway?" he asked, glancing from the pool to the actress.

"Because you and Lizzy are my friends. And you were like best friends and now it's like we've moved to Antarctica, the vibes between you two are so cold."

"It would be like going into Scott's trailer and finding he'd taped your picture to the ceiling," Jared explained.

Amara imagined her picture taped to Scott's ceiling and what he might be doing when looking at it, and a shiver raised every hair on her body. She met his gaze, clearing her throat. "You're upset because she's thinking about you when she...clicks her own mouse?"

This statement gave him pause.

"You don't seriously think she's the only one who's ever done that, do you? From what Lizzy says, your band was a big hit – just short lived."

"No. It was... There were like magazine clippings...and like there were pictures of her family, I guess and pictures of other people I don't know – like actual four by six photos. And there I was, this stranger, mixed into all the real stuff. And please don't ever bring up that thing about clicking her own mouse again."

"Because you like her," Amara accused happily. "And you want to click it for her?" she prodded with a knowing grin.

He pinned her with a look that stopped her teasing cold.

"Wow. That is a strong response to some kindergarten style ribbing." She stirred the melting drink around in her cup.

He pursed his lips, staring down at her, arched a brow, and shook his head. His voice lowered. "I'm telling you that until it's happened to you, you can't understand."

"Maybe." She watched the other actors in the pool and snickered as Scott pretended to be a shark alternately chasing both Catherine and Sean. The little girl was mocking his impression of the sea beast. Her lack of a reply prompted Jared to expound.

"And then on the way to the studio," he continued, words coming together more quickly, "she said she was going to take them down that night and that no one would have my picture on their wall anymore."

"Isn't that what you wanted?" Amara was enjoying the sight of him squirming as he struggled not to admit that his feelings for their costume designer were changing. Or at least she expected that was what kept him from meeting her eyes.

He shrugged, toying with the drawstring on his shorts.

"So are you just never going to talk to her again?"

"I haven't decided. I just want to get through this movie. We've got a week of filming left, and I can't lose my focus right now." Jared paused.

Amara understood this better than she cared to admit, and her eyes wandered toward Scott in the pool again.

"I assume this is why you haven't gone after Scott," he said softly.

Amara's eyes whipped toward him. "Shut up," she ordered just as quietly as he'd said it. "No one gave you permission to be insightful." She saw the pride covering his face and considered shoving him into the pool, but she was afraid of the retaliation.

The music dwindled suddenly, and Amara saw the DJ booth was empty. She swung one leg over the side of the chair to investigate. A faint drumming had started. The song sounded almost familiar, but she couldn't place it, and Jared held up a hand. "This is what I mixed for the party. He's taking a break. It'll go for about an hour."

Amara arched a brow, settling back down and craning an ear toward the nearest speaker. The tones built, becoming more complex, one song swirling around another until a catchy rhythm took over. She beamed at him. "This is sort of amazing," she praised.

Jared's smile shined brightly, and he jumped up, holding out a hand to her.

She accepted, and the pair began dancing right between their chairs, and she felt swept away by his enthusiasm.

Other guests seemed to catch the excitement as well, rising to dance at their chairs. She saw Sean launch himself from the pool, dancing with his eyes closed, jumping to the beat. Amara forgot everything for just a moment, enjoying the music, the dance, and the joy of those around her. She barely even noticed when Scott joined them poolside until she found herself sandwiched between her two costars.

She laughed brightly. If it hadn't been a private party, she'd be waiting for the press to leak that she and Scott had found a new third. Pushing the thought aside, she lifted her arms, dancing between the pair happily.

Nineteen

Amara's House: Amara

Elizabeth couldn't help but yawn as she shifted in her lounger. Christopher had tugged his chair closer 'til they were touching, and now she was leaning against his side with his arm around her. The sun had gone down, but the party seemed to be winding up. The child actors and their parents had departed before sunset, leaving the adults to hit up the bartender in their wake.

The karaoke machine had suddenly whirred to life, and Amara sprang up on the little stage, sashaying from side to side as she prepared to whip the crowd into a frenzy. She began singing a sultry tune, grinning at her crowd as she mimicked a lounge singer, pointing at random people and leering and using her hips to advantage.

"You want to leave?" Christopher asked softly. "You sound tired."

She shook her head. "Not yet. Lack of sunlight does me in every time. But maybe it's time we get a little food," she suggested. "Might perk me up."

He agreed, stretching beneath her and slowly sitting. Elizabeth did the same, rising with a stretch. She felt her borrowed sarong slipping down her hips, and she adjusted it quickly.

"I'm going to wash up and meet you back here," he told her.

She nodded, making her way to the buffet where a pair of servers hooked her up with a plate of barbecue, and she made her way back to the seats they had vacated. She found Scott at the foot of hers and switched to Christopher's seat.

Scott was flipping through a binder of plastic-coated sheets, completely absorbed until she'd said hello. "Oh, did I take your seat?" he worried. He started looking around, eyes landing on empty chairs across the yard

She nodded. "It's okay." She speared a bite on her fork. "Picking out a song?" she asked.

"I'm torn. There are like three I want to do. I'm just trying to decide how aggressive to be." He winked toward the stage. "Amara's good. I'm just...trained."

Elizabeth laughed. "I like this competitive side of you," she applauded. "You should get Jared to do a duet. You know he's trained, too."

"So I've been told, but I've never heard." His fingers slipped over the laminated pages, and his gaze caught on the actress. He actually sighed, and Elizabeth nearly choked.

"You've got it bad for her," she blurted after swallowing carefully.

He didn't answer, transfixed by the end of Amara's song as she posed seductively. Her motions were fluid and knowing, somehow, and Scott seemed unable to tear his eyes away. He sighed again as she exited the stage and turned back to the book. "I wish I didn't," Scott admitted. "But she's all work and no play."

Elizabeth frowned, knowing about Amara's escapades. "The work is pretty important to her. She has a lot riding on this."

Scott didn't look up. "Yes, I've heard that one." He flipped a page roughly.

Pity filled her as she felt the frustration rolling off him. "Did she actually turn you down?" Elizabeth asked gently.

He shook his head. "No. I never even got the chance to ask before I got the speech about how she doesn't date coworkers."

The seamstress eyed the actress as she took a bow, and her mouth curved upwards. "She strikes me as the type that can be worn down," she propounded.

Scott's gaze flicked from her then back to his companion. "I hope you're right."

"Filming's done in a week according to the schedule. That gives you time to form a plan," she encouraged.

Scott said nothing as the next song started, and they both spotted the next performer. Jared was fidgeting with the microphone, and Elizabeth grinned. The cheesy, flashing, colored lights from the karaoke machine lit him at odd angles, and she noticed the sunburn developing on his shoulders. The song was unfamiliar, but she grinned anyway. "I haven't heard him sing live...well, ever," she admitted.

"Really? I thought you were a fan," Scott asked with surprise.

"I was thirteen, and they never came to my city. My parents barely approved of me buying the magazines. They weren't going to find and take me to a concert. Which is why I went to several of yours to make up for it."

Scott's head snapped up from the book in surprise. "How have I never heard this before?"

She grinned and puffed out her chest. "Because I don't tell everything I know. I was a card-carrying member of your fan club for a while."

He blinked at her. "I don't know how to respond to that."

"Point being, this is the first time I'm getting to see him perform." She said no more, turning to the karaoke machine where Jared now stood preparing to perform. She couldn't help but think about their last conversation. Amara hadn't been wrong about the change in the temperature between them. Dressing him had been surprisingly easy. She had worried that he'd be difficult or snarky, but he hadn't been. Just eerily quiet. No more jokes or comments. No more Pepsis delivered just because. He had come in, changed clothes, said thank you, and headed out to set. Even Dana had noticed the difference, but they hadn't discussed it past her saying it was odd and Elizabeth agreeing.

He moved to the unfamiliar tune and then began singing. Chills ran through her, and she wished for a lining in her bathing suit suddenly as her body responded. She tucked up into the chair drawing her legs to her chest and setting her plate on the foot of Christopher's chair to watch.

Jared paced back and forth, tugging on his invisible collar as he sang the opening lines.

Elizabeth thought she felt his eyes land on her as he sang about falling in love with strangers, and she cheered, patting Scott's forearm in the process. The crowd was starting to join in on the "uh-uhs," and Elizabeth wished she knew the words so she could join too.

Scott turned to her with a grin and nodded. "He's actually pretty good."

"I know, right?" Elizabeth beamed at Scott. "And don't sound so surprised," she scolded before looking back to Jared as he continued. She clapped and cheered with the rest of the guests, unfolding herself so she had free hands to throw in the air. "Go, Jared!" she squealed. When he winked in her direction, Elizabeth nearly melted. She felt her cheeks warm as Scott turned around to laugh at her.

For a moment, Elizabeth forgot where she was, jumping to her feet to wiggle to the beat along with everyone else. She loved the confidence on his face, despite that he was sliding around in Spiderman swim trunks which strangely did nothing to detract from his very grown-up physique. He threw in a couple of dance moves between lines, and she jumped in delight, clapping.

The way he sang, she felt like he was talking to her via lyrics, and she tried to chalk it up to his charisma. His body twisted as he swayed to the music, blue eyes slits over his rounded cheeks. "Everything will be alright, if you keep me next to you. You don't know about me, but I'll bet you want to."

She froze momentarily, looking around at the rest of the guests. He was looking at everyone, right? Not just her. But as the song continued, and he sang about ditching the whole scene to end up dreaming instead of sleeping, it felt like the lyrics described their suddenly fraught relationship. She thought she must be imagining things, and sighed relief when Christopher rejoined her, plate of food in hand.

"I didn't know your actors could sing," he remarked, taking a large bite.

Elizabeth nodded guiltily and pressed her shoulder to his. "Well two of our three principals were pop stars in a past life," she pointed out.

Scott turned back to the pair, leaning closer to be heard. "I was about to brag and say I was going to outdo him," Scott interjected, "but...."

Jared started the chorus for the second time, the crowd cheering him on. One hand reached out in her direction, and her heart leaped into her throat. The lyrics taunted her as he sang about someone wanting to get to know him better.

She blinked and stared. Surely, she was seeing things, but part of her mind followed him down the rabbit hole. Yes, she did want to know about him, despite her best efforts not to. She glanced at Christopher with a smile and touched his thigh with the tip of her toe.

He returned her affectionate action before he continued eating, but she could see something was wrong.

Jared's voice was hard to ignore as he sang. "It feels like one of those nights...I gotta have you."

Elizabeth cheered with the rest as he finished before reaching for her plate. Out of the corner of her eyes, she saw Scott half-way to his feet. "You going in?" she asked.

"I think someone else beat me to the punch." He sighed, sitting back down.

"I wouldn't want to go on after that." Christopher pointed his fork at the makeshift stage where Jared was accepting praise from the crew while the next singer bludgeoned the opening lines of the next song.

Elizabeth cringed. "Scott, you should jump in there and save that poor tech."

He threw up both hands defensively. "No way. I refuse to upstage this guy."

Elizabeth loved his answer. "Did you at least settle on a song?"

He nodded, wagging his eyebrows. "I'm gonna wear her down," he replied.

Her mouth formed an "o" of delight. "I can't wait."

Scott stood. "I'm gonna get in line and congratulate our boy."

Christopher moved to the chair once Scott vacated it. He eyed Elizabeth, the off-key serenade seeming to fade into the background. "So that was some song, your boy chose."

She felt suddenly guilty, and she wasn't even sure why. "He's not my boy," she countered, "And I've never heard it before."

He pushed the food around on his plate, not meeting her eyes. "I have a feeling there's no way I can compete with him."

"Compete?" she repeated. "With Jared? In what way?"

"Elizabeth," he said, setting down his plate. He leaned forward and met her eyes. His voice was quiet, and he articulated his next words clearly. "I saw the way you were looking at him, and I saw the way he looked at you. Like a man dying of thirst staring at a glass of water."

She frowned, shaking her head. "We're just friends. We have been since day one on set."

He tilted his head at her. "Lizzy..." he scolded softly. "Be honest with yourself and with me. I have never walked in a room and watched you react like that. And I'm the one jetting you off set like a secret body-guard at the drop of a hat."

"But I like you," she protested.

He reached for her hand. "You're a nice woman," he complimented. "And I like you, too. I just think your heart is somewhere else. And I want someone to feel that way about me."

Her frown deepened to a scowl. "Are you breaking up with me?" she asked.

He nodded. "I'm afraid so. I'm glad I was in the movie, and I'm glad we met. And I'm glad we tried. But I think it's run its course."

Feeling suddenly emotional, Elizabeth didn't know what to say.

"I'm not mad," he continued. "I'd rather know before things get any more serious than lunches and making out in a rooftop garden." He stood, kissing her forehead. "I wish you the best of luck. I'll get Amara to call you a ride, but I'm heading out."

"Now?" she squeaked. "Like this moment?"

He nodded. "See you around," he offered, and without any further ado, he was gone.

She watched him retreating until he found Amara, hugging her lightly. She couldn't hear anything that was said, but she saw the confusion over the other woman's face before she began nodding, and then he waved and slipped inside the house.

What had just happened? Elizabeth's gaze was motionless as she mulled it over again. The party faded away from her perception as she replayed his words. She barely felt Amara's arms wrapping around her shoulders.

"Are you okay?" she questioned.

Elizabeth didn't answer. Her brain said she should be sobbing uncontrollably and making a scene. Why wasn't she? Her face felt pinched as she pondered. "Did he just... did we just...?" she stammered.

Amara pulled away. She felt the other woman searching her face and met her eyes.

"We broke up," Elizabeth finally mumbled.

The actress frowned. "I know. You can stay here tonight," she insisted.

"No. I think I'm okay."

Amara shook her head adamantly. "You're like a patient with a concussion. I want to keep an eye on you."

Elizabeth tittered. "I'm okay. I feel like I shouldn't be, but I think I am," she mumbled.

Amara's brows knit. "What happened?"

Past her friend, she saw Scott and Jared high fiving each other, laughing. "That," she clarified, pointing at the boys.

Amara cast a sheepish expression her way. "I was hoping you wouldn't notice it."

"Well, I didn't," Elizabeth denied, feeling a little guilty that the statement wasn't entirely truthful. She doubled down. "My fangirl just came out. I've been idolizing him for over twenty years, and this is the first time I've ever seen him sing in person. I never made it to a concert or anything. And Christopher just..."

"He was right."

Elizabeth would've felt less shocked if someone had dumped a bucket of ice-water over her head. She stared at the actress.

Amara's expression was almost smug as she continued. "I like Chris. But you only have eyes for one person, honey."

That couldn't be right, Elizabeth thought. She wasn't supposed to catch feelings for Jared – especially knowing that it would go unrequited. "But he doesn't have eyes for me," she countered. "What am I supposed to do with that?"

"I don't know," she answered. "He'll be out of your hair soon, and maybe you can get past it?"

Elizabeth stared at nothing, and she almost missed it when the song changed, and another singer took over. It wasn't until Scott's voice rang through the speakers that she gave the stage her attention. The tune was instantly recognizable, and she burst out laughing as he launched into *Pour Some Sugar on Me* by Def Leppard. Scott didn't shy away, pointing at the crowd and drawing them all in as though this was second nature for him.

Which she supposed it was, given his history. Her eyes bugged out as his hips began thrusting to the beat to emphasize the lyrics. It was the accompanying grunt that had her staring in disbelief. He barely glimpsed the screen for the lyrics, throwing his head back and running a hand down his torso as he dove into the chorus.

For a moment, Elizabeth thought he was looking at her and realized with a sigh of relief that this was his play for Amara. He had promised to wear her down, and from the looks of the goosebumps running all down her friend's arm, it was working.

Elizabeth stood, grabbing her host by the shoulders and guiding her closer to the show. At this, Scott tipped an invisible hat to her and turned all his attention to the actress. It was obscene, she thought, but it was as if neither of them noticed they weren't alone as he thrust his pelvis in her direction. As the song neared the ending chorus, he dropped to his knees, hand running down his torso and just barely missing his thrusting hips as he finished off. He slipped forward to all fours, crawling toward her as he sang.

Elizabeth noticed the actress wobbling and reached out a hand to steady her.

Twenty

Amara's House: Amara

As the classic 80s anthem poured out of the karaoke speakers, Amara was in full-blown heat. Scott's silver blue eyes pierced her, and she was afraid if he came any closer, she might just explode. Her body was shivering, and she was vaguely aware of Elizabeth's hand on her arm. But her brain was somewhere else entirely. Watching his hips thrusting into the air she imagined what it would feel like to straddle him.

She noticed it was having a similar effect on him. Her tongue flicked over her lips, and she smoothed a hand over her sarong.

The song ended, and Scott actually dropped the mic. It squealed against the padded stage floor. Picking himself up, he eyed her directly as he caught his breath.

Her guests were going crazy, cheering and whistling. Jared was leading the charge, and she heard Elizabeth clapping madly beside her.

Scott held out a hand to Amara, and against her better judgment, she placed her fingers into his. He led her away into the house to the applause of everyone.

Amara's heart fluttered, and she thought it was distinctly possible that she was floating.

"I feel like some privacy is in order," Scott burbled closing the door behind them.

She pressed him lightly against the wall, just out of sight of the patio doors. His body was hot against hers, and she ran her hands up his hard torso until she twined her fingers in the back of his hair and crushed her mouth against his. She felt his hands in the small of her back, fingers pressing into her flesh.

Amara wanted to throw him to the floor and have her way with him. But she couldn't. He was her coworker. She felt him pressing against her thigh, and she knew he was primed and ready. She longed to take him up on the offer. If she didn't stop, they'd be peeling each other down and making noises she wasn't prepared for the rest of the cast to overhear. She pulled his hands away, pinning his wrists to the wall beside his hips.

"No," she told him quickly, pulling away slowly. Her eyes began at his ankles, moved to his strong thighs, up his torso, across his chin until their eyes met.

He was gasping for breath and didn't fight her. His mouth was wet as he stared down. "Why not?" he asked.

"I've told you," she asserted, releasing him and turning her back. She stepped away, opening the fridge door and pretending to look for something. Her body was ready to go, and Amara fought to tell herself no, too. She gulped in the cold air, trying to squelch her lust. Her skin puckered against the sudden change in temperature. She pulled a bottle of water from the appliance and closed the door. Facing him again, she steeled herself to lay eyes on his beautiful body. The way he was looking down at her made her heart race all over.

It took every ounce of restraint for her to walk out of the house. She flitted from guest to guest, one eye on Lizzy, but the other woman seemed just as fine as she'd proclaimed to be. She sneaked out the backyard just outside of prying eyes, pressing herself against one of the hedge bushes. She doubled over, pressing her head against her knees. She had very nearly let things happen.

How was she supposed to get this out of her system? Frankie hadn't done the trick. Her last fling hadn't worked. She was going to have to find her little black book.

"What're *you* doing out here?" a voice questioned.

She spun to see Jared leaning against the bushes. "Where did you come from?"

"Where all the superheroes do," he stated, plucking at his shorts. "Obviously. Why are you out here and not ripping that man's clothes off? He practically propositioned you in front of everyone!"

She snickered. "I don't shit where I eat," she said practically, straightening up. Somehow, in front of Jared, she did not want to expose her vulnerable side. It was easier to tamp it all down when she had an audience.

He nodded and held up his hands. "Fair enough." He looked over his shoulder to the raging party and back at her. "So, how come you're out here?"

"Just needed a minute alone. Not sure where else to find it."

"Ah. Should I leave?"

She shook her head. "You can stay."

They were silent for a moment, before Jared spoke again. "I figure it's never a good thing when the host is trying to escape her own party."

She chortled. "Yes, well..." She searched for something to do with her hands and find her mouth something to do besides talk. "It's times like these that make me wish I smoked."

"Glad you don't," he praised.

She eyed him for a minute as he stayed with her, trying to think of something other than a direct request to get him to leave to prevent the awkward silence. She realized she knew something he didn't and was suddenly bursting to tell him. "So, I have news," she declared. "Christopher broke up with Lizzy."

His expression was skeptical. "How do you know that?"

"He told me right before he left." She watched his face for a reaction but was disappointed when he made none.

"Didn't she come with him? How's she supposed to get home?"

The look of worry that was creasing his forehead made Amara grin as she nodded. "I've demanded she stay here tonight. I'll get her a ride in the morning."

His face scrunched up.

"She's safe with me," Amara assured.

"I'm not sure after the last time she stayed over here. She came back with all these weird ideas," he accused.

She rolled her eyes, turning the focus back on him. "Don't think we all didn't see what you did with that song," she accused. "I think that's what pushed Chris to end it."

"That's not what that song was about," he objected. "Why does everyone keep trying to push us together?"

"Because you're like magnets," she answered smoothly. "Eventually the attraction will be too strong to stay apart."

He arched a brow. "Look who's talking." He took a deep breath. "You do understand you're sending him mixed signals with this," he stated, gesturing to her barely-there bikini. "You can't wear this, sing like a minx, follow him inside after he begs, and then tell him no."

Amara scowled. "How I'm dressed should be no indication of how I am required to act."

"If you were dressed as a mummy, sang the way you did, and responded the way you did after his plea, you would still be sending mixed signals. Do you want him or not? If not, you're going to have to stop teasing him."

While not liking it, Amara took his point. He wasn't wrong. "Why did you have to be the voice of reason?"

"It's what we superheroes do," he teased.

Amara swatted his arm.

Jared jumped, rubbing at the tender spot, but grinned at her. "I'm going back in. Find me if you need anything," he offered.

Amara nodded, then paced the few feet of her hideout behind the bushes. The conversation had calmed her down, and she made her way inside to find something to cover up just a little. When she emerged in black lounge pants and a thin halter stretched over her bikini, she was surprised to find Scott at the end of the hallway. He was staring at her, unwaveringly. She arched a brow, approaching him slowly.

When he spoke, his voice was clear and cool. "I accept that you aren't willing to date a coworker. I do not believe you aren't interested."

Amara passed him slowly, not expecting him to reach out and grip her wrist lightly. She turned to face him.

"When the shoot wraps, I want a chance with you," he stated plainly.

She blinked. She wanted to ask what gave him the impression she was willing to give him a chance, but her brain still felt short circuited after she'd smashed him into the wall and treated him to a cavity search with her tongue. "I'm not sure you can handle me," she finally admitted.

The corner of his mouth turned up. "That's because you don't know me at all. Yet."

The actress cleared her throat to keep from choking as her body tried to launch itself at him, and she held it back. She licked her lips, trying to dispel the sudden dryness. "After it wraps," she conceded. "And you get *one* chance."

"That's all I'll need," he purred, releasing her wrist. He headed out of the house back to the party.

She leaned back against the wall for support. What had she just done? She needed air, and headed back to the party herself, surveying her guests. Fewer people were in the pool now that the sun had set. The buffet was beginning to look sparse, and the bartender was busier than a long-tailed cat in a room full of rocking chairs.

She growled inwardly as her eyes landed on Scott again. He was chatting with Jared, and they were going through the karaoke binder together. She wasn't sure she could take another act like the one he'd performed earlier and not break down entirely.

She struck up a conversation with the hair and makeup crew, listening as they traded tips about some new fingernail polish they'd all fallen in love with. She laughed as only a character actress could, slipping outside of herself for whoever fit in best with this small group at the moment. Minutes later, she was holding court with the camera crew who were all grateful that their director hadn't wanted to join them prior to the end of filming.

Amara clung to anything to distract herself from the beautiful actor wandering the same party who wanted her back. He never bothered to hide the fact, and she wondered what it said about her that all she wanted to do was hide.

Twenty-One

Amara's House: Elizabeth

Around midnight, the party began to wind down. Elizabeth had already changed back into her street clothes and was waffling between staying the night with Amara and calling her own car to pick her up. She couldn't blame her now-former beau for abandoning ship, but she strongly disliked the feeling of being stranded. She despised having to ask for help.

She wandered around the patio and the house, picking up stray cups or plates and tucking them into the trash. The caterers intervened, pressing her out of the way, and she eventually found herself curled into a lounge chair staring at the now-still pool as the stragglers began to clear out. She hadn't seen her hostess in more than an hour, and she wondered if she had finally given into her feelings for Scott and absconded to her bedroom for more privacy. This made Elizabeth more uncomfortable, and she pulled out her phone to begin assessing the options.

"Hey."

Jared, bounced from foot to foot as he stared at the chair next to her. She smiled tightly and nodded. "What's up?"

He seemed to prance for a moment longer before taking up residence in the vacant chair. "I thought we might clear the air," he recommended.

She gulped, glancing at her feet before meeting his eyes. "I'd like that."

Neither of them spoke, and Elizabeth began chewing her lip, twining her fingers together, unsure if she should go first, or what he had planned.

After another agonizing moment, he spoke. "I haven't seen my pictures on someone's wall since long before I was old enough to drink," he started. "And never on someone's wall that I knew."

She nodded, trying to see things from his point of view.

"When we first met, I knew you were a fan, so I guess I should've expected that, except that we're both adults now," he continued.

"It's just those few," she justified. "It's not like I have you papered over every surface like I did when I was a kid." She bit her lips together before she could carry on over-explaining the situation.

"After I got to know you, I sort of forgot about the fan thing."

"Even though I ask you fan questions all the time?"

He nodded. "I've gotten pretty comfortable around you. And when I saw that...it all just came rushing back. And I've had to ask myself if you're my friend or if you're just still carrying a torch for someone that turned you on during puberty."

She held her breath for a moment, waiting for him to continue. "And what did you decide?"

He pursed his lips. "I think we are friends. And I guess I'm not a stranger on your mirror anymore."

She shook her head. "You've seen me sleep in your car. Strangers don't see me sleep," she clarified.

He chuckled.

"Honestly, they've been up so long, I kinda forgot it was you. And in all the time we've been getting to know each other, you've never once offered me a picture so I can put up something real," she added, almost accusatory. It felt like a joke she'd have been able to make before their falling out.

His eyes blinked rapidly, and the next thing she knew, he'd pulled out his phone, joined her chair, scooching up beside her. He reached a long arm above them with his phone and snapped a crazy selfie with an arm around her shoulders. When it appeared on his screen, he let go and began tapping the handheld device.

Elizabeth's phone dinged, and the picture popped up.

"There," he announced. "Now you've got a real one."

She wasn't sure how to reply. Part of her wanted to fangirl again, and the rest of her just thought it was one of the sweetest things anyone had ever done for her.

"Thank you," she said simply. "I'll have it printed and put it up."

He slipped back to the opposite chair. "Can you even still print pictures?" he asked.

She nodded. "Yes, of course! I know all the places."

He shook his head slowly, leaning on his elbows and setting down his phone. "I've missed you, Lizzybeth."

"I've missed you too. Set is no fun without you," she agreed.

"So, Amara tells me she's ordered you to stay the night since you no longer have a ride."

She nodded averting her eyes, a little ashamed at her predicament. "She called me a concussion patient and claimed I needed to be kept overnight for observation."

Jared groaned and cocked his head to one side, assessing her. "You don't look very upset."

She debated how much she wanted to own about the event. She edited down the story as she told it. "Super nice guy. But I couldn't argue with him. He just wasn't feeling it. And I'm not heartbroken surprisingly. I thought I would be. And maybe that's a sign that we did the right thing." She waited for him to say something sympathetic, but when he didn't, she felt mischievous as she added, "It's a shame. He was a good kisser."

His brow arched, and he shook his head. "How bout as a sign of our renewed friendship, I'll take you home? After all, I still have the address in my map history."

"You don't have to do that," she excused. There was very little more in the world that she wanted that moment more than to be safe in his little BMW again, but she worried that she was taking advantage of his good nature.

"If I'm going to wear the superhero shorts, I had better live up to the brand," he teased. "Just a friendly neighborhood Spiderman taking care of his people."

She gulped at the thought of being one of his people. "Well, it would be nice to sleep in my own bed."

"What do you say we get out of here before we're the last?"

Elizabeth didn't give herself long to think about it. "Okay. But you have to tell Amara. I'm chicken."

He laughed at this, helping her up and leading her into the house. They found Amara with the head caterer, signing the man's electronic notepad with her finger.

"Looks like you two are on speaking terms again," she pointed out, turning toward them and away from the kitchen where leftovers were being stored.

They both nodded, and Elizabeth sighed relief inwardly as Jared broke the news to her.

"I'm gonna take Lizzybeth home," he told her. "I think she probably needs her own space tonight." He eyed the actress, a smirk wrinkling one cheek. His eyes scanned her up and down. "And I'm betting you might need yours," he added.

Amara froze like a deer in the headlights to Elizabeth, and she snickered at the self-assured woman's inability to articulate. The actress recovered quickly. "Are you heading out now?" she asked.

Jared nodded. "I had a lot of fun. More than I've had in a long while."

"Me too," Elizabeth added, stepping forward to hug her. "Thanks for the invitation."

"Of course. It was my pleasure. I think it was very successful," she added, winking at Elizabeth.

The seamstress blinked, unsure if the wink was for what she thought it might be and embarrassed to maybe be right.

Jared fished his shirt from his duffle and slipped it over his head then jangled his keys. "See you tomorrow."

Elizabeth followed him to his car, settling in happily. She hadn't realized she'd missed his car 'til this moment after thinking she'd ridden in it for the last time. "So, once the movie makes a mint, do you think you'll upgrade?" she asked.

"Definitely. This baby's gotten me through a lot, but she's ready for retirement."

She petted the dashboard. "Sorry, old girl," she teased.

"Eh, I think she'll be glad to get rid of me. I'm a bit of a hard case some days," he confessed.

"You?" Elizabeth teased. "I don't believe it."

Jared looked surprised at her statement, glancing from the road to her and back. "What was that for?"

She shrugged. "It's just what I do with my friends. If you leave a door open, I'm liable to walk through it."

A dimple punctuated his cheek as he smirked. "Uh-oh. The gloves have come off."

They were quiet for a moment, and despite the hour, Elizabeth was beginning to buzz back to life. "So, tell me what you were like when you were twenty-two," she probed.

"That's random," he cited.

"You were the one up there on the machine singing your heart out about being twenty-two. I just wondered if you'd changed much since then."

He barked a laugh. "Of course I have. I was a complete dick then. I let myself get derailed by the dumbest things. When I think about all the opportunities I passed on..." he trailed off.

"Oh really? Like what?"

He paused briefly. "Did you know I had a chance to work with Scott back in the day? Writing his group's third album? And I passed."

She squealed. "Why?"

"I was dating some girl, and I wanted to show her she was more important to me than some job."

"Well, that's only a dumb reason in hindsight. I'm sure you were making some grand gesture."

The corners of his mouth curved up wryly. "You give me too much credit," he denied.

He sounded sad, and Elizabeth wanted to cheer him up. She wondered what he'd been up to in the last two decades that had broken his heart. She stared openly at him as he drove. "That's what friends do, right?"

"Friends also give rides to damsels in distress at the midnight hour," he added as they reached the freeway, and he opened up the engine. "Tell me about you at that age."

She took a deep breath, shifting gears as she considered the request. "Sewing like a mad person. I had just gotten my first job on a TV show," she recollected. "I was like replacing needles in sewing machines and cutting patterns. Nothing exciting. But I got my foot in the door."

"Then you're a veteran in the biz."

"You could say that. Just now hitting my stride though."

He risked a peek at her from the road. "No boyfriend to distract you?"

She shrugged. "That came later, and it was dull, and I was so dumb."

"Weren't we all at that age?" he asked.

She wanted to nod but refrained. "Then why'd you pick that song?" she queried.

His fingers drummed against the steering wheel for a moment. "I don't know." He paused for a moment. "It was fun and almost current. The tracks on that machine were really out of date. It was hard to find anything good from this century."

Elizabeth wanted to know if it had anything to do with the lyrics. If it had anything to do with wanting to get to know her better. With no subtle way to ask, she dropped the subject, trading stories about learning to drive and other inane topics that sprang to mind as he drove and pointing at random fireworks lighting their way.

When he arrived at her place, he pulled up next to the staircase nearest her apartment. "If I was to come use your bathroom again...would I be shocked still?" he asked.

Elizabeth was grateful to have her hand on the door handle already. She tugged quickly, leaped out of the car, and leaned down. "Goodnight!

Thanks for the ride!" she replied. She slammed the door and dashed up the stairs, waving when she'd reached the balcony.

He flashed the headlights, and she let herself inside to fan the flush from her face. She pulled out her phone, opening up the text he sent her at the party and staring at their photo. It was such a candid image. Unrehearsed, honest, and real. She was surprised she wasn't beaming more beside him. She realized that his luster as the elusive teen idol Jared Rains had waned, and instead, he was just her friend Jared who was at the pool party to celebrate the birth of their nation.

Clearly, she discerned as she touched her hot cheeks, she still had feelings for him, but it wasn't because of his connection to her childhood. It was because he was thoughtful, and funny, and kind, and never dull. He held doors and gave rides and was kind to her assistant.

Despite the time and a trip to the studio looming in less than six hours, she had trouble falling asleep. And when she did, she was running errands all over town with the man on her phone. And not once did she think about the breakup.

Twenty-Two

On Set, Reading Room/ Cafeteria: Amara

Amara had never been so grateful to see a buffet as she walked toward the Kraft services table for lunch break. All morning, Scott had been blowing her kisses, teasing her, touching her shoulder or her hand. She could hear the crew resetting the stage for the next scene they were scheduled to shoot, and she wondered how long it would take them to finish.

She picked out a few items and wandered to the corner, contemplating hiding out in her trailer. However, the room was quiet enough, and the summer sun was unbearable even just walking between the set and her trailer, so she settled in.

"It's quiz time," Scott announced, taking a seat across from her and setting his plate down.

Amara sighed as she eyeballed the enormous Dagwood style sandwich he'd built. Condiments from the were beginning to roll down his fingers, slowly approaching his wrists. "If you get that on your clothes..." she warned.

"I won't," he swore, tucking a napkin into his collar and setting two more over his lap. "Least favorite food?" he asked.

Amara wasn't sure what he was driving at, but she played along. "Hazelnuts," she grunted, making a face. "Can't stand 'em."

He eyes widened in shock at the suggestion, then shrugged. "More Nutella for me."

She groaned. "Stop it, or I'll lose my appetite."

"Fine, fine. Indoor or outdoor?"

"Indoor."

"Fancy or casual?"

She hesitated at the answer. "I need more information."

"Just in general. Do you prefer fancy or casual?"

"I don't like this question. I like both in different settings."

"Morning or night?"

"Probably somewhere in the middle, but night is good."

He wrestled the sandwich to his face and took an enormous bite.

"These are very random questions," she observed. At least he had stopped blowing her kisses, but his questions were somehow equally unnerving.

He grinned wickedly. "I know, aren't they?" He took another bite, nearly losing his grip. He set the monstrosity down to lick his fingers.

Amara's eyes focused on the act, watching his nimble tongue slip around each digit meticulously. She imagined the other exacting things he may be able to accomplish with it. She reached for her plate. "I don't know what you're up to, Harper, but I'm not getting tangled up in it."

"Yet," he vowed, meeting her eyes. His face split into an enormous grin, and for a moment, she didn't even notice the sauce on his cheek.

She tapped her cheekbone as she stood. "You got something here," she pointed out.

To her surprise, he made no motion to address the smudge. "I like it messy," he answered.

Amara nearly dropped her plate. "I'm in my trailer in case anyone's looking," she answered. She retreated toward the trailer, but then changed course when she was sure she was out of sight and scurried for wardrobe and a friendly face.

She found Elizabeth alone in the area, propped up between two chairs that were facing each other and somehow slouching between them. She had her phone in her hands, giggling as her thumbs flew over the keys. "Whatcha doin'?" Amara asked taking a seat in the remaining chair and resting her plate on her knee.

"Ooh, that makes me nervous," Elizabeth cautioned, eyeing the precariously balanced plate. Vaulting up, she produced a terry cloth towel to place under the plate and cover Amara's costume.

Amara stared at her when she seated herself more properly. "Who's on the phone?"

"Just Jared," Elizabeth answered, not volunteering more. "Not that I mind the company, but what are you doing back here? Your costume looks like it's all in order."

"I needed a reprieve, and it's too hot to walk to the trailer," she explained.

"A reprieve from what?"

Amara just growled, not willing to say his name and lend credence to the growing feeling that she was not about to win this round with him. "Hey, so I was wondering if I could enlist you to help me with some clothing for the press junket."

"Well," Elizabeth contemplated, "I have a bridal gown to do after filming ends. Tell me what you were thinking, and if you trust me I'll see what I can do."

"I trust you," she confirmed with a smile, then began to detail what she'd like to see in an outfit. As she began describing it, she secretly began detailing what she'd like to wear on her pending date.

Elizabeth listened patiently, reaching for a notebook from her rolling cabinet and began sketching as Amara spoke. When the seamstress turned the pad around, Amara squealed.

"Yes, that's it!"

Elizabeth's face hinted at a smile. "This looks a little double duty, if you ask me," she poked.

Amara relaxed her face then met Elizabeth's face. "I have no idea what you're talking about."

"Are you sure? Because I saw you last night follow that man off stage into the house." Elizabeth waggled her eyebrows and smiled. "You wouldn't be describing a perfect date outfit, would you?"

Amara rolled her eyes. "Stop it." She fidgeted, chewing on a carrot stick. "Why can't it be both?" she asked with a pout.

Snickering, Elizabeth set the notepad down. "I got you. How many days of press do you have scheduled?" she asked.

"A few. I think it's safe to plan for at least three. We'll be doing some as a family. So, it can't be all sex pot."

"I know what I'm doing, darling," she promised. "It's actually a little bridal, if you think about it. Demure but ready to rock a man's world."

Amara arched a brow, and she wondered what it was like up in Elizabeth's head. The woman seemed so innocent, and then she'd just equated a wedding dress to sex. Before she could contemplate further, they were joined by her costar, and she fought the urge to growl.

"Here you are," Scott proclaimed, then jammed a lollipop between his lips. He held onto the stick, and Amara felt his eyes lock onto hers.

He twirled it in his mouth, and the corner of his lips quirked up slightly.

Her whole body contracted at the sight, heat racing from head to toe. Heat pooled in her belly, and she imagined pouncing on him, right then and there. Her brain treated her to images of yanking the sucker from his mouth and replacing it with her tongue and other random body parts. "Stop it," she demanded.

He pulled the candy from his mouth slowly, face projecting inno-cence. "Stop what? I'm just eating a piece of candy. Catherine gave it to me." He stretched out his tongue to grab the sucker and pulled it back in his mouth.

"That's impressively generous," Elizabeth replied from somewhere in the distance. "I didn't think Catherine had it in her."

Scott nodded, but never took his eyes from Amara. He tugged on the stick, and the candy made a popping noise as it exited. "I'd offer you one, but this was the last," he apologized, sucking on it again.

Amara gulped. Her nerve endings were doing a happy dance, prick-ing up all over her skin to wave hello at this beautiful specimen of man.

She twisted in her seat, setting the plate aside to put her back to him. She twined her fingers together in her lap on top of the towels Elizabeth had covered her in. "Did you need something?" she asked pointedly.

Scott was suddenly in front of her, pulling out the sucker so he could speak. "No. Just wondered why'd you'd left me all alone."

"That seems a bit harsh," Elizabeth agreed, looking up from her phone.

"Whose side are you on?" Amara accused pinning the costume designer with a glare.

Elizabeth shook her head, looking back at her phone as her thumbs continued flying. "There are no sides in my area," she replied.

Amara reached for the phone, grabbing it nimbly and reading aloud in an exasperated voice, "You're missing the best show. Bring suckers!" Amara jumped up dumping the phone in Elizabeth's lap. "I thought we were friends," she sassed.

"Oh, we are," Elizabeth groaned, grabbing up her device. "Don't get your knickers in a twist."

"Why," called Max's voice over the rising chaos, footsteps thundering toward the wardrobe area, "whenever my actors are missing, do I always find them back here with you?" he accused.

Elizabeth shrugged. "I am minding my own business."

"Texting your other actor," Amara tattled.

Max stared hard at Elizabeth. "I will be so glad when this movie is done. You're all just a bunch of hormonal teenagers in your thirties," he rambled. He pointed at the actors. "You two. We're ready." He led the way out, mumbling about child actors being more reliable.

Amara pointed at the other woman then to her eyes and back. "Watching you," she called.

Scott kept pace beside her, twirling the sucker around with two fingers and smirking down at her. He slipped it to one side of his mouth. "Does this bother you?"

"Me?" Amara asked. "Why would it?"

"I don't know. But you're awfully red," he said, pointing the candy at her, circling her whole face.

She rubbed at her own cheek, feeling the heat there, and pushed the emotions down. "I don't know what you're talking about."

"Red is a color," he described. "It's a primal – I'm sorry, a *primary* color. Like the color of blood rushing to a single place on your body. I could get you a mirror," he proposed.

Amara thanked him with a slap on the upper arm.

Scott leaned down toward her ear as they approached the set. "Lower next time, please," he whispered. He straightened up, sucking hard on the lollipop one more time before lobbing it at a trash can. The hard candy thudded against the bin's edge as it landed in the receptacle, and Scott cheered, "Two points!"

"Good shot," Sean complimented.

"Don't encourage him," Max scolded. "Places!" he called.

Scott shook out his arms and jumped onto his cue. "Ready!" he sang. And in one quick moment, he was suddenly her on-screen husband. His face was serious, and she believed he was a businessman. A very vanilla businessman, she added to herself. Amara thought she was going to cry, her brain whirling over his comment while also trying to become her character, ignoring the heat that had gathered between her thighs.

The clapboard snapped, and Max called for action.

Twenty-Three

Local Bar Near the Studio: Elizabeth

"A chocolate martini for the mistress," Jared ordered as he and Elizabeth stepped into their usual haunt, "And a Corona light with lime for me."

Used to their order, the bartender filled Jared's drink first then went to begin mixing Elizabeth's. They leaned against the counter as they waited, and she sighed. "I can't believe it's nearly over." Her words were followed with a pout.

"Max is a task master," he agreed, pressing his lime into the bottle. He licked his thumb then took a swig.

Elizabeth's eyes were glued to the sight. She jumped when the bartender pushed a nearly full martini glass toward her, and Jared slid a credit card to the mixologist. He turned to the tables, and she followed, trailing behind him. She waited 'til they were seated to sip her drink.

"Something's off with you tonight," he commented. "I called you mistress in front of the bartender, and you didn't even yell at me."

She sneered. "I'm getting a little morose," she confessed. "There's barely five days left."

He sniggered. "You want me to flub some lines and draw it out?"

She laughed with him, warmed by the idea that he would even suggest it. "No. Of course not."

"Well, don't say I didn't offer." He took a long swig.

"How am I going to get a proper chocolate martini after this?" she whined.

"Well just 'cause the movie's over doesn't mean we won't hang out again if that's what you're worried about."

Elizabeth eyed him warily. She believed his intention, but life had taught her that this was exactly how people grew apart. She frowned. "You're gonna be so busy after this movie hits, you'll completely forget about me."

"How could I forget about my longest surviving fan?" He smiled gently. "I'm afraid you're stuck with me now."

Stuck indeed, she thought and sipped her drink. "What are you going to do with your first day off?" she asked.

"Probably stock the fridge," he replied. "After that, I'm not sure. I hadn't given it a lot of thought. What about you?"

"I don't get a day off. I have a fitting with a bride-to-be first thing Monday morning."

"Ooh…" He scowled. "That sounds awful."

She shook her head. "I'm not worried about it. The bridal business is a good pay day. Makes up for the inconvenience a little."

He arched a brow. "Wow, I thought I was cynical, but you've got me beat."

"I'm not cynical. I'm capitalistic. I'm a big fan of eating and having a place to sleep where I'm not afraid I'm about to be murdered."

He laughed. "All work and no play, Lizzybeth. You need some balance."

"Hey, I spent a lot of hours watching movies with you. I'll call that a lot of play."

He pouted. "I miss our movie marathons. What series can I rope you into next?" he mused.

"I think it's my turn."

"No – you're the fan. I pick the movies."

"No," she countered. "I'm the mistress. You said so."

He laughed, killing his beer and raising his hand to order another. As he did so, his phone began dinging.

Elizabeth noticed the texts flashing over the device but didn't look too closely until a giant picture flashed on the screen that she wished she had never seen.

Jared scrambled to flip his phone over before pulling it under the table, but it was too late. Elizabeth couldn't unsee the close-up selfie involving a provocative birthday suit and a lot of pouting.

"Sorry," he moaned, tapping at it under the table. His brows were knit in concentration, and a frown curved his mouth.

"Um," Elizabeth hesitated. "Do you need to take that?"

There was a lot of throat clearing as he continued his reply via text.

The phone dinged several more times, before he answered, his jaw clenched hard enough to make the vein at his temple protrude. He worried his lips worried his teeth. In a voice almost too low for her to hear, he snarled, "What part of no is the hard part? Is it the N or the O?"

She raised an eyebrow. "Trouble in paradise?"

He frowned. "Booty call," he mumbled.

She was surprised at the confession, but she could have guessed that from what she'd seen on his text. A little part of her was pleased that he was refusing such an attractive offer. "You sure you don't want to get that? Seems like a sure thing."

He rolled his eyes. "No. I'm pretty tired of not being first on the list."

She nodded, contemplating that statement. "You get a lot of these?"

"That would be telling," he retorted, bowing to the waitress as she brought another beer. He pressed the lime into the bottle and sucked on his thumb for a moment.

Elizabeth's mind went wild thinking about a booty call with him and then watching him suck the tip of his thumb for the second time. She should be used to it by now, but outside of the quality time, it had become her favorite part of their nights at the bar. Each time he got a fresh beer, she got treated to him cleaning lime juice from his thumb, and she would be lying if she said she hadn't thought about it many times trying to fall asleep.

"Don't get me wrong," Jared said, breaking her out of her contemplation. "A sure thing is great. But...it's not satisfying anymore."

She sighed sipping her drink and thinking he and Amara had a lot in common. "How *did* you end up with just a side piece?" she asked. "I always thought you'd be the serial type."

He shrugged. "Life beats you up and sometimes all the pieces don't fit back like they used to," he theorized before taking a long drink.

She frowned. "Slow down there unless you want me driving the beamer."

He shook his head, lifting a hand. Within moments, their usual waitress sidled over to the table.

"What you need, gorgeous?" She leaned down onto the back corner of his chair, allowing her hair to flip over her shoulder and treating him to an eyeful of her low-cut ribbed tank.

Jared seemed unfazed by the attention. "Could we get an order of fried something to keep us sober?"

"Pickles, onions, or wings?" she replied.

"All of it," he requested, turning his full bright smile on her.

Elizabeth heard her gasp over the music. "You got it, babe," she complied, turning with a flourish of her hip to place the order.

"And some mozzarella sticks," Jared called after her, tilting his head to one side.

"You should've just ordered *her* to go," Elizabeth mumbled.

Jared waved her off. "She looks like one of my exes," he revealed.

It was her turn to gasp, and she forced her jaw shut. "All this time we've been coming to this place, you never told me that."

"Why would I?" He began peeling the label off his bottle in a tiny strip, slowly turning the bottle to elongate it. "It was a long time ago."

"And I'm just a fan, and you don't tell personal stuff to fans." Elizabeth stared at her own drink as she spoke, afraid to see the truth of her statement on his face.

"We're friends," he corrected.

Elizabeth looked over the rim of her glass. "Do you want to talk about it?"

"It's just not a particularly good story. It was after the network canceled us and everything fell apart. I just sorta felt like a starter kit for a star hunter." He finished pulling the label free of the bottle took another long pull.

"I'm not sure what that means," Elizabeth replied softly. She sipped her drink again. This was sacred territory he was sharing, she realized.

"When the money ran out, so did she. And she made off with some investment banker who could buy me over and never miss the change. Like, next thing I knew, they were off in his house in the Maldives." This time, he finished the bottle. "Don't worry – I'll wait to order another 'til after the food gets here," he promised.

"Thank you." She took another sip, glancing toward the kitchen. "How long were you together?" she asked.

He frowned. "I don't remember exactly. More than a year. We went through my birthday twice."

Elizabeth perked up at the mention. "Oooh. Your birthday is right around the corner. Do you have big plans?"

He shook his head. "Neh. I usually do something low-key with friends. You should come. I'll even pull out the grill. We'll probably watch a movie," he tempted.

"I'll clear my schedule," she said, laughing.

He balled up the label, flicking it across the table at her and nodded. "I'm going to hold you to that, Mistress or not."

"You'd better. It might be the sole way I get through these doldrums." She took a deeper drink than normal, fanning her face as the alcohol warmed it. "This is why I drink so slowly," she admitted. "Too fast, and I turn into a tomato. It's not pretty."

"You're really getting those end of shooting blues, aren't you?" he questioned.

She nodded. "I'd have said it's more like finishing high school, but you didn't do that like most kids, did you?" she asked.

"Like most kids in the biz," he replied. "But my parents are both teachers, and I finished at sixteen. Easy peasy."

She oohed at him, reaching for a napkin and using it to create a bigger breeze on her face. "Here I thought I was special finishing college a whole semester early. I didn't realize I was drinking with Doogie Howser."

He clapped when the food arrived and their waitress set another bottle in front of him with a wink.

"She's not your ex," Elizabeth noted. "You should go after her. She clearly likes what she sees."

"Is that what you think?" he asked, reaching for an onion ring.

Elizabeth turned all her focus on reaching for a pickle chip, dipping it in ranch sauce and nodding. She was getting used to him having feelings for other women, and she remembered his booty text. "Oh, right. You've got the sure thing waiting for you."

He chewed thoughtfully on the onion ring, and his next words were quiet. "I ended that."

Her hand froze midway to her mouth, and she was vaguely aware of sauce dripping to the tabletop. She popped it in her mouth, willing herself not to ask why...willing herself not to hope. "Oh," she murmured.

They each nibbled on several hot, gooey fried foods silently.

"I'm surprised you don't have more to say about that," Jared said.

"Why?" she questioned. "I'm just here to listen and support. And I clearly have no idea how it's done, so on this topic, I have no advice for you either." She took another large drink.

He reached for a wing and bit into it without a word.

"Just wait until something happens to you that I know anything about – you won't shut me up," she promised.

"I'll count on it."

Elizabeth relaxed under his watchful eye, focusing on the food and remarking how surprisingly good it was and how there was no way the two of them could possibly finish it all.

Twenty-Four

On Set: Amara

"That's a wrap!" Max called out over the silent set.

A deafening cheer followed, and Amara sighed with relief, relaxing her shoulders truly for the first time in nine weeks.

Beside her, Scott bounced, grabbing her in a hug and swinging her around. "We did it!" he yelped.

Amara squealed, hanging onto him for dear life until he set her back on her feet. He kissed her forehead and then went to high five the rest of the cast, the lighting crew, the sound techs, and finally Max who he swung around as well.

She watched him go on his happy rampage with a smile. His enthusiasm was contagious, and worst of all, adorable. She hugged the people nearest her, congratulating their efforts.

"Come on, Ms. Baker," Scott called in her direction, and she saw him jogging toward her. "Let's get de-costumed for the last time." He held out an arm to escort her to wardrobe.

Amara took it cheekily. "Trying to get me out of your hair faster?" she sassed.

They walked several feet before he answered. "Who says I'm not just trying to get you out of your clothes?" he murmured.

Her eyes bugged wide, and she realized they were surprisingly alone.

Her body revved its engine, and she felt virtual sparks between her fingers and his forearm. "You wouldn't."

His reply was an arch of his brow as he patted her hand on his arm and smirked.

Elizabeth greeted them cheerfully in total disagreement with the frown on her face.

"What's wrong, darling?" Amara questioned.

The woman's lower lip popped out before she answered. "It's really over." She held out a bag to Scott. "Usually I say ladies first, but I do have a little more to do with Amara."

He nodded and disappeared behind the screen.

Elizabeth turned to a rack behind her and pulled it forward. "I've got some outfits for press started for you here. I want to see how they fit unless you don't have time."

Amara's eyes went wide, glancing at the screen then back at the designer. "Sure, I've got time," she answered softly.

"I heard that," Scott called. "How come she gets special press clothes?"

"Because she asked," Elizabeth replied. "And maybe this is part of my new line. You don't know."

Amara's insides twisted happily at the sound of Scott's deep laugh in response. She moved to the rack, grateful for the distraction. She liked what she was seeing. "Lizzy, you don't fail to impress."

Scott emerged to join them. "I kept the socks," he proclaimed.

Elizabeth gave him a thumbs-up. "Great – we were just going to throw them away."

Without waiting for an invitation, he stood beside Amara and began investigating the outfits on the rack. "Wow. You're totally going to upstage me," he complimented. "I'll have to pull out all my tricks," he added, holding up a hanger. The dress was nearly black, but as Scott turned it in the light, the satiny material gave the illusion of glowing emerald green. "This. You will wear this on Saturday when I pick you up at four. I'll text you the details," he promised, placing it back on the rack. He moved to the designer and hugged her quickly. "I will see you at the cast party Friday, and we will definitely be in touch after."

Elizabeth nodded with a weak smile. "Bye, Scott. Pleasure working with you."

He waved, winking at Amara and exited the building.

"Go get changed," Elizabeth encouraged, wiping at her eyes.

Amara obliged, pulling off the costume for the last time. She hung it neatly on a hanger before slipping into the outfit Scott had selected. It hugged her curves almost to her knees and was simple enough to work for press, but with the right accessories, it could suit any fine establishment. She hurried out to the riser to admire herself. The reflection did not disappoint.

Elizabeth swarmed around her, plucking and tugging at the neckline, the waistline and the hem. "I think it's right," she determined.

Amara agreed. "If this isn't in your new line, it should be."

Elizabeth chuckled. "As long as you photograph it before your date."

"Why?" Amara questioned. "Are you afraid I'll spill something?"

"No," the seamstress reasoned. "I'm more concerned that it'll be in shreds."

Amara drew back. "You have quite an imagination."

"Just eyes," Elizabeth countered.

She wanted to protest to stop adding pressure to an already volatile situation and pinned the designer with her gaze. "Where's Jared?" she asked pointedly.

"At the grocery," Elizabeth answered immediately.

Amara balked. She hadn't expected an answer and certainly nothing as mundane as the grocery. "You got a tracker on him?"

"No. He texted me from the store. And don't change the subject. Where are you going Saturday at four in that dress?"

She shrugged. "No idea. It's a surprise."

"Ooh. A mystery date. I like his style."

"You would," Amara grumbled.

"Go try on the others," Elizabeth insisted.

Amara followed orders, returning to the changing area and stripping down to try on the jumpsuit. The material was light and flowed around her as she stepped into it.

"I don't understand why you're putting up such a fight about this," Elizabeth noted.

Part of Amara didn't understand either. "It's just not appropriate."

"Why?"

The question was simple enough, but Amara didn't have an answer. She stepped out and in front of the mirrors.

"Amara," Elizabeth said firmly, "If you want to be girlfriends, this is the kind of thing girlfriends discuss. It's hard for me to support you if you're not forthcoming with details."

Amara frowned at the other woman through her reflection. "What is it with people on this set making sense? First Jared and now you? What's the world coming to?" she sassed.

Elizabeth's expression softened as she plucked at the back of the garment, straightening the shoulders and neckline. "It's so much easier to see someone else's issues than to see your own. And there's wisdom in a multitude of council."

Amara stared at the top of the other woman's head. "No one ever wants to hear the council, though."

"Fair," the seamstress conceded. "But even if you don't want to tell me, you should probably figure out why you're protesting so much."

Amara turned in the mirror, liking what she saw. "You put the back from the costume in this," she noticed.

"You liked it so much on set, I thought you might enjoy it for other occasions. And I thought I'd put this one in the new line."

As Elizabeth changed the subject, Amara was grateful for the woman's intuition. Unfortunately, the question she'd posed was stuck in Amara's mind. She knew all the reasons that she had used to eschew his attention. But as of today, her excuses had officially run out of steam. Part of her did worry that they were still too embroiled in their spousal character roles, and the feelings would fade if given time. That must be it, she reasoned. She wasn't prepared for it to mean anything else that she was suddenly considering if her house would accommodate a nursery. She hadn't thought about having babies since she was one.

Not surprisingly, all the press outfits worked, and Amara finally changed into her street clothes, folding the new items into her monogrammed bag. She took one last stroll through the set, hugging a number of the staff as she went through. She packed up the remainder of her gear and called for a car to take her home.

Amara dragged herself around the house, hanging up her new outfits and taking a dip in her pool. The water was soothing, but her memory of the party came rushing back, and she remembered the feeling of pushing Scott against the wall of her kitchen. She closed her eyes, letting her imagination go to the place she had not let herself that day.

She rushed to her bedroom, letting her brain run the full course she wished she had allowed herself that night. Her hands roamed body until she reached the desired effect, gasping Scott's name.

Amara felt tears rolling down her cheeks. It wasn't fair. She didn't want her life controlled by another person – beholden to their whims and their presence to satiate her. But here she was, unable to connect with another partner at the mere thought of this man who'd invaded her life, taken her spotlight, and was holding her pleasure at bay.

She wanted to throw a temper tantrum at the realization, but instead Amara went shopping. She bought jewelry for her date and booked a hair appointment and a spa treatment and any other thing she could think of to spoil herself. She even made a stop for some grown up lingerie to wear underneath.

If Scott insisted on having a date, she was going to be irresistible.

By the time she went to bed that night, she had everything prepared.

Twenty-Five

Cast Party, Restaurant: Elizabeth

Max groaned when Elizabeth walked into the back room of the restaurant he'd rented for the party, Jared right behind her. "Whatever you two get into now is your business."

"For the last time," Elizabeth groused, "There is no business."

Dana met her, interceding with a hug for each of them. "Lighten up, Max," Dana scolded, pinching his cheek.

"Which way is the bar?" Jared questioned, head on the swivel. "Need one, Dana?" he asked.

She lifted her glass and shook her head. He darted into the crowd, shaking hands as he made his way toward the bartender.

"Elizabeth," Max gushed. "Wait till you see the preview. Johnny got a rough cut ready for us to show tonight. It looks amazing! You are not going to ever have time to sleep again."

She shook her head gently. "Thank you. That's very kind."

"You ever need a recommendation, you let me know. I'm your second biggest fan." Max flitted away to blow smoke up someone else's skirt, and Dana stayed behind.

"He's third after me," Dana clarified.

Ignoring the reference to someone who liked her better than these two, Elizabeth hugged her assistant's shoulders from the side and rested her head atop the white pixie cut. "Pretty soon, you'll have your own set, and I'll never find a replacement," she flattered.

Dana chortled but nodded toward Elizabeth's chauffer. "Far be it from me to ever side with Max, but...you are here together," Dana pointed out, turning her gaze to where Jared was ordering drinks.

Elizabeth waved it off. "It's our routine. You know we go out for drinks at least three times a week. How we aren't both the size of houses is anyone's guess."

Dana stared at her. "I've just not seen you this way before. For all these years I've been begging for more responsibility, and you always say you're going to give it to me, but you haven't 'til now."

"Maybe you're ready now." Elizabeth smirked at her assistant.

Jared leaned against the makeshift bar in their private room. She had spent a legitimate amount of time assessing his assets during fittings, but she had not tired of it yet. His street clothes fit him like a glove, and she admired how long his legs seemed in his skinny jeans. He was just wearing a Kiss T-shirt tonight, but it was under a geometrical black and white leather jacket that made all her senses dance, and she forced her eyes back to Dana.

Her attention was diverted as the group broke out into cheers as Amara entered the room, and the actress bowed, passing out hugs to those nearest the door.

Dana seemed a bit put off by this. "No one cheered when Jared came in," she pouted.

"It's okay," Jared replied out of seemingly nowhere as he returned with drinks. He passed one to Elizabeth. "I carry around my own personal cheerleader," he countered, raising his glass to hers.

"Here, here," she toasted, clinking their glasses carefully and ignoring Dana's eyes on her.

Dana clinked her glass with theirs, and they all drank. The crew applauded again when Scott arrived a few minutes later, and in moments, they were inundated with crew members introducing their families to the leads and posing for pictures. Elizabeth found herself Jared's unofficial photographer, snapping pictures with more than a dozen phones. She barely had a chance to see either Amara or Scott before food started being delivered to tables, and everyone crowded in to get their portion. Max took the opportunity with everyone seated to say a few words of thanks for everyone's contributions. He called out lead members of the team, including Elizabeth. And once that was out of the way, he played the rough cut of the trailer for them.

Elizabeth's jaw hit the table. She watched the video, barely recognizing the actors or the set. It looked like something real, and for a moment, she couldn't believe she'd been a part of it. The camera zoomed in on Amara, and Elizabeth was distracted by how perfectly the costume fit both the actress and the film. Elizabeth was excited to watch the movie when the trailer ended. She bumped Jared with her shoulder to get his attention and gave him two thumbs up. He beamed back at her, nodding.

Amara was on her feet, cheering and whistling at the screen when the clip ended.

As the lights came back up, a waiter with a cart full of what appeared to be books, rolled into the middle of the room, and Max joined him.

"I know a lot of you were annoyed with the all the cameras wandering around the set, but there was a purpose." He picked up a hard bound book and held it up. "I made some memory books for everyone to memorialize the fun we did have on set. I know it was a grueling shoot, but you guys were amazing. Spouses, thank you for your sacrifice. I hope you enjoy this too, seeing your partners on the pages here. Most of them are even awake." The group laughed, and Max opened the book to reveal the last several pages were blank, then reached to a basket on the bottom shelf of the cart. "I brought some markers in case you want to treat it like a yearbook and have your very best friend draw mustaches on your pictures."

Dana squealed on Elizabeth's right side launching herself toward the cart. Several others followed suit, and, forgetting their food, swarmed the cart to collect their book. Dana was an early adopter, returning to her seat with three books and three pens. "I insist you both sign my book," she declared.

Jared arched a brow while chewing a bite of fajita. "That's a big honor. I have to find the perfect place first. I promise to sign it before I leave," he replied.

Elizabeth began flipping pages as she chewed, choking as she spied a picture of Jared sitting in one of the wardrobe seats from her area. He had one leg in the air, holding onto the chair for dear life as Elizabeth wrangled a sock over his toes. She remembered that day. It had been early in filming, and he was protesting socks again, and in a fit of laughter, she'd pressed one onto him. Frozen in that single image, she saw the expression on both their faces as she never would have seen in the moment. That was the picture she wanted on her mirror.

"Who took this one?" she mumbled.

Dana sank onto one elbow, shielding her face as she tucked into her dinner voraciously.

Elizabeth felt Jared lean in to see the photo then lean across her to her assistant. She sucked in a breath at his nearness, torn between pulling away to give him more space and remaining still to keep him close.

"Did you do this?" he asked the assistant.

"Do what?" she countered, batting her eyelashes and looking at her plate. "I can't believe Max sprang for steak *and* shrimp," she enthused, taking a large bite. She made happy food noises, pointing at her full mouth. About the time she would be swallowing, she grabbed her book and a marker and darted to the opposite side of the room, begging for signatures from the other wardrobe assistants.

Elizabeth watched her go, shaking her head. "I'm almost afraid to see what else wound up in here."

Jared eased back slightly but remained close to look at the book as she turned pages. "I'm curious," he noted. "Honestly, I barely noticed the photographer. There's just so much going on during filming. It's kind of cool to see it from an outsider's perspective.

"Some of these have to be stills from camera shots. Look, this one has to be from Max's phone. Look at the angle," she noted.

He agreed, leaning away for a moment to take another bite.

Elizabeth giggled, closing the book and setting it on Dana's empty chair. Her heart needed to calm itself. "You know, this will be the first autograph I've ever asked you for."

Blinking, he nodded with a smile at her. "I just realized. I think I'm impressed with your restraint. I mean, except for having pictures of me on your bedroom mirror."

She rolled her eyes and focused on her food instead. Max sat in the empty chair across the table from them, and Elizabeth complimented him on the ingenious gift.

The director beamed. "I'm glad you like it. I just realized early in that I was taking a lot of pictures, and I had challenged a select few to submit like at least five a day. I was combing through those every night."

Elizabeth's mouth formed an "o" of delight. "So that means you could like, get me a digital copy of a picture so I could have it printed?"

Max leaned back proudly. "If you check the front cover, there's a link that's available to you guys for thirty days where you can download all the pictures as long as you don't sell them. I figure some of you might want to have some prints made."

"I swear I'm older than both of you, and I didn't know you could still get prints," Jared grumbled.

"Well, it's that or tear up the book, and I couldn't have that," Max rationalized. "But don't wait too long. I will kill that link in exactly thirty days so they don't all wander out onto the world wide web."

"Oh, you know these will get leaked," Jared persisted.

Max sighed. "Some of them. But there's nothing compromising. The only ones who really have to worry are you three leads, and frankly, this isn't all about you guys. Even I make an appearance or ten in those pages."

"Well," Elizabeth said, "since you're not eating, at least sign my book so I don't miss you in the press of your admirers." She thrust her book at him and peered toward Amara and Scott who were suddenly swarmed. Everyone's spouse and a few of the crew were asking for their autographs.

Max took the book from her, flipping to the very first page and writing a lengthy note next to his name as director. The party devolved into groups eating and groups flitting around for signatures.

Elizabeth found herself pushed out of the space to allow everyone to reach Jared. She didn't mind, enjoying the sight of him in the middle of anything resembling a throng. He was so relaxed, and the easy smile that curved his mouth was intoxicating. She could see he'd done this before, and he was a natural. She was so transfixed, that she wasn't aware Amara had peeled off Scott's side until she felt herself accosted with an arm around her shoulder.

"You didn't think I'd let you get out of here without a signature in my yearbook, did you?" Amara cooed, passing her a pen.

Elizabeth smiled softly, taking the book in front of her. "I'm not sure what to say. I haven't signed a yearbook in more years than I care to admit."

Amara reached over to turn the pages until she found a photo of the two of them. "Here," she pointed out.

Thinking for a moment, Elizabeth left a kind note, signing it with a flourish and her phone number. She closed the book and passed it back. "It's not Shakespeare," she apologized.

"Where's yours? I intend to sign it."

Elizabeth passed it to her, and the actress excitedly signed in the same spot she'd asked for in her own book, brandishing the pen in large, curly strokes across the page as she composed.

"Miss Elizabeth," a small voice interrupted.

She turned to see the child actress standing in front of her, a book poised between her miniscule hands.

"Why, Catherine. I'm glad to see you could make it."

"Would you please sign my book? I really loved the costumes you designed and how you fixed mine. I hope to work with you again some-day," she stated.

Elizabeth felt her eyes wet as she reached for the book. "I'd be honored," she warbled. She flipped through to the back, finding a blank corner. "Catherine, it's been such a delight working with you on this film. I hope we work together again soon!" She signed her name beneath and passed it back. "Would you sign mine too?"

Catherine's face quirked into a genuine grin. "Of course." She turned her gaze on Amara who was still writing. Her tiny eyebrow quirked up, and she uncapped her pen loudly in preparation.

Amara snickered. "I'm finished." She passed the book to the child. "Did you get Jared and Scott to sign?"

"First," she noted, taking the book impatiently and setting it on the table where she could reach better.

Elizabeth and Amara giggled quietly, and like a tiny tornado, the child actress scrawled in the back of Elizabeth's book. Then she was gone.

Amara snagged it before Elizabeth could see what the girl had written. Amara gaped. "Little monkey," she objected. "All I got was her name, but you got a whole note about the pretty clothes you make."

Giggling, Elizabeth shrugged. "I'm not her competition. You are. And I did make pretty clothes," she added. "Are you ready for tomorrow at four o'clock? Do you have any details yet?" She fought not to laugh as the actress flushed.

"Never you mind that," Amara shushed.

The party lasted another hour as the food ran out and everyone had snapped all the selfies and acquired the necessary signatures. Jared indicated he was ready to leave, and Elizabeth said her goodbyes, meeting him outside.

He passed his key to the valet, then joined her leaning against the restaurant wall, waiting for his car to arrive. "I'm a little hurt that you didn't ask me to sign your book," he said. "You had me all geared up for it."

She chortled. "Well, the night's not over. And someone's a celebrity. I didn't get much of a chance once the crew and their partners noticed you." She elbowed him gently.

He rewarded her with a smile as his eyes drifted down to her arm against his.

"You were charming," she added. "A complete natural."

"I've had some practice," he reminded her softly.

Elizabeth noticed the tone of his voice, and her heart fluttered. She stared back for a moment, trying not to get caught up in the idea that he could be implying anything. "Did you at least sign Dana's?"

He nodded as his car rounded the corner, and he pushed off the wall, holding the door open for her. She slipped in, buckling up as he closed it and joined her in the driver's seat. She plucked the book from his hands as he did so, stacking it on top of hers for safekeeping while he drove. "I won't get them mixed up," she promised. "Yours is on top."

Jared cleared his throat, and the car lurched forward.

"And I kept a pen," she added. "You can sign it when we get to my place."

"I can, eh?" he chuckled. "Very generous of you."

"I thought so." She was feeling a bit smug as she clutched the pair of books in her lap. She fought the urge to flip through his to see what signatures he'd collected.

"You're not gonna fall asleep on me again, are you?" he questioned.

"No," she vowed. "I've only had one drink, and it's not that late. Thanks for driving tonight, by the way."

He nodded. "If you haven't figured out by now that I like to be in control of things, now you know."

Touching her lips to hide her grin, Elizabeth bit back a giggle. "I didn't want to be the one to say it," she teased. Unable to resist the urge any longer, she opened the cover of his memory book, then stopped for his approval. "You don't mind if I flip through your book, do you?"

He shook his head. "Be my guest. I haven't read them all yet."

Elizabeth flipped the pages slowly. She shook on her phone's flashlight to see the pages. A lot of the pictures simply had signatures beside them, but as she got toward the back, she started to giggle. "Do you know how many phone numbers you picked up?" she asked. "There's at least a dozen in here, and at least half of them were the hair and makeup girls."

"They just like me because I know how to sit still. Better than Scott, I've been told."

"You had a lot more hair than Scott's ever had," she reasoned. "I miss it," she confessed.

"I've been thinking I'll let it grow a little," he said, running one hand over his head. "It's time to reinvent myself."

She arched a brow. "Funny you should mention that." She paused, screwing up her courage. "Because...I was wondering if I could beg a favor of you."

He glanced from the road to her and back. "Maybe. What'd you have in mind?"

"Well, I've been plotting a line of clothes. Something chic but accessible. And originally, I was just going to make it a women's line–"

"I'm sorry. I'm done modeling dresses," he interrupted.

"Oh, rats," she said as she giggled. "You played such a good-looking girl back in the day." The thought conjured images of him dressed as a girl in several comedy sketches he and the others had done.

"There were five of us. Someone had to play the girl – and we all took a turn more than once."

"I remember. But what I was going to say was that I have been reconsidering the line, and I was thinking I might do a little menswear too. And I was wondering if you wouldn't mind modeling some of it for me."

"Really? Me? Are you sure I'm your target demographic?"

Elizabeth wanted to tell him he'd inspired the change, but she didn't have the guts to do so. "Let's see, you're in perfect shape, you look like a twenty-year-old, and you're about to set the world on fire with this movie so... yes. I think you're perfect."

He covered his face. "Lizzybeth," he scolded. "If you keep this up, I won't be able to get my head through the door."

"That's my job." She was quite pleased with herself for evoking his reaction, but she waited for him to stop before she spoke again. "I don't think I want to have any kind of runway show. Amara convinced me that selling online would be the way to go."

"I'd be honored," he accepted. "And if you need some other models, I have connections."

"Thanks. Amara already offered to model for the price of clothes."

"Same," he agreed. "Same! I want to keep whatever I model, please."

"Of course." In Jared's case, she would've felt incredibly weird keeping things he'd worn. If Max hadn't insisted she preserve his costumes from the set in case of a potential spin off, she would have found herself in a similar dilemma when they'd torn down their set at the studio.

Jared began suggesting poses and settings for the clothes, and by the time they reached her place, both of them were red faced and trying to stop laughing. "I hate to say it, but I have to brave the bathroom again," Jared announced when he'd parked.

She invited him up, grateful she'd cleaned her place earlier in the day. The bridal gown she was building was spread across the dining room, but she didn't even consider that chaos as a mess. He darted in past her, already knowing the way.

She busied herself in the kitchen, setting down her bag and book, realizing that she had accidently brought his inside as well. She waited on the couch, reading his inscriptions more closely. It was evident that people liked him. She landed on the page of their picture in wardrobe of her tugging a sock over his toes. It was a classic Jared moment, and she remembered it. She would be lying if she said she hadn't enjoyed just getting to experience how playful he was. Part of her had always wondered if the actor side him was the funny bit or if it had been the script, but now having spent so much time with him, she was sure it was just who he was. The effervescence she saw on the screen wasn't faked; it was just Jared.

"Boy, you move fast," he called from her bedroom.

Realizing what he was doing, she joined him. He was standing at her dresser staring at the new picture of them from Amara's party. "I told you I knew where to get pictures printed," she teased. "And for the record, I'm going to add the one of us from this new book." She held out his copy. "I accidentally brought yours in. Didn't want you to lose all these valuable numbers."

"I think you're just making that up," he accused, flipping through the book.

Elizabeth scooted closer. "Am not. Look." She rifled through the pages, pointing out all the ones she could find without trying too hard. "Everybody wants you."

He closed the book. "I almost feel guilty for writing, 'Have a great summer,' in so many of theirs now."

"You didn't!"

He smirked. "I did. And now, I think, I need to write something in yours." He plucked the book from her hand and walked toward the front room. "Where's yours and where's that pen?"

She followed after him, pulling it from her purse and handing it to him. He skimmed through her few signatures and stopped on a page near the front with a photograph of him on set.

"Okay, go pour me a drink or something. You can't watch while I sign."

"You are so weird." She kicked off her shoes under the coffee table and padded into the kitchen to see what she had to offer in an attempt to comply with his instruction. "You want water or something stronger?" she called.

"Water. In a bottle if you've got it."

She did, and she pulled one for each of them out of the fridge door. She peeked in on him from the doorway. "Can I come back yet? Or are you mid-novel?"

"Just about finished," he promised. He blew gently across the page for a moment. Then, apparently satisfied, he snapped it shut. "Ready!" he called, standing. He set the book on her coffee table.

Elizabeth rejoined him, passing him a water bottle. "Thanks."

"You're still coming tomorrow, right?" he questioned, referencing his birthday cookout party and taking a step toward the door as he untwisted the cap on his water.

"Yes. In fact," Elizabeth held up a finger and darted back into the kitchen. She pulled two containers out of the fridge and held them out in his direction. "These are for tomorrow's party. Something sweet and something savory."

He arched a brow. "Well, you're gonna have to walk me out then, because I'm not carrying both down those steps."

She drew back the salad and passed him the smaller container. "I can do that."

He reached for the door, leading her down the stairs toward his car. His footsteps were slow, she thought.

"You okay to drive?" she asked as they reached the bottom of the stairs.

"Yeah, you know I'm a night owl."

She laughed. "I think you just never sleep."

He gurgled with her. "Too much to do." He opened the passenger door and set his things inside before taking the bowl from her hands. "So, I've told my friends to expect you tomorrow," he stated. "You'd better not make me a liar."

"How many friends?" she asked, now a bit nervous.

"Like six other people and maybe a couple neighbors will drop in."

She sighed relief. "Good. Not a huge fan of large crowds."

"I've met you," he replied. For a second, Elizabeth thought he was about to get in the car and leave. Instead, his footsteps hesitated, and he twisted back to reach for a hug. "Goodnight, Lizzybeth. Noon tomorrow if you want hot food."

A bit stunned from the surprise hug, she gave him a thumbs-up as he slipped into the driver's seat, and in moments he was gone. She watched his taillights until they disappeared then hurried back upstairs and pulled the memory book free to search for his signature. She found it relatively quickly.

> *To my Mistress Lizzybeth. So glad we met. I've enjoyed*
> *getting to know you. Please don't be a stranger! I think there's*
> *more to know. Yours, Jared Rains*

Elizabeth reread the autograph at least a dozen times. She wasn't sure which part of it was throwing her for a bigger loop. Was it the reference to their inside mistress joke? Was it the fact that there was more to know? Or was it that he had called himself hers?

Head swirling, Elizabeth stared at the ceiling of her bedroom for hours in a vortex of confusion, worry, and hope before exhaustion took her to blackness.

Twenty-Six

Amara's House: Amara

At 4:00 Saturday afternoon, Amara received a text to come out front of her house. She was thinking that not coming to the door was relatively rude until she stepped outside to find a waiting limo. She blinked in the late afternoon sun, then locked her door and slipped into the back seat. The driver shut her in, and she reached for her phone, thumbs flying as she texted Scott. "On my way."

She set down the phone, looking over the spacious interior and noting a bouquet of lollipops in one of the cup holders. She reached for one and unwrapped it quickly. In moments, she was posing for selfies with it until she found the right shot and texted it back to Scott.

The reply after the photo was quick. "Tease."

Amara eased back, sucking on the candy as she watched the city pass by through the windows. She had no idea where she was going, but she trusted that Scott had a plan. For as helpless as he had seemed in the short time she'd known him, she was starting to believe that when it came to knowing what he wanted he was anything but weak.

When the limo came to a stop, she smoothed the skirt of her dress. Showtime. The door opened, and she found Scott waiting for her, dressed in a tight, black shirt, and she noted at least one more button than was appropriate was undone, flapping in the breeze. The shirt was tucked into a pair of pinstriped trousers. But her eyes were glued to his as he leaned down, reaching out a hand to her.

Amara leered around the sucker in her mouth, accepting the offer and unfolding herself from the limo's interior. She would never admit to having bowed a bit lower than necessary to taunt him with her ample cleavage.

To her surprise, Scott reached for the sucker stick, pulling it from her mouth while he shook his head. "You'll spoil your dinner," he scolded.

She blinked. "You shouldn't have left it there for the taking if you didn't want me to eat it," she disputed, noticing the way their hands were still together.

He nodded. "You are absolutely right." He turned slowly leading her to the building behind him. "Well, the good news is you can work up an appetite as we walk," he added.

Amara nearly choked when he lifted the sucker to his mouth and popped it in.

He stared at her face for a moment grinning around it and nodding toward the venue.

She stood up taller, pretending there was nothing abnormal about what he'd just done. "Where are we?"

He led her to the door, holding it open for her. "It's called *The Van Gogh Experience*. It's an immersive walk-thru using all kinds of cool tech to be part of his artwork."

Amara looked back at him with surprise. "I've heard of this."

He smiled. "Well, I hope you like it. I managed to get it all to ourselves for an hour."

On this note, she could not hide her surprise as the curators waved them inside, holding a pair of doors open for them to pass through. "How did you swing that?"

"Well, I bought all the tickets for this time slot."

She laughed as he waggled his eyebrows at her. "Oh no! That is too much."

"Don't worry. I got the group rate."

Amara held onto his arm, laughing more as he pulled her forward. "Big spender," she teased.

"You told me I had one chance. You're worth it." He twirled the lollipop between his lips as they walked.

Overhead projectors were casting images onto walls and over their bodies, some stationary and some wandering over the room. However, it was his hand resting lightly on the back of her neck that had her attention. His thumb and forefinger were stroking along its center, gently massaging the hair at the nape of her neck. She was trembling from the attention and was saved when they found the room of Van Gogh's famous sunflowers. Yellow light danced over her body, and she twirled into the center of the room, arms splayed wide as if to absorb the painting.

She watched Scott as he ambled toward her. "You are a sunflower," he confirmed. When he reached her, he swept her into his arms, twirling her around the open space. She squealed, wrapping her arms around his neck, shivering as their bodies fit together in that moment. Her breath went shallow as she searched his eyes. The warm lights playing over his skin tempted her to follow them with her fingers, but she refrained, swirling out of his grasp just before his hands could graze the side of her hips.

Amara gave chase, following the projector's gentle glide across the room, delighted when Scott followed suit. With his long arms and legs, she was no match, and he caught her easily, drawing her into the next room. She was surprised how little they said, meshing into the exhibit and allowing her eyes to follow the images. When they reached *Starry Night*, Scott laid himself out in the middle of the floor, beckoning her to join him. Amara wasn't sure how long they lay there, watching the painted stars twinkling around them, ebbing in and out of the flow of the animated breeze.

Scott pulled the sucker from between his lips, holding it up to the light. "These are actually pretty good," he remarked.

"I had been enjoying it," she admitted wryly.

He turned to one side, holding it out over her mouth, then tracing it slowly over her lips. Her tongue darted out to follow the sugar coating.

Scott pulled it away. "No! I really mustn't spoil your dinner. After all, those reservations cost me three favors."

She arched a brow. "Is that what we're doing next?"

He nodded, sucking the candy back into his mouth and smirking down at her.

It hadn't felt like an hour when they heard the double doors open again and footsteps began to fill the hall.

"I guess that's all for tonight," he sighed then helped her up.

They dusted off and followed a member of the exhibit staff guiding them out a back door where the limo that had picked her up was waiting. Scott tossed the end of the sucker into a nearby bin and followed her into the car.

"Finally decided to stop torturing me with a sucker?"

He beamed as the car rolled away from the exhibition. "I don't need props to torture you," he declared smoothly, taking her hand from the seat beside him. He ran a thumb over it, following the line in her palm until he reached the back of her wrist.

Amara shivered, drawing her hand back. "You're not playing fair," she complained.

"That was not a condition of our agreement," he pointed out.

She blinked at him. "I'm doomed, aren't I?"

"Doomed is not the word I'd have chosen. I was thinking more like delighted, in for a treat, resigned to pleasure."

She choked on air, coughing a little.

Dinner was an extravagant affair with half a dozen small courses. She had heard of the restaurant before but had never been able to get a reservation. If Scott had to call in three favors, she assumed even he had trouble finding a spot – but he had found a way for her.

Amara was barely able to eat. It seemed like everything they ate was gooey or sticky and required him to lick something studiously. The good news was that this particular tool worked both ways, and it was no coincidence that she ordered a pasta dish just to suck the long noodles between her lips and watch him shift uncomfortably in his seat.

She should've seen it coming, she thought, when their ride stopped at the next destination. It was an exclusive night club she had never been able to get into before. She'd spent hours standing in line, waiting to get in, but never once had stepped beyond the doors. Now, as they approached, the bouncer exchanged a complicated handshake with Scott and ushered them both in immediately with a smile.

The entire space was alive with music and light and a hint of smoke running throughout. It smelled like spices and a touch of something sweet she couldn't place. Scott had his hand in the small of her back, guiding her toward a table. "VIP?" she yelled back to him.

He nodded, gesturing for her to have a seat. The velveteen booth was remarkably comfortable, and she was shocked at the speed of service. A waitress was already taking his order and slipped away just as quickly.

"Did you just order for me?" she asked. The music was quieter here, and she could almost hear herself think.

He nodded. "I like a little lubrication before dancing in public."

She scoffed. "Why? You used to dance for crowds all the time."

"That was choreographed and very different from what I plan to do with you tonight," he clarified, scooting closer until they were touching. He crooked a finger under her chin, caressing her cheek and then her jaw before he slid it over her one bare shoulder. "I owe Elizabeth a wine basket for this. You look amazing."

She smirked. "Well, you owe some of that to me. A great dress doesn't account for everything."

He nodded. "I thought I'd thank you with vodka and dancing."

She arched a brow. "This had better be some dance."

"Oh, you know it will be," he replied, leaning in. "I've been wearing you down all evening. You'll have nothing left to resist me with."

They were interrupted by the waitress returning with a pair of drinks. He winked at her with a smile and pressed a folded bill into her hand. Scott reached for his drink, swallowing it down in a single pull.

Amara followed suit, and they both set their empty glasses hard against the table.

Scott slipped a hand boldly up from her knee to her thigh and then to her waist. "You ready to have your world rocked?"

"I dare you," she answered, meeting his blue gaze directly.

Scott apparently needed no further encouragement, pulling her to her feet and to the dance floor. There was no way to talk, but that didn't stop them from communicating. He whirled her around the floor 'til they found a comfortable spot. Amara's heart was racing as his hands slid over her body, molding them together. She laced her fingers through his hair, arching back against him. His hands settled on her behind, gripping her hips tightly against his own.

Amara let herself go, pouring all her attention into the dance. Her body thrummed with desire and heat, and she rolled in his arms to grind herself back against him. She squealed, feeling his hand slap hard against her backside in encouragement. She wasn't sure how long they had been on the dance floor, but when she straightened up, lifting her arms overhead, Scott turned her around, crushing her to his body.

His hand tangled in the hair at the nape of her neck, and he leaned in, kissing her harshly, tongue searching for hers.

Amara kissed him back unabashedly and twined her arms around him. She lifted one leg over his hip, lost in him, forgetting they were on the dance floor. She felt his interest hard against her and ground into it. She was virtually naked against his trousers. She swallowed Scott's groan with her mouth, as his free hand ran up the back of her thigh, cupping her behind. His pelvis thrust against hers, and he bit her lower lip.

Amara drew back with a smile, licking the tender spot. She raised up to meet his ear. "Let's go," she begged.

"Yes," he replied nibbling her earlobe. His hand was hooked behind her knee, and he pulled her tighter to him.

Amara's eyes scanned the room, looking for exits. Her eyes lit on the door to the alley, and she remembered early in their relationship how he'd talked about his time between a pair of dumpsters. She pulled away, gripping his hand and tugging him toward the exit. Scott kept pace easily, pinching her behind as they went.

They burst through the doors, and Amara heard him growl as he grabbed her around the waist. Inching her skirt up over her hips, he kissed her and pressed her into a corner of the building.

"Condom," she groaned against his jaw.

"In a minute," he hissed, kissing her neck. His left hand was wedged between her thighs, fingers boldly exploring her most sensitive of places.

Amara was lost in sensation, nearly losing her ability to speak. He nipped at her collar bone, hand driving her wild. "Tell me what you want," he murmured against her ear.

"You," she whimpered in reply.

Scott nibbled her earlobe and held up a condom up in his free hand. "Open it for me," he bade.

"Yes!" she groaned, grabbing it from him and peeling it open. She heard his zipper in the dark, his belt jangling as his pants lowered, and he grabbed the rubber from her hands. In the next moment, he had hoisted her up against the wall, his body pressing her in place as he finally took her.

Amara didn't even bother to hide her passion as she gave in to the need she'd been holding back since the first day on set. They were both grunting softly as he thrust. Before she had time to worry they would be seen, he had covered her with his mouth, and Amara didn't care if there was a crowd and a film crew standing by. She simply didn't want it to stop. In minutes, she was shrieking his name against his ear with each wave rolling through her body. She finally sagged between Scott and the concrete block wall of the club and gasped for breath, watching his face pinch with release before he buried his head in her chest.

He eased her to her feet gently, chuckling when she grabbed his forearms for balance.

He kissed first the corner of her jaw then rained sloppy kisses over her neck.

Amara nibbled his collar bone. "I'm still hungry," she growled.

"That was just the appetizer," he purred against her ear, tugging her top and skirt back into place. "I'll call the car."

Amara ran her hands over his chest as he pulled his pants up and fished the phone from the back pocket. Within the hour, they were tucked into his bed, panting and moaning in delight. Amara was virtually having an out of body experience, humming to herself in the afterglow. The single thing tethering her to reality was her hand on his calf.

She was vaguely aware of the bed shifting beside her, and Scott maneuvering her against his chest. "So do I warrant a second date?" he whispered against her ear.

"Mmmm," she hummed, turning to face him. "Let's see if lightning strikes twice."

When Amara woke, the sun was baring down between the curtains, lancing across the bed. It sliced across the hand laying limp over her belly. She remained still, not wanting to disturb the moment. She couldn't remember the last time she woke with a body beside her that she wasn't trying to get away from. In fact, she wanted to roll over and rain kisses across his face. For the first time in a decade, Amara was satisfied. The gaping need for intimacy that she'd grown to think of as normal was quiet, curled into a happy ball at the pit of her stomach.

The moment was broken as Scott stirred, his grip on her tightening as he slowly stretched back to consciousness. She felt warm kisses on her shoulders and hummed happily. "Good morning," he whispered against her ear.

She leered, rolling slowly to face him. "Morning." She wriggled until her head was resting on his chest, and he was half beneath her. "I'm sorry I pushed you away for so long."

He kissed the top of her head, one hand making lazy patterns over her shoulder. "The important part is that we got there."

Twenty-Seven

Jared's Apartment Complex: Elizabeth

Elizabeth parked her car in the first available spot she could find at Jared's apartment complex. She hoped her car wouldn't get booted, but he was worth the risk. She was about fifteen minutes early, intending to help with any last-minute set up. She already felt like she was imposing. It was the least she could do. Well, that and the bottle of whisky she'd brought as a birthday gift.

She checked her phone again for the apartment number when she noticed the pool. Barbecue smoke wafted toward her, and she detoured in hopes of finding Jared outside.

She was not disappointed, spotting him behind a stainless-steel pit dressed in a crazy pink and blue gingham apron covered in yellow sunflowers. Despite the blue frills ruffling over his bare shoulders, he managed to look perfectly comfortable in the ridiculous apron.

"Lizzybeth!" Jared called, closing the lid. He set down his spatula, wiping his hands on his apron. He met her at the gate with outstretched arms for a hug.

He was warm from the sun, and she could smell lunch in his hair and sunscreen on his neck, and she squeezed him tightly. She thrilled at the feel of his bare skin under her hands as she patted his back, trying not to giggle at the slapping noise it made.

"I'm so glad you made it. And you're even early. I guess my warning about hot food made an impression." He laughed as he released her then gestured toward the bag on her shoulder. "I know our pool's not as nice as Amara's, but I'm hoping that's a change of clothes so you can swim with us."

She nodded happily. "Happy birthday," she greeted, reaching for the shoulder strap on her bag, then presenting him with the bottle of whisky. The ribbon she'd tied around its neck fluttered in the breeze as she handed it over.

Jared accepted the bottle reverently, hugging it to his chest. "This is very nice! Thank you!"

Folding her hands in front of her, she gawked at the concrete. "You're welcome."

He beamed. "Come meet my friends," he encouraged, holding out an elbow to her.

She accepted without hesitation. He squeezed her hand against his side with his elbow, and she glimpsed up to see his face glowing proudly. It made her suspicious, and she wondered what he was up to. When they rounded the corner of the grill, she understood, nearly losing her balance.

His friends were waiting for them, chatting casually and brandishing cups and bottles. His friends happened to be three of his four former bandmates: Kevin, Andy, and James.

She barely recognized their adult selves from the ones she had admired as a teenager. Two of them were shirtless, and one sported a cut off T-shirt that she was pretty sure was there to cover his adult stomach.

"Guys, this is Lizzybeth," Jared announced, flourishing the bottle she'd just handed him. "And she gives the best gifts."

She balked, looking between them as he slowly released her hand and pressed her a step closer to them. One by one, each guy introduced themselves with a handshake, and she accepted, shell-shocked by each press of the palm.

Jared burst out laughing when they finished. "I got you," he mocked.

She had the good grace to chuckle as she agreed, "You did."

Keven took a step closer, drawing her attention as he pressed, "Jared says you made the candy."

For a moment, Elizabeth forgot she'd sent her contribution to the potluck ahead with Jared the night before, and she nodded. "Yes, I did." Wait. Had they been talking about her prior to her arrival? Was she awake?

Before she could pinch herself, Kevin dropped to one knee, taking her hand. "Marry me," he begged.

Elizabeth squealed, pulling her hand back. "Um...no. Not over candy," she refused.

In a flash, Jared flicked his friend's ear, and Kevin launched back to his feet, rubbing his offended ear.

"Back off," Jared warned.

"You didn't happen to bring any more, did you?" Andy asked hopefully, scooting closer. "'Cause we kinda killed it already."

She shook her head sadly. "If I had known...it's really quick to make. I could whip up some more," she offered, wondering if he had a candy thermometer and the right ingredients in his apartment.

"Not necessary," Jared declared, turning to Elizabeth and nodding toward the complex stairs. She felt his hand light on the small of her back. "Come on. I'll show you where you can change and then you can shove them all in the pool." He turned to the group and pointed at the grill. "And don't let that burn."

"Oh, sure," Andy called. "Now if they're not perfect, it'll be our fault."

Jared snapped his fingers and touched his nose. "Now you're catching on," he teased.

Elizabeth waited a few paces before she pinched his upper arm. "That is a cruel joke you've played on me," she scolded with a smile. "Inviting all the guys without telling me."

He jumped, rubbing the spot with a grin. "It's not cruel. I thought you'd be pleased."

She shrugged. "I didn't say I wasn't. But you can admit it. You liked shocking me."

"Lizzybeth, you're barely blushing. I'm a little disappointed. I thought I'd get more of a reaction out of you than that." He led her up the stairs to his place and opened the door.

"It's extremely cool, but I'm over *them*," she asserted, stepping over the threshold. She expected him to poke at the statement, but he did not, and she turned to see a stunned smile on his face.

He exhaled and turned to his kitchen. "This is my sister Nicole and her friend Ruby."

Elizabeth hadn't expected to see any other guests, but she was pleased to see two women. They were busy prepping the last few dishes of food, hands busy with their tasks and unable greet her. She waved at each of them. "Elizabeth," she introduced.

They smiled back but continued working without a word.

Jared guided her by the elbow into the bathroom. "Meet me downstairs when you're finished?" he asked, one hand on the doorknob.

She nodded and remained still for several moments after he'd closed the door. There was so much happening, and the spot where he'd touched her arm tingled. She wasn't sure if she was in more disbelief over the party guests or the frosty welcome she'd received in the kitchen.

She stared at herself in the mirror once she was changed, fussing with ring on the single shoulder of her suit until it was straight. She adjusted the hips and congratulated herself for remembering a sarong this time. She knotted it, collected her bag, and took one last look in the mirror before giving up the safety of the bathroom.

Jared's apartment was sparse but neat, she noted as she stepped back out to the living room. She set her bag and beach towel next to the couch and turned to the kitchen. "Can I help? I'm not bad in a kitchen, and I'll do whatever you need if you tell me."

Ruby, clearly not Jared's sister with her olive-toned skin and coal black hair smiled at her. She was dressed in a traditional triangle style bikini with a simple gold bar between the cups and a pair of shorts that left little to the imagination. Somehow, she made it exotic. "We might have it just about finished," she replied. "Nicky?"

Nicole stopped chopping and began scooping her cutting board contents into a bowl. "Yeah. We're about done."

Elizabeth tried again. "I saw a table downstairs. I can carry food down if you're ready."

"Sure. Knock yourself out." Nicole gestured to the fridge, and Elizabeth sneaked between the two in the small space to extract anything she guessed was relevant from the fridge. With a nod of approval from Ruby, she started down the stairs, laden with a pair of bowls and a tray balanced on top of them.

She heard James as she reached the bottom of the stairs.

"Come on, dummies," he scolded. She heard the slap of skin on skin before she saw the two of the guys jogging toward her. Upon arrival, they instantly relieved her burden.

"Oh, well, I guess I'll go see if there's more," Elizabeth fussed.

"No," Kevin insisted. "This is our job. And we're just slacking."

"Well, I have to get my beach towel anyway," she persisted.

Andy joined her. "Where is it? I'll grab it."

"And not his sister," James ordered.

Andy stopped, tilting his head. "Jimmy – I mean, really. Why would I do that?"

"Because you always have," James scolded.

Andy snickered. "Where's your towel?" he asked Elizabeth. Armed with details, he darted up the stairs, two at a time.

Elizabeth made her way to the pool, as Jared began expertly pulling burgers off the grill and stacking them onto a platter.

"Back at the pool as instructed," she pronounced with a sloppy salute.

His gaze touched her briefly before turning back to his task. "Sorry about my sister. She's a little wary of strangers."

Elizabeth wondered how he knew what had happened and realized this must be her M.O. "She loves you."

"She remembers my exes," he added. He jumped suddenly, sucking a knuckle into his mouth.

Elizabeth rushed to his side. "Did you get burned?"

He didn't answer with his mouth full of knuckle and nodded.

"So, you never doubled as a line cook," she teased.

He chuckled, finally releasing the finger from his lips. "No. Waiter, janitor, gopher...never line cook. This is just something I learned to do for attention when I was a kid. It's easy to blend into a pool full of gorgeous kids and never be seen. But everyone wants to kiss the cook," he explained.

"You want me to finish up?" she offered.

He shook his head. "No. I refer to everyone wanting to kiss the cook," he replied. "And I'm already wearing this stylish apron." He plucked at one of the ruffles.

She snickered. "I didn't want to say anything."

"It's my sister's idea of a joke."

"It's a pretty good one. I can make you something more masculine if you like," she suggested.

He shook his head. "I could just wear a T-shirt, but then what would be the fun in that?" He slipped the corner of his apron down his shoulder, making a silly face, lips forming an "o" before he covered his mouth with a naughty expression.

Elizabeth grinned so hard her cheeks hurt, but she eyed his bare skin peeking out from beneath the full apron and silently approved.

In minutes, the food began arriving as the guys walked up and down the stairs until finally, they were all seated in folding chairs at the table. Elizabeth found herself squeezed between Kevin and Jared, and she was having trouble focusing as Jared's bare arm rubbed hers.

"Perfect as always, bro," Nicole complimented happily as she neared the end of the food on her plate.

Jared held up his drink to receive the compliment. "Thanks for doing all the rest of the work and making me look like a hero."

The siblings clinked bottles, and shortly thereafter began the cleanup. Despite her best efforts, Elizabeth was pushed out of the mess, and she resigned herself to simply being a guest. She sat at the pool's edge, dangling her feet in the cool water as she nursed her drink. "I'm feeling pretty spoiled at your birthday party," she noted as Jared sat beside her, dipping his legs into the water.

He grinned thoughtfully at the pool. "Nicole likes to be in charge more than I do. Other people are usually just in her way. And that's her choice." He swigged his beer. "I think you're a big hit with the guys," he noted.

"Well, cool. But I think I'd better refrain from pushing them in the pool. I don't think we're there yet."

He scoffed. "Between Nicole and Ruby...it will be happening. Just a warning."

"If I was your sister, you'd be the first to go in. Maybe I'd better keep my distance." She started to scoot away.

He slipped an arm around her side, impeding her motion. "Nope. Not going anywhere," he teased.

Goosebumps puckered over her arms and legs, and her mind whirred to find a way to distract him so he wouldn't notice. She reached a single finger into his arm pit to tickle him. What Elizabeth hadn't counted on was the fierce squirm that resulted from the gesture. For one long moment, they teetered, squealing, before landing in the pool, drinks and all.

Elizabeth sputtered to the surface to the sound of laughter as the rest of the party were emerging through the gate after clearing the food.

"Aww, man! You beat me to it!" Nicole called out.

Elizabeth grabbed for the pool's edge with one hand, wiping her eyes with the other. "Not on purpose," she promised.

Just behind his sister, Andy broke into a sprint, caught Nicole around the waist, and leaped sideways into the deep end with a huge splash as they went under.

She heard Jared howling happily as he pulled himself to the edge beside her. He set his bottle on the patio with a groan then fished out Elizabeth's cup while she clung to the side for dear life.

"Birthday boy needs a little help here!" he called out to his friends, waving Elizabeth's cup.

"What, you baby? Your legs don't work?" Kevin teased, collecting the items from him and making to replace them.

"Not on my birthday, they don't," Jared proclaimed, kicking out his legs. "Lizzybeth needs one, too."

Kevin arched a brow. "She was a given. It's you I have to think about."

The teasing continued for several hours, all of them languishing in the long summer daylight. Elizabeth extracted herself to a nearby lounge chair to relax wrapped in her beach towel. Jared was in the middle of playing keep away with James's hat. The sound of a chair being dragged across concrete pulled her attention from the pool to person responsible for offending her eardrums. Nicole was at the helm.

She sucked in a sharp breath as the other woman plopped down beside her. "So. Elizabeth. What is it that you do again?"

"I'm a clothing designer," she identified.

"And how did you meet my brother?"

Elizabeth blinked, uncomfortable in the other woman's unwavering gaze. "I was the head costume designer on the movie he just starred in."

Nicole nodded. "You know he's got nothing right? There's no bank for you to break."

Elizabeth drew back. "Excuse me?" She wanted to glance at Jared to let him know his sister was crossing a line, but she realized with a start that she didn't need his help.

"If you're after him for his money, there's nothing there. He spent it all years ago. He and Kevin used to share a roll of toilet paper." Nicole's gaze was piercing, and Elizabeth recognized the challenge.

"First of all, I'm not a gold digger. I have my own money. I just sold a ten-thousand-dollar wedding dress. And second of all, most importantly, your brother and I are just friends." Elizabeth dared her to make more accusations.

At this, Nicole laughed in her face.

"I don't understand what's happening," Elizabeth stated, watching as Nicole covered her mouth.

"Really?"

"Yes, really. Why does no one believe us?"

Nicole caught her breath for a moment, leaning on her knees. "He told you that you were just friends?"

"It's one of the first things he said to me," Elizabeth frowned. "Am I the butt of some joke here that I don't know about?"

Nicole's face relaxed. "No." She sighed. "Look, whatever happens, he hasn't taken a risk on anyone in a long time. Please don't break him."

Elizabeth nodded slowly, waiting to see what other insinuations were about to be lobbed at her. She considered defending herself further but decided the swiftest course of action was to simply acquiesce. "Okay."

"Because I might be his little sister, but that doesn't mean I won't make your life miserable if you hurt him." She sneered. "You need sunscreen." With that, she stood and dive-bombed into the pool, directing the splash at her brother.

Elizabeth thought about leaving. The whole encounter had just been weird. She inspected her shoulders noticing that Nicole was right. Her bag with the sunscreen was still upstairs, and she headed for it, thinking a moment alone to collect herself was warranted.

His apartment was cold after being outside for so many hours, and she shivered as she let herself in. Her brain was still reeling from the scolding she'd just taken as she fished the lotion out of her bag and began to apply it.

The front door opened, and Jared stepped in. A towel was wrapped around his hips, and Elizabeth noted the way his hair dripped over his bare chest. "Oh, good. You're here. I was afraid you'd left."

She grinned. "Afraid?"

He smirked. "You missed a spot." He closed the gap between them, taking the tube from her. "May I?"

She nodded, turning as he gestured for her to do so and lifting her hair off her shoulders.

"I saw Nicole talking to you before she jumped in," he stated, and she heard the unmistakable sound of sunscreen being squirted from the container.

"Yes. She pointed out that I needed some protection."

"From her?" he teased.

Elizabeth felt his hand warm against her shoulder as he began to rub in the lotion. "From the sun," she countered after a beat, grateful that he was behind her and couldn't see her eyes squeeze shut as she measured her words. His hands were warm, and his touch firm against her shoulders. She bit her lip to prevent the moan from escaping her lips as he massaged her neck.

He sighed. "Lizzybeth, I know who my sister is."

"She loves you fiercely," she defended. She was sure if she had a brother, she would feel the same, and suddenly felt less attacked by his sibling.

There was silence for a moment as he worked. She shivered as his fingers slipped just under the edge of the shoulder on her suit, and she stared at the floor.

"This okay?" he asked, peeking into the corner of her vision.

She nodded. "Just cold in the AC."

He stroked his hand down her arm, and Elizabeth frowned when he pulled his hands away until she heard another blob of sunscreen being ejected from the container.

This time, both his hands were on her lower back between the strap at her mid back and her bottom. She worried suddenly about him tracing the edge of her suit again, but she shouldn't have. He did run his hand beneath the strap at her mid back, but he seemed to know his boundaries, and her behind went unmolested.

Jared covered her remaining shoulder in the white goo. "I think I got it all," he declared.

Elizabeth turned, watching him trying to rub the excess from between his fingers onto his own arms. "Thank you."

He beamed at her. "My pleasure." He swiped the tip of one white finger along the bridge of her nose.

She squealed, reaching to rub it in then grabbed for his hands, rubbing them between her own to remove the excess. She twined her fingers through his, attempting to get all the lotion from the crevices.

Jared stilled her hands, curling his fingers over hers, and she met his gaze turned suddenly serious.

Elizabeth thought the world may have stopped turning as time seemed to slow. Her pulse soared, and she swallowed hastily. He was so close now she could feel the heat emanating from his body. And then she was aware of the damp towel pressed against her hips as he drew her in by the hands. Her brain whirred. This wasn't happening. But she saw him staring at her mouth. She'd wanted this to happen for so long, and now, in the privacy of his living room with nothing but a few bathing suits and a towel between them, she couldn't deny it was about to. She struggled to catch her breath, eyes slipping shut in surrender when he was mere inches away.

He kissed her gently. Her entire body shivered, frozen in this moment, wishing it to last an eternity. His lips were soft, and she was keenly aware of their hands locked together. She wanted to squeal but knew if she did it would all end, and she wanted more.

When he pulled away, she felt his eyes searching hers, and then he placed her hands on his hips and cupped her face, kissing her again.

Elizabeth sighed against his mouth, getting lost in its warmth, the taste of his tongue teasing her lips, the noises created by their kisses. She was afraid to move – that the spell might break, but she realized she was pulling him closer, and she might have moaned, but she would never admit it.

He pulled away, resting his forehead against hers, not breaking eye contact. His mouth was curved in a satisfied smile, but Elizabeth couldn't look anywhere but his cerulean eyes, melting into them.

So many questions rattled her brain. He only saw her as a friend. Right? He'd told her that more than once. He'd told her that recently. But now, he was kissing her intimately. Her heart thrilled, silencing anything she wanted to say.

"That was…" He paused, as if searching for the right word. "…better than I expected."

She giggled, suddenly remembering that this was Jared, her friend, and the absurdity of the statement punctuated her mirth with a snort.

"And you still went for it anyway thinking it was going to be bad?" she teased, biting her lower lip.

His eyes followed the path of her tongue as he stroked his thumb over the corner of her jaw. "Well, more practice couldn't hurt."

Elizabeth thought she might float away. "It does make perfect, they say."

He purred. "But what do *they* know? I say we test the theory for ourselves." He pulled her hands from his hips to his shoulders, hugging her around the waist.

She laced her fingers together behind his neck, feeling him shift infinitely closer, and she felt her body react to his nearness. His next kiss was far less chaste, parting her lips with his tongue. This time, she definitely moaned, rewarded with a similar noise that she felt rattle in his chest. They had a blissful minute to explore before the commotion of his friends approaching the front door broke the spell, and they pulled apart slowly. He passed the sunscreen to her as the front door burst open.

"We're getting crispy out there," Kevin announced.

Nicole pressed past the others. "Just friends," she mumbled, and Elizabeth felt a hard stare penetrate her forehead. "On that note, I think Ruby and I are gonna head out." She disappeared into the back room of the apartment then returned with two backpacks, tossing one at her friend.

"Happy birthday," Ruby congratulated, hugging Jared's shoulder. She reached out a hand to Elizabeth. "Nice to meet you." She presented similar greetings to Jared's other friends, and the girls ducked out.

Andy sighed. "Yeah. Happy birthday, man, but we should go too."

The three guys exchanged knowing looks, first with each other, then with Jared, tittering as they discreetly gave him the thumbs-up.

"Yeah," Kevin agreed. "That's enough party for me for one day."

"Me too," James added. There was a flurry of activity as they cleared out.

Jared chuckled once he'd shut and locked the door behind them. "Guess I got you all screened up for nothing." He pulled the towel from around his waist, chucking it at the kitchen linoleum where it landed with a wet thud.

"I wouldn't say for nothing." Now that they were alone, Elizabeth couldn't hold back her question any longer. "What about us just being friends?"

Jared stepped forward, and Elizabeth fought the urge to shrink under his obvious assessment. He combed his fingers through her hair, pushing it behind one ear. "I've never stopped to be friends with a woman first before. I get the feeling you might be stuck with me for a long while."

"I'm not afraid of time with you. I've got a twenty-year head start."

He smirked, shaking his head. "I guess Max was right about us after all."

"I won't tell him if you won't."

Jared shook his head, pulling her closer till their hips met. "I don't plan to hide us from anyone, Max or otherwise." He pulled her tightly against himself, and Elizabeth melted into his arms and another exhilarating kiss.

~ THE END ~

EPILOGUE

Amara's House:
Amara

"Stop fidgeting," Elizabeth scolded, "or I'll poke you with a pin, and I can't even promise it won't be on purpose."

Amara laughed down to where the seamstress was hemming her gown. "I'm trying," she promised.

"Stay still, or I'll spank you," Scott ordered from across the room where he was lounging on Amara's living room couch. He held a magazine over his head, reading.

"Not helping," Elizabeth called back as Amara wriggled her behind and mumbled something about being threatened with a good time.

Since their first date, Scott and Amara had been bouncing between their homes, each unwilling to be out of eyesight of the other. Elizabeth had borne witness to the increasingly intimate relationship as she began using Amara, Scott, and Jared for models in her clothing line. All three of her principals had begged to participate, and she was dividing her time amongst them.

The movie had taken the internet streaming service by storm, and had been so successful, the network had optioned a spin-off series based on Jared's character's discovery and subsequent torture of the patients used as part of the gruesome experiments conducted during the technology development. Amara had been inconsolable until her agent sent over piles of manuscripts offering her lead roles.

Six months later now, Elizabeth was fitting the actress for another charity ball gown, the third in as many months. Amara screwed her attention together. "Are you close?"

"Yes," Elizabeth replied pulling the last pin from between her lips. She tucked it into the hemline and pushed herself to her feet. "Okay, go get changed. If I'm late tonight, I'll tell Jared it's all your fault."

Amara rolled her eyes. "Not afraid of him. And besides which, he would wait for you."

"Maybe so, but what does it say about me to let him?" Elizabeth countered.

That logic couldn't be argued with, and Amara changed quickly then passed the pinned gown gingerly to Elizabeth and eyed her as they stood in the foyer. "Are you gonna be okay at a family birthday dinner?" she asked.

Elizabeth nodded. "I can handle Nicole. She invited Jared, and we come as a package deal now," she reasoned. She leaned in closer with a wicked smile. "But part of me can't wait to see her lemon face when she opens the fabulous gift I got her."

Amara giggled. "But his parents will be there tonight. That's a first, right?"

Elizabeth nodded. "I think he's more nervous than I am."

"Oh really?" Amara asked, brow arched. "You don't think..." she trailed off.

"Think what?" Elizabeth asked as she zipped a garment bag closed around the gown.

"If he gets down on one knee...you had better video call us."

Elizabeth waved her off. "And risk seeing whatever happened for you to both have those marks on your backs? No thank you."

Amara frowned. "I'm serious. Parents are a big deal."

"Parents, I've got," Elizabeth promised. "And he's not going to propose. It's only been six months." She glanced at her fitness band, seeing the time. "I've got to go." She hugged Amara then dashed toward her car.

Once alone with Scott, Amara plucked the magazine from his hands and settled into his lap on the couch. "Hey," she greeted.

Pride colored his expression as he met her gaze. "Hey, yourself." He caressed her cheek with his palm.

She hummed happily, leaning in to his touch. "So...I've been thinking about the holiday coming up, and I was wondering how you felt about inviting everyone here for Thanksgiving."

"Who's everyone?" he questioned, moving his hands to her thighs and stroking lightly.

Amara ran a thumb over his chin. "I was thinking maybe my family...your family...blood or otherwise."

He arched a brow. "That could get to be a pretty big affair," he mused.

"As big as you'd like," she elucidated.

Scott rewarded her with a happy glimpse of his pearly whites as he complimented, "I'm impressed with your willingness to meet the family."

She shrugged. "I realized how much I regret putting you off for so long, and I didn't want to make the same mistake with getting to know the people who made you."

He stared at her for long enough that she started to backpedal.

"If you're not into it..." she began, but he stopped her.

"I am. I'm just...in awe of you and how lucky I feel to be here with you now."

She relaxed against him, leaning down to kiss him softly.

"Amara," he crooned, "I love you."

His words didn't surprise her. What surprised her was how quickly she conceded. "I love you, too."

About the Author

Laura Christian is a fangirl. And when she's into something or someone, she's all the way in for life. She has been writing since she was eleven and earned her bachelor's degree in English with a minor in Psychology. Laura has been entertaining her friends and others from mutual fandoms for years. She, her husband, two cats and dog call Houston home. When she isn't writing, Laura is probably sewing, knitting, or playing Fortnite. Want to know more? Visit her website.

www.TheLauraChristian.com

Acknowledgments

Big thank you to Kay Springfield, my editor. Thanks also to my beta readers and the Twitter community who helped me pick up the pace and give me the confidence to move forward.